DE⋯⋯⋯⋯⋯!

Your quest to recover the fabulous Fireseed has led you and your islander partner, Rami, deep into the side of the sleeping volcano. Making your way quickly through the gruesome Cave of Bones, you follow a corridor that leads even deeper into the bowels of the huge volcano.

Suddenly the corridor spills onto a ledge high on the inner wall of the ancient volcano's crater. Directly in front of you, in the middle of the ledge, you see a gigantic circular nest with a gentle haze of steam rising from it into the sky. You can't see into the nest from where you are, but loud scratching noises are coming from inside its tightly woven walls.

"I'm going to have a look at that nest," Rami says quickly and immediately scrambles out of the corridor toward the huge nest.

What will you do?

1) If you want to follow Rami to investigate the nest, turn to page 122.

2) If you decide you'd better leave the nest alone, turn to page 135.

Whatever choice you make, you are sure to find adventure as you seek
THE FIRESEED

THE FIRESEED

BY MORRIS SIMON

A DUNGEONS & DRAGONS™ ADVENTURE BOOK

Cover Art by Larry Elmore
Interior Art by Jeff Butler

TSR, Inc.

For Sean—
a good hunter, mason, and mandolineer

THE FIRESEED
©Copyright 1985, TSR, Inc.
All Rights Reserved.

Distributed to the book trade in the United States by Random House, Inc., and in Canada by Random House of Canada, Ltd.

Distributed in the United Kingdom by TSR UK, Ltd. Distributed to the toy and hobby trade by regional distributors.

First printing: October, 1985
Printed in the United States of America
Library of Congress Catalog Card Number: 85-90156
ISBN: 0-88038-171-X

9 8 7 6 5 4 3 2 1

TSR, Inc.
P.O. Box 756
Lake Geneva, WI 53147

TSR UK, Ltd.
The Mill, Rathmore Road
Cambridge CB1 4AD
United Kingdom

ou are about to set off on an adventure in which YOU will meet many dangers—and face many decisions. YOUR choices will determine how the story turns out. So be careful ... you must choose wisely!

Do not read this book from beginning to end! Instead, as you are faced with a decision, follow the instructions and keep turning to the pages where your choices lead you until you come to an end. At any point, YOUR choice could bring success—or disaster!

You can read THE FIRESEED many times, with many different results, so if you make an unwise choice, go back to the beginning and start again!

Good luck on YOUR adventure!

In this book, you are Davin Farold, a young adventurer returning to your home port of Baysend after a long, hard campaign on the battlefields of far-off Forlund. You should be looking forward to your long-delayed homecoming, but you know it can only lead to yet another confrontation with your father over your chosen career as a mercenary.

At the moment, though, you're even more concerned about the angry storm clouds rapidly approaching off the stern of the ship. . . .

The sky looks stranger today than it ever has on your long voyage from the battlefields at Forlund to your home port of Baysend. After two months at sea, you've learned to recognize some of the signs of a storm—the hurried flights of gulls, the panicked schools of bluefish.

More than anything else, there's the odd silence among the crew of experienced heavy-weather sailors. You've stopped asking questions about the strange purple color of the sky because the hardened men just squint at you and grunt. "Aye, it'll be blowin' come night. Ye'd best secure yer gear below, an' that includes yerself!"

As you join the crowd of passengers and crew gathering on the rear deck, you notice that the captain has veered off the course for Baysend. He wants to keep the purple and rose clouds to the ship's rear for as long as possible. When the storm hits, you know he'll bring the *Salt Castle* about and head into the gale to ride it out.

"We won't outrun the storm, Davin Farold," says a voice at your shoulder. "Pona, the storm god, is angry."

At the sound of your name, you glance around to find the superstitious fool who thinks of the weather in terms of angry gods to be placated.

To your surprise, you see the calm, tanned face of Orson, the courageous young cleric from Baysend who served as chaplain to your force of mercenaries in Forlund.

"I don't believe that nonsense! I'm a professional fighter. I deal in realities, not in myths," you say scornfully.

Orson's long blond hair billows in the rising wind, uncut and loose except for the two braids at his temples that mark him as a warpriest. He studies you with unflinching gray eyes.

"Davin, are you so angry with your father that you must reject his gods as well as him?" he asks.

You're not surprised that the cleric knows of your feud with your father, the wealthiest shipbuilder in Baysend. Taran Farold's public denouncement of your decision to become a mercenary has been a source of common gossip for three years. He publicly disinherited you, his only heir, on the cathedral steps when you were sixteen years old.

"My father's gods and his gold are his own, Orson. I want neither of them! With the plunder we recovered on this trip, I have no need of Taran Farold's wealth, nor his superstitions!"

"Nor his love?" Orson suggests.

You feel your face darken with a mixture of emotions, and you clench your fists. The cleric has touched a tender spot.

In fact, your return to Baysend, decorated with battle honors and laden with treasures, is a final attempt to settle the differences with your father. You want to prove to him that your choice of a profession is a good one so that he will stop insisting that you settle in the city and take over his business.

"I'm not one of your sheep, priest," you tell the cleric, "and I won't discuss my private concerns with you. Find someone else to babble to about your gods and myths."

"Listen to me, Davin Farold. I have glimpsed at least a small portion of your future, and I have seen much danger there."

"So now you're a fortune-teller?" you scoff in disbelief.

"I cannot tell the future because there is always more than one," Orson replies calmly. "Our futures are decided by the choices we make. Only the number of choices is predetermined."

"Then which of my futures have you seen?" you ask lightheartedly.

"I have seen you and another man trapped within a great cloud of burning vapors, forced to choose between immortality and death!" answers the cleric forcefully.

You wait a moment, expecting him to elaborate, but he has turned away to look at the approaching storm clouds.

"Is that it?" you demand. "Where was I? How old did I look in your 'vision'?"

Orson mumbles his reply without turning around to face you. "You were no older than you are now, and you were in some rugged, barren place I've never seen before. There were other images, but they were jumbled and hazy. All of them involved a shadowy thing of great evil with a blood-red heart pulsating at its darkest core."

Then he turns toward you and stares into your eyes with a penetrating gaze.

"No matter what else happens, beware the fiery fog!" he warns. "It hides a force more evil and powerful than anything you can strike with your sword—a force strong enough to destroy you and everything you know!"

You try to ask him more questions about the disturbing prophecy, but the cleric vows he can tell you nothing else. For the rest of the evening, you're as silent as the superstitious sailors who await the fury of the storm god, but your thoughts are elsewhere. You finally manage to drift into a troubled sleep—and into nightmares of a flaming fog.

The wild swaying of your hammock wakes you shortly after midnight. Your fellow passengers are beginning to realize that the ship is in the midst of no ordinary storm. Some of them start to pray aloud, and others joke nervously about the seaworthiness of the vessel and the skills of her crew.

You're no seaman, but you do know a little about how to handle a ship's rigging, and you could be of help to the crew on deck.

On the other hand, you wonder if you might not be of more use where you are. Most of the men in the ship's hold are your comrades-in-arms from your recent campaign. You've seen their great courage and strength on the battlefield, but in this cramped cargo hold, they're out of their element. When seasoned warriors grow nervous, tempers flare, and you may be needed to prevent their tension from turning into panic or a riot.

1) If you decide you could do more good topside during the typhoon, turn to page 142.

2) If you think it would be wiser to ride out the storm below decks, turn to page 41.

"I have to attack them!" you decide. "I can't let them take me to their den." You still can't see more than their long, bulky outlines in the dark water beside the dinghy, so you wait with your cutlass raised for an opportunity to strike.

Finally, one of the maned heads breaks the surface just in front of you. You swing the sword as hard as you can, cleaving the monster's skull in one stroke. The beast flips violently against the side of your skiff, throwing you to your knees. Then its tremendous body flops into the small vessel on top of you. As you squirm away from the dying mass, your hands touch slippery scales rather than wet fur! It isn't a seawolf at all!

You stare in horror at the face of a large lion, its snarling death mask of wild fury frozen in the bright moonlight. Its bloody mane drapes over a scaled back, and its clawed forepaws resemble those of a crocodile. A long tail ending in a single fin is still thrashing in dying muscle contractions against the side of the dinghy.

You've slain a sea lion—one of the fabled creatures chosen by Pona, the mythical storm god of island natives, as his personal guards. Not even the least superstitious pirate would think of harming one of these rare and sacred monsters!

Suddenly you realize that the lifeboat has slowed its forward movement. The sea lions have stopped. You peer over the scaly carcass into the moonlit water. All at once, the ocean explodes beneath your flimsy boat. A tremendous waterspout is lifting you and the dinghy high into the clear night sky!

Far below, you see the shadowy forms of the surviving sea lions forming a circle around the mysterious column of water. They remind you of hounds at bay, waiting expectantly for their master to shoot their prey from a tree. Just then, a larger shadow rises from the depths of the sea just outside the circle of monsters.

A storm giant, shrouded in seaweed and caked with sand, raises a single, dripping arm and points to you! A sound like thunder rolls from his mouth, and the cloudless night sky around you is suddenly filled with small bolts of lightning.

In the next instant, the waterspout vanishes from beneath your boat. You fall free of the dinghy, plummeting toward the dark water where the storm giant's angry pets wait to have their vengeance upon you for killing their pack mate. Your body plunges into the deep salt water in the center of the ring of sea lions. The fall is so great that the water slams into your chest as if it were a solid wall!

Though you're stunned almost senseless, you try to raise the cutlass as the force of your fall drives you deep beneath the sea. The attack you expect from the sea lions doesn't come. Instead, you feel a giant, cold hand catch you near the sandy bottom!

The storm giant's palm is so large that it covers your entire back. The monster grips you firmly, but not painfully, his huge thumb and fingers reaching around your torso. You realize suddenly that the giant could crush your rib cage as easily as you might break an egg!

"Storm giants are the most powerful members of their species," you recall as the hand lifts you from the depths of the ocean. "They're not evil, but I've killed this one's pet!"

Your shoulders suddenly break through the surface of the waves. Your ears are popping from the change in depth, and you fill your lungs with fresh night air before you squirm around in the giant's fist to face the monster.

The creature's sea-green skin is glistening in the moonlight. Huge clumps of seaweed are draped in his sand-caked hair and beard. He's holding you level with his chest, your legs dangling just above the water.

"IS THIS HOW YOU REPAY PONA, LORD OF THE SEA, FOR TRYING TO SAVE YOUR PUNY LANDS FROM CATASTROPHE?" the giant roars. His voice is deep and rumbling, like distant thunder that you can feel as well as hear. "MUST YOU HUMANS KILL EVERY CREATURE YOU DO NOT RECOGNIZE IMMEDIATELY?"

"I—I thought it was a seawolf," you try to explain. "I'd just seen one, and I thought that your sea lions were a pack of them!"

"FOOL! IT WAS I WHO SENT BOTH THE STORM AND THE SEA LIONS TO BRING YOU HERE, DAVIN FAROLD!"

The storm giant's use of your name stuns you. "Do you mean that you wrecked an entire ship and drowned all those men just to get me here?" you demand, twisting your body in the creature's grasp.

"YOUR VESSEL REMAINS AFLOAT. IT WILL LIMP INTO YOUR PORT OF BAY-SEND SEVERAL WEEKS LATE, BUT SAFELY," replies Pona. "AS FOR THE MEN, ONLY A FEW WERE LOST TO SEA TROLLS OR SHARKS. THEIR LIVES WERE SMALL PRICES TO PAY TO SAVE THEIR FAMILIES AND THEIR LANDS FROM TOTAL DESTRUCTION!"

"What kind of destruction?" you cry, trying to recall exactly what the cleric Orson had said about an evil force more powerful than your sword.

"THAT IS NO LONGER A CONCERN OF YOURS!" thunders the angry giant. "I IMAG-INED THAT THE DESCENDANT OF ENNIS FAROLD WOULD HAVE GREATER WISDOM THAN TO SLAY MY BELOVED PET! YOU WOULD NEED SUCH INSIGHT TO UNDERTAKE THE MOST IMPORTANT QUEST OF FACING THE SPIRIT OF YOUR ANCESTOR'S ANCIENT ENEMY."

Pona's mention of your famous ancestor, the Archcleric of Baysend, confuses you more. Ennis Farold was revered throughout the western countries for his banishment of Hektor, the evil sorcerer, but that had been nearly three hundred years ago!

"Do you mean the spirit of Hektor?" you ask the storm giant. "The sorcerer whose evil power once summoned demons to the streets of Baysend?"

"IT IS THE SAME HEKTOR, FOOLISH HUMAN," answers Pona. "HIS SPIRIT STILL LIVES ON STORM ISLAND, BUT NOW HE DABBLES IN GREATER POWERS—POWERS FAR TOO AWESOME FOR ONE WITH AS LITTLE WISDOM AS YOU!"

"That's impossible!" you shout. "He's been dead for—"

Your protest is stifled as Pona opens his huge fist and drops you into the sea. When you recover from the shock of the water and swim to the surface, you see the giant's massive shoulders moving away from you. His sea lions dive like porpoises around their master's great head, then follow him beneath the dark waves.

1) You think your only chance for survival is to follow the storm giant. Turn to page 21.

2) You're eager to get as far away from Pona as possible. Turn to page 149.

"All right, let's see your great power," you demand. "Get us out of here!"

"Wait!" says Rami. "I don't trust him. Hektor was a master of deception. His shade will be even better."

"Your friend is correct, young Farold," adds the shade. "My skills in illusions are more powerful now than they were during the two centuries I was alive on this island!"

"How could you, or Hektor, have lived for two hundred years and not age?" you ask.

"The power of Pona bestows immortality upon me and my followers!"

"I've heard legends about that," says Rami. "It is said that whoever breathes Pona's fiery fog will never die."

"Fiery fog!" you think. "That's what Orson warned me about at the beginning of this adventure!"

"What is this fiery fog?" you ask the shade.

"Its name is quite appropriate," the shadowy figure answers. "Each month, when the tides are at their height, the sea of lava beneath this island shifts toward an underground pocket of rare minerals from the earth's youth. When the molten rock cooks those minerals, hot gases escape into Ponai's crater like a fiery fog. Creatures who breathe those fumes will never die."

"I think you're lying," Rami challenges the shade. "You or Yolmat couldn't have kept such a thing a secret for so long."

"Have you not seen the results of Yolmat's

madness?" asks Hektor's shade. "After the witch Nivida slew my earthly body and imprisoned my soul in a drop of dragon's blood, Yolmat went insane. He used perverted magic to take control of my followers. Then he decreed that their tongues must be fed to Pona."

"Do you mean he cut out their tongues and threw them into the volcano?" Rami asks.

"No," replies the shade. "He forced them to eat their own tongues so that no one would ever reveal the secret of the fiery fog! That was the beginning of their practice of eating human flesh."

"But the children—"

"Must wait until they become adults in the cult before they are made to eat their own tongues. Anyone who tries to leave the valley is eaten by the others!"

You feel a wave of revulsion at the thought of what awaits the children growing up here. At the moment, however, your concern has to be for Rami and yourself.

"Right now, we have to get out of here. How do you plan to arrange our escape?" you ask the shade.

"Stand away from the door," it replies.

You and Rami move to one side. The shadow images of Hektor's shade raise their dark arms simultaneously. A string of phrases in some unknown language echoes in the closed granary. Each of the seven figures seems to be contracting into the center of the pie-shaped building, where the partitions separating the supplies of rice meet.

"They're merging into one figure!" says Rami.

The shadow images are concentrating themselves into a single jet-black entity in the center of the granary. This new form is much more distinct than any of its hazier copies. You can even see varying shades of gray to represent different colors in the living Hektor's eyes and clothes.

"That's the real shade of Hektor!" you gasp. "It seems to draw its energy from all the shadows in the room, including its own images!"

"If I only had my spear—" begins Rami.

"You'd get us both killed!" you interrupt. "You can only wound a shade, not destroy it. Look!"

All around the sorcerer's shade, a thin aura of silver light begins to shimmer and expand. In a sudden explosion and a blinding flash, the walls of the granary blast outward, knocking the startled guards to the ground.

"Get their weapons, Rami!" you shout, pouncing on the nearest cannibal warrior.

You grab the unconscious man's double-ended spear and charge another native who is coming from one of the compound's walkways. He raises his own spear just in time to block your thrust with his trident tip. Then he sweeps the spear end upward, almost slicing your throat before you can dodge the jab.

Seeing how effective such a dual-ended weapon can be, you begin to use it like a quarterstaff with steel teeth, backing the painted cannibal against a wall and killing him with a quick thrust of the trident. You brace your feet on his carcass and rip out the barbed points just as Rami appears at your elbow. He's carrying two of the cannibals' spears.

"I brought one for you," he says, brandishing one of the weapons, "but I see you've already found one of your own. Where's Hektor's shade?"

The walls of the granary have completely disintegrated. Neither the shade nor its shadow images are anywhere in sight. "Gone for now," you answer. "Let's get the Fireseed. Yolmat said it was in the Council Hut, which must be that big one."

Just as you turn toward the central building, more warriors pour into the courtyard from the walkways. Yolmat is standing in the doorway to the Council Hut, a frown creasing his broad forehead. You're completely surrounded by the cannibals!

What should you do?

1) If you think you can fight your way out of this situation, turn to page 148.

2) If you'd rather try to talk your way out of it, turn to page 43.

The thought of being alone again on the open sea at night is frightening. The dinghy is nowhere in sight. Everywhere you look, there's nothing but a waveless stretch of ocean glimmering in the moonlight.

"Wait, Pona!" you scream. "Don't leave me here!"

You start swimming after the storm giant, hoping that he will forgive you for killing his pet sea lion. Your warrior's strength permits you to swim for a long time without stopping.

The moon has traced a wide arc across the heavens when your muscles finally begin to cramp. Forced to stop, you let your body relax and go limp in the warm water. You lean your head backward to rest your neck muscles but jerk it upright when you spot the dark shape on the horizon behind you.

It's a ship! It's a frigate, just like the *Salt Castle*, its sails drooping in the quiet waters of the doldrums! You can't tell how far away it is, but it doesn't matter. You begin swimming once more, taking long, slow strokes so that you won't tire quickly.

You know it would be useless to hail the vessel until you're almost at its hull, so you just swim as long as you can, then rest with your eyes on it, then swim some more. You can hardly believe it when you see the ship come your way!

Your strength begins to fail you completely just as the first dawn light appears on the eastern horizon. You're still more than a mile away from the ship, but can go no farther. The only sound you can make is a faint "Help!" which you're sure no one can hear.

You can no longer hold your head up, and you lie back in the water. As exhaustion takes over, your body floats loosely on the waves, and your mind floats into the gray void of unconsciousness.

The sound of a ship's bell is the next thing you hear. You're lying on a table of some kind, with a soft cushion beneath your head.

"Ah, yer awake!" someone says from near your feet. You try to raise your head, but your muscles are much too sore. "Ye just lie still, lad," says the same voice. "This here's the *Sea Ranger*, bound fer Baysend. We'll have ye in port in two days' time.

"Yer the luckiest man I ever knew," adds the unknown man. "A wind blew us right to ye, straight as an arrow, in the middle of dead doldrums!"

You close your eyes and whisper a silent word of thanks to Pona, the storm giant who befriended your ancestor and now, it seems, has forgiven you for killing his sea lion.

"Perhaps you'll give me another chance to face Hektor," you add as you feel the wind rise, speeding the ship toward Baysend.

THE END

The swimming figure almost disappears into the thick fog before you realize that he may have been frightened by your own movements!

"Hey! Come back!" you shout. The swimmer doesn't respond. "What's the matter?" you call. "Are you injured?"

The fog around you suddenly fills with a long, low wail that slowly rasps into an inhuman growl. "There IS something else in the water that scared him!" you think. "And whatever it may be, it's not human!" You dread your thoughts. Other than the pants and shirt in which you were sleeping, you're naked and defenseless, without arms or armor!

You scan the water, hoping to see something you might use to defend yourself. The only thing nearby that even resembles a weapon is the broken shaft of a heavy oar. It has splintered just above the paddle, forming a pointed end that you can use as a crude spear. You grab the shaft just as a loud splash comes from your right, so near that you feel spray on your face!

The splash sounded as if something very large rose from the water. You squint, and you think you can make out a huge shape glistening darkly through the lifting fog. Whatever it is, it seems to be standing motionless on the surface of the sea!

Just then, you hear two more splashes, which seem to come from behind you. Cling-

ing to the barrel, you jerk around—only to freeze in fear. You're staring into the fierce maw of a hideous blue-green creature with scaly skin! Two more of the things hover near it, their huge torsos extended out of the water at the waist.

After a moment, you recognize the gruesome creatures as marine trolls, called scrags by sailors in these tropical waters.

Reflexively, you hurl the pointed oar shaft at the nearest scrag. You aim is perfect, and your strength drives the makeshift spear into the sea troll's thick hide.

The monster screams in pain and grabs the wooden shaft in its taloned fists. To your amazement, the scrag pulls the stake from its scaly chest and flings it away. Then, almost instantly, the gaping wound begins to heal itself! These vile aquatic creatures have the power of regeneration!

All at once, the sea around you explodes as dozens of the monsters break the surface and begin to converge on you. In a last desperate attempt to save yourself, you push away off the barrel and try to dive away from the sea trolls. But when the talons dig into your back and the evil scrags begin to drag you to the bottom of the sea, you know your adventure has come to . . .

AN END

The storm giant's ominous words about Hektor and his evil plans are ringing in your ears. Taken with Orson's mysterious warning on board the *Salt Castle*, Pona's story seems to have issued a challenge that only you can meet.

"Even if the natives are cannibals, as the legends warn, there aren't many of them in that village," you think. "Maybe I can find somebody who knows something about Hektor and his plans."

You wade from the water onto the beach and slip silently toward the overhanging shadows of the largest hut. From the darkness under the veranda, you can hear several voices from inside the thatched house. They're speaking a trade dialect you recognize.

"Did you find them, Rami?" you hear a man asking.

"No, Uncle. Their tracks led to the caves. I'll go back in the morning light."

"No!" exclaims a woman's voice. "My son will not enter the Cave of Bones! No one ever returns from that place of death!"

Their strange conversation intrigues you so much that you don't notice the fisherman pause by your hiding place until it's too late.

"Aiee! Barakin! The thieves are back! One is under your house!"

Other voices start yelling from neighboring huts, and you see more men running to join the fisherman on the beach.

Above you, the mat covering the hut's doorway is thrust to one side, spilling lamplight onto the veranda and upon your startled face beneath its bamboo rails. A muscular young man wearing a yellow sarong over his deeply tanned skin steps onto the porch with a spear in his hand. You whip the cutlass from your waistband and dodge back into the shadows beneath the large hut.

You begin to inch your way back toward the surf as the man from the hut climbs down the ladder from the veranda. You recognize the catlike grace of a skilled fighter in his deliberate movements. Behind you, there are the ominous sounds of other feet and splashes in the surf. Without having to look, you know you're completely surrounded by native warriors whom many sailors say are cannibals! With a shrug, you hand your weapon to the spearman.

"Who is it, Rami?" asks a woman from the door of the hut above you. "It can't be the thieves. They'd never return here, to the Council Hut."

Through the widely spaced poles of the deck, you can see her outline against the lighted interior. She's a middle-aged woman, perhaps between forty and fifty years old.

"I don't think it's a thief, Mother," the young man replies. "Maybe a pirate."

You start to protest that you're not a pirate, but decide not to complicate matters. Most of the village men seem to have gathered on the beach and in the water. They all have weapons, but no one has threatened you—yet.

"Follow me into the Council Hut, Westerner," the man named Rami says in the calm voice of someone accustomed to authority. He turns his back on you, perhaps because there are so many other men around, or maybe because he trusts you. You climb the bamboo ladder onto the veranda and enter the large hut.

Please turn to page 36.

"I think you're lying!" you shout into the dark corners of the chamber at Hektor's shade. "You want us to throw the Fireseed into the molten rock at the bottom of that pit so that your prophecy will come true! It won't work, Hektor! We're taking the gem back to Moffid."

You wait for a reply, but all you hear is the dying echo of your own voice. You turn to your fellow warrior, who is scanning the walls of the cavern for any sign of the nebulous evil creature.

"You see, Rami? It's gone! Hektor's shade knows that it's powerless now that the Fireseed has been found. Let's take it back to Sala before the shade can try to stop us."

At the mention of his mother's name, Rami smiles. "Let me see the stone again, Davin," he urges. You open the bag and remove the giant ruby crystal. To your amazement, it has begun to glow brightly. Rami takes the gem and stares at its inner radiance with moist eyes.

"My mother's shame will now be erased," he says solemnly. "We can return the Fireseed to its place inside the sorcerer's skull and banish Hektor's shade. My quest is done, thanks to you!"

"And mine as well!" you exclaim. "Together, we've managed to defeat Hektor's prophecy! We've faced both the 'fiery fog' of Orson's vision and Hektor's evil spirit of the storm god Pona's prediction."

"Who is Orson?" asks Rami. "And what's this 'fiery fog'?"

You tell the islander about the cleric's warning aboard the *Salt Castle*, and then about Pona's challenge to you in the sea. "Don't you see, Rami? The 'fiery fog' is the glowing smoke from the lava pit in the fissure. If we had done what the shade wanted us to do, the prophecy would have come true!"

You're grinning so broadly that Rami starts smiling, and then chuckling. Within seconds, you both are doubled over with relieved laughter. It's several minutes before you can recover from the attack of delirious joy and find your way to the front chamber.

At the entrance of the Cave of Bones, you point to the skeletons with their ancient gold and gems. "As soon as the Fireseed is safely back inside Hektor's skull, we'll return for this treasure," you tell Rami. "I guess we've demonstrated how silly that taboo has been all these years. Now we can take this treasure and make everyone in Moffid wealthy!"

When you get back to the village, Rami summons Sala, Barakin, and the other elders to the Council Hut so that you can return the Fireseed publicly to Hektor's skull. As soon as everyone is assembled, Rami asks his mother to bring the skull. She takes the sinister relic from the wooden cabinet and places it in the center of the circle of elders, between you and her son.

"My brother warned us," she begins, "not to

let this kinsman of Ennis Farold help my son
find the Fireseed. Barakin said that Hektor's
shade would use them both to make his terrible prophecy come true." Sala pauses to be
sure that all the elders are listening to her
account of Rami's and your exploits.

"But they have returned to Moffid with the
sacred gem. They defied both Hektor and the
taboos of the Cave of Bones to find the Fireseed and return it to the sorcerer's skull."

The elders begin to mumble excitedly when
Sala mentions the forbidden cave. Barakin's
face is red with embarrassment because his
sister has proven him wrong before the entire
Council of Elders.

"Your son and his friend are great warriors,
Sala!" commends one of the councillors.

"Show us the relic, Sala!"

"Yes! Return it to Hektor's skull so that we
will be rid of his evil shade forever!"

Sala nods to you both. Rami extends his
palm as you open the small leather pouch. You
put the enormous red jewel, its throbbing
inner light even brighter than you remember,
into your companion's hand. But as the elders
begin an excited murmuring, the enchanted
glow dies, leaving behind a dull, glassy surface.

A chorus of gasps fills the Council Hut, followed by an awkward silence. Rami's mother
rushes forward and snatches the huge ruby
from her son's palm.

"What is it?" you demand. "What's wrong?"

The councillors frown at each other, and Sala stands with her head bowed. Only Barakin is smiling as he points to the gem.

"Hektor has deceived you," he gloats. "That isn't the Fireseed! His shade cast a spell to make it glow. You have failed to recover the sacred gem. The shade is now more powerful than ever!"

Rami puts his arms around Sala, trying to console her in this new disgrace before the elders. You turn away. Barakin is right. You've failed your quest, and the evil sorcerer's spirit has won—for now, anyway. But you vow silently that you won't rest until the true Fireseed has been restored to its place inside Hektor's flayed skull!

THE END

The darkening sky seems to be having a strange effect on the man in the water. At first, you think it's merely an illusion, but it makes you so uneasy that you snatch up a broken paddle wedged in the bottom of the dinghy and begin to propel the boat away.

When you glance back at the creature, you see that its nose and mouth are actually growing longer, its ears are becoming pointed, and fur is beginning to cover the lupish face!

Suddenly, you recall one of the more frightening sailors' legends you've heard since childhood: the tale of seawolves, aquatic werewolves with lupine heads and the bodies of seals. And you begin to paddle furiously.

According to the legend, the changeling creatures were once humans who were bitten by other seawolves. They're driven to roam the ocean lanes in packs. They try to sneak aboard ships in order to attack unsuspecting mariners at night. Once bitten, their victims hurl themselves into the sea in the throes of their first changing, thereby joining the lycanthropes' packs!

The animal snarls in rage when it sees you moving off, and it dives toward you. You stop paddling immediately and draw your cutlass, ready for an attack.

Suddenly there's a great splash at the stern of your boat, and you whirl in time to see the huge creature, twice the size of a man, outlined against the darkening sky. You whip your blade forward and plunge it to the hilt

into the seawolf's furry chest. Then you jerk
your sword arm back, pulling the cutlass from
the tough hide just as the lycanthrope sinks
beneath the ocean's surface.

You peer cautiously over the side, hoping
that your steel blade had enough iron in it to
kill the monster. According to every seawolf
legend you've ever heard, they can be slain
only by weapons made of silver or iron.

All at once, the water beneath your boat is
swarming with huge shadowy forms with long
tails and massive maned heads! "It must be
the seawolf pack!" you think.

There are four giant shapes on each side of
your lifeboat, but the water has gotten too
dark to get a good look at them. You feel several hard bumps on the hull. Then your dinghy begins to turn and move in a straight line.
The creatures seem to be herding you with
their heavy but streamlined bodies toward
some unknown destination!

You glance from your sword to the broken
oar. Should you try to fight, or flee?

1) If you want to attack the creatures with
   your cutlass, turn to page 11.

2) If you want to try to paddle away from
   them, turn to page 70.

The interior of the Council Hut is a large round room, bare except for woven mats scattered around the floor, a wooden chest against the rear wall, and some utensils hanging in the windows. An old man dressed in monkey skins squats on one of the mats. The younger native, Rami, watches you carefully with his spear balanced in his hand.

"I'm not an enemy," you tell Rami and the woman in the pidgin language they're using.

"He's not a pirate, Rami," says the woman. "Listen to him. Pirates don't learn our words."

"She's right, Rami," you add. "I'm not a pirate. I'm a warrior. I was thrown from my ship during a storm at sea and drifted in the ocean until I saw the lights of your village."

You hesitate to tell them about your encounter with the storm giant because you don't know yet who or what is involved in your quest to confront Hektor's spirit.

"A warrior!" Rami exclaims. "Then you can help us. Thieves took an important tribal relic. I tracked them to a cave not far from here."

You quickly seize the opportunity to win these people's hospitality and trust.

"If you need an extra sword, I'll go with you. I've had a little experience fighting thieves," you add modestly.

"Praise Pona!" exclaims the woman, handing you your cutlass. "I am Sala, guardian of the Fireseed and Rami's mother. Welcome to our village, Moffid. What are you called?"

"Davin Farold, of Baysend," you reply.

The old man suddenly leaps to his feet and rushes between you and Sala. He raises a quivering finger and points to your face. His faded brown eyes are wide with excitement.

"He is the one!" exclaims the elder. "The one who will feed Fireseed to the boar!"

"What are you talking about?" you demand of the old man. "What is this 'Fireseed'?"

The elder shakes his bony finger in your face. "I am Barakin, shaman of the sorcerer's skull and headman of Moffid," he says. "I will not let you make the prophecy come true!"

Rami steps between you and the priest. He raises his hand to silence Barakin. "Your story is a myth, Uncle. This warrior is here because he was lost in a storm and washed ashore on our island by accident."

Barakin stares around Rami's shoulder at you. "Do you come from the line of Ennis Farold of Baysend, the holy man who sent the evil wizard Hektor to our island?" he demands.

Barakin's knowledge of your famous ancestor, the Archcleric of Baysend, shocks you. It also sends you a warning signal. Apparently, both Orson's prophecy of a "fiery fog" and this one involving a "Fireseed" are related to the storm giant's quest!

"Ennis Farold was my ancestor," you admit to the old man.

The village headman-priest scowls suspiciously. "My people lived with the evil he sent here! Hektor brought his foul magic to Storm

Island. Many died before my mother's sister, the druid priestess Nivida, killed Hektor and put his spirit in a drop of blood from the wizard's own red dragon familiar."

"Then this Fireseed—" you begin.

"Is only a giant ruby!" interrupts Rami. "Old people like my uncle believe it is the crystallized drop of red dragon's blood that holds Hektor's evil life-force."

"As it does!" thunders Barakin. "The wizard foretold that the world will end when blood kin of both Ennis Farold and Nivida feed the Fireseed to a dragon in the stomach of a wild boar!"

"What kind of nonsense is that?" you ask hesitantly. The prophecy of Orson, with its mention of a "shadowy" thing with a "blood-red heart," is beginning to take on a sinister new meaning.

"My elder brother remembers all the legends of our ancestors, especially those of our aunt Nivida," says Rami's mother. "Her magic saved the people of Moffid from Hektor's terror. The theft of the Fireseed has made many people in our village think the end of the world is near. Now that a Farold has come to Storm Island, they'll be sure of it!"

"Yes!" spats Barakin. "If he stays here, Hektor's words will come true."

The old man's logic is good. The strange prophecy could not occur if you were somewhere else and never touched the gem called the Fireseed. You're beginning to wonder if

Pona knew about the prophecy when he arranged for you to come to Storm Island.

"Uncle!" Rami says angrily. "This is a warrior, not an unwelcome merchant! He has agreed to help me find the Fireseed."

"That's true, Barakin," says Sala. "Rami needs the help of an experienced fighter, and this is such a man."

The argument among these people has confused you. One thing seems clear. The stolen gemstone—the Fireseed—is a dangerous magical relic of some kind. You've begun to think perhaps that Hektor's spirit WANTS you to seek the Fireseed with Rami so that the evil sorcerer's prophecy will come true.

"I know I promised to go with you," you tell Rami, "but perhaps it'd be better if I had nothing to do with the Fireseed. As your uncle says, the prophecy can't be fulfilled if I'm not with you."

Rami's face flushes. "Don't you see the disgrace my mother is facing because the Fireseed was in her care when it was stolen? What kind of warrior lets an old man's words make him afraid?"

"Rami! Don't speak like that to a guest!" says Sala sternly. "The Fireseed is our worry, not his."

The young native glowers at you once more, then heads for the door. "Where are you going?" asks his mother.

"Back to the volcano," he answers sharply. "The thieves' trail is already two days old, and I want to start at sunrise—with or without help!"

"Don't go to the caves alone, Rami!" Sala cries. "It's too dangerous!"

"I have to go into the caves, Mother. That's where the thieves went. I go alone because everyone here is afraid of old taboos and superstitions!" he adds with a sneer at you just before he rushes out the door.

Sala turns immediately to you. "Please go with him! The thieves of the Fireseed are evil clansmen who have gone to join Hektor's secret cult of cannibals!"

1) If you decide your destiny lies in helping Rami find the sacred gem called the Fireseed, turn to page 93.

2) If you choose not to risk fulfilling the prophecy and want to avoid contact with the Fireseed, turn to page 131.

"I'd better stay with my comrades," you think. "My loyalty is to them."

Just then a powerful bolt of lightning blasts a hole in the ship's side only a few yards away from you! You're hurled against a crate and knocked unconscious as tons of seawater gush through the large opening. You barely feel your body being lifted by a mighty current and carried out the jagged hole.

You're dimly aware of cargo and human bodies swirling around you. Feebly you grab an empty water cask before your senses merge with the darkness of the night.

A grayish light and the cool clamminess of water are the next things you're conscious of. You see that your left hand is looped inside a rope attached to the side of the water barrel. The cask has saved your life, apparently keeping your head above water as a life buoy would do.

You're floating in a calm sea, surrounded by bits of flotsam, which seem to be all that remains of the *Salt Castle*. The sun must be almost up, but you can't see it because of the thick fog bank encircling you.

The image of the bodies of your fellow crew members rushing past you into the dark sea is the last thing you remember. You glance around the choppy water for signs of other survivors. Just then, a loud splash from your left makes you twist your head in that direction. Through the fog, perhaps twenty or thirty yards away, you can see the silhouette of a head and shoulders swimming away from you.

You open your mouth to call out to the man, but you notice that he seems to be flailing the water in panic and turning frequently to look back. "It's one of the warriors from the *Salt Castle*," you realize, "and he's swimming as if he's afraid of something in the water!"

1) You want to yell to the swimmer and try to calm him. Turn to page 23.

2) You'd rather remain quiet behind the barrel until you can see if anything's chasing the swimmer. Turn to page 118.

Rami has turned and raised one of the dual-edged spears to hurl it at the nearest cannibal. You nudge him with your elbow and whisper an idea that has just occurred to you.

"These people are following Yolmat blindly," you tell Rami. "If they knew that even Hektor thought he was insane, they might rebel against his cruelty."

"Try it," Rami urges. "I have no better idea."

You nod and turn to the crowd. "Listen to me, children of Hektor! My friend and I have spoken with your master's shade. It was Hektor's power that destroyed the granary, and it was his wish that we be released. Hektor is angry with Yolmat because he has been cruel to you and to your children. The master wants us to destroy the Fireseed according to his prophecy so that his spirit will be free to punish this fat tyrant!"

The mute cannibals look at each other and then at Yolmat. A few of them converse with rapid hand signals.

"Wait!" calls Yolmat. The headman is sweating, and you can see the fear in his eyes "You must not believe the kinsman of Ennis Farold. He came to steal our master's soul in the enchanted gem! Remember that Hektor has promised to restore your speech once he is free!"

"No!" you shout. 'Hektor told us of Yolmat's insane custom of making your children eat their own tongues, just as he forced you with sorcery to eat your own You must not believe such a creature as this. Even Hektor himself has denounced Yolmat!"

Your mention of the cruel mutilation of their children has the impact you intended on the tribesmen. Yolmat backs away, raising his hands, and starts to chant in a language you don't recognize.

"Stop him!" Rami yells. "He's casting a spell!" You raise your spear to hurl it, but you're not quick enough. Before you can kill the madman yourself, a dozen cannibal spears strike his chest.

Suddenly released from their spellbound slavery to Yolmat, the warriors throng around the evil tyrant's carcass. You turn away from their disgusting revenge on the monster who forced their children to eat their own tongues.

"The Fireseed!" you whisper to Rami.

You both run into the central hut and see a glowing gem in the middle of the room, mounted on a carved bamboo pedestal as if it were some kind of idol. It radiates an inner brilliance, as if it had a living source of energy within its cold crystalline walls.

Rami grabs the stone from the pedestal and tosses it to you. Its glassy surface is so cold that it seems to hurt your hand to hold it. You thrust the gem into a pocket of your trousers and run from the hut with Rami just behind you.

The cannibals are still too busy with Yolmat's corpse to care what you do. No one seems to notice as you slip from the compound's enclosure and race toward the forest. Once you're at a safe distance from the village, you stop to rest in the deepening shadows of sunset.

"Let me see the Fireseed," Rami says, joining you on the ground next to a huge tree. You reach for the enchanted jewel, but it's gone! Your pants pocket must have been torn in the fight with the cannibals.

"It fell out of my pocket somewhere between here and the village!" you cry. "We'll have to retrace our steps to find it!"

You've backtracked only a few hundred yards when you spot the unusual glow of the Fireseed at the side of the trail.

"There it is!" exclaims Rami. The islander lunges for the enchanted gemstone just as a huge wild pig bursts from the bushes in front of you. The animal seems almost hypnotized by the glow of the Fireseed, making you wonder if Hektor's spirit is completely powerless inside the bright crystal.

"Stop that pig!" you yell to Rami. "Don't let it near the jewel!"

Your companion throws himself at the beast, but he's too late. The boar has already reached the Fireseed and wolfs the enchanted gem down his throat! Then the frightened pig grunts and runs from the trail into the darkening shadows of the forest.

"After him, Rami! Remember the prophecy!" you shout.

You bound from the trail, trying to head off

the animal. As you crash through the thin underbrush, the words of the prophecy are ringing in your brain: "The blood kin of Ennis Farold and Nivida will feed the Fireseed to a dragon in the stomach of a wild boar!"

Just ahead of you, the beast leaves the forest and starts to run across a wide rice field. The swift Rami is only a few yards behind the animal and gaining with every step. He has one of the trident spears poised for the kill.

Suddenly the sky above you darkens. You hear the sound of great wings a moment before a strong wind blasts fine volcanic ash into your eyes. Rami's shouts and the boar's squeals reach your ears while you're stumbling blindly forward.

"Look, Davin! The dragon! It's got the wild pig with the Fireseed in its stomach, just as Hektor foretold!"

"Of course!" hisses a familiar voice. You finally rub the ash from your eyes, to see an even dozen of the shade's shadow images on the fringe of the forest.

"There was no way you could have prevented this event from happening, except by your deaths," says the shade. Once more, its voice is muffled so that you can't identify its source.

"I wasn't sure of the day, but I knew it had to be on one of the nights when the fiery fog seeps into Pona's Mouth from the chimneys beneath the dragons' nests. That's how the Fireseed will fall into the subterranean fires,

you see. The dragon and its young will feast on the boar until the gemstone falls through the nest to the lava below."

"Davin!" Rami exclaims. "If we try to recover the Fireseed, we'll breathe the fog of fire and become immortal, like Yolmat and his cult!"

"Precisely," says the shade, "but I forgot to tell you about something else. Anyone who breathes the fiery fog can never take the air from the other side of Ponai into his lungs again. He must remain in Ponai's crater forever or die as soon as he leaves! That's what happened to many of my followers soon after Yolmat's insanity began."

"The skeletons in the Cave of Bones!" you exclaim. "They were trying to leave and got as far as the entrance of the cave before—"

"Exactly!" interrupts the shade. "They lived only as long as they breathed the fumes of the fiery fog that were trapped inside the crater and the caverns. They died instantly when normal air entered their lungs at the cavern's mouth."

A cold feeling sweeps through you as the shade's meaning becomes clear. You turn to Rami.

"We have to choose between following the dragon to its nest or going back to Moffid tonight," you say. "If we try to recover the Fireseed in order to block Hektor's prophecy, we'll breathe the fog of fire and have to stay here forever. But if the prophecy's only a superstition, there will be no destruction of the world. We can return to Moffid right now."

"That's an excellent statement of your dilemma," calls the shade in a laughing voice.

"But you won't be alive to see how we solve it!" shouts Rami. He hurls one of his spears at one of the dark figures by the trees. The deadly shaft strikes the shadowy form but passes through it without resistance.

The booming laughter of Hektor's shade fills the forest as the shadow images merge with the darkness among the trees. The sorcerer's shade has left you alone with what may be the ultimate decision of your quest for the Fire-seed.

1) If you decide to chance the fiery fog to recover the Fireseed, turn to page 129.

2) If you believe that the prophecy is probably just a superstition and not worth the risk of breathing the fiery fog, turn to page 53.

There's something odd about the man in the water, a reminder of something you heard in childhood but can't quite recall. You find a broken oar wedged under a seat and use it to keep the dinghy a few feet away from the stranger.

"Who are you?" you demand suspiciously. "How did you get here?"

"Help me, friend! Pull me into your boat!" the man calls, extending his hand toward you. Instinctively, you reach for it, but stop when you see the webbing between his fingers. You glance from his webbed hand to his face and nearly drop the broken paddle. His nose is no longer human—it's a snout!

All at once the childhood stories burst from your memory: stories of sea monsters and demons, of giant creatures from the ocean depths, and stories of SEAWOLVES!

According to ancient sailors' legends, aquatic werewolves wait as human castaways in the sea for ships to pick them up. Then, at night, they transform themselves into creatures with the heads of wolves and the bodies of seals! Their bites infect their victims, who begin to change almost instantly into seawolves and hurl themselves overboard to join the growing packs of the monsters who bit them.

You clench the hilt of the cutlass. Superstitious sailors warn that only silver or iron blades can stop a seawolf, and you hope that the steel sword contains enough iron to have the magic effect.

"Give me your hand, sailor!" the creature commands. Its voice is now more bestial, almost a growl. You step into the prow of the dinghy as it approaches the wolfish head protruding above the ocean's surface. There are no doubts left in your mind. You draw your cutlass just as the monster hurtles out of the sea at you!

You dodge the creature's lunge and hack at its furry hide with four quick slashes of the curved blade. The cutlass bites into the seawolf's side, nearly severing the flipper that has replaced the webbed hand. The seawolf snarls viciously as its huge body crashes into the lifeboat.

Being careful to avoid the fangs that would infect you, you swing your blade right and left as rapidly as you can without upsetting the boat. The razor edge bites deeply into the creature's flesh, causing its blood to gush onto the deck.

The snarling monster is trying to rise onto its two front flippers, but your powerful blows with the cutlass have made it too weak. You see the seawolf drop its head slightly and expose its neck by accident.

You swing the blade, catching the monster on the back of the neck. In seconds, the battle is over. You're horrified anew when the creature begins changing back into the youthful form of the human it once was

Satisfied that the seawolf is dead, you dump the corpse over the gunwales of the small rowboat. Almost immediately, the sea swarms with long brownish figures. You count six, seven, then eight of the huge creatures!

"It must be the seawolf pack!" you mutter.

They're swimming so close to the wobbly boat that you can feel their heavy bodies brush against the hull. A chill races through your blood when you realize that they've wedged themselves against the sides of the dinghy and are taking you with them!

You're not anxious to go wherever the pack is heading, but you're also doubtful whether you can stop so many of them.

1) If you want to attack the creatures, turn to page 11.

2) If you'd rather try to break free of them and choose your own destination, turn to page 70.

"Rami, I'm beginning to doubt that Hektor's occult powers are capable of the kind of destruction he prophesied," you tell the islander. "His shade has some limited magical power, but I haven't noticed anything to suggest an ability to destroy the world."

"My uncle Barakin says that most of his powers are locked inside the Fireseed," Rami replies. "What you and I have seen of his shade's abilities are those few that leaked from the crystal prison. Even those were controlled as long as the Fireseed remained within Hektor's own skull."

You study the darkening sky for a long moment, wondering in which of the ancient nests the dragon is eating its special meal. Finally you grip Rami's shoulder firmly.

"I know how important the Fireseed is to you and your mother, but so is your life, Rami. We've got to get out of here before that fiery fog covers the crater valley. I'm going back, Rami, and I want you to come with me."

The native warrior shakes his head. "I have to stay here," he says stubbornly. "The village elders blame my mother for the loss of the Fireseed. I must do what I can to get it back, even if it means I might never leave this crater alive!"

"Listen to me, Rami!" you exclaim. "The prophecy of the end of the world must be nothing more than superstition. If Hektor's spirit is released, why would he want to practice his sorcery in a destroyed world? Come back with me before it's too late!"

Rami shakes his head and smiles grimly. "You must go. It's almost dark, and the fiery mists will be starting soon if Hektor's shade was truthful. I'll find the dragon's nest and get the Fireseed. You must tell my mother and the elders that it's safe with me."

You squeeze the courageous warrior's arm and turn hurriedly toward the crater wall. "I'll be back for you," you call, "between the tides, when the fiery fog is gone. I won't rest until we figure out a way to get both you and the Fireseed out of Ponai's crater!"

"I know you will, Davin!" your friend shouts as he turns away and runs toward the spot where the dragon flew with the enchanted Fireseed inside the boar's belly. You cast one last look after the bold native, then hasten for the safety of Ponai's outer wall so that you may attempt your quest again one day in the future.

THE END

You decide that the storm giant's tale about your grandfather and the sorcerer Hektor is too fantastic to believe. The thought that the evil wizard might still be alive after more than two centuries sounds like superstitious nonsense to you. The stories surrounding Storm Island, though, are a different matter.

"If just half of the legends have some truth in them, those villagers are worse than any evil Orson or Pona could have foreseen," you reason.

The stories of the Storm Island cannibals convince you that it would be a mistake to try talking to them. You're confident that you could handle as many as a half dozen untrained fighters, but there would be many more than that, even in the small village on this beach. You decide to wait until everyone is asleep and then try to steal one of the outrigger canoes to sail to a neighboring island.

You crouch in the water with only your head breaking the surface, watching the fires on the beach die, one by one. You wait another half hour after the last flame has died, then move silently toward the village.

The building straight ahead is the largest hut on the beach, but there aren't any canoes under it. A bamboo ladder on the water side ascends to a wide veranda hanging over the surf and running all around the large building. You slip into the shadows beneath the big porch to scout your surroundings.

There are two outrigger canoes in the shallow water beneath the next hut, as well as several rows of cleaned fish drying on a string between the pilings.

"With that food, I could stay alive in one of those canoes until I reach a friendlier island," you think.

You start to cross the patch of moonlight leading to the next hut but stop when you notice some jugs hanging in an open window just off the veranda above your head. The large building seems deserted, and you'll probably need some containers for drinking water aboard a canoe in the open sea.

1) If you think it's necessary to get the water jugs before stealing a canoe, turn to page 126.

2) If it seems too risky to take the jugs, turn to page 107.

"Let's go back to the sea cave where you lost the thieves' trail and start there," you suggest. "Whatever killed the people in the Cave of Bones might still be in there."

You and Rami leave the ledge with its tabooed Cave of Bones and return to the seawater inlet. When you're both up to your waists in the warm salt water, you peer into the darkness of the jagged cave cut into the black lava rock.

"I can't see anything from here," you tell Rami. You wade into the mouth of the sea cave, moving slowly so that you won't splash and warn anyone of your approach. You've gone about ten yards into the cave when you spot a pile of strange objects against the left wall.

"Look, Rami," you whisper, pulling him closer. "There's something over there on that rock shelf, above the water."

You both climb onto the slippery ledge to investigate the articles heaped on the stone floor and covered with seaweed. At first you can't identify the items, but then Rami rubs one, and diamonds gleam in the light from the cave's mouth.

"A necklace!" you gasp. "Worth thousands of gold pieces!" You both drop to your knees and rummage through the treasure trove. There are magnificent weapons with finely made hilts and scabbards, jewelry of every description, and even some ancient coins.

"How could these things have gotten here?"

asks Rami. "They couldn't float."

Just then, a mountain of mottled green flesh rises from the warm inlet, dripping gallons of seawater from its slimy hide. The monster is one of the most hideous creatures you've ever seen. It's covered with warts and growths, and two writhing mandibles protrude from its cheeks, guarding a drooling, fang-filled maw.

"What's that?" Rami gasps as you both drop the treasures in your hands and back away from the gigantic monster.

"A vodyanoi!" you whisper.

The creature's huge bulk blocks out nearly all the sunlight from the cave's entrance. Its fan-shaped ears are flexing while its gills wheeze in the dank cavern air.

The sea monster's beady eyes are adapted for hunting in the deep ocean, and you doubt if it can see you very well. You must act quickly, before the giant creature hears or smells you.

1) If you want to attack the vodyanoi, turn to page 128.

2) If you decide to try to escape in the darkness, turn to page 115.

"We might as well wait a bit," you tell Rami. "We'll have to breathe that fog no matter when we go for the Fireseed, and there's no point in fighting one of those creatures if we don't have to!"

Rami nods, and the two of you take turns watching for the adult pterodactyl to leave its nest unguarded. The fiery mist has just begun to creep over the rim of the dinosaur's woven lair when you turn away to rest while Rami keeps watch.

You recall Orson's warning about the fiery fog and the shadowy thing with a glowing red heart. Now you know what the young cleric was seeing in his vision—Hektor's shade with the sorcerer's evil life-force trapped inside the Fireseed.

"Davin!" Rami whispers urgently. "It's leaving!"

You leap to your feet and find that the fog of fire is all around you. The entire sky of the crater is now ablaze with the cold blue and purple flames. The mother pterodactyl has just soared away to circle in the eerie fog with others of her ancient kind. Rami has already crossed the cliff toward the undefended nest by the time you start after him.

The fiery fog is thicker near the reptile's lair. You can't avoid breathing the odorless fumes, but you feel only a slight lightheadedness mingled with a sensation of high energy. Fatigue vanishes, and you feel as if you could go on indefinitely without resting.

Rami has reached the rim of the nest when you arrive at its base. "Davin, I can see the Fireseed!" he whispers. "It's still in the pig's carcass. I think I can get it."

"Wait for me!" you call, but the islander has already vanished from the edge of the aerie. You start up the wall of interwoven branches, but you freeze when you hear Rami's blood-curdling scream mingled with excited squawks from the baby dinosaurs.

"Hold on!" you yell. "I'm almost there!"

When you reach the top edge of the nest, you see a gruesome sight by the light of the fiery fog. Rami is lying at the bottom of the nest, and two huge young pterodactyls are gnawing on his legs with their crocodilian teeth.

You hurl your spear at the closest nestling. The barbed trident's points enter the young creature's side just below its immature wings. At the instant the spear strikes, the nest explodes with fury. The wounded beast thrashes around so wildly that it knocks its sibling away from Rami's legs.

Seizing your opportunity, you drop to the bottom of the nest. In the eerie light of the fiery fog, you can see that Rami's injuries look serious.

The wounded dinosaur stops its frenzied thrashing and squawking suddenly. You glance at it just in time to see the creature's eyes glaze in death. The other young pterodactyl is cowering beneath its nestmate's body.

"Can you hear me, Rami?" you ask the

native warrior, whose tanned face seems to be burning with the multicolored cold flames of the fog. "Did you get the Fireseed?"

Rami nods weakly and tries to hold up his left hand. You see the bright red glow even before he opens his fist.

"Give it to me," you tell your injured friend. "This time it goes in the other pocket!" The islander smiles and hands you the precious gem, then loses consciousness.

When the Fireseed is safely in your untorn pocket, you rip several strips of cloth from Rami's sarong and tie them tightly around his gashed legs. Once you're satisfied that the tourniquets have stopped the bleeding, you brace yourself and lift the warrior slowly out of the nest.

Now you must choose whether to try and leave the crater, or get help for Rami where you are.

1) If you feel you must risk the fog's effect to save Rami, turn to 108.

2) If you think it's already too late for you to leave Ponai and survive, turn to 106.

"Let's get some fresh air!" you exclaim, pointing toward the passage with the strange scratching noises in the distance. "At least there's something alive down that way."

Rami grins and turns from the corridor with the horrible stench. "Dead things can be much safer than live ones!" he jokes, but he joins you in front of the more pleasant corridor. As soon as he enters the other tunnel, the torch flame starts to flicker in a strong breeze.

The passage slopes upward immediately. In places, it's so steep that you have to brace yourself against the rock walls to keep from sliding backward. After several hundred yards of strenuous climbing, Rami gasps excitedly.

"I can see an opening just ahead!"

The islander quickens his steps, climbing the last thirty yards as if he were anxious to see the sunlight again. You hasten your own pace so that you both burst into open air at the same time.

The corridor spills onto a ledge high on the inner wall of the ancient volcano's crater. Directly in front of you, in the middle of the ledge, there's a gigantic circular nest with a gentle haze of steam rising from it into the sky. You can't see into the nest from where you are, but loud scratching noises are coming from inside its tightly woven walls.

From the ledge, the view of Ponai's center is breathtaking. Instead of a barren core, the collapsed volcano contains a lush valley, complete with shimmering streams and thick tropical forests. Many wisps of either steam or smoke curl upward into the blue sky above the ancient volcano, coming from more of the huge nests scattered across the rugged interior slopes of the crater.

Thin streams of smoke waft upward from cleared sections of jungle in the central valley. There are people living in the center of Ponai! You're so surprised that all you can do is stand and stare for a few minutes.

"What is this place, anyway?" you mutter finally. "Who are those people down there?"

Rami is just as dumbfounded as you are and shakes his head numbly. "I don't know. Some people say that Hektor and his cannibal cult were banished to the core of Ponai. I never believed them. But now . . ."

"What kind of monstrous bird could have made those nests?" you ask him.

"I don't know that, either," he says, "but we can find out right now!" He steps onto the ledge and heads for the huge nest with its strange scratching sounds.

You know you have a choice to make.

1) If you want to follow Rami to the nest, turn to page 122.

2) If you decide you'd better leave the nest alone, turn to page 135.

In desperation, you lunge for the nearest outrigger canoe. You fumble in the darkness with the hide cord that ties the lightweight but sturdy craft to the pier. It loosens finally, and you're able to push the canoe away from the pilings.

There are several long paddles with blades on each end, and you grab one. As you guide the boat through the surf and out to sea, the native warriors are shouting and hurling spears at you.

"Into the canoes! After him!"

You glance over your shoulder long enough to see several canoes filled with natives shoot into the surf behind you. The experienced islanders paddle with synchronized teamwork, propelling them rapidly toward you.

You paddle even harder, turning toward the beach in an effort to outmaneuver your pursuers. The strategy fails. Two of the canoes turn just as you do and cut you off while another one circles around behind you.

The night air is filled with the excited cries of warriors and the dark shafts of their spears. You have the cutlass halfway out of your waistband when the first spear strikes your back. Your numb, dying brain knows only a little pain as many others find their marks with bone-jarring thuds.

THE END

"What do you think, Rami?" you ask your companion. "Should we enter one of these passages, or split up and explore both of them at the same time?"

"I've heard stories of people getting lost in the many caverns inside Ponai's walls," replies Rami. "Let's stay together. Which one do we want to explore first?"

You nod and step closer to the dark opening on your right. You pause, sniffing the air and listening for suspicious sounds. You smell the distinctive odor of fresh air and hear a distant scratching sound.

The other tunnel is more unpleasant. From it, a horrible smell of decaying flesh nearly overwhelms you. The stench is so repulsive that you jerk your head away from the opening quickly.

"Whew! That's bad!" you exclaim, screwing your face into an expression of disgust. The foul odor doesn't seem to bother Rami as much as it does you. In fact, he's peering into the second passage, trying to imagine what could be the source of such a stench.

1) If you prefer to trace the horrible smell, turn to page 102.

2) If you'd rather take the passage leading to fresh air and distant scratching noises, turn to page 63.

Sala's description of Hektor's evil is etched in your memory. You can believe nothing his shade tells you.

Disregarding the trail toward the volcano, you continue on the narrow path that leads deeper into the island jungle.

You follow the faint trail for nearly an hour. Finally, you stop and crouch beside the path, looking desperately for any sign of Rami's footprints.

When your raise your head, you're sure that something about the jungle has changed, but you can't tell what exactly. You move down the trail a little way, and you have a stronger sense of something being wrong—very wrong. Just then, from the corner of your eye, you spot a huge clump of vegetation moving closer to you!

An idea pops into your head: "I'll bet that Hektor's shade is hiding in that mound of rotten leaves!"

Turning your back to the shifting pile of vegetation, you grasp your cutlass and prepare to charge the spectral creature. You count silently to three, tensing your muscles with each number.

"One . . . two . . . THREE!" You spin around and raise your sword to hack at the hidden shade—but face a massive monster made of rotten leaves, moss, and writhing roots! It towers several feet over your head and is sending scores of tendrils to entangle your arms and legs.

It's a shambler, a semi-intelligent monster whose brain is located in the center of its vine-encrusted midsection! You recall numerous tales of the carnivorous plant creatures in the eastern provinces but have never seen one yourself.

You hack with fury at the roots and creepers the shambling mound is shooting at your body. Your blows have little effect on the vegetable creature. They merely knock a few leaves to the ground while the monster's mass continues to press itself against you.

Your arms begin to tire as several sets of thick vines coil themselves around your body and draw you tightly into the stinking mound of rotten leaves. More tendrils twine around your limbs and neck. The pressure is more than you can stand, and you slip into blessed darkness as you become a meal for the hideous shambler.

THE END

The sinister shapes crowded against the small hull are too far below the surface to use your cutlass, so you try to paddle away from the monsters. But they're much too powerful. The dinghy moves so fast that a white spray churns as it knifes through the dark water.

"I'll just have to wait until they slow down," you think desperately.

When one of the beasts' wide back breaks the surface, you see large scales gleaming in the moonlight instead of the wet fur of a seawolf! When the heavy head rises from the water with a deep roar, it has the muzzle of a giant sea lion, the creatures of legends kept by storm giants as pets and guards!

Just when you're considering leaping over the side in a last-ditch attempt to escape, the sea lions suddenly vanish, and the prow of the dinghy settles down into the waves. In the distance, you can hear the roar of heavy surf. The sea lions have brought you within swimming distance of an island!

You peer over the gunwales into the water. In the bright moonlight, you can see brilliant white sand on the shallow bottom, perhaps only twenty or thirty feet below the surface. Thousands of fish are scurrying around the hull of your boat, darting in and out of clumps of seaweed. There are no sea lions.

White-capped breakers are crashing against a coral reef a mile or so in front of you. Just beyond the reef, moonlight gleams on a beautiful lagoon and beach. The dark shadows of a thick jungle lie just beyond the sand. Above the tops of the trees, a wall of bare stone rises dramatically into the night.

"THAT IS THE MOUNTAIN HUMANS CALL PONAI, THE 'VOICE OF PONA'—MY VOICE!"

The booming words sweep over you like thunder rolling across a hilly pasture. You were so interested in the island that you didn't notice the giant creature who has approached you from the rear.

It's a storm giant, one of the most powerful beings on earth! Even in the moonlight, you can see the greenish cast of his skin and beard, and his glowing emerald eyes. Seaweed is stuck to his face and shoulders, the only portions of the giant visible in the water.

"Pona, the sea god?" you ask in disbelief.

"NATIVES OF YOUR SPECIES CALL ME THAT," he admits, "BUT I AM NOT A GOD AT ALL. I BELONG TO THE ANCIENT RACE OF STORM GIANTS, THOSE BEINGS WHO INHABIT CLOUDS AS WELL AS THE SEA!"

"Then those sea lions—"

"THEY WERE MY PETS! I SENT THEM FOR YOU, DAVIN FAROLD, TO BRING YOU HERE—TO STORM ISLAND!"

The giant's use of your name and his mention of the legendary island of terror send tingles to your scalp. "Why did you want me to come to Storm Island?" you ask Pona. "How did you know my name?"

"THE SEA IS FILLED WITH MY SER-VANTS," thunders Pona. "THERE ARE NO SECRETS FROM ME IN MY OCEAN DOMAIN. THAT IS WHY YOU ARE HERE, AND THAT IS WHY I SENT THE STORM TO INTERRUPT YOUR HOMEWARD VOYAGE! ONLY YOU CAN PREVENT SOMETHING THAT MUST NEVER HAPPEN!"

"People died in that storm!" you protest. "Brave warriors and mariners who served their country well!"

"AS THEY WILL AGAIN!" booms the giant. "YOUR VESSEL IS STILL AFLOAT, DAMAGED BUT SEAWORTHY. ONLY A HANDFUL OF YOUR COMRADES SACRI-FICED THEIR LIVES TO GET YOU HERE, DAVIN FAROLD."

"What do you mean?" you demand. "Why me?"

"ARE YOU NOT THE DIRECT DESCEN-DANT OF ENNIS FAROLD, THE HOLY ARCHCLERIC?" Pona thunders.

All that you know of your priestly ancestor is that he gained fame by banishing a power-ful evil wizard from Baysend more than three hundred years ago. The wizard's name was Hektor, and it is said that he had the power to summon demons.

"Archcleric Ennis was my ancestor," you admit. "Why? What does that have to with your bringing me here to Storm Island?"

"ENNIS FAROLD WAS ONE OF THE FEW HUMANS I EVER BEFRIENDED IN MY

LIFETIME," answers the storm giant.

"But he's been dead for centuries!" you cry.

"MY RACE DOES NOT COUNT LIFE-TIMES IN THE BLINK OF AN EYE," Pona explains. "WE LIVE MUCH LONGER THAN HUMANS, AND PAY LITTLE ATTENTION TO THEIR AFFAIRS. BUT SOMETHING EVIL IS GROWING ON STORM ISLAND FROM THE SPIRIT OF YOUR ANCESTOR'S UNDEAD ENEMY, HEKTOR!"

"That's impossible!" you protest. "The sorcerer Hektor—"

"LIVES!" interrupts the giant. "AND HIS EVIL POWERS THREATEN TO DESTROY ALL THE LANDS YOUR NOBLE ANCESTOR ONCE DENIED TO HIM! HE HAS BECOME MORE POWERFUL THAN EVER, AND ONLY A DESCENDANT OF ENNIS FAROLD CAN STOP HIM!"

Suddenly you recall the cleric Orson's prophecy of the fiery fog and the evil shadow with its red heart. You look at the mountain called Ponai and wonder if that was the place Orson saw in his vision.

"How could I stop a sorcerer?" you demand. "I'm a warrior. I fight physical evils, not magical ones."

"ENNIS FAROLD'S WISDOM LIVES IN YOU," Pona replies. "YOU WILL KNOW WHAT TO DO WHEN THE TIME COMES!"

Before you can ask more questions, the storm giant raises two massive hands from the sea and claps them together. Suddenly the world seems to explode. A huge wave nearly thirty feet high looms above you, then crashes powerfully over the small dinghy.

You're washed out of the boat by the force of the mysterious lone wave, and you try to swim against its great undertow. Just when you think you'll be able to break free, another huge wave crests beneath you, lifting you completely out of the water. With the speed of a typhoon, it rushes your helpless body toward the forbidding coral reef.

It all happens in less than a minute. The wave vanishes from beneath you, sinking back gently into the sea and leaving nothing but sizzling foam behind. There's no sign of either the storm giant or the dinghy, and you're in the gentler surf of the quiet lagoon, only a few hundred yards from the beach.

You swim forward until you can stand on the sandy bottom. The beach is dotted with fires and stilted huts, with huge outrigger canoes tied to the hut pilings.

You're faced with two choices.

1) If you wish to approach the natives in the huts and find out what you can about Pona's tale, turn to page 26.

2) If you prefer to ignore the storm giant's story and try to steal a canoe to sail away from Storm Island, turn to page 55.

You glance at the nearest outrigger, but see that the native warriors down the beach are already pushing several war canoes into the surf. You realize with a sinking feeling that you'd have no chance at all to outrun the islanders, even if you were an expert paddler.

"Wait!" you yell, raising your arms high above your head. "I'm not a thief!"

The natives become silent for a moment while you walk toward them in the shallow surf. The beach is now so crowded with torch-bearers that you can feel the heat even before you step from the water. The closest islanders step back, as if they fear touching you.

"Let me through!" calls a commanding voice from the crowd. A tall, well-muscled man around your own age is pushing his way toward you.

"It's one of the men who stole the gem from the skull, Rami!" someone exclaims.

The man named Rami glances at your face and at your cutlass. Then he raises his steel-tipped spear. "This man isn't one of those who took the Fireseed. Maybe he's a pirate."

Rami then gestures toward your sword with his spear. "Give me your cutlass," he orders. "We will go to our Council Hut to my uncle, Barakin, our village headman and shaman. He won't talk to an armed stranger."

You hesitate, but you decide that you have little choice in the matter. There are far too many warriors for you to fight, and your only alternative is to meet with the headman. Mur-

murs run through the crowd of villagers as
you surrender your blade to the young fighter
whose body looks as powerful as your own.

The nephew of the village headman escorts
you through the mob of onlookers to the front
of the large hut you almost burgled for water
jugs. There's a light on inside it now, and the
silhouette of a woman with waist-long dark
hair is framed by the doorway. Rami nudges
you up some wooden steps on the beach side
and ushers you past the woman into a large
room with woven mats on the floor.

Please turn to page 36.

You stare at the immense ruby in your palm and turn to Rami. "Are you sure that the Fireseed glows?" you ask him. "Is it possible that what you call a 'glow' is only a reflection from other light?"

Rami looks more closely at the gem, examining it from every angle. Finally he sighs and shakes his head. "There's only one way to know," he says. "If this is the real Fireseed, it will glow in the dark like fire."

"That's it, clansman of Nivida!" hisses the voice of Hektor's shade. "Extinguish your torch and test the trinket."

"If you want us to have the Fireseed, then tell us where it is!" you shout, but the shade is silent. "Go ahead," you urge Rami, "douse the light."

The islander crushes the flaming tip of his torch against one of the pumice boulders. With the flames reduced to embers, you can see that the gem in your hand lacks the Fireseed's fabled glow. It's nothing but a worthless piece of glass!

"The shade was right," you tell Rami, and you hurl the counterfeit gem into the deep abyss. As it shatters against the chasm walls, Rami blows on the torch until the embers burst into bright flames again.

Please turn to page 63.

You look at the huddled shapes of the feeding beasts and are reminded of a flock of vultures you once saw ripping apart the carcass of a dead rabbit. You also see that the fiery fog is getting thicker every minute.

"I think we'd better move quickly," you tell Rami. "The fiery fog is really starting to fill the crater. And, from the sounds of that feast next door, the Fireseed will be rattling inside that boar's skeleton in no time at all."

You both check your spears for the coming battle and slide from your ledge to the face of the cliff. You run silently toward the nest where the pterodactyls are much too busy gnashing and tearing at the pig's fresh, warm meat to notice either of you. The fiery mist is hovering at the top of the aerie, so you are still shrouded in semidarkness.

"If one of us can draw the adult away from the nest, the other might be able to reach the boar's body and get the Fireseed," Rami suggests quickly.

"Good idea," you tell him. "I'll go for the gemstone if you'll keep that dragon thing off my tail!"

Rami leaps forward and grabs a branch protruding from the nest, then pulls himself up to the rim. His head pops into the thickening fog of fire for only an instant. You see him prod something with his spear and hear a loud, hissing roar from inside the aerie. The woven wall shifts as the angry monster bursts out of its lair into the fiery haze. Rami flings himself away from the side of the nest and drops to the dark ledge.

"Go when I yell!" he calls to you. Then he pokes his spear at the monstrous crest of the pterodactyl, framed in the glow of the dangerous fog. "Here I am!" he screams as loud as he can. The monster's gigantic wings unfurl as the creature hops down from its perch to land beside Rami. You start to charge the beast to save the islander from the dinosaur, but he waves you away.

"Get inside the nest! Get the Fireseed!" Rami yells bravely.

You follow the plan, ignoring whatever might be happening to the islander, and climb the nest wall as easily as if it were a ladder. When you reach the top, you hold your breath to avoid drawing the fog of fire into your lungs.

Just below you, at the bottom of the nest, you see the half-eaten pig being devoured by the two young dinosaurs. Still holding your breath, you climb closer and thrust your spear at it.

The barbed trident end sinks into the dead boar's skull, but half your breath is forced out of your lungs by the force of the thrust. With a hurried glance at the fiery fog, you test the weight of the carcass against the strength of the barbs and find that the trident is expertly made. With the barbed prongs set in the skull, you begin to pull the wild pork cadaver out of the nest.

"Hold on, Davin!" you mentally command yourself, desperate to control your need for air. "Don't breathe the fog!"

The two young pterodactyls start squawking when they see their dinner escaping, but they seem too frightened to attack you. Your tortured lungs give out just as you haul the heavy carcass onto the rim of the nest. You hang your head down on its outer side and fill your chest with normal air.

Feeling refreshed and stronger, you jerk the carcass over the side at the same moment you hear a terrible shriek from the adult pterodactyl. Rami has just whacked the dinosaur on its long beak with his spear shaft and is trying to drive the monster away from the nest with the spear's pointed end.

You drop to the ground, wishing you had your cutlass now. All you have to dissect the pig is the sharpened edge of the spearhead. You plunge the point into the boar's midsection and rip the stomach open.

Fireseed's bright red glow is like a flare in the darkness. You grab for the enchanted jewel just as Rami screams in horrible pain only a few feet away. Clutching the gemstone, you charge toward the battling pair. In the ghostly glow of the spreading fog, you see the huge creature's pointed beak tearing at your companion's legs with its reptilian teeth.

"HEY! COME HERE!" you shout, prodding the pterodactyl's leathery hide with the trident end of your spear. The monster turns away from Rami, whose unconscious form slips to the ground in a pool of his own blood.

You continue teasing the giant creature until it starts to follow your every movement. Finally, you step over the pig's corpse so that the dinosaur has to reach over it to get to you. The smell of the boar's blood excites the monster's small brain. It stops chasing you and resumes its feast on the fresh pork.

Rushing to Rami's side, you quickly tear some cloth strips for tourniquets from his own sarong and tie them above his gushing leg wounds. Then you hoist your friend in your arms and try to decide the best thing to do for him.

1) Despite what you've heard about the effect of the fiery fog, you opt to take Rami and the Fireseed back to Moffid. Turn to 151.

2) Fearful that you've already breathed the fiery fog, you feel you can't take Rami out of the volcano. Turn to 106.

Despite the confusion of the three shadow images, it suddenly dawns on you that Hektor's shade was probably telling you the truth about Rami's location.

"Hektor wants us to find each other because he prophesied that descendants of BOTH Ennis Farold and the druid priestess Nivida would destroy the Fireseed!" you think.

The shade's reasons for directing you to Sala's son are chilling, but you decide to follow its advice anyway. You need an ally against this powerful evil creature, and Rami is a natural warrior. You return to the junction of the trail where it begins to climb into the loose rocks of the great volcano.

"If I stay close to the side of the volcano, where I can spot his footprints in the bare dirt, I can pick up his trail again," you reason quickly.

The sharp rubble is painful to your bare feet, which are accustomed to the protection of heavy boots, and you pick your way gingerly. You're almost at the vertical wall of the ancient cone when you spot a movement behind you. In a split second, you roll to one side, causing your attacker to land on the hard rocky ground instead of on top of you. It's Rami!

You're on your feet instantly, your cutlass raised over Rami's stunned head and a foot clamped firmly on the shaft of his spear.

"Make a move, and I'll split your skull!" you warn him. Rami clenches his jaw and says nothing. Most men would betray some sign of fear, but he remains totally calm.

"I thought you would not seek the Fireseed," he says casually. From his relaxed voice, no one would suspect that this man is facing death. "Did your evil master change his mind and send you after me, or did you decide to do it yourself?"

"Hektor's shade did send me to you, but not as his henchman," you admit to Rami. You then tell him of your encounter with the sorcerer's shade and its shadow images.

"I think he intends to help us find the Fireseed," you tell Rami, "in order to destroy it through us, as he prophesied."

Rami's expression doesn't change, but you can tell from his long silence that he's considering whether or not to believe what you've just told him. You decide to be the first to demonstrate mutual trust. You release his spear shaft from your foot, lower your cutlass, and offer your hand to the native fighter. He hesitates for a moment, then grasps it and lets you pull him to his feet.

His grip is just as powerful as yours, and you catch yourself wondering who would win if you ever had to fight this agile and strong warrior, especially without the advantages of modern armor. Rami is studying your physique, too, probably trying to weigh your fighting skills in the same fashion.

"Maybe we can teach each other a few things after we return the Fireseed to Hektor's skull," you suggest with a grin.

Rami frowns for several seconds until he understands your meaning. Then he smiles, too, and clasps your shoulder with a friendly hand. "I'd like that," he tells you earnestly. "I've always wanted to learn more about western weapons and ways of fighting."

You find yourself liking the native's honesty and directness. "Not many people in Baysend are as open and relaxed as Rami," you think as the warrior gestures toward the sheer rock face of Ponai.

"The caves are this way," he tells you. "I'll show you where I lost the thieves' trail."

The wall of the volcano forms a sheer gray face extending into the morning fog high above your head. It's such a smooth vertical side that you doubt if you could climb it without special ropes and other equipment.

"Don't worry," says Rami, smiling at your doubtful frown. "We won't have to climb it."

He leads you along the narrow apron between the mountainside and the jungle for several miles. The trail goes up a slight incline, and you can see that the jungle is thinner just ahead. Rami shows you an occasional footprint along the edge of the volcano's base.

"They lead past a sea cave, where the jungle disappears," he says. "There are a few more tracks on the other side of the cave, but they all head back this way."

When you reach the next curve in Ponai's walls, you see what Rami was talking about.

The ocean extends into the side of the volcano at a narrow inlet, forming a craggy sea cave. The jungle is split by the inlet, and the trail along Ponai's base continues just beyond the mouth of the cavern.

Rami slips into the water at the cave, nodding for you to follow. The shallow inlet is filled with warm salt water, heated not by the sun but by underground fires of the great volcano. As you tread silently across the inlet in the sheltered mouth of the large sea cave, you peer into the blackness but see nothing.

On the opposite side of the inlet, you note other footprints, all but one pair headed toward you. "Those prints are mine, from yesterday," says Rami, pointing to the ones that continue on past the mouth of the cavern. "The others lead this way from the direction of the Cave of Bones. Come on, I'll show you."

Beyond the sea cave, the jungle reappears, but the apron trail is higher than before. Rami points to a dark cavern on a ledge above the path. "That's the tabooed Cave of Bones. Its name comes from the human skeletons just inside its mouth. No one knows what happened to the dead people, or where they came from. We would know if that many island people died or disappeared."

"Perhaps it's the lair of some kind of flesh-eater," you suggest.

"No," Rami replies. "The skeletons are lying just as they died, with only a few bones chewed by cave rats. A flesh-eater would have moved them."

You agree with your companion's logic and wonder what mysterious force might have killed so many people in the same place. "What do we do now?" you ask.

"The Cave of Bones and the sea cave are the only routes the thieves of the Fireseed could have taken into Ponai's caverns," Rami answers. "We must enter one of them."

1) If the sea cave seems the better way to go, turn to page 57.

2) If the Cave of Bones, despite its apparent danger, seems a more likely route to the Fireseed, turn to page 110.

"I don't like the idea of stealing the gem," you tell Hektor's shade. "I'm a fighter, not a thief. Still, it may be the only way we can get past all those guards out there."

"And you, clansman of Nivida?" the shade asks Rami. "Do you prefer to be released from this makeshift jail at night rather than now?"

Rami shakes his head. "No, but I agree with Davin. There are too many cannibals to risk a fight. Our quest is to get the Fireseed. I don't care how we do it, but I have to take that gem back to my village!"

"So you choose to steal the gem. Excellent!" the shade exclaims. "Rest now. I shall return for you after midnight."

The dark forms in each of the seven compartments of the granary begin to fade. In less than a minute, there's no sign at all of the shadow images.

"Why are we trusting that thing?" Rami asks. "Hektor would do anything to destroy the Fireseed! Why should he want us to have it?"

"I've thought about that, too," you reply. "It looks to me as if Hektor's shade has been mixing the truth with half-truths and lies. I think the only way the Fireseed can be destroyed is by casting it into Ponai's lava. And for some reason, only you and I can destroy it—and the world, if the prophecy is true. It must have to do with our ancestors' magical powers and wisdom, and releasing Hektor's spirit."

"So Hektor's helping us steal the Fireseed

just so we'll be able to destroy it!"

You nod. "That's the way I see it. Once we have it, he'll probably do everything he can to keep us from returning it to your mother. If she puts it back inside the skull, the shade will be completely powerless."

Rami frowns and shakes his head. "If the shade has any power at all with Hektor's energy being locked in the Fireseed, it'd use it. I think the shade has very few magical powers and must use lies to get its way. We shouldn't trust it at all!"

You consider your companion's words very carefully. "He's probably right," you think. "Hektor's shade wouldn't tell us everything, but right now we don't have any other choice."

"Well, whether we trust it or not, the shade was right about resting," you tell Rami. "Let's try to doze until midnight."

You both make yourselves comfortable in the piles of rice, and you drift to sleep just moments after Rami's soft snores echo in the next grain stall.

"Wake yourselves. It's time to steal the gem!" The shade's voice appears in your brain, but you don't really hear it. Rami is stirring in the next compartment, so you assume that he's sensing the same words in his thoughts. The interior of the granary is lit by a ghostly glow from outside the straw walls, as if the entire compound were on fire.

Before you can ask the shade about it, there's a heavy thud on the other side of the door, and the panel opens silently onto a curious sight. The air is burning! There seems to be a thick fog covering everything, and the fog is burning with violet and blue flames!

"Those are the strangest flames I've ever seen," says Rami. He extends an arm into the air. "They do not burn!"

"The guards are gone!" you exclaim. "Let's go to Yolmat's council chamber and get the Fireseed."

The two of you cross the courtyard quickly so that you won't have to remain within the fiery air any longer than is necessary, and enter the large Council Hut.

"Look at that pedestal," says Rami. "I'll bet the Fireseed was there, but it's gone now!"

He's pointing to a tall platform made of bamboo that's standing upright in the very center of the spacious room. On top of the platform is a soft pillow of woven cloth with an egg-sized depression in it.

"You're probably right," you whisper. "They must move the Fireseed during the night to protect it from thieves like us! Where would they put it?"

"In a chest like that one," Rami replies. He indicates a small wooden chest against the wall. "It's like the one my mother keeps Hektor's skull in."

You hurry to the chest, but you can't find any way to open it. "There's usually a trick to these things," you mutter. "There's a piece that moves with the pressure of your fingers and then—"

Your forefinger suddenly slips into a crevice. "Ouch!" you cry, sucking the tip of your finger. "There's a needle of some kind hidden inside."

"A needle!" Rami exclaims in a hoarse whisper. "That means the chest is trapped! That needle is probably poisonous!"

You stare at the single drop of blood on the tip of your finger. As your vision begins to fade, you begin to have new respect for professional thieves.

The last image in your dying mind is a shadowy thing whose heart is a shining, pulsating red jewel, and the last sound you hear is that of distant, hollow laughter.

THE END

You've never run from a fight before, and you're starting to feel very strongly that you're not meant to run from this one.

"I didn't come here by accident," you tell Sala. "The being you call Pona, the storm god, brought me to this island for a special quest—to face Hektor's evil spirit and stop his plans for vengeance upon my ancestral homelands. From what I've heard here, it seems that your son's quest for the Fireseed and mine are intertwined. Perhaps we can help each other."

Tears flood the woman's brown eyes. "May the gods of our people guard you as they do my own son," she whispers.

"I'm warning you for the last time," says Barakin, pointing at you with a trembling finger. "This man is the one in Hektor's prophecy. It will be his hand that feeds the Fireseed to the dragon and brings the end of the world!"

"Be quiet, my brother!" Sala demands. "We both know that Hektor's cannibal cult is behind the theft of the sacred jewel. They will stop at nothing to have their evil leader back among them. I don't want Rami to seek the Fireseed alone, and this man is a warrior."

Barakin's frown deepens as he listens to his sister's words. Then he snorts rudely and stalks from the hut, just as Rami did a few minutes earlier.

Rami's mother shakes her head sadly. "Barakin is a priest. It's his duty to remember the sacred stories and to pass them on to our children. My brother is worried because he

believes devoutly in the myths and legends of our people."

"What about you?" you ask Sala. "Do you believe them? Do you believe this prophecy about the end of the world?"

The woman doesn't answer you right away. She turns to a carved wooden chest in the center of the rear wall. Kneeling in front of the cabinet, she releases a hidden catch that loosens the entire front panel. She lowers it to the mat on the floor, then reaches inside for something.

"Behold the head of the most powerful sorcerer in the world!" she exclaims with much emotion. She places a gruesome object on the mat in front of you. It's a human skull, with shriveled skin and strands of black hair still clinging to the face. The rounded top of the skull has been sliced away, and you can see the empty braincase in the flickering light.

A disturbing image forms in your mind of the person whose brain once filled this skull. The picture is one of incarnate evil, of a totally corrupt human with access to the darkest and most powerful forces on earth!

"You see?" exclaims Sala. "Even without his life energy, Hektor still commands your thoughts. His shade is near, waiting to be reunited with his body when the Fireseed is destroyed!

"My aunt Nivida used her powerful druid skills to capture Hektor's spirit in a drop of red dragon's blood, in the Fireseed. As long as the

Fireseed remained inside the sorcerer's skull, his shade was confined. With its theft, Hektor's spirit now roams the world again, seeking vengeance upon the descendants of his captors."

"You mean me, because of Ennis Farold?"

"I fear so," says the woman, "and upon my family because Nivida was our clanswoman. That's why I want you to help Rami. The shade of Hektor will use any power at its command to destroy the Fireseed before Rami can return it to this skull."

"You never answered my question about the 'end of the world' prophecy," you remind Sala. "What does that have to do with the Fireseed, and Hektor, and our quests?"

"Before Hektor was slain, he swore a terrible vengeance upon the world. He prophesied that a descendant of Ennis Farold, the great holy man who banished him from Baysend, and a child of Nivida's clan would one day feed the Fireseed to a dragon in the stomach of a wild boar. The dragon, in turn, would feed the gemstone to the volcano, Ponai, which would explode, destroying the entire western world of Baysend and this island."

"So that's what Pona meant!" you exclaim. "He wants me to prevent that prophecy from happening somehow, and to confront Hektor's spirit.

"I'm beginning to see that my quest and Rami's aren't separate at all! The gem called the Fireseed is the key to both of them. I'll do whatever I can," you promise the woman. "What does Hektor's shade look like?"

"A shade has the normal body of its previous lifetime, except that it is colorless and drab. It's nearly powerless in a bright light or total darkness, where shadows do not exist," says Sala. "Hektor's shade is crippled because his life-force is trapped within the Fireseed, but it still has some of the sorcerer's evil power. You can attack it as you would any other creature, but it will heal itself almost as soon as you wound it."

"Then it will be most dangerous where shadows are common, and at times of the day when they are more numerous?"

"Exactly," Sala agrees. "That's why you must hurry. Dawn is approaching, and that is one of the times when shadows are everywhere."

Minutes later, you're on the beach, studying the sand by torchlight to find Rami's footprints. His trail leads to a jungle path just a few yards off the beach. You follow the path, which seems to lead directly to a vertical wall of the volcano called Ponai.

Just as the first gray haze of dawn is beginning to creep into the thick forest, the trail ends abruptly at the sheer face of volcanic rock. The ground at the base of the wall is loose enough for footprints, but you don't see any. Rami hasn't passed this way at all!

"There are probably dozens of side trails I missed in the darkness!" you think, angry at yourself for being careless. "Now I've got to backtrack until I pick up Rami's trail!"

The morning shadows grow stronger as you try to find Rami's tracks on the overgrown jungle floor. Sala's warning about Hektor's shade spurs you to move faster, before the sun rises over the trees and brings new shadows.

You've taken several running steps back toward the jungle when a dark figure suddenly detaches itself from the shadow of a large tree and blocks the trail just ahead of you. It's the silhouette of a slender man.

The shadowy form turns its head, showing you a profile of its gaunt cheekbones and balding forehead. You recognize the features instantly. They're the same as the ones you saw on Hektor's mutilated skull in the Council Hut!

"The man called Rami has not come this way, Davin Farold!" the shadow-thing tells you in a voice that belongs only in dreams. "He has gone to the volcano and is seeking the trail of my followers who have stolen the gem known as the Fireseed."

After what Sala told you, you don't trust the evil shade, especially since it knows your name! Drawing your cutlass, you stalk forward threateningly, hoping to drive the ghostly figure from your path.

"What do you intend to do with that antique blade, scion of Ennis Farold? Don't you know it's useless against me? I've attained immortality, you young fool!"

"Let's test that immortality of yours, Hektor!" you shout. You lunge, swinging the cutlass in a powerful arc. The silhouette makes no attempt to move, and the steel blade passes through it, doing no damage whatsoever.

"Try again!" calls a second voice from your rear, although the first image is still in front of you. You whirl around just as a duplicate shadowy form assembles itself in the path, drawing its substance from lighter shadows of shrubs and leaves.

"Or here!" sounds a third cry to your right as another silhouette clones itself in front of your confused eyes. Now there are three identical shades on the jungle trail, each one just as nebulous as the others.

"Relax your weapon, Farold!" The new voice seems to come from the treetops themselves, from everywhere yet from nowhere. "The images you see are but copies of myself. They speak with my words but have no substance of their own. I made them from forest shadows."

"Where are you?" you demand, looking past the three images for Hektor's real shade.

"Come now!" it replies. "You can't expect me to reveal myself to you and your blade, can you? Surely the blood of Ennis Farold is not that diluted in your veins! Your grandsire was a worthy opponent, young man. What you have in the way of physical strength, Ennis Farold had ten times over in wisdom!"

You ignore the taunt, remembering that

your immediate mission is to find Rami and help him recover the Fireseed. Paying no attention to the vague images blocking the path, you stride directly toward the first one, passing through it just as you would any other shadow.

"STOP!" The real shade's voice is louder this time, and so clear that it seems to be inside your head. "My image told you the truth, Davin Farold! Rami is at the mountain called Ponai. You're wasting your time in the jungle if you want to help him find the Fireseed!"

You suspect a trick from the evil Hektor and demand more details of Rami's location.

"Tell me where he is at the volcano. It covers the whole island!"

You stare at the treetops, waiting for the shade's reply, but hear only the chattering voices of birds and small monkeys. Looking at the trail, you see that the three shadow images have completely vanished. You stand alone, unsure whether to believe what you have heard.

1) You believe Hektor's shade and want to return to the volcano. Turn to page 84.

2) You think the shade is trying to trick you and want to search the jungle for Rami. Turn to page 67.

The odor of rotting flesh is ominous, but it tells you that something has died recently enough to be putrifying in the bowels of the volcano. Rami knows it, too, and motions to the tunnel on your left.

"The smell of death is strong in this passage, Davin, and it may mean that our quest is over. The thieves may have come this far and died inside the caverns."

You nod. "That's exactly what I was thinking, Rami. Let's see if we can find out what's happened."

The islander steps into the gloomy corridor, the torch in one hand and his spear in the other. You're filled with new admiration for this bold native warrior, whose courage and sense of duty drive him onward in the face of death itself. You follow him with your cutlass drawn, ready to fight at his side against whatever evil forces the spirit of Hektor may have summoned. The stench becomes worse as you near a wider place in the passage.

"It's a chamber!" calls Rami. Hundreds of porous boulders are strewn around the floor of a cavernous room. The huge rocks are made of volcanic pumice and are light enough to float on water.

"I see something," you tell Rami. "Hold your light toward the right by that large smoking crack in the floor."

He lowers the torch to the floor near a wide, glowing crack that divides the chamber in half. It's a fissure so deep that you can smell the hot gases of molten rock wafting from it. The torchlight illuminates what caught your eye—two human legs protruding from behind a large boulder.

You're no stranger to death, but neither you nor Rami is prepared for the horror of your discovery. A man's body has been ripped apart and has already begun to rot in the warm, damp air of the cavern.

"See those marks?" you exclaim, looking at long, bloodless gashes in the corpse's chest and at huge holes in its arms and legs. "What could have done that?"

"Ghouls," replies Rami. "Those wounds were made after that man died, not before. There's no blood along some of the gashes."

"Was he one of the thieves?"

"I don't know. There's not enough left of his face to be sure. We'll have to search his body."

Rami's suggestion is unpleasant, but you know that he's right. If this was one of the thieves, the Fireseed might still be on the body.

You clutch your nose to prevent the sickening fumes from entering your nostrils and reach for a fat pouch still attached to the dead man's belt. You cut the strings of the purse and hold it closer to the torch while you dump its contents into your hand.

A stream of precious gems pours from the leather bag onto your palm, some of them spilling with a clatter to the stone floor. But the one that captures your attention is a gigantic ruby, larger than a hen's egg, which glitters in your outstretched hand!

"The Fireseed!" you exclaim. "We've found it!"

Before Rami can say anything, you hear a fiendish moan from the darkness near the corpse. You cram the ruby and a few of the gems into the pouch, letting the rest drop to the ground. Then you whirl around—and face four slobbering ghouls!

"You take the two on the right," you mutter to Rami. "I'll handle the other ones."

"Don't let them touch you!" Rami warns. "The touch of a ghoul can paralyze even the strongest warrior!"

The loathsome creatures have splotchy, greenish white skins, colorless eyes, and fangs. The undead monsters shuffle toward you, their deranged minds devoid of any fear of your weapons.

The battle is a quick one for you. Your cutlass slashes your two ghouls to ribbons. But to your right, you see that Rami can't get one impaled creature off his spear tip to fight the other one! The second ghoul is stalking toward the islander with a clumsy, stiff-legged gait.

You leap across the chamber just in time to hack the ghoul's arm off as it slaps the air inches from Rami's face. A moment later, Rami forces the impaled creature over the edge of the smoking crack in the floor. The ghoul clutches at the spear shaft, trying to pull itself up, but Rami shakes the spear vehemently. The monster slips from the steel tip and drops into the deep volcanic abyss.

"We've got the Fireseed!" you tell Rami. "Let's get out of here before any more of those things are attracted to that rotten carcass!"

Rami looks puzzled. "Let me see the jewel," he says. You remove the magnificent ruby from its pouch and hand it to your fellow warrior. He studies it for a long while, then shakes his head and returns it to you.

"It looks like the Fireseed, but it doesn't have the magical glow of the sacred stone stolen from my mother's care," he says.

Before you can reply, a sinister but familiar voice echoes around you, coming from all of the deepest shadows at once.

"The kin of Nivida is correct, Davin Farold! The gem you hold in your hand does not contain my spirit," says Hektor's shade. "It's a mere replica, fashioned by foolish thieves to deceive the elders of Moffid. Cast it into the bowels of Ponai where your friend discarded the ghoul, or it will bring you great misfortune!"

1) If you think this is the real Fireseed and choose to ignore the warning of Hektor's shade, turn to page 29.

2) If you're afraid the shade might be telling the truth, turn to page 77.

"I've got to get some help for Rami," you think. "We've both probably breathed too much of the fiery fog to leave Ponai and live. That means we'll have to survive here, among the cannibals." Then you carry your companion into the shadows, away from the nest of the winged creatures.

Rami's eyelids twitch and open. The native warrior is frowning with an anxious expression. "Do . . . you have the Fireseed?" he demands weakly.

"No, WE have the Fireseed!" you reply. "And as long as we have it, Hektor's shade can't come near us."

Rami frowns. "The sorcerer's shade may go to Moffid, seeking revenge on my clan," he mumbles.

"Not if we get the Fireseed to your mother so she can return it to the skull," you answer. "Hektor's shade told us that the fiery fog comes only during the high tides. That means that the warriors from Moffid can come and go safely between the tides. All we have to do is get a message to them somehow!"

Rami smiles through his pain. "We will do it, my friend. We managed to stop Hektor's prophecy from coming true."

"Right! Besides, we immortals have lots of time to plan our next move!"

THE END

"I don't dare wake anyone," you think. "Better to take a canoe along the coast to a less populated area, then find some water as well as containers." You leave the shadows of the larger hut and swim silently across the moonlit patch of rolling surf toward the tethered boats.

When you're halfway to the canoes, a dog inside the nearest hut begins barking loudly. Within seconds, all the other dogs in the village join in the alarm. Lights appear in every hut amid the confused shouts of wakened sleepers.

"The thieves of the Fireseed have come back for the skull!"

"There he is! Near the pier!"

You glance quickly around you and see that the village men are running from their huts with spears, axes, and other weapons in their hands. You're completely surrounded, except for the sea behind you. It would be useless to fight so many people. There are only two things you can do.

1) If you feel you still have a chance to escape in one of the canoes, turn to page 65.

2) If you feel your only chance is to surrender and try to talk your way out of the situation, turn to page 75.

"I don't care what happens, Rami," you whisper into his unhearing ear. "You'll die unless I get you back home. If there's even the slightest chance that Hektor's shade was lying about the fog, we have to risk it!"

You hoist the islander's limp form onto your shoulders for the perilous journey back to Moffid. Then you press yourself against the face of the cliff and inch your way silently from the ledge with the pterodactyl's aerie.

The fiery fog is all around you, casting its violet light over the entire crater and the valley far below. You've quit worrying about the mysterious effect of the fog since it's too late to do anything about it.

You finally reach the cave entrance you recall from your trip through Ponai's wall. You enter the caverns expecting to be in total darkness but see that the fiery mist has already spread its glow into the caves. Rami moans with pain when you lower him gently to the ground to rest your back.

"Hang on, Rami," you tell the warrior. "We're only a few minutes away from the Cave of Bones. Hektor's shade can't touch us as long as we have this."

You pull the Fireseed from your pocket and stare in wonder at the crimson glow from the gemstone. It blends with the blue and violet rays of the fog's cold fire, producing a vivid purple halo around the powerful jewel.

"Even if we don't make it out of here," you mutter, "we'll still have the Fireseed, and

Hektor's evil-life force will be trapped with us." Feeling rested, you return the gem to your pocket and lift Rami's body again to your shoulders.

When you reach the Cave of Bones, the skeletons are there, just as you left them. Their grinning teeth glisten in the violet light of the fog that granted them both immortality and death. Even their filthy gold and jewels shine in the cold blue flames.

Just ahead, inside the mouth of the cave, you see a dark edge in the air where the wind from outside is billowing into the opening and preventing the fog from leaving the Cave of Bones.

"Well, here goes nothing!" you mumble to Rami. You take three quick steps into the area of fresh air and breathe deeply. The salty sea air is balmy, and its breeze caresses your bearded face as you collapse on top of the skeleton nearest the entrance. The shade was telling the truth about the fiery fog! The normal sea air has filled your changed lungs and is killing you both!

Your last thought is of the gem in your pocket—the Fireseed glowing with Hektor's evil spirit, waiting for the next descendant of Ennis Farold to help fulfill the sorcerer's prophecy.

THE END

"We might as well start with the Cave of Bones," you tell Rami. "Whatever killed all those unknown people might still be in there, but we have to check it for the thieves' trail. How do you feel about violating a clan taboo?"

Rami smiles grimly. "No taboo will stop me from finding the Fireseed. I'll get a torch."

The islander vanishes into the jungle across from the cave's mouth just long enough to find some resinous wood to use as a firebrand. He also has a handful of dry tinder that he ignites by rubbing the butt of his spear against the wood. As soon as the torch is flaring brightly, Rami steps onto the ledge and into the Cave of Bones with you behind him.

Just inside the mouth of the cavern, you see that Rami's description was no exaggeration at all. Everywhere you look, there are human skeletons. They seem to have been mostly men, and for some reason they seem to all be lying with their heads toward the mouth of the cave, as if they died trying to get out of the cavern.

"Maybe they were lost and starved to death," Rami suggests in a solemn whisper. You can hear the awe in his voice, and realize that the brave warrior may be more concerned about breaking the taboo than he admitted. You admire the extra courage it must have taken for him to enter the cave.

"That's impossible," you object. "They're only a few feet away from the exit. They could have gotten outside within seconds."

"Unless something was keeping them inside!" Rami mutters, scanning the cavern walls. You step over the grisly remains and begin scouting the rest of the entry chamber. At the rear of the cavernous room, you find two separate corridors leading farther into Ponai's heart.

Please turn to page 66.

The surface of the ocean has grown so dark that it's difficult to see the man in the water. His head seems shrouded in shadows, reminding you of the cleric's warning of a "shadowy thing of great evil." You shrug off your uneasy feelings and paddle the lifeboat close enough to save the drowning man.

"Take my hand," you call out.

Just as you reach into the water to grab him, you see that he has no arms! Instead of human muscles and flesh, your hand grasps a wet, furry flipper! You jerk your hand away, but not before the strange creature buries its fangs in your forearm!

The pain is almost paralyzing, as if you were being bitten by a cobra. You rip your arm away from the monster, tearing the flesh even more. As you fall back into the dinghy, the early moon casts its bluish light on the face of the creature you were going to help.

Instead of human features, you see the cruel snout and glaring eyes of a wild beast. It's a seawolf! These aquatic lycanthropes, or werewolves, are said to roam the seas searching for human victims that they add to their packs by their contagious bites! The legends claim that seawolves can be killed only by weapons of silver or iron.

Clutching your steel cutlass, you hope that there's enough iron in its blade to slay the monster. You crawl to the gunwale and raise the sword. Your left arm is throbbing strangely where the seagoing werewolf bit it.

Instead of charging you, the huge creature with the head and mane of a wolf on a giant seal's body just floats on the surface several yards away. Its luminescent eyes are focused directly on you, and it seems to be waiting for something.

All at once, your body is wracked with pain! Your bones feel as if they're bending out of shape and threatening to burst through your flesh. Your legs and arms seem to be shrinking, while your head is swelling around your nose and mouth.

You can't bear the pain any longer! The dark seawater beckons you, promising to soothe the horrible transformation occurring inside your body. With a muffled cry that sounds more like a growl, you tear off your clothes and tumble over the side of the dinghy. The cool salt water feels wonderful against your new skin, which has begun to sprout fine brown hairs.

With a toss of your growing mane, you whip the flat tail that has replaced your shriveled legs and slice smoothly through the ocean to join the seawolf pack—your pack!

THE END

"We can't fight something that big!" you yell to Rami as you grab his arm. The fearless warrior is poking at the giant vodyanoi with his spear as if he were a lion tamer. "Come on! The darkness is our only chance! Those things have terrible eyesight!"

You pull him back into the shadows with you, away from the light at the mouth of the sea cave. To your horror, the rock shelf narrows to nothing only a few yards farther into the cave.

"What do we do now?" Rami asks, his voice crackling with excitement.

"We hit the water!" you tell him quickly. "Our only chance is to swim into the darkest part of the cavern so that the vodyanoi can't find us. There's no way we can get by it!"

You dive into the inlet, hoping that Rami will follow. In the murky light, you see his body knife into the salt water seconds after your own plunge.

The two of you swim side by side underwater until the water's so dark that you can't see, and your lungs are bursting for fresh air. Then you let yourself drift slowly to the surface. Your head bursts into the darkness above a small pool, and a moment later, Rami breaks the surface next to you.

"Where are we?" he whispers.

"In a different cavern," you reply. "The inlet led underground from the vodyanoi's lair into this pool!"

A mixture of cool air and foul odors is all

around you. Distant light of some kind is seeping into this new cavern from your left. You paddle silently toward it, and are delighted when you feel solid rock beneath your bare feet at the side of the warm pool.

You step from the water to find yourselves in a gruesome cavern piled high with human skeletons! Everywhere you look, there are the rotted remains of hundreds of people. Most of them appear to be men, and they all seem to have died less than twenty feet from the sunlit entrance to this chamber of horrors!

"We're in the Cave of Bones!" exclaims Rami.

"What could have killed these people?" you wonder aloud. "There are no signs of violence, and they seem to have had plenty of food and other supplies."

You can see sacks whose sides have rotted away, revealing their contents of water jugs, dried food, and other vital items, as if they had been packed for a long journey. There's also the glint of precious metals and gems adorning the dust-covered corpses.

"My people have known of this cave and its treasures for centuries," Rami whispers, "but it's a tabooed place because of the death in it. Our legends say that this treasure is cursed and that anyone who touches it will die. It is also said that no one ever returns from the Cave of Bones—and now we are inside it!"

"Well, since we're here, let's try to find a trace of the thieves who stole the Fireseed," you suggest. "I doubt if Hektor's shade is resting right now."

Rami nods. From the wide-eyed look on his face, you realize that the atmosphere of death inside the tabooed cave has had some effect on the fearless native after all.

"We'll need a torch, Davin. Wait here," he says. Confidence has returned to his voice, and you know the islander has won his battle with superstitious fears.

The warrior darts outside and into the jungle across from the mouth of the cave. While he's gone, you stare at the grisly remains with their ominous treasures. Rami's mention of the curse looms in your mind.

"Something very powerful killed these people," you think with a frown, "and until we find out what that something was, it might be wise not to disturb these corpses!"

Rami returns in a few minutes with a flaming firebrand of resinous wood. You step over the skeletons and begin scouting the rest of the entry chamber. At the rear of the room, you find two separate corridors leading farther into Ponai's heart.

Please turn to page 66.

You'd prefer to discover what's panicked the man before you draw attention to yourself by calling out. "He's trying desperately to get away from something in the water," you think. You remain quiet and look all around you in the fog, trying to spot the danger.

"AAAIIE! It's got my le—" The sudden scream of pain from the swimming man comes an instant before his struggling head and arms vanish beneath the choppy surface of the sea.

Your automatic reaction is to freeze to avoid attracting whatever has just attacked your fellow survivor from the *Salt Castle*. Very slowly, you hoist yourself over the rim of the half-submerged barrel and crouch inside it. Weaponless and clad only in your sleeping pants and shirt, you know you have to identify the danger before attempting to help the man.

Peering over the edge of the water keg, you're horrified to see a patch of dark crimson appear on the sea's surface. Either the swimmer or his attacker seems to have scored a hit with sword, claws, or fangs. For a tense moment, you wait, watching the ocean for a sign of victor or victim.

Suddenly, a pale hulk breaks the surface of the bloody water only a few feet from your makeshift lifeboat. It's the upper body of the swimmer, his now-sightless eyes staring glassily into yours! Beneath his drained torso, there's only emptiness where his legs had been moments before. The man's cutlass is still in its scabbard—he had no time to draw it.

You watch the sea around the mutilated corpse for a moment to see if the attacker will retrieve the rest of its gruesome meal. Then you reach over the rim of the barrel and grab the hilt of the cutlass. As you start to draw it from the scabbard, a huge shape appears beneath the man's carcass!

Deftly, you whisk the sword from its wet holster and crouch back inside the half-submerged keg. At the same time, a tremendous splash sends a fountain of seawater high into the foggy sky above you.

The torrent nearly swamps the barrel. You tense your muscles, ready to swim free and fight the unseen sea monster to death if the waterlogged cask sinks. The waves slap at the outside of the barrel, continually sloshing water over the rim.

For long minutes, you scarcely breathe while the unknown predator finishes feeding on your shipmate's corpse. You hear other splashes all around you, accompanied by the snarling, wheezing sounds of more sea scavengers, probably drawn by the scent of fresh blood.

Just when your legs are growing numb in their cramped position, you realize that everything seems quiet again. You press your ear against the soaked wood of the barrel, but hear only the steady lapping noise of normal waves.

"I'll wait a few more minutes, just to be

absolutely sure that it's safe," you decide.

Finally you shift your weight and stand up in the cask. The ocean surface is quiet, and there are no signs of either the dead man or his killer. The morning sun has climbed higher, drying the fog clouds and warming the surface of the water. You thrust the cutlass through your waistband and begin to bail water from the barrel, hoping you can stay afloat in it long enough to be rescued.

In the late afternoon, you spot the hull of a boat bouncing on the gentle blue waves. It's only a capsized dinghy, but your eyes swell with grateful tears because water has begun to seep into the keg faster than you can bail it out.

You remain inside the sinking cask as long as you can, then push away from it into the warm salt water. When you reach the dinghy, you see that its once-white sides are now covered with green slime and mildew. They're so slippery that it takes you a long time to get a good grasp on the gunwales and flip the craft.

You hoist yourself over the side and collapse on the wet deck. Then you shut your eyes and let the sinking afternoon sun bake the water wrinkles from your salty skin. You're almost asleep when you hear a gasping voice from the water.

"Help me! I'm drowning! Here! Here!"

Jerking your head toward the frantic hail, you see a man's head and arms bobbing a few dozen yards away from the dinghy. In the failing light of dusk, you see that it isn't anyone you recognize from the *Salt Castle*. His face is long and lean, and his dark hair streams behind him in the water like the mane of a wild animal.

There's something brutish, almost wolflike, about the stranger's features, and a memory dances at the edge of your mind—something about wolves and the sea. You hesitate, trying to decide what to do.

1) If you are so suspicious that you want to leave the stranger in the sea and take the boat away from this place, turn to page 33.

2) If you prefer to challenge the man in the water before offering to help him, turn to page 50.

3) If you decide to help the drowning man immediately, turn to page 113.

"Wait for me!" you call to Rami, who's already at the huge nest. When you join him, you see that the sides of the structure are actually built of sapling trees.

"What kind of bird could have torn those trees from the ground and then twisted them this way?" you ask your native companion nervously, knowing that the builder must be extremely strong.

The islander shakes his head. "I thought I knew every bird on Storm Island. Well, there's one way to find out!"

Rami leaps upward and grabs a protruding branch. He swings himself against the woven saplings and starts to climb the nest's outer wall. You follow him.

On the other side of the woven wall, the scratching noises grow louder. Rami is the first to reach the rim and peer into the steamy opening at the top of the nest.

"Great Pona!" the warrior exclaims.

"What is it?" you call from below. "What do you see?"

"Dragons!" Rami replies. "Baby dragons!"

In seconds, you join Rami at the rim of the nest and stick your head into the cloud of rising steam. Two brownish figures are huddled against the opposite side of the nest, their beaks rubbing against some of the branches to make the scratching noise you've been hearing. You can't tell how big their featherless, scaly bodies are, but their heads are larger than yours!

The bottom of the nest consists of a loose mesh of branches laid over an opening in the rock ledge, which is belching warm steam into the sky. The creature that built the nest had either the instinct or the genius to place it over a natural steam geyser so that its eggs would be hatched by volcanic heat.

Rami swings his legs over the edge of the nest and hangs on the inner wall.

"What are you doing?" you ask.

"I'm trying to get them to move so that we can get a better look at them," he answers. The nimble warrior inches his way closer to the huddled nestlings and pokes one of them with the butt end of his spear.

Suddenly the reptilian infant starts shrieking and flapping its thin, batlike wings. The creature's alarm startles its sibling, who joins in the commotion. They're so frightened that they fly into each other and bounce off the walls of the nest in a frenzied attempt to get away from the strange monster clinging to its side.

"Get out of there!" you yell to Rami just as one of the giant babies crashes into him. The islander loses his handhold and falls through the opening at the base of the nest!

"Rami!" you shout, hoisting yourself into the nest to help him. You clutch at the steep inner wall, descending rapidly but carefully. The cloud of steam clears momentarily, and you can see Rami's hands clinging to one of the loose crosspieces at the bottom of the nest. He hasn't fallen all the way through—not yet, anyway!

One of the panic-stricken reptiles is squawking loudly only a few feet from your head. It's a deafening sound, and you try to frighten the nestling farther away by swinging one arm at it and yelling.

"MOVE!" you scream, but the frightened infant only shrieks louder. Suddenly, a great winged figure blots out the sunlight, and the wind from its huge wings blasts your face with dust and rock particles. The nestlings' mother has returned!

You hug the side of the nest, hoping the winged reptile won't see you. From the corner of your eye, you get your first look at the "dragon" of Storm Island legends.

It's a flying dinosaur that sages call a pterodactyl. The crested, birdlike head is several times larger than your body, with rows of dagger-shaped reptilian teeth in its black beak.

You glance down at Rami to see if he's still holding on to the bottom of the nest. He's looking up at you, and his eyes suddenly widen with horror at something behind you. In the next instant, the pterodactyl plucks you both from its nest to feed you to its ravenous infants.

THE END

You'd better get the jugs. Even if you steal a canoe and reach an uninhabited stretch of beach, you'll need containers to collect water.

Darting from shadow to shadow, you reach the bamboo ladder leading to the back veranda and climb it. Halfway up the rungs, you hear the sound of heavy breathing!

You peer cautiously over the edge of the porch floor. A young man no older than you is sleeping in the middle of the veranda, but his face is turned away from the top of the ladder.

You pull yourself stealthily onto the porch behind the sleeping man. Then you inch your way along behind his back. Your hand rests on the hilt of your cutlass, ready to draw it if it is necessary.

Finally you get to the open window with the clay jugs hanging from the sill. You reach out very gently, watching the sleeping guard all the while. As your fingers brush the nearest jug, a hand grabs your wrist!

"I've got one of them!" someone yells from inside the hut.

The man sleeping on the porch leaps to his feet and pins your free arm behind your back before you can draw the cutlass. A light appears inside the window, and you can see a long-haired woman placing a lamp on a chest.

Dogs are barking throughout the village, and a crowd is beginning to gather on the beach in front of the large hut.

"You can let go, Uncle," says the man who was asleep. His strength is as great as that of any warrior you've ever fought. He has your right arm locked so tightly in a wrestler's hold that you can't move it at all. You jerk away from the hand inside the window, but the man behind you snares your left arm, too.

"Don't struggle," he warns you, "or I'll snap your arms out of their sockets!"

The threat is a real one. You've wrestled with many good fighters, but you've never felt such pressure on your shoulders before. You test the hold with a few slight movements, but the pain in your shoulder joints is unbearable.

"Bring him inside the Council Hut, Rami! We must question him."

The woman with long hair is standing in the lighted doorway. The man called Rami nudges you forward without relaxing his powerful hold. The woman steps aside while Rami pushes you into the hut, releasing your arms.

You reach for your cutlass, but Rami is already pressing a sharp spear point against your chest, aiming straight for the heart. "This native warrior knows how to use weapons as well as wrestling holds," you think. You relax and let the woman take your sword.

Please turn to page 36.

"Let's get it!" you yell to Rami, who immediately hurls his spear at the towering monster. The tip of filed steel penetrates the slimy green hide, but it's no more than a pinprick to such a giant creature. The vodyanoi bellows in rage at the sight of intruders in its lair and makes a vicious swipe at Rami with a webbed hand larger than the islander's chest.

"Look out!"

Your scream echoes in the dank sea cave but it was unnecessary. Rami springs backward with the agility of a cat. You run to his side with your cutlass drawn just as the vodyanoi tries to hit you both with another lethal slap.

You dodge the blow, which is powerful enough to shatter the hulls of huge sailing ships, and hack at the scaly wrist. Your blade bites into the green flesh at the same instant a monstrous claw catches Rami's head with a savage swipe and tosses the dying warrior into the water.

The creature roars with pain, its oily black blood spilling from the wrist wound onto your leg. Then the vodyanoi's webbed fingers close tightly around your upper arms and raise your struggling body toward its drooling jaws.

THE END

The fact that Hektor's occult powers were strong enough to predict the exact events that have been happening is frightening. It makes you disinclined to doubt his prophecy about the destruction of the world.

"Come on!" you call to Rami, breaking into a run after the giant, bat-winged form swooping over the distant edge of the rice field. "We've got to keep it in sight! We have to stop that beast from ripping the Fireseed out of the boar's stomach, even if it means we can never leave the crater!"

Tracking the beast's flight against the face of the crater cliffs, you see that what you're chasing isn't a dragon but a type of flying dinosaur called a pterodactyl. The prehistoric monster soon dives to one of the steam-heated nests on a ledge high above you.

"There it is!" you shout to Rami. "Let's get up there!"

The vents all around you on the slope of the volcano have begun to spew more steam into the air. If Hektor's shade was telling the truth, the lava must be shifting beneath the surface. As dusk fades to night, you might finally get a glimpse of what Orson called the fiery fog, and know if you have traded your life outside the crater to save the Fireseed.

It's even darker by the time you reach a ledge adjacent to the one holding the flying dinosaur's aerie. You can see a swarming mass of leathery flesh in the nest, and you can hear the tearing sounds of feeding reptiles, but you can't tell how much of the boar has been eaten.

Suddenly, the air above the nest is filled with fire! Tiny tongues of blue and violet flames lick the dragon wings of the pterodactyl and flash on the beaks of its nestlings. Then you realize that it isn't fire at all, but a cloud of steam from the vent below the monster's nest.

Just as Hector's shade had said, the effect is one of a fiery fog, which has already begun to spread from the pterodactyl's nest to the surrounding air. Before long, it will seep down to the crater valley to bestow immortality upon all who breathe those fumes that seem to be burning without fire.

"We've got to get over there right now!" you tell Rami. "The fog will be pouring out of that nest any minute!"

"We'll have to fight those things to get that carcass if we make our move before they eat their fill!" Rami replies.

1) If you want to wait for a better opportunity to slip into the nest, turn to page 60.

2) If you decide to attack the monster before the fiery fog gets any thicker, turn to page 78.

You decide that you'd better not help with Rami's quest just yet The Fireseed seems to be related to Hektor's spirit in some mysterious way, and some deep part of you is afraid the prophecy could come true.

Sala is so worried about her son's decision to seek the Fireseed alone that you try to reassure her.

"I think Barakin's right," you tell her as gently as possible. "It may be more dangerous for everyone, including Rami, if I join in his quest for the Fireseed. That may be exactly what Hektor wants us to do."

There's a thick silence in the Council Hut. You see tears in Sala's dark eyes but don't know if they're tears of sadness or anger. Barakin is wearing a stony smile, as if your words please him.

"Yes!" he exclaims. "If you aren't near the Fireseed, then the prophecy cannot come true."

"You're a fool, my brother!" Sala challenges the smug priest. "He can't get away from Storm Island until the trade ship anchors beyond the reef—four days from now! Till then, Hektor's shade will have whatever opportunities it needs to draw this Farold into its plot to destroy the Fireseed! We haven't won yet, and Rami is facing the sorcerer's soulless shadow alone!"

Barakin's superior smile fades as he turns to face you. His eyes glaze in a strange way, and tiny beads of sweat pepper his forehead. You can almost smell the fear oozing out of his pores.

"My sister speaks the truth," he tells you in a low monotone. "There's only one way to stop the prophecy from coming true!"

His hand slips to the bone hilt of the dagger at his waist.

"Don't, my brother!" cries Sala. "Rami needs the westerner to help recover the sacred gem!"

"No, Sala," he replies, drawing the thin blade of steel. "That's what Hektor's shade wants us to think. If this one goes to help Rami, then the wizard's prophecy will be at hand! His death is the only way to block the evil forces!"

The crazed shaman crouches and begins to stalk toward you. You whip the cutlass from your waistband and hold it in front of you.

"Stop, Barakin!" you warn the old priest. "I don't want to hurt you. Put the dagger away, and let's discuss this whole thing a little—"

Before you can finish your sentence, Barakin lunges forward, jabbing the knife at your chest. You sidestep the older man's attack easily and hit his head with the handguard of your cutlass. The blow is only enough to knock the aged man down, but he strikes his temple on a corner of a carved wooden chest as he falls.

"Barakin!" screams his sister. She rushes to his side, cradling his bloody head in her arms. Then she presses her ear to his chest.

Her face tightens as she listens for a heart-beat.

"He's—he's dead! You've killed him!" she exclaims.

You take a step toward her, but she bounds backward, pointing at the cutlass in your hand. "Hektor's shade sent you here! You're one of his evil servants!"

Before you can reply or stop her, Sala runs to the door of the hut and begins screaming.

"Help! He has killed Barakin!"

You burst through the doorway after her, your cutlass still in your hand.

"There he is!" "See his sword?" The cries from the beach below the veranda are those of an angry mob. You raise your hands high in the night air, trying to soothe the crowd, but your action only exposes your chest to the cluster of native spears that end your role in the Fireseed legend forever.

THE END

"Rami, wait a minute!" you call to the curious warrior. "Anything large enough to weave sapling trees into a nest is too big for us to handle. Besides, I doubt if the Fireseed is in that giant basket. Let's try the valley."

The islander casts a look at the nest, then shrugs his shoulders and follows you along the right side of the cliff. You pass many steam geysers on your way down the slope, with huge nests built over most of them. Some of them spew hot mists into the air constantly while others spit steam under pressure at different intervals. The entire internal crater wall of Ponai seems alive with these sporadic geysers warming the gigantic nests.

The valley reminds you of a heated greenhouse. The fertile black volcanic soil at the base of the crater is moist and warm from the steam, and you enter a lush field of dry rice.

"Let's see if we can find the people who cultivated this field," you suggest.

"I don't think we have to look very far," Rami mutters in a wary tone of voice. You follow his gaze to your rear, where more than two dozen men have slipped silently onto the fringe of the field! A shiver races up your spine when you remember Rami's story of Hektor's cannibals living in the volcano!

The men's bodies are painted with bright blue and yellow designs, and the sides of their heads are shaved so that their greased hair stands erect in the center of their scalps. They're all armed with strange double-tipped spears, one end having the usual point while the other bears a barbed trident.

"It looks like farmers aren't the only people living in Ponai's crater," you mumble to Rami. "Have you ever seen warriors like these before?"

"No. I know the designs painted on their bodies, though," he replies as they approach you with raised spears. "They're tabooed symbols of evil sorcery. They also have filed teeth—the mark of cannibals!"

"Well, we can't fight them all," you add. "Let's save our strength for a better chance to escape. Besides, we still haven't found the Fireseed."

Several of the cannibals grab your weapons and push you roughly toward the trees. They gesture with their strange spears for you to walk in front of them on a well-used trail beside the rice field. They still haven't said a word, even to each other.

"Where are you taking us?" you demand, but the warriors pay no attention to you. At first you become angry, but then it dawns on you that they don't seem to hear you. "Do you think they understand me?" you ask Rami.

He shrugs. "It's strange the way they do not talk among themselves," he replies. "They just make signs to each other. Anyway, you don't need to ask them any questions. That's where they're taking us."

Rami is pointing with his chin to a cluster of straw huts built in the shadows of a large forest. As your captors push you past the first huts, children and elders line the trail to peer at you. You notice that only the children are yelling insults about your light skin, long hair, and beard. The elders say nothing, but bare their pointed teeth in grins at their children's taunts.

They take you to a large compound in the center of the village. It's actually a cluster of separate buildings connected by covered walkways. The cannibals force you both to sit on the ground in a courtyard outside the largest hut in the complex. Moments later, a huge man with rolls of fat and necklaces of human bones and rare gems jiggling all over his body lumbers through the doorway.

"He's a chief of some kind," Rami whispers. "Remember that these people are cannibals, and that one has had lots to eat!"

Your companion's thought is gruesome but true. From his great size, you deduce that the large man is eating better than anyone else in Ponai's crater. He carries a fan made of woven straw and is followed from the hut by four attractive young women, who remain behind him and drop to the ground on their knees whenever he stops.

"So, strangers have fallen into the mouth of Pona!" he exclaims with a sinister grin. His filed teeth are yellow and worn. "It's a special day when outsiders, especially light-skinned ones, offer to feed themselves to the storm god. Pona will be pleased."

"We haven't come to feed Pona!" you tell the fat headman. "We're looking for a gem stolen from the village of Moffid—a huge red jewel called the Fireseed."

"The Fireseed! Did you hear, children of Hektor?" he calls to the warriors around you. "These fools expect us to give up the jewel that has imprisoned the soul of our master! The same gem that I, Yolmat, have recovered by my powerful sorcery!"

From all sides, the painted guards are making hideous moaning noises that you suddenly realize are the sounds of voiceless laughter. They haven't been talking because they're mutes!

"Yolmat!" Rami exclaims from your left. "There was a man named Yolmat from my village who served Hektor before my mother's aunt destroyed the sorcerer. Some of the elders tell stories about him. But you couldn't be that man. He was older than Nivida, and she'd be at least eighty years old if she were still alive!"

The fat man's grin broadens even more. "This is much better than I might have planned!" he exclaims. "Nivida's own kin here in my village! Yes, spawn of a witch's niece, I am that same Yolmat who was banished by Nivida before you were born! I'm more than a century old, thanks to Hektor's sorcery. In fact, some of these warriors are others your aunt banished from Moffid along with the master and myself."

"I don't understand what strange magic has kept you alive and young," Rami cries, "but Davin Farold and I will stop you from freeing the soul of Hektor!"

"Farold? A kinsman of Ennis Farold?" booms Yolmat. "Listen, children of Hektor! Our master's prophecy is at hand. The blood kin of both Nivida the druid and Archcleric Farold are here among us, and the Fireseed is in my hut. It's only a matter of time before Hektor's oath of vengeance is kept! The voice of Pona will speak again, just as your tongues will be restored!"

The moaning from the cannibals becomes even louder. "Lock them in the granary," their leader commands, "and guard them well! I, Yolmat, will pray to Hektor's spirit within the Fireseed to enlighten us. We must do whatever is needed to help bring about the hour of vengeance!"

The cannibals drag you and Rami to a hut across the courtyard that has a thick wooden beam on the door and no windows. They thrust you both inside and bar the only exit. You're in a large circular room with seven wedge-shaped partitions dividing different-sized piles of brown rice.

"This is a chief's granary, where his wives each store their supplies of rice," says Rami after he studies the building for a few minutes.

You can see the moving silhouettes of the guards outside the walls. "We can't do anything until nightfall," you tell Rami. "Let's just hope the spirit of Hektor isn't impatient enough to demand something from Yolmat before then."

"We are not impatient at all, Davin Farold!" The inside of the granary brightens noticeably as the shadows of all seven partitions begin to intensify and take on the wiry, cloaked forms of Hektor's shade. You and Rami are surrounded by seven dark figures, one of whom must be the actual shade of the sorcerer while the others are merely shadow images designed to confuse you.

"Do not attempt to identify my true form," warns the shade in a single voice that seems to come from all the figures at once. "It would be a waste of time, anyway. I can transport myself away from you instantly. Listen to me, and I shall help you to escape, and recover the Fireseed as well!"

"Why should you do that?" demands Rami. "Your followers have both us and the gem. What more do you need?"

"I need for you to be free and to have the Fireseed in your hands," replies the shade. "Isn't that what you want, too?"

"You're planning some kind of trick to make us throw the Fireseed into Ponai's lava beds!" answers Rami.

"What if I am? I'm also offering you a chance to be free."

"Why don't you just order Yolmat to give us the Fireseed and let us go?" you ask the shade.

"Why do we need to escape?"

"An excellent suggestion, young Farold! You remind me more and more of my old enemy, the archcleric. To answer your question, the Fireseed saps my energy. I can't appear to anyone in its presence, but I can help you get out of this prison."

"When?" you ask suspiciously.

"Why, any time you like!" answers the shade. "Now, for instance, if you're prepared to face the guards outside. I personally would wait until dark and try to take the Fireseed by theft. But then again, I'm not as proficient at fighting as you and your friend are."

1) If you wish Hektor's shade to free you now so that you can try to take the Fireseed by force, turn to page 17.

2) If you choose to do as Hektor suggests and wait until night to steal the Fireseed, turn to page 89.

You slip from the hammock to the heaving deck, ready to help the crew any way you can.

Realizing you'll be soaked by the rain and waves as soon as you get topside, you don't take the time to get dressed. Barefoot and wearing the light canvas pants and shirt you sleep in, you head toward the gangway stairs.

You push your way through the milling men, bouncing off several of them as you all try to maintain your balance on the shifting deck. Finally you reach the stairs.

As you climb the steps, you sense someone staring at you. Glancing back, you encounter Orson's steady gaze. His lips move, and somehow his soft voice pierces the mounting noise around you.

"The storm god, Pona, has come for you, Davin Farold. It is your destiny to face the evil thing that waits in the fiery fog!"

The storm sounds and the cries of desperate men from above draw your thoughts away from the young cleric's disturbing words. Tearing your eyes from his hypnotic stare, you hurl yourself up the steps.

The moment you burst through the topside hatchway, wind and rain batter you with such stinging force that you're nearly knocked back down the narrow stairs. Clinging to the frame of the hatch, you manage to turn your back to the fierce wind long enough to find the hatch cover and secure it.

"You there! Grab a line!"

At the quarterdeck rail, a sailor is yelling

and pointing to a row of flapping ropes dangling from a yardarm. Three or four crewmen are crawling along the boom, trying to get a new sail lashed onto it. The original sail must have been torn away by the storm.

You work your way to the quarterdeck gangway. The dangling ropes are threaded through pulleys on a higher boom of the mast nearest the stern. The bo'sun points to the end rope and motions for you to pull it. You signal your understanding and start hauling steadily on the heavy line.

"Look, Bo'sun! Jock's in trouble!"

The frantic shout draws everyone's eyes upward. One of the men on the high yardarm is hanging by one hand from a rope. If he loses his grip, he'll crash to the deck!

"Hang on, Jock! We'll get ye!"

"Don't let go, man!"

"Get up there, Abdul!" screams the bo'sun to a small crewman in a bedraggled turban. The wiry sailor looks up at the yardarm.

"No! It's too dangerous!" he protests. "Let someone else do it."

You see quickly that no one is going to risk climbing the mast in this storm to help the imperiled sailor.

You bull your way through the blinding wind and rain to the Arab's side and hand him the taut rope. "Watch my line!" you yell. Then you shield your face against the stinging spray and work your way to the nearest webbing.

You cling to the slender rope shrouds knitted into a ladder like a spider's web. The wind slams into your body with the full force of the cyclone behind it, dumping hundreds of gallons of seawater and rain on you. You move one hand or foot at a time, climbing with slow, deliberate movements. Finally, you're close enough to touch the trapped sailor's dangling foot.

"I'm right below you!" you shout to the frightened man. "Swing your leg toward me!"

You can see by the seaman's terrified face that he's too afraid to do anything. You inch your way higher in the shrouds until you're even with him. Then you anchor one arm securely in the tarred webbing and grab the paralyzed sailor's waist with the other.

You can dimly hear shouts and cheers from below, despite the shrill whine of the wind in the rigging. You find a loose line and tie it around the man's waist. Then you signal for the crew to lower him to the deck.

Just as you start to climb down, the *Salt Castle* rises high on the crest of a huge wave. The bulky vessel seems to hang in the air for a breathless moment or two. Then the ocean vanishes from beneath the ship, and the craft plummets. Your stomach rises into your chest, and you hug the webbing, trying to prepare yourself for the jolt when the ship hits the sea's surface.

As the *Salt Castle*'s keel smacks the water, the frigate leans on its side into the giant wave it has just ridden. A monstrous shelf of water collapses on top of the vessel, dumping tons of ocean on your exhausted body. The great force of the wave tears your hands from the tarred lines of the shroud and pulls you into the sea.

The weight of the giant wave plunges your helpless body so deep into the dark turbulence that it seems to take an eternity for you to return to the surface, though you're swimming as hard as you can. Your lungs are straining for oxygen by the time you finally burst through the churning foam into the night air. The *Salt Castle*'s great bulk is tossing and twisting more than fifty yards away, and the distance between you and it is growing rapidly.

"Help!" you shout. "Throw me a line!"

But your yells are futile. The ship is much too far away for anyone to be able to hear you above the howling wind and crashing water. Even if they could hear you, it would be nearly impossible for them to see you among the swirling whitecaps. You'll have to try to stay afloat somehow through the typhoon!

"I shouldn't try to swim until the sea is calmer," you think quickly. "I'd get tired too soon. I have to relax and float on top of the waves for as long as I can."

Your body floats easily in the salt water, even if it's difficult to keep your head above the roiling surface. You're so intent upon regulating your movements with the natural motion of the waves that you don't see the round object in the water till just before it slams into your head!

When you come to, the sea is calmer. Dawn is just breaking, but you're surrounded by a thick morning fog. Your head still throbs from the blow of the floating barrel—the same barrel that probably saved your life. Your right arm is tangled in a rope used to tie the cover on top of the cask. The empty barrel must have acted like a life buoy while you were unconscious, keeping your head above water until you woke up!

You wriggle your arm free of the rope and twist your body around to get your bearings. To your astonishment, you spot a man swimming toward you in the foggy sea!

"Another survivor from the *Salt Castle!*" you think elatedly. You take only a few strokes toward him when an expression of horror crosses the man's face, and he starts swimming furiously away from you. You realize he's seen something that terrifies him—but you have no idea what!

1) If you want to remain hidden behind the barrel until you know what frightened the man, turn to page 118.

2) If you'd rather yell to the swimmer before he's too far away to hear you, turn to page 23.

"Hektor's shade must have tricked us!" you shout to Rami. "We'll have to fight our way out of here!"

You charge the cannibal nearest to Yolmat, hoping that you can surprise him long enough to reach the cult leader. If you can just get your spear to his throat, you hope that Yolmat will order his men to lay down their arms.

The fat chieftain sees your charge and holds one of his pudgy hands toward you.

"When this spell be cast
May this sight be your last!"

Almost as soon as Yolmat's words reach your ears, a gray haze clouds your vision, blotting out everything around you.

"Rami! I can't see!" you yell. "Yolmat's blinded me with a spell of some kind!"

Instead of a reply, you hear an anguished scream from your fighting companion. At the same instant, you realize that your quest for the Fireseed has failed, and the cannibals' spears skewer your heart.

THE END

As you watch the waves settle behind the storm giant's departing hulk, your first impulse is to follow him, but you quickly decide you just want to get away from him and his strange talk about a quest.

"He was standing on the bottom!" you think. "Storm giants are big, but they're not tall enough to stand on the bottom of deep ocean with their heads above water. I must be close to land, probably Storm Island, since that's where Pona wanted me to go."

The dinghy is nowhere in sight. You glance at the sky, noting the stars and moon. Then you mentally plot a course opposite to Pona's when he left you. You start swimming with slow, powerful strokes so that you won't get tired too fast.

It's during your second resting period, while you're lying limp and motionless on your back, that you hear the distant sound of the surf. You raise your head quickly and search the horizon for land. Then you see it! A tiny black dot against the night sky!

You estimate that the island is perhaps twenty miles away, so you start for it immediately. Now that you have a destination in sight, it seems that you're moving faster, but you know that it's only an illusion.

During the long swim, you let your mind dwell on everything that the storm giant told you about Hektor, your famous ancestor's mortal enemy. It's difficult to believe that someone from Ennis Farold's time might still be alive, but you know that sorcery can be extremely powerful. Despite yourself, you're intrigued by Pona's words.

It seems as if many hours have passed when you finally near the crashing sound of surf. You swim toward the beach until you can stand with your head above water and scout your landing spot.

It's an inhabited strip of beach, but the village is a small one. You can see perhaps a dozen fires on the white sand and a few huts built on stilts over the lagoon water. Outrigger canoes are tied beneath most of the huts, and other canoes are pulled up onto the sand.

You don't know whether the natives are friendly or not—legend has Storm Island inhabited by cannibals. Maybe you should just steal a canoe and get safely away. The problem is that you feel more and more drawn to investigate Pona's story, and the natives might be able to help you.

1) If you want to ask the natives on the island to help you, turn to page 26.

2) If you decide you should get away from the island as quickly as you can, turn to page 55.

"If we stay here, Rami may die from his wounds," you think, "but if we go back, there's a slim chance that we haven't breathed enough of the deadly fumes to kill us on the other side."

You decide quickly that you must get Rami back to Moffid, and you carry him into the shadows, away from the aerie and the feeding pterodactyl.

The exit you used to enter the volcanic crater is closer than you thought. You duck inside, away from the rapidly expanding fog of fire, which is even beginning to seep into the cave behind you. The blackness is so thick that you can't see your own hands in front of you. Then you remember the Fireseed. Its glow is enough to keep Hektor's shade at bay, so it ought to work as a lamp!

When you take the gem from your pocket, its brilliant internal glare floods the caverns with crimson light. The evil essence of the immortal Hektor trapped within the crystal walls is helping to return itself to its prison inside the sorcerer's own skull!

The island warrior's dead weight is beginning to tire you by the time you reach the Cave of Bones. The stacked skeletons there are grisly reminders of the lethal effects of the fiery fog.

You stop to rest once inside the cavern mouth, letting Rami's body slip gently to the rocky floor. Your dazed companion grunts with pain but doesn't awaken, perhaps because he has lost so much blood. You stare at the fiery glow of the icy-cold gemstone in your hand and wonder how Hektor's evil essence was trapped by Nivida in the perfect crystal.

A thin mist has floated into the cave from the jungle outside its mouth. It has settled like a cloud of smoke over the remains of Hektor's first followers, those who fled the insanity of Yolmat. Fireseed's enchanted glow spreads to the smoky haze, seeming to set it ablaze almost like a . . .

"FIERY FOG!" your brain screams just as the first dust-covered bone begins to move. All around you and Rami's unconscious figure, the skeletons in the Cave of Bones are coming to life! Frozen in a moment of fear, you're unable to tear your eyes from the horror around you.

Hektor's first henchmen, all members of his demonic cult on Storm Island, are dragging their ancient bodies toward you! Dried flesh and hair still cling in gruesome patches to some of the grinning skulls. The red glare of Fireseed reflects on the tarnished blades of primitive weapons and jewelry as the hideous horde closes in upon you!

"Fool of a warrior!" booms Hektor's voice from the figure of a man in front of you. "Did you imagine that I'd let you escape from Ponai with my essence in your doltish hands? Do you think that my power is limited to shadowy apparitions and exploding walls?"

A wave of confusion sweeps over you. "I

thought your shade was powerless in the presence of the Fireseed!" you exclaim as you back away slowly from the advancing undead cultists.

"And so it is!" answers the voice. "I am the real Hektor! Enough of my life-force has leaked from the enchanted gem to perform such minor spells as the one that now threatens you!"

Suddenly, you understand what has happened! As long as the Fireseed remains outside Hektor's skull, its energy can escape into the world through the gemstone's magical glow! That's why Rami's mother keeps it locked in a darkened cabinet even when it's inside the skull!

You lunge forward, crashing through the first wave of skeletons, swinging your spear shaft against their animated bones. Gaining enough time to put your thoughts into action, you hastily cram the Fireseed into your pocket, plunging the cave into total darkness except for the dim moonlight from its mouth.

You press your body against the wall of the cavern, prepared to meet the full attack of the skeleton horde if you're wrong. The fleshless figures take several more steps toward you in the darkness, then begin collapsing with a series of clattering sounds throughout the chamber.

"Come on, Hektor! Where's your great power now?" you yell. "You're not even strong enough to break through my pocket!"

The sorcerer's reply is weak, as if it were coming from the other end of the earth.

"I see that I misjudged the amount of wisdom you inherited from your ancestor, the Archcleric of Baysend!" the voice admits. "But do not think our contest is ended, Davin Farold! You have defeated my prophecy, but only for the moment. The forces that I control are timeless, as you will see. . . ."

The sorcerer's voice drifts away into nothingness as his freezing essence inside your pocket grows weaker, until it seems no colder than any other large gem would feel.

"Wh—what's happened?"

Rami's weak query from the floor beside you is a welcome relief from your final confrontation with Hektor.

"We're in the Cave of Bones," you tell your companion and new friend. You hastily describe Hektor's last desperate attempt to keep you from returning the Fireseed to the skull.

"But how did you stop the skeletons?" Rami mumbles.

"By simply putting the Fireseed in my pocket!" you tell him. "I realized all of a sudden that it was the light of Fireseed that was Hektor's spirit. That's why your mother keeps it hidden away, both inside the skull and inside that special cabinet. I figured that Hektor's spell couldn't work on the skeletons if I turned off Fireseed's glow. It was a risk I had to take, but it worked!"

"Wh—what about the fog?" Rami asks weakly. "We'll die in the outside air!"

"You'll die inside the crater without a healer!" you reply. "The fog is just beginning to seep into the cave behind us. We may not have inhaled enough of it yet to change our bodies. It's another chance we have to take, Rami. Whatever happens, we have the Fireseed, and Hektor's prophecy will never be fulfilled."

"Help me up," he says. "I want to do this on my own two feet."

Together, you hobble out of the Cave of Bones and fill your lungs with the balmy sea air on the other side of Ponai's slopes. You wait for the first deadly sign that your lungs have been altered by the fiery fog of the crater, but nothing happens.

"We're safe!" you shout. "We've beaten Hektor's prophecy as well as the fog of fire! Now we can return to the crater of Ponai between the high tides with enough warriors from Moffid to rid the crater of the cult of cannibals!"

"Right now, I just want to take the Fireseed back to my mother so that she can return it to the sorcerer's skull," says Rami. "Then, I want to rest for about a week!"

"It'll take more than a week to fix your wounds," you tell the courageous islander. "I plan to use the time to go home to Baysend and try to settle the differences between my father and me. Give me a few months to convince him that I'm a better fighter than a shipbuilder. By that time, you'll be fit enough for another adventure!"

"We can start by collecting all of that treasure from the Cave of Bones," says Rami. "No one else will go near the place."

Rami's pained but happy face is gleaming in the moonlight as you lift him in your arms for the journey to Moffid. You step into the jungle filled with the satisfaction of a mission successfully completed and the anticipation of other exciting adventures yet to come.

THE END

SAGA OF OLD CITY
Comes Alive In . . .

GREYHAWK™
ADVENTURES

$3.95

by Gary Gygax

Follow the adventures of Gord, a young thief, as he comes of age in lusty, brawling Old City. A cast of rich wonderful characters waits to welcome you into this exciting novel where danger lurks behind every shadowy doorway and a man always keeps his hand upon the hilt of his dagger.

Distributed to the book trade in the U.S. by Random House, Inc., and in Canada by Random House of Canada, Ltd.

ONE-ON-ONE™ ADVENTURE GAMEBOOKS

by James M. Ward

The ONE-ON-ONE Gamebooks are self-contained role-playing games for two people. Each player becomes the central character in one of the two books. Each book portrays the adventure, step by step, as the two characters stalk each other through a dangerous environment until they reach the final combat!

Play anytime!

Play anywhere!

Play many times!

CASTLE ARCANIA
You are the gallant knight or the powerful wizard, each searching for other in the magical ruins of Castle Arcania.

BATTLE FOR THE ANCIENT ROBOT
You are the human star pilot or the killer robot, racing through space in a desperate search for the powerful parts of the Ancient Robot.

REVENGE OF THE RED DRAGON
You are the vengeful red dragon or the marauding black knight who raided the dragon's lair.

Boxed set of two books includes everything needed to play. All you provide is paper, two pencils, and one friend.

Suggested retail price: $5.95. Available at fine book and hobby stores.

IVAN SERGEYEVICH TURGENEV
was born in Orel in 1818. He
was educated first at home, later at the universities of
Moscow and St. Petersburg. In 1839 he studied at the
University of Berlin where he acquired the Western
values for which he was much criticized in Russia
throughout his life. In 1843 he successfully published
Parasha—a tale in verse. His infatuation with the
famous singer Mme. Viardot caused his mother to
cut off his allowance, and he lived as a Bohemian until
her death in 1850 made him a rich man. In 1852
Turgenev abandoned poetry and the drama; thereafter he devoted himself wholly to fiction. His first
successful novel, *A Sportsman's Sketches* (1852),
contrasted appealing peasants and unpleasant masters.
The next decade produced *Rudin* (1856), *A Nest of
Gentlefolk* (1858), *On the Eve* (1860), *First Love*
(1860), and *Fathers and Sons* (1862)—all of which
drew critics' applause. The radical press, however,
initiated strong and continuing criticism of the "nihilist" Bazarov in *Fathers and Sons*. Deeply offended,
Turgenev left Russia for France, where he became an
intimate of Flaubert and the French literary world.
His novels *Smoke* (1867) and *Virgin Soil* (1877)
show the depth of his bitterness and his loss of touch
with contemporary Russia. However, his last visit to
Russia (1880) marked a triumphant homecoming.
He died in 1883, at Bougival, near Paris.

Ivan Turgenev

FATHERS AND SONS

A NEW TRANSLATION BY
George Reavy

WITH A FOREWORD BY
Alan Hodge

A SIGNET CLASSIC

Published by THE NEW AMERICAN LIBRARY

Published by arrangement with
FARRAR, STRAUS AND GIROUX, INC.
No part of this book may be reproduced without permission.
For information address Farrar, Straus & Giroux, Inc.,
19 Union Square West, New York, New York 10003.

Fourth Printing

SIGNET TRADEMARK REG. U.S. PAT. OFF. AND FOREIGN COUNTRIES
REGISTERED TRADEMARK—MARCA REGISTRADA
HECHO EN CHICAGO, U.S.A.

SIGNET CLASSICS *are published by*
The New American Library, Inc.
1301 Avenue of the Americas, New York, New York 10019

PRINTED IN THE UNITED STATES OF AMERICA

Foreword

FOR Western readers Turgenev is the most engaging of the great Russian novelists. Open any of his novels, and from the first chapter one's sympathy and curiosity are aroused. Take the beginning of *Fathers and Sons*. A middle-aged landowner is affectionately waiting to welcome his son, freshly down from the University. In very few words Turgenev conveys the amiable but ineffectual charm of Nicholas Kirsanov. This is done not so much by the summary of his life, all to the point though that is, as by the lightly drawn contrast between Nicholas in his dusty overcoat and his foppish and pretentious valet.

As Nicholas waits on the porch, lost in the warm glow of reverie, a plump gaudy chicken struts by on sturdy yellow legs, eyed with hostility by a marauding cat. Is this just a telling stroke in the picture of a rural posting-house—the sort of realistic item Defoe might have thought of? Or is not Nicholas himself a kind of plump gaudy chicken, upon whom hostile fate is about to spring? The book is full of these significant touches in which a bird or a pot of gooseberry jam, a piece of furniture or the cut of a coat—all the adjuncts and surroundings of everyday life—are brought out of the background to suggest the colour of a mood and the shape of expectations to come. When young Arcady Kirsanov arrives, we very soon see who will play the rôle of marauding cat. It is Arcady's formidable college-friend whom he worships and from whom he takes all his opinions, Bazarov the Nihilist. But though we know, or rather guess, that conflict will break out between Nicholas and young Arcady, we have only this neat and light hint to go on. Turgenev never underlines, never over-emphasizes. The plump gaudy chicken struts out of the story, having for the space of one sentence become almost a symbol.

If there is one supreme gift in the novelist's art, it is the capacity for drawing his story out of the very natures of his

v

characters, letting the situation unfold and develop as the various and frequently contrasting sides of their personalities are revealed. This gift Turgenev possesses to the highest degree. Every character in his books, whatever his faults, has the attractive quality of humanity, and it is out of the human contrariety of his people that the story grows. It has been said of Turgenev that he never provides a plot. In the sense in which Trollope builds up his plots, step by step, according to a careful dramatic schedule, this is certainly true. By comparison Turgenev is episodic; seemingly casually, he assembles one telling scene after another. Each one is a portrait of moods and feelings at a moment in time, compounded of memories and of hopes, of conflict and of harmony—between the characters, and within themselves. The scenes are so vivid, and their succession so unerringly presented, that one is left with the impression of knowing every significant detail of the lives of Turgenev's creation. Through his imaginative insight, the slightest characters appear in the round, and the most ordinary incidents acquire their full emotional importance.

It was this mastery of impressionistic realism, in psychology and in background as well, that won for Turgenev his enthusiastic following in France. Flaubert was perhaps his closest friend, Maupassant his most brilliant disciple. Towards the end of his days, Turgenev became practically an honorary Frenchman of letters. All his life he had been a "Westerner," as the Russians defined it. Largely he was so by temperament, but there were other motives. His tyrannical mother kept a firm grip on the family estates; living on them, with her in charge, was never a pleasure for long. For a large part of his life, also, Turgenev was deeply attached to Mme. Viardot, the opera singer—and, curiously enough, to her husband and children too. There were few years when he did not spend many months in her company. But for all his ties with the West, Russia is always the essential subject of his books. In his political outlook—and long before Communist days no Russian author was without one—he was a liberal, an advocate of emancipation of the serfs and, in Tsarist terms, altogether a man of "advanced" views. In his own country his "Westernism" and his liberalism brought him many critics. But never had Turgenev to face such a storm of criticism as was provoked by *Fathers and Sons*. The reason for this was wholly the novel revolutionary figure of Bazarov.

Before and after Turgenev's day, Russian fiction has been full of delightful characters who plan great projects they will never accomplish, of brilliant talkers incapable of managing even their own private lives. Turgenev's own Rudin, in the novel of that name, is one of the most impressive of these "superfluous men"—to use Turgenev's own phrase. To them, Bazarov stands in complete contrast. In a sense he is the literary ancestor of the hard-shelled, self-possessed commissars celebrated in so many early Soviet films and novels. For Bazarov is the rejector of all current beliefs and illusions; only after they have been swept aside, he is convinced, can a new and better world be built. In Turgenev's eyes, Bazarov was the most profoundly sympathetic of his creations—and we shall see in a moment how often and how skilfully he engages the reader's feelings on Bazarov's side. But to the young intelligentsia of Petersburg and Moscow, Bazarov seemed an uncouth caricature of all they stood for. And by the diehards he was considered to epitomize the crudity of would-be revolutionaries. Turgenev was horrified to find himself congratulated by crusty old believers in serfdom, whose friendship he did not welcome, and bitterly reproached by the young reformers, whose views he largely shared.

The dust of this controversy has long since settled—at least for English readers. But its violence is a proof of how brilliantly Turgenev held the scales in the conflict of *Fathers and Sons*. He remained convinced that Bazarov was the most striking of all his characters, and for a long time he kept a diary in which he entered with relish the sort of iconoclastic opinions that Bazarov would have expressed on all sorts of general subjects. But here we need to remind ourselves that Turgenev compiled similar dossiers, though less thoroughly, for most of his characters; and that his supreme interest lay in people, not in opinions. *Fathers and Sons* is not a study in the doctrine of Nihilism, or even a simple story of conflict between parents and children. Its drama lies in the impact on all its characters of one extraordinarily gifted, impatient and caustic man. Bazarov alone is the agent who utterly changes the tenor of existence in the household of the Kirsanovs; in the life of the brilliant, beautiful and cold-hearted Mme Odintsov, with whom he falls in love, and finally in the wonderfully characterized home of his own tedious but adoring parents. The genius of the novel lies in the delicately even balance kept between the rights and wrongs of all parties to the drama. For though Bazarov may be a destroyer, so much that he attacks is false and sham and worthy of destruction.

The Kirsanov household, for instance, is full of fine feelings and good intentions. But their estate is hopelessly mismanaged. What useful purpose in the world do the two elder Kirsanovs serve? Nicholas, for all his liberalism, keeps a former peasant girl for a mistress, like any old-fashioned feudatory, and his brother, Paul, is a touchy dandified romantic, doting on long-lost love. Yet when the conflict finally breaks out between the older and younger generations, one's sympathies go to the old people: it is the old who possess tolerance, good manners, and the desire to understand. On the other hand, while he has been on the estate, Bazarov has succeeded in making Nicholas's mistress, the shy and lovely Fenichka, feel at ease with "the gentry" for the first time in her life; and he has been most kind and attentive towards her baby. . . . In this debate there is no end to the oscillation of rights and wrongs. If Bazarov in Chapter X seems a lout in comparison with Paul Kirsanov, how neatly the tables are turned in Chapter XXIV. There, in a superbly grotesque duel, it is Paul's behaviour that is ridiculous and absurd.

Neat shifts of emphasis, intricate changes of feeling—the story abounds in them. Nothing could be finer, to take another example, than the hardly perceptible stages by which young Arcady Kirsanov begins to doubt some of his friend's judgments, then to question them, and finally to quarrel with him. A simple process, one might suppose, of disillusionment with theories, once they have started to come into conflict with the loyalties of love. But the most straightforward themes in Turgenev have subtle complexities. Arcady's change of mind could not take place without the transfer of his worship to Katya. He would not have fallen back upon Katya had he not imagined himself under the spell of her elder sister, Mme Odintsov. And would he have thought himself in love with her, but for his desire to follow Bazarov's example in everything?

Bazarov's own end is tragic and ironical. Mme Odintsov is delighted to discuss with him everything under the sun.

He is tremendously moved and impressed by the emancipated brilliance of her mind. Has he at last found someone with whom he can really and truly share the great future that lies before him? But Mme Odintsov has the timidity of an intellectual flirt; she is thoroughly frightened by the violence of the passion she arouses in him. Had she been able to respond, he would not have gone sulking off to his father's small village, nor in an idle and disgruntled moment have undertaken to perform an autopsy, cut himself, caught typhus and pitifully died.

By a magnificent piece of alchemy in these last pages, Turgenev manages to convince one that though Bazarov's great talents have been wasted, and his life almost fruitless, here was a personality possessed of fascinating stimulation. Arcady may marry his Katya, and Nicholas at last his Fenichka, but are not these happy endings in a way Bazarov's achievement? And will not the most important thing in the lives of the Kirsanovs, as of everyone else in the book, always be to have known Bazarov? That, at least, is the answer Turgenev would have given to those who accused him of letting the old order of humanity triumph and, in Bazarov's death, of stifling the new.

Alan Hodge

Father and Sons

I

"WELL, Peter, any sign of them yet?" This was the question addressed on the 20th of May, 1859, to his servant—a young and lusty fellow with whitish down on his chin and with small dim eyes—by a gentleman of just over forty years of age, in a dusty overcoat and check trousers, as he emerged hatless on the low steps of a posting-station on the X highway.

Everything about the valet—his single turquoise earring, his pomaded hair of various shades and his studied gestures—proclaimed him a representative of a modern and more perfect age; and, as he stared superciliously down the road, he vouchsafed a reply, "No-o, there's no sign of them."

"No sign of them?" his master queried.

"Not a sign," the valet repeated.

His master gave vent to a sigh and sat down on a bench. While he is sitting there, with his legs tucked under him and gazing pensively around, let us introduce him to our readers.

His name was Nicholas Petrovich Kirsanov. Within ten miles of the posting-station he owned a fair estate—a "farm" as he now called it, having divided his land and rented it out to his former serfs. His father, who had seen service as a general in the War of 1812, had been a half-literate, coarse, but not bad sort of Russian; as a commander, first of a brigade and then of a division, he had led a strenuous life, but had spent most of his time in the provinces where, by virtue of his rank, he had wielded quite an appreciable influence. Nicholas Petrovich, like his brother Paul (of whom we shall speak later), was born in the south of Russia and brought up at home until the age of fourteen in an environment of inexpensive tutors, garrulous and obsequious adjutants, and other such regimental and staff personages. His mother, who came of the Kolyazin family and in her youth had been called *Agathe* and later, when she married a general, Agafokleia Kuzminishna Kirsanov, belonged to

11

the species of "commanding matrons"; she wore brightly coloured caps and gaudy silk dresses, was invariably the first to put her lips to the cross at mass, and was in the habit of holding forth loudly and at length upon having her children kiss her hand in the morning and bestowing a blessing on them at bedtime—in short, she ruled the roost. Although not distinguished for courage—he had even been dubbed "poltroon"—Nicholas Petrovich was under an obligation, as was his brother Paul, to join the army; but having broken a leg on the very day that he heard the news of his success in obtaining a commission, he spent a couple of months in bed and retained a slight limp for the remainder of his life. Giving him up as a bad job, his father let him take up a civilian occupation. As soon as Nicholas had reached the age of eighteen, he took him to Petersburg and registered him at the University. By that time, his brother Paul had got his commission in a Guards regiment. The two young men started their life together, in the same apartment, under the distant tutelage of Ilya Kolyazin, an official of standing who was a cousin on their mother's side. Their father rejoined his division and also his wife; every now and then, he dispatched to his sons a few large sheets of greyish paper scribbled over in an ornate clerkly handwriting. At the bottom, these sheets were decoratively inscribed with the words, "Peter Kirsanov, Major-General," painstakingly ringed by an ornamental scrawl. In 1835 Nicholas Petrovich took his degree. In the same year, General Kirsanov, who had been retired from the service as a result of an incident at a military parade he had commanded, arrived in Petersburg with his wife, intending to settle there. But he suddenly died of an apoplectic stroke when he was on the point of renting a house in the vicinity of the Tavrichesky Gardens and had put his name down for the English Club. His wife soon followed him: she could not get accustomed to a dull life in the capital; the boredom of living in retirement had proved too much for her.

In the meantime, to his parents' great annoyance while they were still alive, Nicholas Petrovich had fallen in love with the daughter of an official by the name of Prepolovensky, his former landlord. She was a pretty and, as they say, "cultured" girl, who was addicted to reading serious articles in the Science section of the *Gazettes*. He married her as soon as the period of mourning was over and, having resigned from the Ministry of Pensions in which his father's influence had procured him a post, lived very happily with his Masha, first in a cottage near the Lesnoy Institute, then in a small but attractive apartment in town, with a clean staircase and a chilly drawing-room. Finally he withdrew to the country, where he settled for good and where his son, Arcady, was born. The young married couple lived very happily and tranquilly: they were almost inseparable, they read to one another, played piano duets and sang together; she planted flowers and kept a poultry-yard, while he sometimes went out hunting and busied himself with the management of the estate. In the meantime, Arcady grew and grew—also very happily and tranquilly. Ten years passed like a dream. In 1847 Kirsanov's wife died. He hardly survived the shock and went grey within a few weeks; then he decided to go abroad for a change . . . but it was 1848, the year of revolutions. Reluctantly he returned to the country and, after a prolonged period of inactivity, set about "reforming" his estate. In 1855 he took his son to the University: he spent three years with him in Petersburg, avoiding social engagements and trying his hardest to strike up an acquaintance with his son's young friends. He had been unable to spend the last winter in Petersburg—and so we meet him, in the month of May, 1859, a grizzled, slightly bent, stoutish, elderly gentleman, waiting for the arrival of his son who, as he himself had once done, had just taken his degree.

Out of a feeling of respect or, perhaps, because he wished to escape his master's scrutiny, the valet strolled under the gateway and lit his pipe. Nicholas Petrovich let drop his head and began to examine the rickety steps of the porch: with an air of dignity, a plump, gaudy chicken was strutting on them, stamping firmly about on his sturdy yellow legs; a filthy cat was eyeing him with hostility as it sprawled posturing on the banisters. The sun was blazing: a smell of freshly baked rye bread was wafted from a shadowy passage in the posting-house. Nicholas Petrovich had surrendered himself to his reverie. "His son . . . a graduate . . . his Arcady . . ." Such were the thoughts ceaselessly spinning in his head; he made an effort to divert his mind to other things, but the very same thoughts came flooding back. He remembered his late wife . . . "She did not live to see this day," he whispered mournfully. . . . A bulky blue pigeon settled on the roadway and waddled off hastily to quench its thirst in a pool next to the well. Nicholas Petrovich directed his attention to it just as a rumble of approaching wheels began to impinge upon his ears. . . .

"Looks as if they're coming," the valet reported, darting out of the gateway.

Nicholas Petrovich jumped up and fixed his gaze on the highway. A tarantass came into view, drawn by three stage-horses; in the tarantass the band of a student's cap gleamed for an instant, and then he caught sight of a dear and familiar face. . . .

"Arcady! Arcady!" Kirsanov shouted, waving his hands and running forward. . . . A few seconds later, he was already pressing his lips on the young bachelor's beardless, dusty and sun-tanned cheeks.

II

"LET me dust myself, daddy!" Arcady exclaimed in a ringing, youthful voice, which the journey had made slightly husky, as he cheerfully returned his father's embraces. "I shall only soil you."

"No matter, no matter," Nicholas Petrovich kept repeating with an affectionate smile as, first of all, he slapped his son's coat a couple of times, and then his own. "Let me look at you, let me see you," he added, standing back. Then he hurried off towards the posting-station, reiterating as he went: "Quick there, quick, bring out the horses."

Nicholas Petrovich appeared more excited than his son; he looked a little flurried and overcome with shyness. Arcady stopped him.

"Daddy," he cried, "allow me to introduce my great friend Bazarov, about whom I have written so often. Very kindly he has consented to stay with us."

Nicholas Petrovich spun quickly round and, going up to a tall man in a longish, loose-fitting country overcoat with tassels, who had just climbed out of the tarantass, he warmly gripped the red, ungloved hand, which his son's friend had been in no hurry to extend to him.

"I am heartily glad," he began, "and grateful, too, for

your good intention in wishing to visit us; I hope . . . May I ask your name and patronymic?"

"Eugene Vassilich," Bazarov replied in a drawling but virile voice and, throwing back the collar of his coat, showed his full face to Nicholas Petrovich. The face was long and gaunt, with a broad forehead, a nose flat above but tapering below, large greenish eyes and bushy whiskers of a sandy colour—the whole animated with a serene smile and expressive of self-assurance and intelligence.

"I trust, my dear Eugene Vassilich," Nicholas Petrovich went on, "that your stay with us will not bore you."

Bazarov's thin lips gave a slight twitch; but he made no reply and merely touched his cap. His fine dark hair, which grew long and thick, failed to conceal the bulges on his large skull.

"Well? What shall we do, Arcady?" Nicholas Petrovich began again, turning to his son. "Shall we have the horses harnessed at once? Or would you prefer to rest here first?"

"We'll rest at home, daddy. Tell them to get the horses ready."

"Immediately, immediately!" his father exclaimed. "Hey, Peter, did you hear that? Get on with it. Look lively."

Peter, as an up-to-date servant, had not ventured to approach the young master to kiss his hand, but had merely bowed from a distance; now he vanished once more through the gateway.

"I have my barouche here, and there is also a fresh relay of horses available for your tarantass," Nicholas Petrovich put in fussily, while Arcady gulped some water from an iron mug which the station-master's wife had brought, and Bazarov, puffing at his pipe, went up to the coachman who had unharnessed the horses. "There is only room for two in my barouche, and I don't know how your friend . . ."

"He'll manage in the tarantass," Arcady interrupted in an undertone. "Please don't be so ceremonious with him. He's a grand fellow and very simple at heart—you'll see for yourself."

Nicholas Petrovich's coachman led out the horses.

"Get on with it, you bush-beard!" Bazarov exclaimed, addressing the coachman.

"D'ye hear, Mityuha," interjected another coachman, who was standing nearby with his hands thrust into the back openings of his sheepskin coat, "d'ye hear what that gentleman was after calling you? 'Bush-beard,' that's what he said."

Mityuha merely gave a pull at his cap and started to drag the reins from the sweating shaft-horse.

"Look lively, lively, my lads. Now come along and lend a hand," Nicholas Petrovich shouted. "I'll see to it you get money for vodka!"

Within a few minutes the horses were harnessed; the Kirsanovs got into their barouche; Peter clambered up on the box; Bazarov leapt into the tarantass, pressed his head against the leather cushion—and both vehicles drove away.

III

"HERE you are, a graduate now, and back in the fold," Nicholas Petrovich said, patting Arcady now on the shoulder, now on the knee. "Home at last!"

"And how is Uncle Paul? Is he keeping well?" inquired Arcady who, despite a sincere and child-like feeling of elation, was anxious to switch the conversation as soon as possible from an emotional level to one of ordinary conversation.

"He's well enough. He wished to come and meet you, but for some reason changed his mind."

"And have you been long waiting for me?" Arcady asked.

"About five hours."

"How kind of you, daddy!"

Quickly turning round, Arcady gave his father a smacking kiss on the cheek. Nicholas Petrovich uttered a subdued laugh.

"You should just see the horse I've got waiting for you!" he began. "You'll see. And we've also had fresh wall-paper put in your room."

"And is there a room for Bazarov?"

"We'll find him one, too."

"Please, daddy, do be very kind to him. I can't tell you how much I esteem his friendship."

"You became acquainted recently?"

"Yes, recently."

"That explains why I did not meet him in the winter. What does he do?"

"The natural sciences are his main subject. But he knows everything. Next year he intends to take his final medical exam."

"Ah! So he's in the medical faculty," Nicholas Petrovich remarked and then paused. "Peter," he added, pointing, "are those our peasants driving along there?"

Peter glanced in the direction his master had indicated. Several carts, drawn by unbridled horses, were rolling at a good pace along the narrow by-road. Each cart held one or two peasants, wearing sheepskin coats flapping wide open.

"That's correct, sir," Peter replied.

"Where are they going? To town?"

"To town most likely. To the gin-shop," he added superciliously, with a slight nod at the driver as if expecting him to confirm this. But the latter did not move an eyelid: a peasant of the old school, he disapproved of the modern outlook.

"The peasants are giving me a lot of worry this year," Nicholas Petrovich went on, addressing his son. "They won't pay their rent. What am I to do with them?"

"And the hired labourers? Are you satisfied with them?"

"Yes," Arcady's father squeezed through his teeth. "But the trouble is they are being led astray; they are not doing their best yet. They only smash the tools. However, in their ploughing they did tolerably well. There should be enough flour when the corn's threshed. Have you become interested in farming now?"

"How unfortunate to have no shade here," Arcady remarked, without replying to the question.

"I had a large awning put up on the north side, over the terrace," Nicholas Petrovich answered. "Now we can even dine in the open air."

"That will make the house look like a summer cottage. . . . However, that doesn't matter very much. The air here is magnificent. How fragrant it is! I do believe the air smells sweeter here than anywhere else in the world! And these skies . . ."

Arcady suddenly paused, glanced quickly back, and relapsed into silence.

"Of course," Nicholas Petrovich remarked, "you were

born here; in these parts everything must seem very special to you."

"But, daddy, what does it matter where a man was born!"

"And yet . . ."

"No, it doesn't matter at all."

Nicholas Petrovich glanced sideways at his son: the barouche rolled on for another half a mile before they resumed their conversation.

"I don't remember if I ever wrote and told you," Nicholas Petrovich began, "about the death of Yegorovna—your nanny."

"You don't mean that she's dead? Poor old soul! And is Prokofyich still alive?"

"Yes, and he hasn't altered a bit. He grumbles as much as ever. On the whole, you won't find many changes at Maryino."

"Have you still got the same steward?"

"That's one of the few things I have changed. I decided that I would not keep any of the former house-serfs about the place once they were liberated, or at least, that I would not entrust them with any jobs involving responsibility." (Arcady glanced significantly at Peter.) *"Il est libre en effet,"* Nicholas Petrovich remarked in an undertone, "but he's merely a valet. My new steward is a man from town; he seems an efficient sort of person. I pay him a salary of two hundred and fifty roubles a year. However," he added, rubbing his forehead and eyebrows with his hand, "though I told you that you would find no changes at Maryino . . . that is not quite correct. I think it my duty to warn you that . . ."

He hesitated for an instant and then went on to speak in French.

"A strict moralist would judge my frankness improper, but, firstly, this thing cannot be concealed and, secondly, as you know very well, I have always had principles of my own as to the relations between father and son. You would be within your rights, of course, to condemn me. At my age . . . In short, that . . . that girl, of whom you have probably heard already . . ."

"Fenichka?" Arcady asked in a clear voice.

His father blushed.

"Please don't mention her name aloud. . . . Well, yes . . . she is now living with me. I have taken her into the house

. . . we had a couple of small rooms to spare. However, we can change all that."

"But why should you, daddy, if I may ask?"

"Your friend will be staying with us now. . . . It might be embarrassing."

"Please don't worry about Bazarov. He is above prejudice."

"It's off my chest, at least," Nicholas Petrovich said. "The rooms in the wing are not so comfortable, that's the trouble."

"But, daddy, you seem to be apologizing," Arcady interjected. "Are you ashamed?"

"Of course I should be ashamed," Nicholas Petrovich replied, getting redder and redder.

"Enough, daddy, enough, I entreat you!" Arcady exclaimed, smiling affectionately. "Why apologize?" His heart filled with a feeling of indulgent tenderness for his kind and sensitive father, mingled with a secret sense of superiority. "Do please stop it now," he repeated, involuntarily enjoying the awareness of his own advanced and emancipated state.

Nicholas Petrovich glanced at him through the fingers of the hand with which he continued to rub his forehead, and felt his heart twinge. . . . But immediately he took all the blame on himself.

"Look! Our fields already," he said after a long pause.

"And isn't that our forest over there?" Arcady inquired.

"Yes. But I have just sold it. It will be cut down this year."

"Why did you sell it?"

"I needed the money; and besides, those lands were part of the peasants' share."

"Of the peasants who won't pay rent?"

"That's their affair; anyway—they will pay me one day."

"I'm sorry about the forest," Arcady remarked, staring round him.

The locality through which they were driving could not be described as picturesque. On all sides, fields upon fields spread as far as the horizon, now sloping gently up, now sloping gently down; scattered here and there, copses could be seen, and winding ravines planted with sparse, stunted bushes, which reminded the traveller of the way they had been indicated on the old maps of Catherine the Great's reign. They also came on streams whose banks had been hollowed out, minute ponds with rickety dykes, hamlets with squat little huts beneath sombre thatched roofs which were only partially intact, tumbledown threshing barns with wattled walls and doorways gaping on abandoned threshing floors, and churches, sometimes of brick with peeling plaster and sometimes of wood with crosses awry and graveyards gone to wrack and ruin. Arcady felt his heart gradually contract. As though to confirm this pattern of neglect, the peasants whom they met on the way looked miserable and their nags wretched; like ragged beggars, the roadside willows stood with their bark ripped off and their branches broken; emaciated cows, shaggy and gnawn with hunger, were plucking greedily at the grass in the ditches. They looked as if they had just escaped from the dread and deadly claws of some wild animal—and, on this beautiful spring day, the heartrending plight of these enfeebled animals evoked the white spectre of a joyless and endless winter, its blizzards, frosts and snows. . . . "No," Arcady mused, "there is no prosperity here. There is no abundance and no hard work; this country simply cannot remain as it is, it will have to be transformed. . . . But how can that be achieved? How should one go about it? . . ."

Such were Arcady's reflections. . . . While he meditated, spring claimed its own. Everything round him glittered gold and green; in the soft breath of a warm breeze everything stirred gently, all things—the trees, the bushes and the grasses; on every side larks trilled endlessly and ecstatically; the plovers called, weaving in flight over the low-lying meadows or skipping from stump to stump in silence; the rooks strutted about, beautifully and blackly outlined against the tender green background of the as yet short spring corn; darting into the rye, which was already slightly tinged with white, they let their heads be seen now and then among its smoky waves. Arcady stared and stared until his thoughts grew dim and, finally, faded. . . . Throwing off his student's greatcoat, he glanced at his father so brightly and boyishly that the latter embraced him once again.

"It's no distance now," Nicholas Petrovich remarked. "Once we reach the top of the hill, the house will be in sight. We shall have a glorious time of it, Arcady; you can help me to manage the estate if that doesn't bore you. We must draw closer, we must get to know each other better, don't you think?"

"Certainly," Arcady replied. "But what a marvellous day!"

"Especially for your arrival, my dear. Yes, spring is at its glorious zenith. Incidentally, I agree with Pushkin—do you remember those lines in *Eugene Onegin*?

> How sad your coming is to me,
> O spring, O spring, the time of love!
> What——"

"Arcady!" Bazarov shouted from the tarantass. "Will you send a match over? I have none left for my pipe."

Nicholas Petrovich fell silent. Arcady, who had begun to listen to the recitation not without surprise and a certain sympathy, hastened to produce a silver match-box from his pocket and to send it over with Peter.

"Would you like a cigar?" Bazarov shouted again.

"Send it over," Arcady called back.

Peter ran back to the barouche and, together with the match-box, handed him a black cigar, which Arcady instantly lit, diffusing such a potent and acrid smell of cheap tobacco that his father, who was no smoker, was obliged to turn away his nose—but this he did very discreetly for fear of offending his son.

A quarter of an hour later, both vehicles pulled up in front of the porch of a newly built wooden house, coated with grey paint and topped by a red iron-sheeted roof. This was Maryino, known also as the "New Suburb" or, as the peasants had dubbed it, the "Will-o'-the-wisp Farm."

IV

No throng of servants swarmed from the house to greet the gentlemen; only a girl of about twelve came down the steps, followed by a lad very like Peter, wearing a grey livery jacket with white crested buttons; he was Paul Petrovich's valet. Silently he opened the door of the barouche and then undid the leather apron of the tarantass. Followed by his son and Bazarov, Nicholas Petrovich passed through the dim and almost bare reception room, behind the door of which they caught a glimpse of a young woman's face, and into the drawing-room, which was furnished in the latest style.

"You're at home now!" Nicholas Petrovich exclaimed, taking off his cap and tossing back his hair. "What you now need is supper and rest."

"Actually, a bite to eat would not be a bad idea," Bazarov remarked, stretching himself and sinking down on the sofa.

"Yes, indeed, we must have supper served. The supper quickly!" Nicholas Petrovich exclaimed, stamping his feet for no apparent reason. "Ah, here comes Prokofyich!"

A man of about sixty years of age, white-haired, lean and swarthy, in a brown tailed coat with brass buttons and a pink handkerchief, entered the room. He grinned, went up to kiss Arcady's hand and, having bowed to the guest, retreated to the door and put his hands behind his back.

"Here he is, Prokofyich," Nicholas Petrovich began. "He has arrived at last. . . . Well? How do you find him?"

"Looking his best," the old servitor replied, grinning once again. Then knitting his thick brows, he inquired significantly: "Do you wish me to lay the table, sir?"

"Yes, yes, please. But, Eugene Vassilich, wouldn't you like to retire to your room first?"

"No thank you, I have no need. But will you be so good as to have my luggage taken there, and this little garment too?" he added, pulling off his travelling coat.

"Certainly. Prokofyich, will you see to the gentleman's coat?" With a look of slight perplexity on his face, Prokofyich picked up Bazarov's "little garment" and, holding it with both hands high above his head, tiptoed out of the room. "Now what about you, Arcady? Do you wish to retire for a moment?"

"Yes, I must tidy myself," Arcady replied. He was about to direct his steps to the door when, at that instant, in came a man of medium height, dressed in an English suit of dark material, a fashionable cravat, and patent-leather shoes. It was Paul Petrovich Kirsanov. His appearance suggested that he might be forty-five: his grey, close-trimmed hair shone dark as silver; his bilious, unwrinkled face, whose lines were unusually symmetrical and clean-cut as though carved by a fine, light chisel, bore the traces of exceptional good looks: his black, glowing, almond-shaped eyes were particularly attractive. The whole mien of Arcady's uncle, elegant and well-bred in appearance, had preserved a youthful uprightness and a certain soaring quality which usually tends to disappear when a man turns thirty.

From his pocket Paul Petrovich drew one of his graceful hands, with long pink nails—a hand whose grace was further enhanced by a snowy-white cuff, linked together by a single large opal. He extended it to his nephew. Having achieved a preliminary European hand-shake, he kissed his nephew thrice in the Russian fashion, that is to say, he brushed his cheeks thrice with his scented moustaches, exclaiming, "Welcome home!"

Nicholas Petrovich introduced him to Bazarov: Paul Petrovich gave a slight inclination with his flexible body and a slight smile, but failed to offer his hand and in fact put it back in his pocket.

"I was beginning to think you would not arrive to-day," he said in a pleasant voice, graciously swaying his body, twitching his shoulders and displaying his fine, white teeth. "Did anything happen on the way?"

"Nothing happened," Arcady replied. "We just took it easy. But, as a result, we are now as hungry as wolves. Will you tell Prokofyich to hurry up, father? I shall be back in a second."

"Wait, I'll go with you," Bazarov suddenly exclaimed, leaping up from the sofa. The young men went out.

"Who is he?" Paul Petrovich inquired.

"A friend of Arcady's and, according to him, a very intelligent fellow."

"Is he staying with us?"

"Yes."

"That hairy creature?"

"Yes, he is."

Paul Petrovich drummed with his finger-nails on the table. "I find that Arcady *s'est dégourdi*," he remarked. "I'm so glad he's back."

There was little conversation at supper. Bazarov, in particular, almost failed to utter a word, but ate a great deal. Nicholas Petrovich related various incidents of his "farmer's life," as he called it, discussed the imminent government reforms, the committees and the deputies, the need for more farm machinery, and other matters of the sort. Paul Petrovich slowly paced up and down the dining-room (he never supped), taking an occasional sip of red wine, and, more rarely, uttering some remark or, rather, some exclamation, such as "Ah! Aha! H'm!" Arcady gave them news of Petersburg, but experienced a slight embarrassment—the embarrassment a young man is liable to suffer when he has just emerged from adolescence and then finds himself in a place where the company is still accustomed to regard him as a child. Drawling his sentences unnecessarily, he avoided addressing his father as "daddy," and once, though with an effort, called him "father"; with excessive assurance he poured out rather more wine than he really wanted, and drank it all. Prokofyich could not take his eyes off him and kept chewing his lips. After supper, the company immediately dispersed.

"What an eccentric uncle you have!" Bazarov exclaimed, as he sat in a dressing-gown near Arcady's bed and sucked a short-stemmed pipe. "Just think, what elegance for the country! And as for his nails—why, they're only fit for an exhibition!"

"You don't realize, of course," Arcady replied, "he was a society lion in his day. One day I shall tell his story. He was as handsome as they make them, and a regular Don Juan."

"That explains it! It's for the sake of old times, then! There are no hearts to captivate here, so much the worse. I just couldn't take my eyes off him: what wonderful collars he wears, they might be made of granite, and he shaves his chin so smoothly. Don't you find him funny, Arcady?"

"Perhaps. But he has really a very good heart."

"He's archaic! But your father's fine. A pity he has a weakness for reciting verse; it's unlikely that he understands much about estate management, but he must be a kind-hearted man."

"My father has a heart of gold."

"Have you noticed he tends to be a little shy?"

Arcady nodded his head, as though he himself were exempt from shyness.

"They simply amaze me, these old romantics!" Bazarov went on. "They excite their nervous systems to the point of irritation . . . well, and that upsets their balance. However, good night! In my room I have an English washstand, but the door of the room won't shut. Nevertheless, it's a thing to be encouraged: English washstands spell progress!"

When Bazarov had gone, a feeling of joy swept over

Arcady. It was sweet to fall asleep in one's own home, in a familiar bed, under a quilt embroidered by loving hands—those of his nanny, perhaps. Oh, those fond, kindly, indefatigable hands! Arcady remembered his nanny—Yegorovna—and sighed, wishing her eternal peace. . . . He said no prayers for himself.

Both he and Bazarov dozed off immediately, but it was a long time before some of the other inhabitants of the house could fall asleep. His son's return had excited Nicholas Petrovich. He did not snuff out the candles before getting into bed and, propping his head with his hand, remained plunged in thought for a long while. His brother sat up far past midnight in his study, in a roomy armchair in front of the fireplace where a few embers still glowed faintly. Paul Petrovich did not bother to undress but only changed his patent-leather shoes for a pair of heelless Turkish slippers. In his hands he held the last issue of *Galignani,* but did not read it; he stared fixedly into the fireplace where, dying and kindling again, a pale blue flame flickered. . . . God alone knows where his thoughts were roaming, but they did not roam only into the past; his face wore a grim and tense expression, and this does not happen when one's thoughts are absorbed merely in recollections. Meanwhile, a young woman, dressed in a warm, pale blue knitted jumper and white kerchief, was sitting on a large chest in a small back room; it was Fenichka, and alternatively she listened, dozed or stared at a door which was wide open—a door through which a child's cot could be seen and the steady breathing of a slumbering infant was audible.

V

NEXT morning Bazarov was the first to wake and be out of the house. "H'm!" he thought, gazing round. "This is hardly an attractive spot." When Nicholas Petrovich had redistributed his lands among the peasantry, he had been obliged to include in his new domain some nine acres of entirely flat and barren fields. Here he had built a new manor house and sunk two wells; but the young trees were tardy, the pond proved shallow, and the water from the wells tasted rather brackish. Only an arbour, contrived of lilac and accacia, had sprouted properly; there tea or dinner was sometimes served. A few minutes sufficed for Bazarov to walk all the garden paths, inspect the cattle sheds and the stables, and to come upon two servant lads with whom he at once struck up acquaintance. With them he set off in search of frogs to a small marsh less than a mile distant from the manor.

"What's the frogs for, master?" one of the lads inquired.

"I'll tell you," Bazarov replied. Though he never indulged common-folk and treated them offhandedly, yet he had the special gift of inspiring their confidence. "I'll split a frog open and see what's going on inside. Except for the fact that we walk about on our hind legs, we are very like these frogs, and that will help me to learn what is going on inside us too."

"But what's it for?"

"To prevent me from making mistakes when you feel sick and I have to doctor you."

"Are you a doctor then?"

"Yes."

"Vaska, d'ye hear that? The master says you and me are like them frogs. Funny, isn't it?"

"They scare me, them frogs," remarked Vaska, a boy of seven, with flaxen hair, bare feet, and a grey cossack coat with a high collar.

"Why be scared? They don't bite, do they?"

"Go on, scramble in, you philosophers," Bazarov said.

In the meantime, Nicholas Petrovich had also wakened and called on Arcady, whom he found already dressed. Father and son went out together and stopped under the awning of the terrace; set among a profusion of lilac bouquets, a samovar was already steaming on the table close to the banisters. A young girl came out—the same as had greeted the travellers at the porch on the previous day—and piped out:

"The young lady, Fedosya Nicolaievna, is not very well, and can't come. She ordered me to ask you if you would be pleased to pour out the tea yourselves or will you have Dunyasha sent for."

"I'll attend to it," Nicholas Petrovich interjected hastily.

"How do you like your tea, Arcady? With cream or a slice of lemon?"

"With cream," Arcady replied and, after a short pause, pointedly said: "Daddy!"

Nicholas Petrovich glanced at his son with an air of embarrassment.

"What is it?" he asked.

Arcady dropped his eyes.

"Pardon me, daddy, if my question strikes you as out of place," he began, "but the frankness with which you spoke yesterday encourages me to be as frank. . . . You won't be angry? . . ."

"Go on."

"You give me the courage to ask you. . . . Is it because I . . . is it because I am here that Fenichka has not come to pour out the tea?"

Nicholas Petrovich turned his face slightly to one side.

"Perhaps," he said at last. "She supposes . . . she feels ashamed. . . ."

Arcady cast a quick glance at his father.

"A great pity if she does feel ashamed. In the first place, you know my views" (Arcady found great pleasure in uttering these words), "and in the second—would I ever dream of upsetting your life by so much as a hairbreadth? Besides, I am convinced that you could not have made a more suitable choice; the fact that you allow her to live with you under the same roof implies that she deserves to do so: in any case, it's not for a son to judge his father, least of all for me, and especially a father like you, who has never restricted my freedom in any way."

Arcady's voice quavered at first. He felt that he was being magnanimous, but at the same time he realized that he was lecturing his father; but the sound of his own speeches has an intoxicating effect on any orator, and Arcady uttered his concluding words firmly and even with emphasis.

"Thank you, Arcady," Nicholas Petrovich replied in a hollow voice, while his fingers danced again over his eyebrows and forehead. "Your assumptions are quite justified. Of course, if the girl were unworthy . . . It is no passing lust of mine. I don't find it easy to talk to you about it; but as you will understand, it was difficult for her to come here, in your presence, especially on the first morning you are here."

"In that case, I'll go and find her myself!" Arcady exclaimed, as a fresh wave of generous sentiments broke over him and he jumped up from the chair. "I shall make it clear to her that she has no cause to feel ashamed because of me."

Nicholas Petrovich also stood up.

"Arcady," he began, "do me a favour . . . how can you . . . there . . . I did not warn you . . ."

But without heeding him, Arcady left the terrace at a run. Nicholas Petrovich stared after him and then, in great confusion, relapsed into his chair. His heart was pounding. . . . It would be difficult to say whether, at that instant, he pictured to himself the inevitable peculiarity of his future relations with his son, whether he realized that Arcady might have shown greater respect for him by ignoring this affair altogether, or whether he was reproaching himself for his weakness; all these feelings stirred within him or, rather, he sensed them—and very indistinctly at that. In the meantime, his face remained flushed and his heart kept beating fast.

There was a sound of hurried steps as Arcady came back to the terrace. "We have made friends, daddy!" he exclaimed with an expression of affectionate and good-natured triumph on his face. "Fenichka is really not feeling too well, but she will come later. But you didn't tell me that I had a brother. If I'd known, I would have kissed him quite as fondly yesterday as I did just now."

Nicholas Petrovich tried to say something, he tried to stand up and open his arms. . . . Arcady threw himself on his neck.

"What's this? Embracing again?" Paul Petrovich's voice sounded behind them.

Both father and son were equally glad at his coming that moment; there are touching situations from which one is nevertheless anxious to escape as soon as possible.

"Are you surprised?" his brother gaily asked. "After an age of waiting, Arcady is with us again. . . . I didn't have my fill of him yesterday."

"I'm not in the least surprised," Paul Petrovich remarked. "I wouldn't mind embracing him myself."

Arcady went up to his uncle and once again felt his perfumed moustaches brush his cheeks. Paul Petrovich sat down at table. He was wearing an elegant morning coat of English cut; a smoking-cap graced his head. This cap and a small, carelessly knotted cravat were the only hint that he led a more relaxed life in the country; but the stiff collar of his shirt, which was indeed not white but striped as befitted morning wear, was cutting as inexorably as ever into his clean-shaven chin.

"Where is your new friend?" he inquired of Arcady.

"He's gone out; he usually gets up early and goes exploring. The main thing is not to fuss over him: he can't stand ceremony."

"Yes, that's obvious," Paul Petrovich retorted, beginning hastily to butter his bread. "Will he be staying with us long?"

"That depends. He's stopped here on his way to his father's."

"And where does his father live?"

"In our province, about fifty miles from here. He owns a smallish estate. He used to be a regimental doctor."

"Tut, tut, tut, tut. . . . And I kept asking myself where I had heard that name before. Bazarov? . . . Nicholas, do you remember? Wasn't there a surgeon of the name of Bazarov in our father's division?"

"I believe there was."

"So there was, so there was. And that surgeon is his father. H'm!" Paul Petrovich allowed his moustaches to twitch. "Well, and what exactly is Mr. Bazarov himself?" he inquired with deliberation.

"What is Bazarov?" Arcady smiled. "Would you really like me, uncle, to tell you exactly what he is?"

"Do me the favour, my dear nephew."

"He is a Nihilist."

"What?" Nicholas Petrovich gasped, while his brother poised his knife in the air with a piece of butter on the tip of the blade, and froze into immobility.

"He is a Nihilist," Arcady repeated.

"A Nihilist," his father said slowly. "As far as I can judge, that must be a word derived from the Latin *nihil—nothing;* the term must therefore signify a man who . . . will admit nothing?"

"Better still—a man who will respect nothing," Paul Petrovich interjected, and then resumed his buttering.

"Who looks at everything critically," Arcady remarked.

"And what is the difference?" his uncle inquired.

"There is a difference. A Nihilist is a man who admits no established authorities, who takes no principles for granted, however much they may be respected."

"Well then? Is that a good thing?" his uncle interrupted.

"That depends on the circumstances, uncle. It's good in some cases and very bad in others."

"So that's how it is. Well, I can see this is not our cup of tea. We men of an older generation assume that, without princ*ee*ples" (Paul Petrovich pronounced this word softly in the French manner; Arcady, on the contrary, pronounced it principle, stressing the first syllable), "without prin*cee*ples, taken as you say on trust, one cannot move a step, one cannot even breathe. *Vous avez changé tout célà.* May God grant you health and a general's rank, but we can only admire you from a distance, gentlemen. . . . Nihil . . . What did you call it?"

"Nihilists," Arcady said distinctly.

"Yes. Formerly we had the Hegelians, and now the Nihilists. We'll see how you will manage to survive in a void, a vacuum. And now, Nicholas Petrovich, will you please ring the bell? It's time for my cocoa."

His brother rang the bell and shouted, "Dunyasha!" But, in place of Dunyasha, Fenichka herself appeared on the terrace. She was a young woman of about twenty-three, white-skinned and soft, with dark hair and dark eyes, red, childishly pouting lips, and small delicate hands. She was wearing a neat cotton dress; a new, pale blue scarf rested lightly on her rounded shoulders. She was carrying a large cup of cocoa and, as she set it down in front of Paul Petrovich, she blushed violently of a sudden: the hot blood gushed in a crimson wave beneath the delicate skin of her pretty face. She dropped her eyes and stopped near the table, leaning on it slightly with the tips of her fingers. She appeared conscience-stricken at having ventured to come in, but at the same time she looked as though she had every right to do so.

Paul Petrovich knitted his brows sternly, while Nicholas Petrovich showed traces of embarrassment.

"Good morning, Fenichka," he mumbled through his clenched teeth.

"Good morning," she replied in a voice that carried without being too loud. Glancing out of the corner of her eye at Arcady, who was smiling at her in a friendly fashion, she quietly retired. She walked with a slight waddle, but that, too, became her.

For a few seconds silence reigned on the terrace. Paul

Petrovich sipped his cocoa and then suddenly raised his head. "Here is Sir Nihilist deigning to pay us a call," he brought out in an undertone.

And sure enough, Bazarov came hurrying through the garden, taking the flower-beds in his stride. His linen jacket and trousers were spattered with mud; a clinging marsh plant had twined itself round the crown of his circular hat; in his right hand he held a small sack, and something was wriggling inside it. He strode up to the terrace and exclaimed with a nod: "Good morning, gentlemen. Apologies for being so late for tea; I shall be back at once; I must put my captives away."

"What have you got there? Leeches?" Paul Petrovich inquired.

"No, frogs."

"Do you eat them? Or do you breed them?"

"I experiment with them," Bazarov replied indifferently as he went in.

"He'll cut them up," Paul Petrovich remarked. "He has no faith in prince*ee*ples, only in frogs."

Arcady glanced reprovingly at his uncle while his father stealthily shrugged his shoulders. Paul Petrovich realized that his jest was misplaced and turned the conversation to the management of the estate. The new steward had approached him the previous day with a complaint about Foma, the labourer, who had been "debauching" and had got out of hand. "He's such an Æsop, this Foma," the steward had added. "He's made a bad name for himself in the district; but he'll live and learn, and shake off his stupid ways."

VI

On returning, Bazarov sat down at table and began hastily to drink his tea. The brothers stared at him in silence, while Arcady stole a stealthy glance now at his father and now at his uncle.

"Have you been far?" Nicholas Petrovich inquired at last.

"You have a marsh here, near the aspen copse. I started

some five snipe. Perhaps you'd like to go and shoot them, Arcady?"

"Then you're not a keen sportsman yourself?"

"No."

"Is physics your chief occupation then?" Paul Petrovich inquired in turn.

"Physics, yes; and the natural sciences in general."

"They say that the Teutons, of late, have done wonders in this domain."

"Yes, the Germans are our masters there," Bazarov replied casually.

Paul Petrovich had used the word "Teutons" instead of "Germans" with ironical intent, but this had passed unnoticed.

"You have a very high opinion of the Germans then?" Paul Petrovich asked with exquisite courtesy. Inwardly he was beginning to feel irritated. His aristocratic nature was revolted by Bazarov's utter detachment. This surgeon's son not only did not quail before him, but even gave his answers brusquely and reluctantly. His voice had a caustic and almost insolent note.

"Their scientists at least know their business."

"Quite so. Then you must hold less flattering views of Russian scientists."

"Very likely so."

"That's very laudable and self-denying of you," Paul Petrovich exclaimed, straightening his back and holding up his head. "But is it true, as Arcady was just telling us, that you admit no authorities? That you have no belief in them?"

"Why should I admit them? And what am I to believe? If they talk sense, I'll agree with them. That's all there is to it."

"But do all Germans talk sense?" Paul Petrovich asked, while his features assumed such a distant and aloof expression that he looked withdrawn into the empyrean.

"Not all," Bazarov replied with a stifled yawn; he was manifestly tired of this inquisition.

Paul Petrovich glanced at Arcady as though he wished to say to him: "Your friend is excessively polite, I must say." "As far as I am concerned," he went on again, not without an effort, "sinner that I am, I hold no brief for the Germans. I don't need to mention the Russian Germans: we all know their kind. But I can't stomach German Germans either.

The old kind of Germans just passed muster; then they had —well, there was Schiller, Goethe, let's say. . . . My brother is particularly taken with them. . . . But nowadays they merely churn out some sort of chemists and materialists . . .''

"A good chemist is more useful than a score of poets," Bazarov interrupted him.

"Really?" Paul Petrovich said, raising his eyebrows slightly as though he were dozing off. "So you don't acknowledge art?"

"The art of coining or that of claiming to banish hæmorrhoids!" Bazarov exclaimed with a contemptuous smile.

"Quite so. A joke, I presume. Evidently you're bent on denying everything? Let's assume it. In that case, science is the only thing you believe in?"

"I have already informed you that I do not believe in anything. And what is science—science in general? There are only particular sciences just as there are particular trades and callings; but science in general does not exist at all."

"Very well then. Now as regards the other socially accepted conventions—do you maintain the same negative attitude towards them?"

"What is this? A cross-examination?" Bazarov asked.

Paul Petrovich turned slightly pale. . . . His brother thought it his duty to intervene.

"Another time we shall discuss this matter with you in greater detail, my dear Eugene Vassilich; we shall get to know your views, and we shall state our own. For my part, I am very glad that you are studying the natural sciences. I have heard that Liebig has made some wonderful discoveries for improving the soil. You may be able to help me in my agricultural work and to give some useful advice."

"I am at your service; but Liebig is far beyond us! We must first of all learn the alphabet and only then attempt to read; as it is, we haven't even so much as glanced at our A B C."

"Well, it's quite clear that you are a Nihilist and no mistake," Nicholas Kirsanov thought. "All the same, you must allow me to apply to you for assistance in case of need," he added aloud. "And now, brother, I think it's time for us to go and have a talk with the steward."

Paul Petrovich got up from his chair.

"Yes," he said, without looking at anyone, "what a calamity it is to have spent five years buried like this in the

country, so far removed from intercourse with great minds!
It's enough to turn one into a fool twice over. One does
one's best to remember what one was taught, but behold—
it all turns out to be rubbish. One is told that people in the
know no longer bother with such trifles, and that one is,
as it were, backward and a dunce. What's to be done?
Obviously the younger generation is really more intelligent
than we are."

Paul Petrovich slowly spun round on his heels and then
slowly left the room. Nicholas followed him.

"Is he always like that?" Bazarov coolly inquired of
Arcady as soon as the door had closed behind the brothers.

"Listen, Eugene, you were a bit curt with him," Arcady
remarked. "You have offended him."

"Do you think I'm going to pander to these provincial
aristocrats! Why, it's nothing but sheer personal vanity,
playing the lion, ostentation. If that's the way he's made,
let him carry on like that in Petersburg. . . . But why worry
about him! I have just discovered a fairly rare specimen of
water beetle. *Dytiscus marginatus,* do you know it? Let me
show it to you."

"I promised to tell you his history," Arcady began.

"The history of the beetle?"

"No, don't be so exasperating, Eugene. My uncle's history. You will then see that he is not the sort of man you
imagine. He's deserving of compassion rather than ridicule."

"I don't dispute that. But why are you so full of him?"

"One must be fair, Eugene."

"How does that follow?"

"Now listen . . ."

And Arcady proceeded to tell him his uncle's history.
The reader will find it in the next chapter.

VII

LIKE his younger brother Nicholas, Paul Petrovich was, to
begin with, brought up at home, and then enrolled in the
Imperial Corps of Pages. From childhood his strikingly
handsome appearance had been his greatest distinction;

moreover, his manner was self-assured, faintly ironical and quite amusingly caustic—he could not fail to please. As soon as he had gained his commission, he began to circulate in society. The environment spoilt him and he started to indulge himself, play the fool, and affect mannerisms; but that also became him. Women lost their heads over him, while men called him a coxcomb and secretly envied him. As we have already indicated, he shared an apartment with his brother, whom he sincerely loved though he did not resemble him in the least. Nicholas Petrovich had a limp, his features were small and pleasant, though a shade gloomy, while his eyes were on the small side and his hair soft and sparse; he was inclined to be indolent and shy of society, but was fond of books. Paul Petrovich never spent an evening at home, enjoyed a reputation for courage and agility (it was said that he had set the fashion for gymnastics among the gilded youth of the city), and had read in all some five French novels. By the age of twenty-eight he was already a captain; a brilliant career lay ahead of him. Suddenly everything was changed.

At that time a woman, a certain Princess R. who is still remembered, occasionally used to frequent Petersburg society. She had a well brought up, respectable but stupid husband, and no children. She paid sudden visits abroad and returned as suddenly to Russia; on the whole she led a strange life. She passed for a frivolous coquette, eagerly gave herself up to every sort of pleasure, danced till she could hardly stand on her feet, laughed and joked with the young men whom she used to receive before dinner in the twilight of her drawing-room. But at night she wept and prayed, unable to find peace of mind anywhere and would often pace up and down her bedroom restlessly till dawn, mournfully wringing her hands or sitting all pale and chilled over a psalter. In the daytime, she was once more transformed into a society lady, went out to pay her calls again, laughed, chattered, and behaved as though she were flinging herself at anything that might afford her the least distraction. She was wonderfully proportioned; her golden tresses —which were also as heavy as gold—fell below her knees, but no one would have called her a beauty. Her eyes were the most striking thing about her face; no, not her eyes— they were grey and less than large—but rather their expression, which was swift and penetrating, carefree to the point of rashness and thoughtful to the brink of despondency: an enigmatic expression. Even when she was engaged in lisping the most fatuous phrases her eyes had the most extraordinary glint. And she dressed with exquisite care.

Paul Petrovich met her at a ball and, after dancing a mazurka with her during which she did not utter a single sensible word, fell head over heels in love. Accustomed to conquests, he very soon gained his objective; but his easy triumph failed to cool his ardour. On the contrary, his passion for her only increased and grew ever more tormenting; for this woman, even after an absolute surrender, seemed to preserve in her depths a sanctum into which no one ever succeeded in penetrating. God alone knows what nestled in her soul! She might have been in the power of some mysterious forces unknown even to herself; they played on her as they willed; her limited intelligence could not cope with their impulses. . . . Her whole conduct was made up of inconsistencies; the only letters she ever wrote, which might have excited her husband's just suspicions, were addressed to a man who was almost a stranger to her, and her expressions of love were tinged with melancholy; she never laughed or joked with the man of her choice, but only listened to him and gazed at him in wonder. Sometimes, usually quite suddenly, her look of wonder would change into a stare of frigid terror; her face would assume an expression of deathly pallor and frenzy; she would lock herself in her bedroom, and her eavesdropping maid would catch the sound of dismal sobbing. More than once, on returning home from a tender tryst with her, Paul Petrovich felt his heart oppressed with a lacerating and bitter nostalgia, such as overwhelms a man after utter failure. "What more do I want from her?" he would ask himself while his heart ached. One day he made her a present of a ring engraved with the image of a sphinx.

"What is that?" she asked. "A sphinx?"

"Yes," he replied. "The sphinx is you."

"Me?" she asked, slowly raising her enigmatic eyes to his. "Do you realize that you are being extremely flattering?" she added with a meaningless little smile, while her eyes gleamed as strangely as ever.

Paul Petrovich suffered torments even when the Princess R. reciprocated his affection; but when, as was to happen soon enough, she chilled off towards him, he almost went out of his mind. He fell into a state of anguish, threw fits of jealousy, gave her no peace, and dogged her footsteps. Tired of his persistent importunity, she went abroad. In spite of the entreaties of his friends and the exhortations of his superiors, he resigned his commission and followed her; he spent some four years in foreign parts, now chasing after her, now intentionally losing her from sight. He felt ashamed of himself, angry at his own lack of fortitude . . . but nothing availed. Her image, that incomprehensible, almost meaningless but alluring image, had bitten too deeply into his soul. They happened to come together again in Baden and resumed their relationship; to all appearance, she had never loved him so passionately. . . . But within a month it was all over: the fire had kindled for the last time and then had died for ever. Having a presentiment of the inevitable break, he wanted at least to remain her friend, as though friendship with such a woman were possible. . . . But she left Baden in secret, and thereafter consistently avoided him. He returned to Russia and tried to resume his former life, but failed to get into the swing of it. Like a drugged man, he strayed from place to place; he still drove out to receptions and preserved all the habits of a man about town; he could boast of two or three new conquests; but he had abandoned all hope of anything either from himself or anyone else, and shunned all serious activity. He grew old and grey. To spend his evenings in the club, to be scathing or bored, to indulge in trivial arguments in the society of bachelors, that was all he required—and, as we all know, that is a bad sign. Needless to say, he entertained no thought of marriage. Ten years passed in this wise, dully, fruitlessly and quickly—terribly quickly. Nowhere does time fly so fast as it does in Russia! In prison, they say, it flies even more quickly. One day, as he was dining at his club, Paul Petrovich learned of the death of the Princess. She had died in Paris in a state verging on frenzy. He got up from the table and for a long time paced up and down the rooms of the club, halting like one rooted to the spot near some card-table, but he returned home no earlier than usual. After a time he received a package: it contained the ring he had presented to the Princess. On the image of the sphinx she had scratched some lines in the form of a cross, and the message it conveyed told him that the Cross was the final solution of the enigma.

This had occurred at the beginning of 1848, at a time when Nicholas Petrovich, just bereaved of his wife, had arrived in Petersburg. After Nicholas had settled in the country, his brother had hardly seen him at all; Nicholas's marriage had coincided with the early phase of his infatuation with the Princess. On his return from abroad, Paul Petrovich had gone to his brother's estate with the intention of spending a couple of months with him and enjoying the sight of his happiness, but he only managed to stay a week. The brothers' ways of life had become too different. By 1848 this difference had narrowed: Nicholas Petrovich had lost his wife, and Paul Petrovich his memories; after the Princess's death, he had tried to forget her. Nicholas could look back on a well-spent life and had a son growing up under his eyes; whereas Paul, the lonely bachelor, was just crossing the threshold of that troubled, twilit period, when regrets come to resemble hopes, and hopes are beginning to resemble regrets, when youth is fled and old age is fast approaching.

For Paul Petrovich this period proved more trying than for most others: in losing his past, he had lost everything.

"I am not inviting you to Maryino," Nicholas Petrovich once said to him (he had called his village by that name in memory of his wife), "because you found it so tedious even when my wife was alive, but now, I am sure, you would just die of nostalgia."

"I was silly and fussy in those days," Paul Petrovich replied. "I have since grown calmer if not wiser. Now, if you will allow me, I am ready to come and settle down with you permanently."

By way of reply, Nicholas Petrovich embraced him; but a year and a half passed from the day of that conversation before Paul Petrovich finally made up his mind to carry out his intention. On the other hand, once he had settled down in the country, he did not forsake it—not even during the three winters which Nicholas had spent with his son in Petersburg. He became an assiduous reader, mostly of English books; in general, he modelled his whole life on English taste, frequented his neighbours but seldom, and visited town only at election time, when for the most part he preserved a discreet silence, only occasionally venturing to provoke and startle the landowners of the old school by his liberal gestures. At the same time he kept the representatives of the new generation at a distance. Both the former and the latter considered him supercilious; but they respected him for his exquisite, aristocratic manners, and for the rumours that had reached them of his former conquests; they honoured him for the superb way he dressed and for always putting up in the best room at the best hotel. They also admired him because he always dined like a lord and had once even sat at table with the Duke of Wellington at the court of Louis Philippe; because, wherever he went, he took with him a dressing-case of real silver and a portable bath; because the perfume he used was out of the ordinary and amazingly 'aristocratic'; because he played a masterly game of whist and invariably lost; and finally, they respected him for his irreproachable honesty. The ladies thought him charming and melancholic, but he avoided them. . . .

"So you see, Eugene," Arcady exclaimed, "how unfair you were in judging my uncle! I shall not dwell on the fact that he has come to my father's help more than once when he has been in financial difficulties—you may not know it, but the property was never divided equally between them. But uncle is always ready to help anyone and, besides, he is always prepared to intervene on behalf of the peasants; it is true, when talking to them, he puckers his face and sniffs eau-de-Cologne . . ."

"Clearly, a nervous case," Bazarov interrupted.

"Perhaps. But he is the kindest of men and far from being stupid. What valuable advice he has given me . . . particularly . . . particularly as regards relations with women!"

"Aha! 'When you scald yourself with your own boiling milk, you start blowing on another's water.' We know that!"

"Well, in short," Arcady went on, "he is deeply unhappy, I assure you. It would be a sin to despise him."

"But who despises him?" Bazarov retorted. "All the same, I maintain that a man who has staked his whole life on the card of a woman's love, and then, when he has lost it, turns sour and lets himself drift—a creature like that is not a man but just a male animal. You inform me that he is unhappy, you know that best; but he just hasn't quite shaken off his former stuff and nonsense. I am convinced that he imagines in all seriousness that he is a capable person, just because he reads *Galignani* and, once a month, intervenes to save some peasant from the rod."

"But you must take into account his upbringing as well

as the times in which he lived the best part of his life,"
Arcady rejoined.

"His upbringing?" Bazarov exclaimed. "Every man
should educate himself—well, just as I did, for example. . . .
As to the times, why should I depend upon them? Much
better they should depend on me. No, brother, all that is
just loose thinking, there's nothing solid behind it! And
what are those mysterious relations between men and
women? We physiologists, we know what sort of relations those are. Just study the anatomy of the eye: how is
one to explain that mysterious glance, as you term it? It's
all sheer romanticism, stuff and nonsense, putrefaction,
artiness. Let us rather go and examine our beetle."

And the friends sauntered off towards Bazarov's room,
in which a sort of medical or clinical smell, mingled with
the reek of cheap tobacco, had already had time to affirm
itself.

VIII

PAUL PETROVICH did not assist long at his brother's inter-
view with the steward, a tall gaunt man with a mellifluous,
consumptive voice and roguish eyes, who, in reply to every
remark of Nicholas Petrovich's, answered, "Certainly, that
goes without saying," and tried to make out that all the
peasants were drunkards and thieves. The recently mod-
ernized system of estate management was creaking as badly
as home-made furniture knocked together out of damp,
unseasoned wood. Nicholas Petrovich did not despair, but
kept sighing and racking his brains: he felt that his enter-
prise would fail to flourish without capital, but all his
resources had already been swallowed up. Arcady had
spoken the truth: Paul Petrovich had helped his brother
more than once. On more than one occasion, when he had
seen his brother in difficulties and puzzling to find a way
out, he had walked slowly up to the window and, thrusting
his hands into his pockets, had muttered through his teeth,
"Mais je puis vous donner de l'argent," and had given him
money. On this particular day, however, he had none to

spare and so had preferred to stride away. The unsavoury details of household management depressed him; moreover, although he could not himself have put his finger on the weak spot, he was often under the impression that Nicholas, for all his eagerness and diligence, was setting about things in the wrong way. "My brother is not practical enough," he would argue with himself. "He allows himself to be cheated." Nicholas Petrovich, on the other hand, had a very high opinion of his brother's practical ability and always asked his advice. "I am too easy-going and lack firmness, I have spent too much time in the wilds," he used to say; "but it's not for nothing that you have mixed with the world and know it so well; you are as sharp-eyed as an eagle." By way of reply, Paul Petrovich merely averted his head and did not attempt to disillusion his brother.

Leaving Nicholas in the study, he walked down the corridor which separated the front part of the house from the back, and, on reaching a low doorway, stopped, reflected for an instant, tugged at his moustache, and then knocked.

"Who is there? Come in," Fenichka's voice could be heard saying.

"It's me," said Paul Petrovich, opening the door.

Fenichka leapt from the chair on which she had been sitting with her child and, handing the baby over to a young maid who carried him out of the room, hastily adjusted her kerchief.

"Pardon me for intruding," Paul Petrovich began, without looking at her, "I only wished to ask you . . . I believe someone is being sent to town to-day. . . . Will you get him to buy me some green tea?"

"Certainly," Fenichka replied. "How much would you like?"

"Oh, half a pound will do. I notice you have made some alterations here," he added, casting round him a quick glance which flitted over her face. "I mean the curtains."

"Nicholas Petrovich very kindly gave them to me; they have been hanging for some time already."

"It's quite a while since I was last in your room. You have now arranged it very cosily."

"Thanks to Nicholas Petrovich," Fenichka whispered.

"Are you more comfortable here than in the wing?" Paul Petrovich inquired politely, but without a trace of a smile.

"Of course I am."

"Who's taken your place there?"

"The laundry-maids are there now."

"Ah!"

Paul Petrovich was silent. "He'll go away now," Fenichka thought; but he made no move to depart, and Fenichka stood in front of him as though rooted to the ground, playing nervously with her fingers.

"Why did you have the baby taken away?" Paul Petrovich asked at last. "I love children; let me have a look at him."

Fenichka blushed with confusion and joy. She was frightened of Paul Petrovich, who hardly ever addressed her.

"Dunyasha," she cried, "will you bring in Mitya, if you please?" (Fenichka was very polite to everyone in the house.) "No, wait a moment: we must first put on his dress for him." And Fenichka made for the door.

"Why bother?" Paul Petrovich asked.

"I shall be back in a second," Fenichka replied, disappearing promptly.

When left alone, Paul Petrovich gazed about him with keen attention. The small low room in which he found himself was very clean and comfortable. There was a smell of paint from the freshly painted floor, of camomile and other dried flowers. Against the wall stood a set of chairs with lyre-shaped backs; the late General Kirsanov had acquired them once upon a time in Poland during one of his campaigns; in a corner next to an iron-clamped chest with a round lid was a small bed under a muslin canopy. In the opposite corner a lamp glowed in front of a large dark icon, representing St. Nicholas, the Miracle-worker; a minute porcelain egg, fastened to the halo with a red ribbon, hung down over the saint's breast. The window-sills were stocked with jars of carefully sealed jam, through which a green light filtered; the jam had been made the previous year and was tied up with meticulous care; on the paper covers Fenichka had written in her own hand, "Gooseberry." Nicholas Petrovich was particularly fond of that jam. From the ceiling on a length of string hung down a cage with a short-tailed greenfinch in it; he was twittering and hopping about ceaselessly, and as ceaselessly the cage swayed and quivered: hemp seeds kept falling and faintly tapping on the floor. On the partition-wall above a small chest of drawers hung several photographs of Nicholas

Petrovich in various poses, all rather unsuccessfully taken by some travelling photographer; here also hung a complete failure of a photograph of Fenichka herself: a sort of eyeless face was straining to smile from a dark frame—it was impossible to distinguish more. Above Fenichka's picture and beneath a satin pin-cushion slipper, General Yermolov, in a shaggy Caucasian cloak, glowered at the far-off peaks of the Caucasus.

Five minutes elapsed; a whispering and rustling was still going on next door. Paul Petrovich picked up a greasy, tattered volume of Massalsky's *The Streltsy*,[1] and turned over a few pages. . . . The door opened and Fenichka came in, holding Mitya in her arms. She had dressed him up in a little red shirt with an embroidered collar, combed his hair and wiped his face: he was breathing strenuously, straining to break away with his whole little body, and jerking his hands as all healthy infants do; but his foppish little shirt had evidently produced an effect on him; an expression of pleasure had spread over his chubby face. Fenichka had also tidied her hair, and wore her kerchief more neatly; but she could very well have stayed as she was. For is there anything in the world really more enchanting than a young and beautiful mother with a healthy-looking child in her arms?

"What a pumpkin!" Paul Petrovich said condescendingly, tickling Mitya's double chin with the tapering nail of his forefinger; the child stared up at the greenfinch in the cage and burst out laughing.

"This is your uncle," Fenichka said, putting her face close to his and shaking him a little, while Dunyasha, after first of all putting down a brass coin on the window-sill, carefully placed a lighted smoker's candle on it.

"How many months is he?" Paul Petrovich inquired.

"Six months; the seventh is not far off—on the eleventh of the month."

"You don't mean it, seven months! How is that possible?"

"Wouldn't it be eight months, Fedosya Nicolaievna?" Dunyasha interposed shyly.

"No, seven; how could it be otherwise!"

The child laughed again, staring at the chest in the corner,

[1] The Streltsy were the Musketeers of Moscow.

and then suddenly gripped his mother by the nose and lips with all the five fingers of one hand.

"You little wretch!" Fenichka exclaimed, without disengaging her face from his fingers.

"He's very like my brother," Paul Petrovich remarked.

"Whom else could he be like?" Fenichka thought.

"Yes," Paul Petrovich pursued, as though talking to himself, "the likeness is unmistakable." He glanced at Fenichka attentively, almost sadly.

"This is uncle," she repeated in a whisper this time.

"Ah! Paul! So this is where you are!" Nicholas Petrovich's voice suddenly rang out.

Paul hastily turned round, frowning; but his brother was looking at him with such joy and gratitude that he could not fail to return his smile.

"A fine little lad you've got," he said, glancing at his watch. "I dropped in here about my tea. . . ."

And assuming an air of indifference, Paul Petrovich at once quitted the room.

"Did he come of his own accord?" Nicholas Petrovich asked Fenichka.

"Yes, he did. He just knocked and came in."

"Well, and hasn't Arcady been here again?"

"He hasn't. Had I not better move back to the wing, Nicholas Petrovich?"

"Why should you?"

"I think it might be better for a time at the beginning?"

"N-no," Nicholas Petrovich replied hesitantly, rubbing his forehead. "Better it had been done earlier. . . . Hello, bubble," he said with sudden animation and, approaching his son, kissed him on the cheek; then stooping slightly, he kissed Fenichka's hand, which stood out as white as milk against Mitya's red shirt.

"Nicholas Petrovich! What are you doing?" she mumbled, lowering her eyes and then suddenly raising them. . . . Her expression was enchanting whenever she looked like that, from under her eyelids, laughing affectionately and a trifle vacantly.

Nicholas Petrovich had become acquainted with Fenichka in the following fashion. One day, some three years previously, he happened to spend a night at a hostelry in a remote district town. He was pleasantly surprised at the cleanliness of the room set aside for him and at the immaculate whiteness of the bed linen. "Is the woman of the inn a German?" was the first question he asked himself; but the woman turned out to be Russian, some fifty years of age, tidily dressed, with an agreeable, intelligent face, and a dignified way of speaking. He chatted with her over tea; he had taken a great liking to her. At that time, Nicholas Petrovich had just moved into his new house and, loath to employ any of his former serfs, was in search of hired domestic staff. For her part, the woman of the inn complained of the small number of travellers who passed through the town and of hard times. Nicholas had therefore suggested that she should take up an appointment in his house as his chief housekeeper; and she had agreed. Her husband had died long ago, leaving her with an only daughter, Fenichka. About a fortnight later, Arina Savishna (such was the new housekeeper's name) arrived at Maryino together with her daughter, and took up residence in the wing of the house. Nicholas Petrovich's choice proved a happy one. Arina put the house in order. No one ever mentioned, and few ever saw, Fenichka, who had just turned seventeen: she lived quietly and modestly, and it was only on Sundays that Nicholas Petrovich would notice the delicate profile of her milk-white face in some corner of the parish church. Thus a whole year passed.

One morning Arina Savishna came into his study and, bowing low as was her custom, asked if he could help her daughter whose eye had been struck by a spark. Like all domesticated people, Nicholas Petrovich dabbled in medicine and had even ordered a homœopathic medicine chest for himself. He at once commanded Arina Savishna to bring in the patient. On learning that the master had summoned her, Fenichka was very startled but nevertheless accompanied her mother. Nicholas Petrovich led her up to a window and took her head in his hands. Having thoroughly examined her red and swollen eye, he prescribed an eyewash, which he then made up on the spot and, tearing up his handkerchief, showed her how to apply the solution. Fenichka heard him to the end and then prepared to leave the room. "Kiss the master's hand, silly," Arina Savishna said to her. But Nicholas Petrovich withheld his hand and, in some confusion, kissed her bowed head on parting. Fenichka's eye was quickly healed, but the impression she had made on Nicholas Petrovich was not to be dissipated so rapidly. He kept picturing that pure, tender, apprehensively uplifted face; the sensation of her soft hair still tingled in his hands; he kept seeing those innocent, slightly parted lips which in the sunlight revealed a moist glitter of diamond-like teeth. At church he began to peer at her more attentively and tried to engage her in conversation. At first she was very shy and once, in the late afternoon, when she happened to run into him on a narrow footpath leading through a field of rye, she had turned aside into the tall, thick rye, all overgrown with cornflowers and wormwood, so as to avoid meeting him face to face. He caught sight of her little head through the golden network of the ears of rye, whence she peeped like a wild animal. He shouted in a friendly tone:

"Good evening, Fenichka, I don't bite."

"Good evening," she had whispered back, without emerging from her retreat.

Though still shy in his presence, she was gradually beginning to get used to him, when her mother, Arina Savishna, unexpectedly died of the cholera. Where was Fenichka to go? From her mother she had inherited a love of order, intelligence and decency; but she was young and lonely; Nicholas Petrovich was himself such a kind and modest person. . . . There is no need to describe the rest. . . .

"So my brother dropped in to see you after all?" Nicholas asked Fenichka. "He just knocked and came in?"

"Yes."

"Well, that's excellent. Just let me rock Mitya."

And Nicholas Petrovich began to throw him up almost as high as the ceiling, to the huge delight of the infant and the great perturbation of the mother who, at each throw, stretched her arms towards his twinkling little feet.

In the meantime, Paul Petrovich had returned to his elegant study. Its walls were covered with wall-paper of a greyish tint and hung with an assortment of weapons on a Persian wall-carpet. The room was stocked with walnut furniture, a Renaissance book-case of ancient oak, several bronze statuettes displayed on a sumptuous writing-desk, a fireplace. . . . He threw himself down on a sofa, put his hands to his head and remained quite motionless, staring almost in despair at the ceiling. Whether he wished to conceal the expression on his face from the very walls or for some other reason, he got up, unfastened the heavy window-curtains, and then again slumped back on the sofa.

IX

THE same day Bazarov made Fenichka's acquaintance. He was strolling with Arcady in the garden and explaining to him why some of the newly planted trees, the oaks in particular, had not taken to the soil.

"What you should do is to plant more silver poplars here and fir trees, and limes maybe, but you must first put down some black earth. Now this arbour here is flourishing," he added, "because acacia and lilac are sturdy fellows and require the minimum of nursing. Ah, there's someone in it."

Fenichka was sitting in the arbour with Dunyasha and Mitya. Bazarov halted while Arcady nodded to Fenichka like an old friend.

"Who's that?" Bazarov inquired as soon as they had gone past. "What a charming girl!"

"Whom are you referring to?"

"It's clear enough: only one of them is pretty."

Arcady, not without embarrassment, told him briefly about Fenichka.

"Aha!" Bazarov exclaimed. "Your father obviously has taste. I quite like your father! He's a fine chap. But I must make her acquaintance," and he retraced his steps towards the arbour.

"Eugene!" Arcady shouted after him in alarm. "Be careful, for God's sake."

"Don't be perturbed," Bazarov replied. "I've knocked about and lived in cities."

Approaching Fenichka, he doffed his cap.

"May I introduce myself?" he began with a polite bow. "A friend of Arcady Nicolaievich and an inoffensive person."

Fenichka rose from the bench and stared at him in silence.

"What a wonderful baby!" Bazarov pursued. "Don't

worry, I haven't cast a spell on anyone yet. Why are his cheeks so red? Is he teething by any chance?"

"Yes," Fenichka replied. "He has already cut four teeth, but his gums are swollen again."

"Let me see them . . . don't be afraid. I'm a doctor."

Bazarov picked up the child in his arms and to both Fenichka's and Dunyasha's surprise, the infant offered no resistance and showed no alarm.

"I see, I see. . . . It's nothing . . . everything is in order; he'll have a strong set of teeth. If there's any trouble, just let me know. And are you in good health yourself?"

"I am, thank God."

"Thank God indeed—that's the best of all things. And you?" he added, turning to Dunyasha.

Dunyasha, who was very strait-laced in the house and an inveterate giggler out of doors, only snorted by way of an answer.

"Well, that's excellent. Here's your little champion."

Fenichka took the child back in her arms.

"How quiet he was in your arms," she said in an undertone.

"Children are always quiet in my arms," Bazarov replied. "I know a trick or two."

"Children instinctively recognize those who love them," Dunyasha remarked.

"That's right," Fenichka confirmed. "Now, as a rule, Mitya will not let anyone handle him at any price."

"May I try?" ventured Arcady who, after keeping his distance for a while, had approached the arbour. He tried to lure Mitya into his arms, but much to Fenichka's perturbation the infant only threw back his head and squalled.

"I'll try again when he's got used to me," Arcady said condescendingly, and the friends walked away.

"And, pray, what is her name?" Bazarov inquired.

"Fenichka . . . Fedosya," Arcady replied.

"And her patronymic? I must know that too."

"Nicolaievna."

"*Bene*. What I like about her is that she doesn't show too much embarrassment. Another might blame her for that. But it's sheer nonsense. Why be embarrassed? She is a mother, and quite right too."

"She's in the right," Arcady remarked, "but my father . . ."

"He's also in the right," Bazarov interrupted him.

"No, I don't agree."

"I suppose you can't stomach a second heir!"

"You should be ashamed to impute such ideas to me!" Arcady retorted hotly. "That is not why I criticize my father; I think he should marry her."

"Aha!" Bazarov said quietly. "What magnanimity! You attach then some importance to the marriage tie; I did not expect that from you."

The friends walked on a few steps in silence.

"I have seen all your father's installations," Bazarov began again. "The cattle are of poor quality, the horses mere hacks. The buildings are tumbledown, and the labourers look arrant loafers; as for the steward, he is either a fool or a rogue, I'm not yet sure which."

"You are very censorious to-day, Eugene."

"Nor will the good peasants fail to cheat your father. You know the proverb, 'A Russian peasant will get the better of God Himself.' "

"I'm beginning to think my uncle was not far off the mark," Arcady remarked. "You have decidedly a poor opinion of Russians."

"As if that mattered! The best thing about a Russian is the poor opinion he has of himself. What's important is that two and two make four, the rest is just trivial."

"And is nature trivial?" Arcady inquired, staring thoughtfully at the far-spread, variegated fields, suffused with the beautiful and mellow light of the declining sun.

"Nature *is* trivial in the sense you mean. Nature is no temple but merely a workshop, and man is the craftsman."

At that instant the lingering notes of a 'cello were wafted towards them from the house. Someone was playing Schubert's "Expectation" with sensibility, but without the professional touch, and, like honey, the melody flowed through the air.

"What's that?" Bazarov inquired in amazement.

"It's my father."

"Your father plays the 'cello?"

"Yes."

"And how old is your father?"

"Forty-four."

Bazarov burst out laughing.

"What are you laughing at?"

"Good Lord! At forty-four, a *pater familias,* in the province of X, playing the 'cello!"

Bazarov continued to laugh: but, on this occasion, Arcady, though he venerated his mentor, did not even smile.

X

ABOUT a fortnight had elapsed. Life at Maryino was pursuing its normal course: Arcady played the Sybarite, and Barazov kept his nose to the grindstone. Everyone in the house had got used to him, to his casual ways, as well as to his curt and brusque manner of speech. Fenichka, in particular, had come to take him so much for granted that one night she even had him wakened: Mitya was suffering from cramp; and Bazarov had come along, as was his wont, partly jesting and partly yawning, spent a couple of hours in her room, and eased the child's pains. On the other hand, Paul Petrovich had developed a violent dislike for Bazarov: he deemed him an arrogant, impudent fellow, a cynic and a plebeian: he suspected that Bazarov held him in little esteem, that he almost despised him—him, Paul Petrovich Kirsanov! Nicholas Petrovich was a shade frightened of the young Nihilist and doubted the value of his influence on Arcady: but he listened willingly enough to him, and assisted just as willingly at his experiments in physics and chemistry. Bazarov had brought a microscope and pored over it for whole hours on end. The servants had become attached to him; even though he poked fun at them, they felt that he was one of them and no "master." In his presence Dunyasha was very ready to burst out giggling and to trip past him like a fluttering quail, casting significant glances at him from the corner of her eyes; Peter, who was an extremely conceited and stupid person with an intent expression and a perpetually wrinkled forehead, a person whose entire dignity depended on his respectful mien, his ability to spell out a text syllable by syllable, and his habit of frequently brushing his jacket—even he grinned and cheered up as soon as Bazarov paid the least attention to him. As for the servant lads, they followed the "doctor" about like puppies. Prokofyich was the only person to dislike him; he served him at table with a sullen expression on his face, called him a "skin-alive" and a "rapscallion," and maintained that he was, with his side-whiskers and all, a regular pig in the poke. In his own way, Prokofyich was no less of an aristocrat than Paul Petrovich.

The year was at its best in early June. The weather was beautiful; in the remote background, it is true, there was a renewed threat of cholera, but the inhabitants of the province had already grown accustomed to its visitations. Bazarov used to rise early and set off for a walk of a mile or two, not just for the sake of exercising his limbs—he could not bear purposeless jaunts—but in order to gather herbs and insects. Sometimes he took Arcady with him. On their way back they usually became engrossed in argument and, though more eloquent than his friend, Arcady usually came out the loser.

One morning they were out longer than usual; Nicholas Petrovich had strolled into the garden to meet them and, as he drew level with the arbour, he suddenly heard the sound of quick steps and young men's voices. They were walking along on the other side of the arbour and could not see him.

"You don't know my father well enough," Arcady said.

Nicholas Petrovich kept in the background.

"Your father is a good-natured old boy," Bazarov replied, "but he's a back number. He's sung his swan-song."

Nicholas Petrovich pricked up his ears. . . . Arcady made no reply.

For a couple of minutes the "back number" stood motionless and then slowly trudged back home.

"A couple of days ago I caught him reading Pushkin," Bazarov went on meanwhile. "Will you please explain to him that this won't do? He's no youth, it's time he gave up such nonsense. Where's the sense in being a romantic nowadays! Give him something practical to read."

"What can I give him?" Arcady inquired.

"I should think Büchner's *Stoff und Kraft* would do for a start."

"I'm inclined to agree," Arcady replied approvingly. "*Stoff und Kraft* is written with an eye on the general reader. . . ."

"So it seems both you and I are 'back numbers,' and our

swan-song is sung," Nicholas Petrovich said to his brother after dinner that day. "Well? Maybe Bazarov is right; but I confess to being hurt by one thing: I had hoped that the time was ripe for me to establish a really close friendship with Arcady, but it turns out that I have been left standing while he has forged ahead, and we cannot understand each other."

"And why should he have forged ahead? In what way is he so different from us?" Paul Petrovich inquired impatiently. "All that's been stuffed into his head by that *signor,* that Nihilist. I can't stand that petty surgeon; in my opinion, he's a mere charlatan; I am convinced that, for all his frogs, he hasn't got very far with his physics."

"No, brother, you mustn't say that: Bazarov is intelligent and knowledgeable."

"But he's so horridly arrogant!" Paul Petrovich exclaimed.

"Yes," Nicholas agreed, "he is arrogant. But evidently he can't do without it. I can't make head or tail of just one thing. I seem to be doing everything possible not to lag behind the age: I have split up the land among my former serfs, I have inaugurated a model farm and acquired throughout the province the reputation of being a Radical; I read, study, do my best, on the whole, to keep level with contemporary demands—and yet here they are talking about my swan-song. And once it has reached that stage, brother, I really begin to think that I have sung it."

"Why is that?"

"This is why. To-day I was sitting and reading Pushkin. . . . Arcady came up and without a word, though with a look of affectionate pity on his face, gently took away my book as he might have taken it from a child, and put another one in front of me, a German one. . . . He smiled and then went out, carrying off my Pushkin."

"Really! What book did he give you?"

"This one."

From the back pocket of his frock-coat Nicholas Petrovich pulled out a volume of the ninth edition of Büchner's celebrated treatise.

Paul Petrovich turned it over in his hands. "H'm!" he growled. "Arcady is trying to educate you. Well? Have you attempted to read it?"

"I have."

"And what do you make of it?"

"Either I'm stupid or it's sheer rubbish. I must be stupid."

"You haven't forgotten your German?" Paul Petrovich inquired.

"I can understand German quite well."

Paul Petrovich turned the book over again in his hands and glanced sideways at his brother. They were both silent for a while.

"By the way," Nicholas Petrovich began, obviously anxious to change the subject. "I have just received a letter from Kolyazin."

"From Matvey Ilyich?"

"From the very man. He's just arrived in town to inspect the province. He's risen in the world and writes to say that, as a relative of ours, he would like to see us, and so he invites you and me, and Arcady, to go and stay in town with him."

"Are you going?" Paul Petrovich asked.

"No. Are you?"

"I won't go either. It's not worth while traipsing thirty miles for that! *Mathieu* wishes to display himself in all his glory. The devil take him! He will have the whole province at his feet, so he can dispense with us. As though a Privy Councillor were such big fish! If I had continued in the service, carrying that stupid knapsack on my back, I'd have been an Adjutant-General by now. Anyway, we are both in retirement."

"Yes, brother. Evidently the time has come for us to order our coffins and to fold our arms," Nicholas Petrovich replied with a sigh.

"As for me, I shan't capitulate so quickly," his brother muttered. "I intend to do battle royal with that surgeon yet, I can feel it in my bones."

The battle royal took place that very day, at tea-time. Paul Petrovich came down to the drawing-room in an irritable mood, all itching for battle. He was only waiting for a pretext to rush upon the enemy, but the pretext was long in presenting itself. As a rule, Bazarov talked little in the presence of the "old Kirsanovs" (so he called the brothers), and that evening he felt out of sorts as he sipped one cup of tea after another in silence. Paul Petrovich was consumed with impatience; but at last his wish was granted.

The conversation turned on one of the neighbouring

landowners. "A rotter, a petty aristocrat," Bazarov, who had met him in Petersburg, remarked indifferently.

"May I ask you," Paul Petrovich began, his lips trembling, "whether, as you understand it, the words rotter and aristocrat are synonymous?"

"I said a petty aristocrat," Bazarov replied, lazily taking a sip of tea.

"Exactly so. But I assume that you are of the same opinion about aristocrats as you are about petty aristocrats. I consider it my duty to declare that I do not share this opinion. I venture to say that I am known as a liberal and progressive person; and that is why I respect aristocrats—real aristocrats. You must remember, my dear sir" (at these words Bazarov raised his eyes to Paul Petrovich), "you must remember, my dear sir," he repeated with exasperation, "the English aristocrats. They never yield a jot of their own rights and, for that reason, they respect the rights of others; they insist on the fulfilment of obligations due to them and, because they do that, they fulfil *their own* obligations. The aristocracy gave England her freedom and have maintained it ever since."

"We have heard that refrain often enough," Bazarov retorted. "But what do you wish to prove by this?"

"By 'phthis' I wish to prove, my dear sir," (when angry, Paul Petrovich used to say deliberately "phthis" and "phthat," though he knew very well that no such words existed in the dictionary. This caprice was a tradition he had inherited from Alexander I's reign. The blades of those days, on the rare occasions when they did speak their native language, used to employ the terms "phthis" and "phthat." "We are, as it were, *real* Russians," they meant it to be understood, "and at the same time nobles who can dispense with grammatical rules")—"by 'phthis' I wish to prove that without a sense of personal dignity, without any respect for one's self—and these feelings are highly developed among the aristocracy—there can be no solid foundation for the social . . . *bien public* . . . for the social order. The personality, my dear sir—that is the chief thing; the human personality must be as strong as a rock, for on it everything else is founded. I know very well, for instance, that you deign to ridicule my habits, my way of dressing and, above all, my neatness, but all that comes from a feeling of self-respect, a sense of duty—yes-s, yes-s, a sense of duty. I live in the country, in the wilds, but I do not demean myself, I respect the man in myself."

"But if you will allow me, Paul Petrovich," Bazarov said, "you may respect yourself and yet you sit doing nothing; of what use is that for the *bien public*? If you had no respect for yourself, you would do the same thing."

Paul Petrovich turned pale.

"That is quite a different question. I am under no obligation to explain to you now why I sit doing nothing, as you are pleased to put it. I only wish to say that aristocracy is a principle, and only immoral or empty-headed people can dispense with principles in our times. I said this to Arcady the day after he arrived, and I repeat it to you now. Isn't that so, Nicholas?"

Nicholas Petrovich nodded assent.

"Aristocracy, liberalism, progress, principles," Bazarov said in the meantime, "just think, what a lot of foreign— and useless—words! Russians have not the least need of them."

"What do you think they need then? To hear you talk, we might all be living outside human society, beyond the pale of its laws. I ask you—the logic of history demands . . ."

"What need have we of that logic? We can get on quite well without it."

"What do you mean?"

"Just that. I hope you have no need of logic to find a bite of bread when hungry. What have we to do with such abstractions!"

Paul Petrovich threw up his hands.

"After that, I fail to understand you. You insult the Russian people. I don't understand how one can fail to admit principles and rules. What is the motive of your conduct?"

"I have already told you, uncle, that we admit no authorities," Arcady intervened.

"Our actions are governed by utility," Bazarov said. "In these days, negation is the most useful thing of all—and so we deny."

"Everything?"

"Everything."

"What? Not only art, poetry . . . but also . . . I am afraid to say it . . ."

"Everything," Bazarov repeated with inexpressible calm.

Paul Petrovich stared at him. He had not expected this, and Arcady blushed with pleasure.

"However, if I may say so," Nicholas Petrovich interjected, "you deny everything or, to put it more precisely, you are destroying everything. . . . But it's essential to construct as well."

"That is not our affair. . . . First, we must make a clean sweep."

"The present state of the people makes it necessary," Arcady solemnly added. "We must fulfil these demands. We have no right merely to indulge in the satisfaction of our personal egotism."

This last phrase evidently displeased Bazarov; it smelt of philosophy, that is, of romanticism, for Bazarov identified the two; but he did not think it necessary to contradict his youthful disciple.

"No, no!" Paul Petrovich exclaimed with unexpected heat. "I will not believe that you gentlemen have any exact notion of the Russian people, that you represent its strivings! No, the Russian people is not what you imagine it to be. It has a holy respect for traditions, it is—a patriarchal people. It cannot live without faith . . ."

"I shall not attempt to dispute that," Bazarov interrupted. "I am even prepared to agree that you are right in this."

"But if I am right . . ."

"That still proves nothing."

"Exactly. It proves nothing," Arcady repeated with the assurance of an expert chess player who had foreseen an obviously clever move on the part of his opponent, and as a result was in no way nonplussed.

"What do you mean—it proves nothing?" Paul Petrovich muttered in amazement. "You are going against your own people then?"

"And even if I were?" Bazarov exclaimed. "When it thunders, the people assume that the Prophet Ilya is riding through the heavens in his chariot. Well? Am I to agree with them? And besides—the people may be Russian, but am I not Russian too?"

"No, you are no Russian after what you have just said! I cannot accept you as a Russian."

"My grandfather tilled the soil," Bazarov replied haughtily. "Ask any of your peasants in which of us—in you or me—he would sooner recognize a compatriot. You don't even know how to talk to them."

"And you talk to them and despise them at the same time."

"Well, and what if they deserve contempt? You deprecate my attitude, but who told you that it was an accidental thing in me rather than something called forth by the spirit of the people themselves, in whose name you are protesting?"

"I don't think so! Nihilists are not so very essential!"

"Whether they are essential or not—it's not for us to decide. You don't regard yourself as quite useless either!"

"Gentlemen, gentlemen, you mustn't be personal!" Nicholas Petrovich exclaimed, standing up.

Paul Petrovich smiled and, laying his hand on his brother's shoulder, made him sit down again. "Don't worry," he said. "I shall not forget myself, just because of the sense of personal dignity which is being so savagely assailed by Mister—Doctor Bazarov. If you will allow me," he continued, turning anew to Bazarov, "perhaps you think your doctrine is a novelty? A pity you imagine that. The materialism you preach has gained currency more than once and has invariably proved bankrupt . . ."

"Again a foreign word!" Bazarov interrupted him. He was beginning to get angry and his face had assumed a coarse coppery tint. "In the first place, we preach nothing; that is no habit of ours. . . ."

"What are you doing then?"

"This is what we are doing. Formerly, not so very long ago, we used to say that our officials took bribes, that we had no roads, no trade, no justice. . . ."

"Well, yes, yes, you are castigators of social maladies—that's what you're called, I believe. I agree with a great many of your criticisms, but . . ."

"And then we concluded that to chatter and only chatter about our maladies was not worth a candle, that it only led to a petty and doctrinaire attitude. We realized that our 'bright men,' the so-called 'advanced men' who castigated social maladies, were good-for-nothings, that we were merely preoccupied with trivialities, debates about types of art, unconscious creation, parliamentarianism, justice, and the devil knows what, when the gist of the matter was our daily bread, when the most vulgar superstitions were stifling us, when our industrial enterprises were failing for lack of honest men at their head, when even the emancipation of the serfs—the emancipation the government is making such a fuss about now—will hardly be to our advantage, because the peasants are only too delighted to filch from each other in order to drink themselves silly in the gin-shops."

"So," Paul Petrovich interrupted him, "so, you are convinced of all this and are resolved to avoid any serious undertaking."

"And are resolved to avoid any undertaking," Bazarov repeated grimly. He suddenly felt depressed at having been so expansive in front of this lordling.

"But only indulge in abuse?"

"To indulge in abuse."

"And that is what you call Nihilism?"

"And that is what you call Nihilism," Bazarov repeated again, this time with emphatic insolence.

Paul Petrovich screwed up his eyes slightly.

"So that's it!" he exclaimed in a strangely calm voice. "Nihilism is a remedy for all our maladies, and you—you are the saviours and heroes. But why do you pick on the others—the castigators of social maladies? Don't you chatter quite as much as the rest of them?"

"Anything you like, but don't lay that particular sin at our door," Bazarov muttered through his teeth.

"Well then? Are you *already* in active conspiracy? Or are you preparing for action?"

Bazarov did not answer. Paul Petrovich quivered, but mastered himself at once.

"H'm! . . . To act, to break up . . ." he continued. "But how can you break things up without knowing even why?"

"We break things up because we are a force," Arcady remarked.

Paul Petrovich looked at his nephew and laughed.

"Yes, a force need give no account of itself," Arcady said, drawing himself up.

"Wretched lad!" Paul Petrovich wailed; he was decidedly in no state to control himself any longer. "If only you gave a thought to *what* you were supporting in Russia by your silly judgments! No, it's enough to make an angel lose patience! A force! The wild Kalmuk and the Mongolian have force—but what do we need it for? We value civilization—yes, yes, my dear sir; its fruits are dear to us. And don't you tell me those fruits are insignificant: the pettiest dauber, *un barbouilleur,* a cheap musician who makes fivepence an evening—even they are of more use than you, because they represent civilization rather than crude Mongolian force! You imagine that you are advanced, but your real home is a Kalmuk tent! A force! And finally, my forceful gentlemen, you must remember this, there are only four and a half of you, whereas the others number millions, and they will not allow you to trample on their most sacred beliefs. They will crush you underfoot!"

"If they do crush us, such is our destiny," Bazarov replied. "Only you can't have your cake and eat it. We are not as few as you suppose."

"What? You seriously think you can deal—deal with the whole people?"

"A penny candle, you know, set Moscow on fire," Bazarov retorted.

"I see. First of all, a pride that is almost satanical, and then a gibing tone. Indeed, that is what attracts young men, that is what conquers inexperienced boyish hearts! Just look, Bazarov, there's one sitting beside you, almost adoring you, just look and admire." (Arcady turned away and frowned.) "That disease has already made great inroads. I am told that our painters in Rome refuse to set foot in the Vatican. They consider Raphael almost a fool —on the grounds that he is, as it were, an 'established authority'; and as for themselves, they show themselves impotent and barren to the point of disgusting one, and, however much they try, their fantasy goes no further than a picture like 'Girls at the Fountain'! And the painting of the girl is rotten into the bargain. In your opinion, they are fine fellows, isn't that so?"

"In my opinion," Bazarov retorted, "Raphael isn't worth a brass farthing; and they are no better."

"Bravo! Bravo! Listen, Arcady . . . that's the way modern young men should express themselves! When one reflects, it's no wonder they follow you! Formerly, young men had to study; they had no wish to be known as ignoramuses, and so willy-nilly they had to apply themselves. Now all they can say is, 'Everything is rubbish!' And they have made their point. The young men are simply delighted.

To be sure, before they were only blockheads, now they have suddenly become Nihilists."

"So, your boasted sense of dignity has failed you," Bazarov remarked phlegmatically, while Arcady went all hot and his eyes flashed. "Our argument has gone too far . . . we'd better stop it. I shall be prepared to agree with you," he added, getting up, "when you confront me with at least one form of our contemporary life, in the family or the social order, which does not call for absolute and ruthless negation."

"I can confront you with a million such," Paul Petrovich exclaimed. "A million! Now take the Peasant Commune, for example."

A cold sneer twisted Bazarov's lips.

"Well, as to the Peasant Commune," he said, "you had better discuss it with your brother. He seems to have had some practical experience of the Commune—of its mutual guarantees, sobriety and other devices of the sort."

"There's the family, finally, the family, as it exists among our peasantry!" Paul Petrovich shouted.

"I suggest you had better not examine that question in detail either. You have, I suppose, heard of the way the head of the family can select his daughter-in-law? Listen to me, Paul Petrovich, take a couple of days to consider it, you won't tumble on it at once. Sift over all our social classes, and ponder well on each of them, while Arcady and I will . . ."

"Will sneer at everything," Paul Petrovich picked him up.

"No, we shall dissect frogs. Let's go, Arcady; good-bye, gentlemen!"

The friends went out. The brothers remained alone and, for a time, only stared at each other.

"There," Paul Petrovich began at last, "there you have the young men of to-day! Such are our heirs!"

"Our heirs," Nicholas Petrovich repeated with a despondent sigh. While the disputation was going on, he had sat as on red-hot coals, stealing now and then a stealthy and pained glance at Arcady. "Do you know what it reminds me of, brother? Once I had a quarrel with our late mamma; unwilling to hear me, she was shouting her head off. . . . I finally told her that she was incapable of understanding me: 'We belong to different generations,' I had said. She was terribly offended, while I thought to myself,

'What's to be done?' It is a bitter pill—but I shall have to swallow it. Now our turn has come, and our heirs can say to us: 'You don't belong to our generation, you can swallow the pill.' "

"You're far too good-natured and modest," Paul Petrovich expostulated. "I am convinced that you and I are much more in the right than these little gentlemen, even though we may express ourselves in somewhat out-of-date, *vieilli* language, and may lack their impudence and self-assurance. . . . They are so swollen-headed, these young men of today! If you ask one of them, 'Which wine do you prefer, red or white?' 'I am in the habit of preferring red!' he will answer in a bass voice and with such a solemn expression on his face as though the whole of the universe were looking at him at that instant. . . ."

"Would you like some more tea?" Fenichka asked, thrusting her head through the door: she had hesitated to enter the drawing-room while voices had been raised in dispute.

"No, you may tell them to remove the samovar," Nicholas Petrovich replied, getting up to meet her. With a brusque, *"Bon soir!"* Paul Petrovich retired to his study.

XI

HALF an hour later, Nicholas Petrovich was in the garden, sauntering in the direction of his favourite arbour. He was oppressed with sad thoughts. For the first time he had clearly realized the gulf that separated him from his son, and he had a foreboding that with each day the gap would widen. Therefore, he felt that he had merely wasted his time when, as he had sometimes done during his winter stay in Petersburg, he had spent whole days poring over the latest books; he had merely wasted his time in listening to the young men talk and in feeling elated at his own success in inserting a word or two into their heated discussions. "My brother maintains that we are right," he thought, "and discarding all personal vanity it seems to me also that these young men are further removed from the truth, and yet I cannot help feeling that they have something we lack, an advantage over us. . . . Is it their youth? No, it can't be only a question of youth. Perhaps their advantage lies in their having fewer traces of the serf-master in their character?"

Nicholas Petrovich lowered his head and passed a hand over his face.

"But to reject poetry?" he asked himself again. "To lack all feeling for art, for nature . . ."

And he gazed about him as though he wished to grasp how it was possible not to share the feeling for nature. The evening was already creeping on: the sun had hidden behind a small aspen grove, some half a mile away from the garden, and its shadow spread endlessly over the motionless fields. A peasant was riding a white horse at a trot along the dark, narrow path that skirted the grove: though he was riding in the shadow, his horse's hooves could be perceived flashing up and down with pleasing precision. The rays of the sun, for their part, filtered into the grove and, forcing their way through the thicket, drenched the trunks of the aspen trees in such a suffusion of light that they began to assume the appearance of pine trunks, and their foliage showed blue beneath an azure sky, slightly tinged by the beams of the setting sun. The larks were soaring on high; the breeze had quite died away; belated bees were buzzing lazily and drowsily among the lilac; a column of swarming gnats was crowding over an isolated projecting branch. "How beautiful it all is, O Lord!" Nicholas Petrovich thought, and some favourite lines of verse rose to his lips. Suddenly he remembered Arcady—his *Stoff und Kraft*—and restrained himself; but he kept his seat, surrendering himself to the bitter and consoling play of solitary reflections.

He was fond of meditation; his life in the country had developed this capacity in him. Only recently he had meditated in this manner when waiting for his son to arrive at the posting-station, but since then things had changed, and how they had changed! their relations, nebulous until then, had now become defined. . . . He conjured up the image of his late wife, not as he had known her through the many years of their married life, not as an efficient and painstaking housewife, but as a slender young maiden with innocent, searching eyes, and a plait of hair knotted tightly over her girlish neck. He remembered his first glimpse of her. He had met her on the staircase leading to his apartment: and having accidentally pushed her, he had turned round intending to apologize, but could only mumble, *"Pardon, monsieur."* At that she had nodded, laughed and run away as though frightened; but at the turning of the stair, she had glanced quickly round at him, looking grave, and had blushed. Then had followed their first shy meeting, the half-uttered phrases, the half-smiles, the perplexity, the depressions and the surges of emotion, which were finally crowned by breathless happiness. . . . Where had all that gone? She had become his wife, he had been happier than most mortals. . . . "But," he thought, "why should not those first sweet moments remain eternal and immortal?"

He made no attempt to clarify this thought, but longed to arrest that blissful time by some means stronger than memory; he yearned to have his Maria near him once more, to feel her warmth and her breath, and he fancied that yonder, above him . . .

"Nicholas Petrovich," Fenichka's voice rang out nearby. "Where are you?"

He started. He felt no pain or shame. . . . He did not even admit the possibility of comparison between his late wife and Fenichka, but he regretted that she had taken it into her head to seek him out. Her words reminded him at once of his grey hairs, his age, his present . . .

The magic world, which he was just entering and which was just looming out from the misty waves of the past, wavered—and vanished.

"Here I am," he replied. "I'll be along soon, don't wait for me."

As he said this, he instantly thought, "That's the serf-master in me talking!" Fenichka peeped silently into the arbour and was gone; and he noticed with surprise that darkness had already descended while he had been musing. In the vicinity everything was dark and quiet; and the glimpse he had caught of Fenichka's face threw into relief its pallor and frailness. He rose and was about to make for the house; but his agitated heart gave him no peace. He began to pace up and down the garden, now staring thoughtfully at his feet, now raising his eyes to the sky where the stars were already swarming and winking at each other. He went on walking till he felt almost exhausted, but his anxiety, an undefined probing and sorrowful anxiety, did not diminish. Oh, how Bazarov would have laughed at him, if he had known what was going on in his mind! Arcady himself would have reproved him. Here he was at forty-four, a gentleman farmer and landowner, shedding tears, inexplicable tears; that was a hundred times worse than playing the 'cello.

Nicholas Petrovich pursued his pacing, unable to make up his mind to return home—to that peaceful and cosy nest whose lighted windows peeped at him so invitingly; he had not the strength to tear himself away from the gloom, from the garden, from the fresh air that played on his face, from the nostalgia, from the anxiety. . . .

At the turning of the path, he ran into Paul Petrovich.

"What's the matter with you?" Paul Petrovich asked. "You look as pale as a ghost. Aren't you feeling well? Why don't you go to bed?"

Nicholas Petrovich explained his state of mind and then walked away. Paul Petrovich strolled as far as the end of the garden, grew pensive too, and likewise lifted his gaze to the sky. But his fine dark eyes reflected only the glimmer of the stars. He was not born a romantic, and his soul, so dry and elegant, passionate and misanthropic in the French way, was incapable of reverie. . . .

"Do you know what?" Bazarov said that night to Arcady. "I've just had a marvellous idea. Your father was telling us to-day of the invitation he had received from that highfalutin relative of yours. Your father does not wish to go; let us make a dash for town—the gentleman in question has invited you too. We could stay there five or six days, and that would be a change!"

"But will you come back here afterwards?"

"No, I'll have to travel on and see my father. As you know, he lives only some twenty miles from town. I haven't seen him for ages, nor my mother; I must cheer up the old folk. They are splendid people, both of them, especially my father: he's a most amusing person. I'm the only son."

"And will you stay long with them?"

"Not very long. I'd find it a bit boring."

"And will you call on us on the way back?"

"I don't know. . . . We'll have to see. Well, are you game? Shall we go?"

"Maybe," Arcady replied lazily.

In his heart he rejoiced at his friend's suggestion, but he thought it his duty to disguise his feelings. He was not a Nihilist for nothing!

The following day Arcady and Bazarov set off for town. The younger folk at Maryino regretted their departure; Dunyasha even shed a tear . . . but the older men breathed a sigh of relief.

XII

THE town which was the object of our friends' visitation was in the charge of a Governor of the younger generation —a man who, as is often the case in Russia, was at once progressive and despotic. Within a year of assuming office he had quarrelled not only with the Marshal of the Nobility. a retired cavalry captain of the Guards, who ran a stud farm and kept open house, but also with his own subordinates. The conflicts engendered as a result assumed such proportions that the Ministry in Petersburg had been finally obliged to dispatch an official entrusted with the task of investigating the pros and cons on the spot.

The choice of the authorities fell on Matvey Ilyich Kolyazin, the son of that particular Kolyazin who had once upon a time acted as guardian to the brothers Kirsanov. He was also one of the "younger men," that is to say, he had just turned forty, but already he aimed at the higher posts of state and displayed a star on each side of his chest. As a matter of fact, one of these stars was of foreign provenance and of a none too illustrious order. Like the Governor, whom he was about to judge, he had the reputation of being a progressive but, as he was already a big shot, did not conduct himself as most of them are wont to do. He had the highest opinion of himself; his vanity knew no bounds, but his manner was simple, his glance encouraging, his attention indulgent and his laughter so good-natured that, for a short while, he might have passed for a "splendid fellow." However, on important occasions he was quite capable, as they say, of "beating the carpet." "Energy is essential," was his favourite maxim at the time. *"L'énergie est la première qualité d'un homme d'état"*; but despite it all, he was extremely gullible, and any experienced official could ride over him rough-shod. Matvey Ilyich used to speak with the greatest respect of Guizot, and tried to instil in all and sundry the notion that he himself did not belong to the category of routine officials and backward bureaucrats; that he never missed any important "manifestations" of social life. . . . All such words and phrases were only too familiar to him. He even followed the development of contemporary literature, though he did so with casual condescension, like an adult who, on occasion, might join in a procession of boys he happened to meet in the street. Actually, Matvey Ilyich was but little ahead of those statesmen of Alexander I's reign who, before attending a *soirée* at Madame Svyechin's, then resident in Petersburg, would peruse a page of Condillac in the morning; but his approach was different by virtue of its modernity. He was a subtle courtier, a man of great wile, and that was all; he had no sense for handling public affairs, no intelligence—only a knack for making ends meet; no one could outsmart him in this domain, and that is what really matters.

Matvey Ilyich greeted Arcady with all the affability— and even playfulness—that becomes an enlightened hierarch. He was amazed, however, to learn that the relations whom he had invited had preferred to stay at home in the country. "Your father was always an eccentric," he remarked, fingering the tassels of his sumptuous velvet dressing-gown. Then turning brusquely to a young official, who wore an undress uniform carefully buttoned up for the occasion, he exclaimed with a worried look: "What is it?" The young man, whose lips were glued together from prolonged silence, leapt up and stared at his chief in perplexity. But having set his subordinate a problem, Matvey Ilyich paid no more attention to him. As a rule, our higher officials like to startle their subordinates; and they employ a great variety of methods to achieve this end. Among others, the following method is in vogue, "is quite a favourite," as the English say: a high official will suddenly fail to understand the simplest words and simulate deafness. For instance, he will inquire, "What day of the week is it?"

He will be respectfully informed, "To-day is Friday, your Ex . . . len . . . cy."

"Eh? What? What did you say?" the high official will repeat with great intensity.

"To-day is Friday, your Ex . . . len . . . cy."

"What? How's that? What is Friday?"

"Friday, your Ex . . . len . . . cy, is a day of the week."

"Well, I . . . Are you trying to teach me something?"

Although he was reputed to be a liberal, Matvey Ilyich was first and foremost a high official.

"I advise you, my friend, to pay a call on the Governor," he told Arcady. "You will understand that I counsel you to do this out of no predilection for the old convention, according to which the authorities must be placated, but simply because the Governor is quite a decent fellow; besides, you would probably like to mix in local society. . . . You're no bumpkin, I trust? The day after to-morrow the Governor is giving a large ball."

"Are you going?" Arcady inquired.

"He is giving it for me," Matvey Ilyich replied almost in a tone of regret. "Do you dance?"

"I do, but not very well."

"That's a pity. There are some charming girls here and, besides, a young man should be ashamed of not being able to dance! I'm not saying this out of prejudice; I don't in the least assume that one's brain should go into one's feet, but the Byronic attitude is ridiculous now, *il a fait son temps.*"

"But, uncle, the Byronic attitude has nothing to do with my . . ."

"I shall introduce you to the young ladies, I'll take you under my wing," Matvey Ilyich interrupted him, laughing in a self-satisfied sort of way. "You'll find it quite warm, eh?"

A manservant appeared and reported the arrival of the President of the Finance Department, a doting-eyed old man with wrinkled lips; he was inordinately partial to nature, particularly in summer when, according to him, "Each bee takes its wee bribe from each wee flower. . . ." Arcady took his leave.

He found Bazarov at the inn where they had put up and

spent quite a time trying to persuade his friend to call on the Governor.

"There's no way out!" Bazarov exclaimed at last. "We must go through with it. Since we have come to spy upon the landed gentry, we might as well inspect them at close quarters."

The Governor received the young men cordially, but did not ask them to sit down and himself remained standing. He was very fussy and always in a hurry; in the morning he donned his tight-fitting undress uniform and an exceedingly stiff cravat; he never found time to finish his meals or drinks, and was constantly issuing orders. In the province he had been nicknamed "Bourdaloue"; this implied no affinity with the well-known French preacher of that name but rather with a muddy beverage called "bourda." He invited both Kirsanov and Bazarov to the ball, and within two minutes repeated the invitation under the impression that the friends were brothers and that their name was Kaysarov.

As they were walking back from the Governor's, a passing droshky pulled up and a squat man in a jacket of Hungarian cut much favoured by the Slavophils jumped out and, with a shout of "Eugene Vassilich!" rushed to meet him.

"Ah! So it's you, Herr Sitnikov!" Bazarov exclaimed without halting in his stride. "What fates bring you here?"

"Just imagine, a pure accident," the other replied. Turning towards the driver of the droshky and waving his hand at him four or five times, he bawled: "Follow us, will you? My father has a concern here," he went on, leaping over the gutter, "well, and so he asked me. . . . This morning I learnt of your arrival and have already called on you. . . ." (As a matter of fact, when our friends returned to their rooms, they found a visiting-card with the corners turned down and the name of Sitnikov printed on one side in French and on the other in a Slavonic scrawl.) "I hope you are not coming from the Governor's?"

"Don't hope. We have come straight from him."

"In that case, I shall call on him too. . . . Eugene Vassilich . . . Will you introduce me to your . . . to him? . . ."

"Sitnikov, Kirsanov," Bazarov growled without halting.

"I am highly flattered," Sitnikov began, sidling up to Arcady, smirking and hurriedly pulling off his over-elegant gloves. "I have heard a great deal . . . I am an old friend of Eugene Vassilich's and, if I may say so, his disciple. I am obliged to him for my regeneration. . . ."

Arcady stared at Bazarov's disciple. The small but agreeable features of his smoothly shining face wore a dull and anxious expression; his smallish eyes, which looked as if they had been crushed into his face, stared restlessly ahead of him, and he had an anxious laugh, a sort of jerky wooden laugh.

"Would you believe it," he went on, "when I heard Eugene Vassilich say for the first time that we must respect no authorities, I was simply bowled over with enthusiasm. . . . It was like having a new vision of the world! Here, I thought, I have at last found a man! By the way, Eugene Vassilich, you must not fail to call on a certain lady here. She is quite capable of understanding you, and your visit would be a real joy to her. I am sure you must have heard of her?"

"Who is she?" Bazarov reluctantly inquired.

"Kukshin, *Eudoxie,* Eudoxia Kukshin. She is a woman of remarkable disposition; she is *emancipée* in the real sense of the word—an advanced woman. Do you know what? Let's go and visit her now. She lives only a couple of steps away. We can have lunch with her. You haven't lunched yet, have you?"

"Not yet."

"Well, that's grand. She's separated from her husband, you know, and is quite independent."

"Is she attractive?" Bazarov interrupted.

"No-o-o, I wouldn't say that."

"Then why the devil are you asking us to call on her?"

"You like your little joke. . . . She's sure to stand us a bottle of champagne."

"That's better! One can see at once that you're a practical man. By the way, is your father still in the liquor business?"

"He is," Sitnikov hurriedly replied, emitting a shrill laugh. "Well? Are you game?"

"I really don't know."

"Since you wanted to see how other people live, you might as well go," Arcady interjected in an undertone.

"And what about you, Monsieur Kirsanov?" Sitnikov asked. "You must come too, we couldn't go without you."

"But wouldn't we be intruding if we all went?"

"That's quite all right. Kukshin is a marvellous woman."

"And are you certain she will provide a bottle of champagne?" Bazarov queried.

"Three!" Sitnikov exclaimed. "I guarantee that."

"With what?"

"With my own head."

"Your father's money-bags would be better. However, let us go."

XIII

THE small aristocratic house in the Moscow style, where Avdotya Nikitishna or Eudoxia Kukshin resided, was situated in one of the recently burnt-out streets of the town; as everyone knows, our provincial towns are ravaged by fire every five years. In the doorway, above a crookedly fixed visiting-card, a bell handle could be perceived, and in the entrance hall the visitors were met by a woman who must have been either a maid or a lady's companion. She was wearing a mob-cap—a manifest sign of the progressive strivings of the lady of the house. Sitnikov inquired whether Madame Kukshin was at home.

"Is that you, Victor?" a shrill voice asked from an adjoining room. "Come in."

The woman in the mob-cap immediately disappeared.

"I'm not alone," Sitnikov replied, as he dashingly threw off his Hungarian jacket, revealing beneath it a sort of sleeveless undercoat or jerkin, and glanced eagerly at both Arcady and Bazarov.

"Never mind," the voice replied. *"Entrez!"*

The young men entered. The room in which they found themselves resembled a working cabinet more than a drawing-room. Papers, letters, thick volumes of Russian periodicals for the most part uncut, were strewn over the dusty tables; white cigarette-ends lay scattered all over the place. On a leather sofa a lady reclined, still young, fair-haired, a trifle dishevelled, wearing a none too tidy dress, heavy bracelets on her short arms and a lace kerchief on her head. She got up from the sofa, absent-mindedly pulling over her shoulders a short velvet coat lined with ermine and, as she shook hands with him, drawled lazily, "Good morning, Victor."

"Bazarov, Kirsanov," Sitnikov said curtly after the manner of Bazarov.

"You are very welcome," Madame Kukshin replied and, fixing Bazarov with her round eyes between which a tiny snub nose was just visible, added, shaking hands with him also, "I know you."

Bazarov knitted his brows. There was nothing ugly about the small, matt face of the emancipated lady; but its expression left a disagreeable impression on the beholder. Instinctively one longed to ask her, "Why are you so hungry? Are you bored? Do you lack confidence? Why are you so fidgety?" Something was continually gnawing at her soul just as it was at Sitnikov's. Her conversation and her movements were disconnected and awkward, she evidently looked upon herself as an affable and simple creature, but her actions invariably gave the impression that she intended the opposite; everything she attempted looked "intentional," as children say—in short, neither simple nor natural.

"Yes, yes, I know you, Bazarov," she repeated. (Like many provincial and Moscow ladies, she was in the habit of calling men by their family names on first acquaintance.) "Would you like a cigar?"

"A cigar's a cigar," interjected Sitnikov who, with one of his legs in the air, was already sprawling in an arm-chair, "but do let's have some lunch. We are quite famished; and tell them also to send up a bottle or two of champagne."

"Sybarite!" Eudoxia exclaimed, laughing. (Whenever she laughed, the gums of her top teeth showed.) "He's a Sybarite, isn't he, Bazarov?"

"I appreciate the comforts of life," Sitnikov solemnly declared. "That doesn't prevent my being a liberal."

"Yes, it does, it does!" Eudoxia exclaimed. Nevertheless she ordered her attendant to see to both the lunch and the champagne. "Now what do you think?" she added, turning to Bazarov. "I'm positive you share my opinion."

"Not quite," Bazarov retorted. "Even from the chemical point of view, a chunk of meat is better than a morsel of bread."

"So you are a student of chemistry? It's my great passion; I have even invented a new compound."

"A new compound? You?"

"Yes, I. And do you know for what purpose? For making dolls—to prevent their heads from breaking off. I'm quite a practical person. But I haven't got quite into shape yet. I have still to read Liebig. *Apropos,* have you seen Kislyakov's article on female labour in the *Moscow Gazette?* Do read it. I'm sure you are interested in the question of women's emancipation, aren't you? And also in the problem of the schools? But what does your friend do? What is his name?"

Madame Kukshin let drop her questions one after the other with feminine insouciance, without expecting any answers; it was the way in which spoilt children talk to their nannies.

"My name is Arcady Nicolaievich Kirsanov," Arcady informed her, "and I don't do anything."

Eudoxia guffawed.

"That's charming! Don't you smoke? Victor, you know I am angry with you."

"Why?"

"They say you've been praising Georges Sand again. She's already out of date and that's the end of it! How can one compare her with Emerson! She has no ideas about education or physiology or anything. I am sure she has never heard of embryology, and in these days what can we do without it?" (Eudoxia even threw up her hands.) "Ah, what a wonderful article Yeliseyivich has just written on that topic! He's quite a genius of a gentleman!" (Eudoxia constantly used the word "gentleman" instead of "man.") "Bazarov, come and sit down beside me on the sofa. You may not be aware of it, but I am terribly afraid of you."

"Why's that? May I inquire the reason?"

"You're a dangerous gentleman; you are so very critical. Oh Lord, oh Lord! How funny! I'm talking like any staid lady-landowner. However, I actually am a landowner. I manage my own estate and, just fancy it, my steward Yerofey is an amazing character, just like Fenimore Cooper's Pathfinder: he has something in common with him! I have now definitely taken up my quarters here; it's quite unbearable, this town, isn't it? But what's to be done?"

"It's much the same as any other town," Bazarov remarked coolly.

"All these niggling interests, that's what is so terrible! Formerly I used to spend the winter in Moscow. . . . But now my worthy husband, Monsieur Kukshin, lives there. Besides Moscow is now . . . I don't know what's the matter, but it's not the same. I am thinking of going abroad; I was already on the point of departing last year."

"To Paris presumably?" Bazarov inquired.

"To Paris and Heidelberg."

"Why Heidelberg?"

"Why? Because Bunsen is there."

Bazarov was at a loss how to cap this.

"*Pierre* Sapozhnikov . . . do you know him?"

"No, I don't."

"But goodness me, *Pierre* Sapozhnikov . . . he still comes regularly to Lydia Khostatova's."

"I don't know her either."

"Well, he's taken it upon himself to accompany me abroad. Thank God, I'm free, I have no children. . . . Did I say 'Thank God'? Not that it matters anyway."

With her nicotine-stained fingers Eudoxia rolled herself a cigarette, licked it, sucked it and then lit it. The attendant entered with a tray.

"Ah, here's the lunch! Will you have a bite? Victor, uncork a bottle; that's your specialty."

"It is, it is," Sitnikov mumbled, laughing shrilly again.

"Are there any attractive women in this town?" Bazarov inquired as he emptied his third glass of champagne.

"There are," Eudoxia replied, "but they are all lightheaded. But *mon amie* Odintzov, for example, is not so bad. What a pity she has such a reputation. . . . However, that would not matter so much, but she has no freedom of outlook, no breadth, nothing . . . of *that*. Our whole system of education needs changing. I have already been pondering on it; our women are all very badly brought up."

"Better give it up as a bad job!" Sitnikov exclaimed. "Women should be despised, and I do despise them, completely and absolutely!" (The chance to be scathing and to express his contempt for anyone was for Sitnikov a most agreeable sensation; he made a particular point of attacking women, little suspecting that within a few months he would have to crawl before his own wife for no other reason than that she was born a Princess Durdoleosov.) "None of them would be capable of understanding our conversation; none of them deserves to be discussed by us serious-minded men!"

"But they have no need to understand our conversation," Bazarov retorted.

"Whom are you talking about?" Eudoxia intervened.

"Attractive women."

"What? You must share the views of Proudhon!"

Bazarov drew himself up haughtily.

"I share no one's views: I have my own."

"Down with all authorities!" Sitnikov shouted, rejoicing at an opportunity to express himself critically in the presence of the man whom he slavishly imitated.

"But even Macaulay—" Madame Kukshin tried to say.

"Down with Macaulay!" Sitnikov thundered. "Are you attempting to defend those females?"

"Not those females, but the rights of women which I swore to champion to the last drop of my blood."

"Down with them all!" Sitnikov cried and then pulled himself up. "I am not against their rights," he added.

"Yes, you are. I can see you are a Slavophil!"

"No, I'm not a Slavophil, though of course . . ."

"No, no, no! You are a Slavophil. You're an upholder of the *Domostroy,* of patriarchal tyranny. You want to rule with the rod!"

"The rod's sound enough," Bazarov remarked. "But we have just reached the last drop . . ."

"Of what?" Eudoxia interrupted him.

"Of the champagne, my most respected Avdotya Nikitishna," Bazarov replied. "Of the champagne—not of your blood."

"I cannot remain indifferent when women are being attacked," Eudoxia went on. "It's terrible, simply terrible. Instead of blackguarding them, you would do better to read Michelet's book, *De l'Amour.* It's a miracle! Gentlemen, let us talk of love," Eudoxia added, letting her hand fall languorously on the crumpled cushion of the sofa.

A sudden silence followed.

"No, why should we?" Bazarov said. "But you referred to Madame Odintzov. . . . That is what you called her, I believe? Who is this lady?"

"She's simply charming!" Sitnikov squeaked. "I'll introduce you to her. She's intelligent, affluent, and a widow. A pity she's not more developed: what she needs is to get to know Eudoxia more intimately. I drink your health, Eudoxia! Let's clink! *Et toc, et toc, et tin-tin-tin. Et toc, et toc, et tin-tin-tin!* . . ."

"Victor, you're a scamp."

The luncheon lasted a long time. The first bottle of champagne was succeeded by a second, then a third, and finally a fourth. Eudoxia chattered away without respite; Sitnikov echoed her. They had much to say about the nature of marriage—whether it was prejudice or crime. They debated whether men were born equal or not. And they discussed the essence of individuality. The proceedings ultimately reached a stage when Eudoxia, all flushed with the wine she had drunk, began to thump with her close-cut fingernails on the keys of an out-of-tune piano and to sing in a hoarse voice, first, some gipsy songs and then Seymour Schiff's romance, "Granada Lies Slumbering," while Sitnikov, a scarf tied around his head, mimed the swooning lover at the passage:

> And when your lips and mine
> In burning kiss shall twine . . .

Arcady could bear it no longer. "Gentlemen," he exclaimed loudly, "this is very like bedlam."

Bazarov, who had contented himself with dropping a sarcastic word every now and then into the conversation—he was more engrossed in the champagne—yawned noisily, got up and, without so much as bidding good-bye to the hostess, strode out from the house followed by Arcady. Sitnikov leapt up and tried to catch up with them.

"Well, well!" he exclaimed, running now to the right, now to the left of them. "Didn't I tell you she was a remarkable personality! There should be more women like her! In her own way, she is a supra-ethical phenomenon."

"And is *that* establishment of your father's also an ethical phenomenon?" Bazarov inquired, pointing to a gin-shop which they were passing at that instant.

Sitnikov laughed shrilly again. He was very ashamed of his origin, and was at a loss whether to feel flattered or hurt by Bazarov's unexpected familiarity of speech.

XIV

A FEW days later the Governor gave his ball. Matvey Kolyazin was indeed the guest of honour. The Marshal of the Nobility made it clear to all and sundry that he had only attended out of respect for him; and the Governor persisted in ordering everyone about even while the ball was in full swing and he himself was standing still. Matvey Kolyazin's suppleness of approach was equalled only by his stately manner. He had soft words for everyone, with a shade of fastidiousness for some and of deference for others; in front of the ladies he sparkled with compliments *en vrai chevalier français* and laughed continuously with a hearty, resounding and solitary laugh, as befits a dignitary. He patted Arcady on the back and in a loud voice dubbed him "nephew." On Bazarov, who was arrayed in an oldish dress-coat, he bestowed an absent-minded but condescending sideways glance, which slipped over his cheek, and a vague but friendly grunt, which sounded something like, "I . . . greatly." To Sitnikov he held out one of his fingers, smiling at him as he turned his head away. Even to Madame Kukshin, who had arrived at the ball without a crinoline, wearing a pair of soiled gloves and with a bird of paradise in her hair, he vouchsafed an *"enchanté."* There were lots of people and no lack of cavaliers; the civilians tended to bunch along the walls, while the officers danced with gusto, especially a certain officer who had spent about six weeks in Paris, where he had picked up a variety of dashing expressions, such as *"zut," "Ah fichtrrre," "pst, pst, mon bibi,"* and others of the sort. His pronunciation was perfect, full of real Parisian *chic,* and yet at the same time he used to say, *"si j'aurais"* instead of *"si j'avais,"* and *"absolument"* when he meant *"certainly"*—in short, he delivered himself in that Franco-Great-Russian jargon at which the French poke fun when they have no need to assure us that we speak their language like angels, *"comme des anges."*

As we already know, Arcady danced badly, while Bazarov did not dance at all: they both retired to a corner and there Sitnikov joined them. With a mocking expression on his face and letting fall a few venomous remarks, he stared round him provokingly; to all appearance he was thoroughly enjoying himself. Then of a sudden his expression changed and, turning to Arcady, he said in an embarrassed sort of way, "Madame Odintzov has just arrived."

Arcady looked round and perceived a tall woman in a black dress pausing in the doorway of the ballroom. The dignity of her carriage astonished him. Her bare arms hung gracefully beside her stately figure; from her glossy hair light sprays of fuchsia fell gracefully upon her rounded shoulders; from under a slightly prominent, white forehead, her bright eyes looked calm and intelligent, calm above all and not pensive, and a barely perceptible smile played on her lips. A sort of affectionate and tender strength beamed in her face.

"Are you acquainted?" Arcady inquired from Sitnikov.

"Intimately. Would you like me to introduce you?"

"If you like . . . after the quadrille."

Bazarov had also directed his attention to Madame Odintzov.

"Who is that figure?" he asked. "She's unlike the other women."

Having waited for the quadrille to end, Sitnikov led Arcady up to Madame Odintzov; but he proved to be anything but intimately acquainted with her: he grew embarrassed as he addressed her and she, for her part, stared at him with a certain amount of surprise. However, her face assumed an affable expression when she heard Arcady's family name. She inquired whether he was not the son of Nicholas Petrovich.

"That is so," Arcady replied.

"I have met your father twice and have heard a great deal about him," she went on. "I am very glad to make your acquaintance."

At that moment some adjutant flew up to her and invited her to dance the next quadrille with him. She consented.

"So you dance?" Arcady asked her respectfully.

"I do. But why should you think I didn't? Or do I seem too old for it?"

"I beg your pardon, I didn't intend . . . But in that case may I invite you for the mazurka?"

Madame Odintzov smiled indulgently. "Certainly," she

replied, glancing at Arcady not so much with condescension as in the way a married sister might look at a younger brother. Madame Odintzov was a little older than Arcady; she had turned twenty-nine, but in her presence he felt himself a schoolboy, a young student, as though the difference of years between them were much greater. Then Matvey Kolyazin came walking towards her with stately mien and flattering speeches. Arcady stepped aside, but continued to keep her under observation: he did not take his eyes off her while she danced the quadrille. She was as unconstrained in her conversation with her partner as she had been with the high official; she made a few gentle motions with her head and eyes, and laughed softly once or twice. Her nose, like that of most Russians, was a trifle thick, and her complexion matt; for all that, Arcady decided that he had never met such an entrancing woman. The sound of her voice haunted his ears; the very folds of her dress, it seemed to him, hung down in a way no other woman could imitate, in a fashion more stately and flowing, and all her movements seemed particularly smooth as well as natural.

Arcady felt inwardly a little shy when, at the first strains of the mazurka, he sat out with his partner and, as he was on the point of engaging her in conversation, he could only stroke his hair without uttering a single word. But his shyness and agitation did not last long; Madame Odintzov's self-possession communicated itself to him also: within a quarter of an hour he was already talking quite freely about his father, his uncle and his life both in Petersburg and in the country. Madame Odintzov listened to him with obliging readiness, opening and shutting her fan a little as she did so; his chatter was interrupted whenever a new partner claimed her for a dance; Sitnikov, incidentally, invited her twice. She would return, sit down again and pick up her fan, without appearing to breathe any faster; Arcady would resume his chatter, feeling full of happiness at finding himself so close to her, talking to her, gazing into her eyes, at her lovely forehead, at the whole of her charming, grave and intelligent face. She herself spoke little, but her words showed a wide knowledge of life; from some of her remarks Arcady concluded that this young woman had already experienced and pondered on many things.

"With whom were you standing," she asked him, "just before Monsieur Sitnikov brought you over to me?"

"You noticed him then?" Arcady inquired in his turn. "What a fine face he has, don't you think? That's Bazarov, a friend of mine."

Arcady launched into a description of "his friend."

He spoke about him in such detail and with such enthusiasm that Madame Odintzov directed her gaze on Bazarov and attentively scrutinized him. Meanwhile the mazurka was drawing to an end. Arcady felt sorry at having to give up his partner: for almost an hour he had been very happy with her! It is true, during that time he had a persistent feeling that she was being indulgent to him, that he should have been grateful to her . . . but such feelings do not weigh heavily on youthful hearts.

The music came to a stop.

"Merci," Madame Odintzov murmured, getting up. "You have promised to visit me; do also bring your friend with you. I am very curious to meet a man who dares have no belief in anything."

The Governor came up to Madame Odintzov, announced that supper was served and, with a worried look on his face, offered her his arm. As she departed, she glanced back with a smile of farewell and a nod to Arcady. He made her a low bow and, following her with his eyes (how well proportioned her figure seemed, sheathed in the greyish glitter of black silk!) he thought to himself, "By now she's already forgotten my existence." As he did so, a feeling of exquisite resignation welled up in his heart. . . .

"Well? How goes it?" Bazarov inquired of Arcady, as soon as the latter had rejoined him in a corner. "Did you get any pleasure out of it? A certain gentleman was just telling me that the lady in question was—'quite hot'; but he looks a fool. Well? What is your opinion? Is she really—'quite hot'?"

"I completely fail to grasp the allusion," Arcady replied.

"Come, come! What innocence!"

"In that case, I fail to understand your gentleman. Madame Odintzov is very charming—there is no doubt on that score, but her manner is so cold and reserved that . . ."

"Still waters . . . you know the rest!" Bazarov exclaimed. "You say she is cold. That merely improves the flavour. You're fond of ices, aren't you?"

"Maybe," Arcady mumbled. "I'm no judge of such things. She would like to make your acquaintance. She has asked me to bring you along when I pay her a visit."

"I can imagine the portrait you daubed of me! However, you have acted sensibly. Take me along. Whatever she may be—a mere provincial lioness or just an *emancipée*, like Kukshin—she has a pair of shoulders I have not seen this many a day."

Bazarov's cynicism jarred on Arcady, but—as happens often enough—the reproach he levelled against his friend did not correspond exactly with what he really held against him. . . .

"Why are you unwilling to admit that women are capable of freedom of thought?" he asked in an undertone.

"Because, my dear brother, my observations lead me to suppose that free-thinking women are monstrosities."

On that the conversation ended. Both the young men departed immediately after supper. Madame Kukshin gave vent to a nervously spiteful but rather faltering laugh in their wake: her vanity had been deeply hurt because neither of them had paid the least attention to her. She was among the last to leave the ball, and towards four o'clock in the morning she and Sitnikov danced a polka-mazurka in the Parisian style. With this edifying entertainment the Governor's festival culminated.

XV

"WE shall soon find out to what category of mammals this personage belongs," Bazarov said to Arcady next day as they mounted the staircase of the hotel where Madame Odintzov was staying. "I can smell something not quite right here."

"You amaze me!" Arcady exclaimed. "What? To have you, Bazarov, of all people, uphold the narrow morality which . . ."

"What a queer chap you are!" Bazarov interrupted carelessly. "Don't you realize that, in our jargon and for people like us, 'not quite right' signifies 'quite all right'? It implies

that some advantage can be gained. Did you not say yourself earlier on that she had made an odd marriage? Though,
as I see it, to marry a rich old man is not in the least odd;
on the contrary it is a sensible decision. I distrust the gossip
of the town; but I should like to think, as our cultured
Governor puts it, there is some foundation in it."

Without replying, Arcady knocked at the door. A young
manservant in livery conducted our friends into a large
room, which was furnished in as bad taste as the majority
of rooms in Russian hotels but was embellished with a
profusion of flowers. Very soon Madame Odintzov in
person appeared on the scene in a simple morning dress.
The spring sunshine made her look younger than ever.
Arcady introduced Bazarov and noted with concealed surprise that his friend exhibited signs of embarrassment,
whereas Madame Odintzov remained as self-possessed as
she had been on the previous day. Bazarov became aware
of his confusion and felt ashamed. "Well I never!" he
thought. "Here's a woman who has put the wind up me!"
Thereupon, sprawling in an arm-chair in the Sitnikov manner, he began to hold forth in an exaggeratedly free and
easy tone, while Madame Odintzov kept her glowing eyes
fixed on him.

Anna Sergeyevna Odintzov was born the daughter of
Sergey Nicolaievich Loktyev, a speculator and gambler,
who had been renowned for his good looks. Having succeeded in staying the course and gaining some notoriety in
Petersburg and Moscow, Loktyev had ended by losing all
he had at cards and by being obliged to retire into the
country; there he soon died, leaving a tiny income to his
two daughters—Anna, aged twenty, and Katerina, aged
twelve. Their mother, a descendant of the impoverished
line of the Princess K, had died in Petersburg while her
husband was still at the height of his prosperity. After her
father's death, Anna found herself in a very difficult situation. Her brilliant Petersburg education had not fitted her
for the worries connected with the management of an estate
and a manor house, or for the dull life of the provinces. She
had absolutely no friends in the neighbourhood, and there
was no one whose advice she could ask. Her father had
done his best to avoid contacts with his neighbours; he
despised them and they returned the compliment, each in
his own way. However, she did not lose her head and at

once wrote to a maternal aunt of hers, the Princess Avdotya Stepanovna K, a spiteful and conceited old lady, inviting her to come and stay in the house. This the Princess did, appropriating to herself all the best rooms, growling and grumbling from morning till night, and even going to the lengths of having herself accompanied whenever she went out for a stroll in the garden by her one and only serf-retainer, a sulky footman in a threadbare, pea-green livery trimmed with pale-blue braid and in a three-cornered hat.

Anna bore patiently with her aunt's oddities, supervised her young sister's education in her spare time, and seemed resigned to the idea of withering away in this wilderness. . . . But fate had other things in store for her. She happened to meet a certain Odintzov, a very wealthy man of about forty-six, eccentric, hypochondriac, bloated, ponderous and sour, but neither stupid nor ill-tempered; he fell in love with her and proposed marriage. She consented to become his wife; after living with her for some six years he died, bequeathing to her his whole fortune. For about a year after his death Anna Sergeyevna did not leave the country; then she went abroad with her sister, but stayed only in Germany; becoming homesick, they returned to their favourite estate at Nicolskoye, some thirty miles from town. There she kept up a sumptuous, excellently furnished house with a lovely garden and conservatories: the late Odintzov had denied himself nothing. Anna Sergeyevna visited town but rarely and then for the most part on business which did not take up much time. But she was not liked in the province. Her marriage with Odintzov had caused quite a stir, and the most incredible rumours about her were in circulation. It was affirmed that she had helped her father in his nefarious deals, that she had an ulterior motive for travelling abroad—that of concealing the unfortunate consequences . . . . "You know what," the indignant interlocutor would exclaim. "She's been through fire and water," others said of her; and a notorious provincial wit usually threw in: "And through a brass band." All this gossip reached her ears, but she paid no attention to it: she had a firm and independent character.

Leaning back in an arm-chair with hands clasped, Madame Odintzov listened to Bazarov. He was talking more than his wont, garrulously and, to Arcady's great surprise, obviously trying to intrigue her. He could not make up his mind whether Bazarov was succeeding in his purpose. From Anna Sergeyevna's face it was hard to guess her thoughts: its expression remained unchanged, cordial and sympathetic; her beautiful eyes were bright with attention, yet her glance seemed imperturbable. At first, Bazarov's attitudinizing produced a disagreeable impression on her, like a bad smell or a too strident note; but she quickly realized that he was ill at ease, and this even flattered her. Paltriness was the only thing that revolted her, and Bazarov could not be accused of paltriness. That day Arcady was destined to be in a state of recurring amazement. He had expected Bazarov to converse with Madame Odintzov as with an intelligent woman about his convictions and opinions: she herself had expressed the wish to listen to a man "who dared have no belief in anything," but instead Bazarov discoursed on medicine, homœopathy and botany. It turned out that Madame Odintzov had not wasted her time in solitude: she had read through several good books and spoke faultless Russian. She brought the conversation round to music, but perceiving that Bazarov did not relish art, quickly veered the conversation back to botany despite the fact that Arcady had already begun to discuss the significance of folk melodies. Madame Odintzov continued to treat him like a younger brother: she seemed to appreciate his good qualities and youthful simplicity—and no more. Their leisurely, varied and animated conversation lasted for over three hours.

At length the friends rose to go and began to take their leave. Anna Sergeyevna eyed them amiably, held out her beautiful white hand to each of them in turn and, after a moment of reflection, said with a hesitant but impressive smile, "If you are not afraid of boredom, gentlemen, come and visit me at Nicolskoye."

"How can you say that, madame!" Arcady exclaimed. "I shall be delighted. . . ."

"And you, Monsieur Bazarov?"

Bazarov merely bowed—and Arcady was again amazed: he noticed that his friend had blushed.

"Well?" he asked when they were out in the street. "Are you still of the opinion that she is—'quite hot?'"

"One can never tell! Just look at the way she has put herself on ice!" Bazarov retorted, and after a pause added: "A regular duchess, a commanding personality. She only needs to have a train trailing behind her and a coronet on her head."

"Our duchesses don't speak such faultless Russian," Arcady remarked.

"She's been through the mill, my lad. She's tasted of our common bread."

"And yet she's beautiful," Arcady rejoined.

"A really opulent body!" Bazarov pursued. "Just ripe for the dissecting table."

"For Heaven's sake, Eugene, shut up! This won't do."

"Well, you mustn't be angry, you ninny. First class—that's what I really meant. We must go and pay her a visit."

"When?"

"The day after to-morrow, if you like. What is there to do here! Drink champagne with Kukshin? Or listen to your relative, the liberal big-noise? . . . We'll make a dash for it the day after to-morrow. By the way—my father's property is not very far from here. Isn't Nicolskoye on the X road?"

"Yes."

"*Optime.* Why dawdle then? Only fools delay—and the wise. Didn't I tell you, she's got an opulent body!"

Three days later, the friends were on the road to Nicolskoye. It was sunny without being too hot, and the well-nourished post-horses raced along in good fettle, gently swishing their knotted and plaited tails. Arcady stared at the road and, for some unknown reason, smiled to himself.

"You must congratulate me," Bazarov suddenly exclaimed. "This is the twenty-second of June, my name-day. We'll see how well my Patron Saint will watch over me. They are expecting me at home to-day," he added, lowering his voice. . . . "Well, they can wait a little longer—it's not so important!"

XVI

ANNA SERGEYEVNA'S country house stood on the slope of a bare hill, within easy reach of a yellow stone church with a green roof, white columns and a fresco of the Resurrection painted in the Italian style over the main entrance. The figure of a swarthy warrior in a helmet, lying prostrate in the foreground, was particularly remarkable for its well-rounded contours. Behind the church a village spread for some distance in a double row of houses, whose chimneys projected here and there over the thatched roofs. The manor house was built in the same style as the church, the style so well known in Russia as the "Alexandrine"; this house was also painted yellow and had a green roof, as well as a row of white columns and a pediment with an escutcheon. The chief architect of the province had erected both buildings with the approval of Anna's late husband, who could not bear any "pointless and arbitrary innovations," as he called them. The house was flanked on each side with the sombre trees of an ancient park, while an alley of clipped fir trees stretched towards the main porch.

Our friends were met in the hall by two stalwart footmen in livery; one of them at once ran off to fetch the butler. The butler, a stout man in black tails, appeared promptly on the scene and directed the guests up a carpeted staircase to the room reserved for them, which already contained two beds as well as all the essential toilet requisites. Order evidently reigned in the house: everything was spick and span, and everywhere there was an odour of respectability such as is to be found in ministerial reception rooms.

"Madame would like you to call on her in half an hour," the butler reported. "Have you any instructions for me in the meantime?"

"No instructions at all, my worthy fellow," Bazarov replied, "unless you will deign to serve us with a glass of vodka."

"Certainly, sir," the somewhat puzzled butler replied as he went off with boots creaking.

"What *grand genre!*" Bazarov remarked. "I believe that's what it's called in your parlance? A regular duchess, that's what she is."

"A fine duchess," Arcady retorted, "to have invited at first sight two such obvious aristocrats as you and me."

"Me in particular, a country doctor in the making, and the son of one, and the grandson of a deacon. . . . You knew, didn't you, that I was the grandson of a deacon? . . ."

"Like Speransky,"[1] Bazarov added, after a brief pause,

---

[1] Speransky (1772-1839)—A Russian statesman of "westernizing" and reformist tendencies.

with a wry smile. "Anyhow, she's pampered. Oh, how she has pampered herself, this lady! Hadn't we better don our dress clothes?"

Arcady merely shrugged his shoulders . . . but he also felt slightly embarrassed.

Half an hour later Bazarov and Arcady descended into the drawing-room. It was a spacious, lofty room, furnished fairly luxuriously but without any distinctive taste. The ponderous, expensive furniture was set out in the usual, rather frigid order along the walls, which were covered in a buff wall-paper with golden arabesques; the late Odintzov had ordered the furnishings from Moscow through an agent friend of his, a wine merchant. Over the centre sofa hung a portrait of a somewhat flabby, fair-haired man—he seemed to stare rather disapprovingly at the guests. "It must be *him*," Bazarov whispered to Arcady and, wrinkling up his nose, added, "Shall we beat it?" But at that instant the lady of the house came in. She was wearing a summery muslin dress; her hair was smoothly brushed back behind her ears, imparting a girlish expression to her pure, fresh face.

"I am grateful to you for keeping your word," she began. "You must stay with me for a while: it is really not at all unpleasant here. I shall introduce you to my sister, she plays quite well. That is of no interest to you, Monsieur Bazarov; but I believe that Monsieur Kirsanov is fond of music; besides my sister, I have living here an old aunt, and one of our neighbours drives in occasionally for a game of cards: that is the whole of our society. And now let us sit down."

Madame Odintzov uttered the whole of her little speech very precisely, as though she had learnt it by rote: then she turned to Arcady. It transpired that her mother had known Arcady's mother, and had even acted as her confidante when the latter had fallen in love with Nicholas Kirsanov. Arcady began to speak with great warmth of his late mother, while Bazarov proceeded to inspect some of the albums. "I've grown quite tame," he was thinking.

A handsome borzoi with pale-blue collar ran into the drawing-room, tapping on the floor with its paws; it was followed by a girl of eighteen, with black hair, an olive-complexioned, slightly oval but winsome face, and dark eyes. In her hands she held a basket full of flowers. "This is

Katya," Madame Odintzov said, with a nod in her direction.

Katya made a slight curtsy, sat down beside her sister and began to sort out the flowers. The borzoi, whose name was Fifi, approached each of the guests in turn, wagging its tail and thrusting its cool muzzle into their hands.

"Did you pick them yourself?" Madame Odintzov inquired.

"Yes, I did," Katya replied.

"And is auntie coming down for tea?"

"She's coming."

Katya, when she spoke, had a charming smile, at once bashful and candid, and she had an amusingly severe way of looking up at one: everything about her was still innocently fresh; the downy bloom on her face, her rose-pink hands with white palms, and her rather compact shoulders. . . . She was constantly blushing and apt to catch her breath.

Madame Odintzov turned to Bazarov. "You are looking at those pictures merely out of politeness, Monsieur Bazarov," she began. "They don't really amuse you. You had better come closer, and then we can start an argument about something."

Bazarov moved closer. "What shall we argue about?" he inquired.

"Anything you like. I warn you, I'm a fierce wrangler."

"You?"

"Yes, I am. You seem surprised. Why?"

"Because, as far as I can judge, you have a calm, cold temperament. Argument implies an excitable nature."

"How can you sum me up so quickly? In the first place, I am very impatient and obstinate—you'd better ask Katya; and in the second, I am easily carried away."

Barazov looked at Anna Sergeyevna.

"Perhaps, you know best. So you would like us to have an argument—all right then. I was examining some views of German Switzerland in your album, and you remarked that they could not possibly interest me. You said that because you assumed that I had no artistic sense—yes, I really have none. But those views might have interested me from a geological standpoint, for instance that of the way mountains are formed."

"If I may say so, as a geologist you had better consult a manual, some special work on the subject, rather than those drawings."

"A drawing may provide a visual image of what it takes ten pages of text to describe."

Anna Sergeyevna was silent for a moment.

"And so you have no drop of artistic sense in you?" she brought out, leaning on the table, and, as a result of that movement, bringing her face nearer to Bazarov's. "How can you do without it?"

"And may I inquire why I need it?"

"It might help you to read people's characters."

Bazarov smiled.

"First, one's experience suffices for that; and secondly, may I state that it's not worth the trouble to make a separate study of individuals? All men are similar in body and soul; each one of us has a brain, a spleen, a heart, and identically formed lungs; and the so-called moral qualities attributed to us are the same in all: slight variations only prove the rule. One human specimen affords an adequate basis for judging all the rest. People are like trees in a forest; no botanist would dream of studying each birch tree in detail."

Katya, who was leisurely matching the flowers one by one, raised her eyes in perplexity and, encountering Bazarov's quick, casual glance, flushed to the tip of her ears. Madame Odintzov shook her head.

"The trees in a forest," she repeated. "According to you, then, there is no difference between a stupid and an intelligent man, between a good and a bad man."

"Oh yes, there is: it's like the difference between a sick and a healthy man. A consumptive's lungs, although identically formed, are differently conditioned from ours. We know approximately the cause of physical ailments; but moral ailments are induced by the wrong sort of education, by all sorts of rubbish with which it has been the custom to stuff people's heads, by the monstrous state of society—in short, if society is put right, then the ailments will vanish."

As Bazarov delivered himself of this, he had the air of thinking, "Believe me or not, it's all the same to me!" As he slowly stroked his side-whiskers with his long fingers, his eyes flitted round the corners of the room.

"You assume then," Anna Sergeyevna said, "that when society is put right, no more stupid or bad people will be left?"

"In a properly functioning society, it wouldn't matter a

jot whether a man were stupid or intelligent, good or bad."

"Yes, I understand. They will have identical spleens."

"Exactly so, madame."

Anna Odintzov turned to Arcady. "And what is your opinion, Monsieur Kirsanov?"

"I agree with Eugene," he replied.

Katya looked at him from under her eyelids.

"You amaze me, gentlemen," Madame Odintzov said, "but we shall discuss this further. And now I can hear auntie coming down for tea; we must be merciful to her."

Princess K, Anna Odintzov's aunt, a thin, little woman with a clenched fist of a face and glaring spiteful eyes under a grey wig, came in and, with barely a bow to the guests, sank into a roomy velvet arm-chair which no one but herself was privileged to use. Katya placed a hassock under her feet; the old lady did not bother to thank her, she did not even so much as glance at her, but kept twitching her hands under a yellow shawl, which covered almost the whole of her infirm body. The princess was fond of yellow, and her cap was also hung with bright yellow ribbons.

"Did you sleep well, auntie?" Madame Odintzov inquired, lowering her voice.

"That dog is here again," the old lady growled in reply. Then observing that Fifi had taken a couple of hesitant steps in her direction, she exclaimed, "Go away, go away!"

Katya called Fifi and opened the door.

Fifi rushed out joyously, expecting to be taken for a walk, but on being left alone outside the door, began to scratch with her paws and to whine. The princess frowned. Katya was on the point of going out. . . .

"I think tea is served," Madame Odintzov said. "Gentlemen, let us go. Auntie, please come and have some tea."

The princess silently vacated her arm-chair and was the first to leave the drawing-room. Everyone followed her into the dining-room. The little Cossack boy in livery noisily pushed back from the table another sacred arm-chair, laden with cushions, into which the princess sank; Katya, who was pouring out the tea, served her first with a cup emblazoned with a coat of arms. The old lady put some honey in her tea (although she never spent a penny of her own on anything, she considered it sinful and expensive to drink tea with sugar), and suddenly inquired in a husky voice:

"And what does *Preence* Ivan write?"

She received no reply. Bazarov and Arcady soon divined that, although she was treated with respect, no one paid any attention to her. "They keep her for the sake of appearances, because she comes of a princely house," Bazarov concluded. . . . After tea Anna Sergeyevna suggested a stroll, but a drizzle had set in, and the company, with the exception of the princess, returned to the drawing-room. Then the neighbour arrived. A squat, grizzled old man, with short spindly legs, very courteous and humorous, he was Porfiry Platonich by name, and a great lover of cards. Anna Sergeyevna, who talked with Bazarov more than anyone else, asked him whether he would not care to pit himself against them in a game of old-fashioned preference. Bazarov consented, remarking that it behoved him to train in advance for his impending duties as a country doctor.

"Take care," Anna Sergeyevna said, "Porfiry Platonich and I, between us, will rout you. As for you, Katya," she added, "play something for Monsieur Arcady: he likes music, and we shall listen too."

Reluctantly Katya approached the piano; and, though fond of music, Arcady followed her as reluctantly; it had occurred to him that Madame Odintzov was sending him away—and his heart, like that of every young man at his age, was beginning to seethe with a sort of vague and nostalgic sensation akin to a foreboding of love. Katya raised the lid of the piano and, without a glance at Arcady, asked him in an undertone:

"What shall I play for you?"

"Whatever you like," Arcady replied indifferently.

"What music do you prefer?" Katya inquired again, without changing her position.

"Classical," Arcady replied in the same sort of tone.

"Do you like Mozart?"

"Very much."

Katya brought out Mozart's Sonata Fantasia in C minor. She played very well, although a trifle too mechanically and dryly. She sat motionless and stiffly, without taking her eyes off the music, her lips tightly pressed, and it was only as the Sonata neared its end that her face began to glow, and a small tress of hair fell uncoiling over her dark brow.

The last part of the Sonata in particular impressed Arcady—the part where transports of the most woeful and almost tragic grief come suddenly bursting through in the middle of the enchanting joyousness of the heedless refrain. . . . But the reflections which were stimulated in him by the music of Mozart bore no reference to Katya. As he looked at her, he merely concluded, "This young lady doesn't play at all badly, and she is not bad-looking either."

When she had come to the end of the Sonata, Katya asked him, without taking her hands off the keys, "Will that do?" Arcady declared that he did not dare to impose on her any further, and began to talk to her about Mozart; he asked her whether she had selected the Sonata herself or whether anyone had recommended it to her. But Katya's replies were monosyllabic: she was hiding herself, she had withdrawn into herself. Whenever this happened to her, it took her a long time to come to the surface again; her very face as a result assumed an expression of obstinacy and almost of blankness. She was not so much shy as distrustful, and somewhat intimidated by the sister who had brought her up—a fact which the latter did not even suspect. For the sake of appearing at ease, Arcady finally fell back upon Fifi, now back in the room once more; calling her over to him and smiling benevolently, he stroked her head. Katya busied herself again with the flowers.

Meanwhile Bazarov was losing one game after another. Anna Sergeyevna was an expert player, Porfiry Platonich could also hold his own. Bazarov came out the loser of a sum which, though it was by no means considerable, he nevertheless found regrettable. Over supper Anna Sergeyevna once more broached the subject of botany.

"Let us go for a stroll to-morrow morning," she said to him. "I should like to learn from you the Latin names of various wild herbs and the properties."

"What do you want with Latin names?" Bazarov inquired.

"There must be order in everything," she replied.

"What a wonderful woman!" Arcady exclaimed as soon as they were alone in their room.

"Yes," Bazarov replied, "a woman with brains. I'm sure she's seen quite a lot."

"In what sense do you mean, Eugene?"

"In the good sense, in the good sense, my dear friend Arcady! I am also persuaded that she is an excellent estate manager. But it's her sister, not herself, who is the miracle."

"What? That little dark thing?"

"Yes, that little dark thing. She's fresh, untouched, apprehensive, anything but talkative, and whatever else you like. But she would be worth a lot of trouble. You could shape her to your fancy; but the other is too spry." Arcady made no reply. They went to bed, each pondering his own thoughts.

That night Anna Sergeyevna was also thinking about her guests. She had taken a liking to Bazarov—his lack of airs and the downright severity of his judgments appealed to her. She detected something new in him, something she had never encountered before, and her curiosity was roused.

Anna Sergeyevna was an odd enough person. Free from all prejudice, she yet lacked strong convictions; and though she was not put off by obstacles, she had no goal in life. She had clear ideas about many things and a variety of interests, but nothing ever fully satisfied her; nor did she seek complete satisfaction. Her mind was at once probing and apathetic: any doubts she may have entertained were never banished to the point of oblivion; nor were they ever allowed to provoke a state of inner alarm. If she had not been rich and independent, she might have thrown herself into the battle of life, experienced passion. . . . But she had an easy life, boring as it may sometimes have been, and continued to pursue her daily round without haste or undue agitation. From time to time a rainbow would loom in her sky, but when the mirage had faded she rediscovered peace and did not pine. Her imagination ranged beyond the bounds of what was considered permissible by the laws of conventional morality, but even then the rhythm of her blood pulsed no quicker as it circulated through her magnificently proportioned and tranquil body. Sometimes, emerging all warm and languorous from a fragrant bath, she would begin to muse on the insignificance of life, its sorrows, labours and evils. . . . Her soul would be filled with sudden resolve and would seethe with noble ardour; but a draught from a slightly open window was enough to make her shrink, complain, and almost be angry; in a moment like that her most urgent desire was to prevent the horrid draught from blowing on her.

Like all women who had failed to fall in love, she expeperienced a yearning for something she could not define. In reality, she yearned for nothing, although she seemed to long for everything. She could hardly bear her late husband (she had married him for practical reasons, although she probably would not have consented to become his wife unless he had been, as she imagined, of a kindly disposition), and had developed a secret revulsion for men, whom she represented as being all untidy, clumsy, limp and impotently wearisome creatures. On one occasion, somewhere abroad, she had met a handsome young Swede with a chivalrous face and a pair of honest pale-blue eyes beneath an open forehead; he made a powerful impression on her, but that did not prevent her from returning to Russia.

"What an odd man that doctor is!" she thought as she lay in her sumptuous bed, on lace pillows, beneath a silk quilt. . . . From her father Anna Odintzov had inherited a propensity for luxury. She had been very fond of her sinful but indulgent father; and, in his turn, he had adored her, joked with her as a friend and equal, confided in her and sought her counsel. She hardly remembered her mother.

"What an odd doctor!" she repeated. Stretching herself, she smiled, clasped her hands behind her head, and then, after letting her eyes stray over a couple of pages of a silly French novel, dropped the book and fell asleep, all pure and frigid in her spotless and fragrant linen.

Next morning, immediately after breakfast, Anna Odintzov set out on a botanizing expedition with Bazarov and came back just before dinner: Arcady did not venture to go out and spent about an hour with Katya. He did not feel bored in her company. She had suggested of her own accord that she might play yesterday's Sonata for him again; but when Madame Odintzov returned at last, when he saw her—his heart instantly contracted. . . . She was walking through the garden with a somewhat tired gait; her cheeks had flushed crimson and her eyes beneath the round straw hat shone more brightly than usual. In her fingers she was twirling a slender stalk of some wild flower, a light mantilla hung down to her elbows, and the broad grey ribbons of her hat clung to her bosom. Bazarov strode behind her, looking as self-confident and casual as ever, but the expression of his face, though cheerful and even affectionate, displeased Arcady. With a muttered "Good morning!"

Bazarov stalked off to his room. Madame Odintzov absent-mindedly pressed Arcady's hand and also went past him.

"Good morning," Arcady thought to himself. . . . "As if we had not seen each other earlier!"

XVII

TIME, as we all know, is sometimes a bird on the wing, and sometimes a crawling worm; but men are happiest when oblivious of time's quick or slow pace. In this mood Arcady and Bazarov spent about a fortnight at Madame Odintzov's. Her regular life and the order she had instituted in her household were partly responsible for this. She adhered strictly to her time-table and obliged others to observe it. There was a fixed time for everything throughout the day. In the morning, at eight o'clock punctually, the company assembled for morning tea; from tea-time till lunch everyone followed his own bent; the lady of the house attended to the steward (her estate had been put on a rent basis), the servants and the head housekeeper. Before dinner the company gathered again for conversation or reading; the evening was given up to walks, card-games and music; at half-past ten Anna Sergeyevna would retire to her room, give her final instructions for the following day and go to bed.

The measured, rather dignified precision of this daily round was not to Bazarov's taste: "It's like rolling on rails," he used to declare: the footmen in livery, the decorous butlers and servants, offended his democratic sentiments. According to him, the next logical step would have been to dine in English fashion, in evening dress and white ties. One day he broached the subject to Anna Sergeyevna. Her manner disposed everyone to express his opinions frankly, and without reserve. When Bazarov had had his say, she rejoined, "You are right from your point of view, and maybe in this particular case I am too much of a 'lady'; but one cannot live in the country without routine, otherwise it would only lead to boredom." And she pursued her course. Bazarov grumbled, but the reason why Arcady and he found life so smooth at Madame Odintzov's was that every-thing in her house did "roll on rails." Nevertheless, since the day of their arrival at Nicolskoye's, both the young men had undergone a change. An unfamiliar anxiety had overtaken Bazarov, whom Anna Sergeyevna treated with obvious favour, even though she hardly ever saw eye to eye with him: he was easily irritated, reluctant to talk, bad-tempered in his looks and, as though impelled by an inward anguish, could hardly sit still for a moment. Arcady, who finally made up his mind that he was in love with Anna, began to suffer from subdued fits of depression. However, his depression did not prevent him from becoming more in-timate with Katya; it even helped him to establish affection-ate and comradely relations with her. "Anna doesn't think much of me! So be it! . . . But this good-hearted creature does not spurn me," he thought to himself, and his heart once more indulged in the sweetness of magnanimous sensations.

Katya vaguely grasped that he was seeking some consola-tion in her company, and she did not deny either herself or him the innocent pleasure of a half-shy, half-trusting friendship. In Anna Sergeyevna's presence they refrained from talking to one another. Katya invariably shrank into herself under her sister's probing glance, and Arcady, as befits a young man in love, had no eyes for anything but the object of his passion; but he felt happiest of all when alone with Katya. He knew that it was not in his power to hold Anna Sergeyevna's interest; when left alone with her, he grew shy and lost his poise; nor did she know what to say to him—he was too young for her. On the other hand, Arcady felt himself quite at home with Katya; he treated her indulgently, allowed her to air the impressions excited in her by the music, the reading of novels, verse and other such "trifles," without observing or, rather, failing to realize that these trifles also amused him. Katya for her part did not inhibit his feelings of melancholy. Arcady felt happy with Katya, Anna—with Bazarov; and this usually resulted in the two couples, especially when they went for a stroll, going their different ways so as to enjoy their intimacy for a while. Katya *adored* nature, and Arcady loved it too, though he did not dare to admit it; like Bazarov, Anna Sergeyevna was fairly indifferent to it. The fact that they were almost continuously separated from each other was not without its consequence for our friends: their relationship underwent a change. Bazarov stopped referring to Anna Sergeyevna when talking to Arcady; he even stopped railing at her "aristocratic ways"; he continued, it is true, to praise Katya as before, counselling his friend to tone down her sentimental inclinations, but his praise was hurried, his counsels dry, and, on the whole, he chatted with Arcady far less than was his wont . . . it looked as though he were avoiding him or felt ashamed in his presence. . . .

Arcady noted all this, but kept his observations to himself.

.   .   .   .   .

The real cause of all these "innovations" was the feeling inspired in Bazarov by Anna Sergeyevna—a feeling which tormented and enraged him, and which he would have at once repudiated with scoffing laughter and cynical vituperation if anyone had even distantly hinted at the possibility of what was going on in his mind. Bazarov was a great lover of women and feminine beauty, but love in the ideal sense or, as he would have put it, in the romantic sense, he called tomfoolery and unpardonable idiocy; he regarded chivalrous feelings as something in the nature of malformation or disease. On more than one occasion he had voiced his amazement at the fact that Toggenburg, with all his Minnesingers and Troubadours, had not been locked up in bedlam. "If you are attracted by a woman," he used to say, "try and gain her; but if that proves impossible—well, don't bother, drop her. A forest is not made up of one tree."

He liked Anna: the rumours about her, the freedom and independence of her mind, her undoubted penchant for him—all these seemed to argue in his favour; but he was quick to grasp that he could not "gain her." Moreover, to his amazement, he discovered that he lacked the resolution to "drop her." His blood took fire as soon as her image impinged on his mind; he could have controlled his blood easily, but something else had got into him, something he would not admit at any price, something which he had always scoffed at and which revolted his pride. In his conversations with Anna he used to indulge to an even greater extent than usual in his scathing indifference to everything savouring of romanticism; but when left to himself, he became indignantly aware of the romantic strain in his own composition. On these occasions he would set off into the forest and walk about there with large strides, breaking off any branch that barred his way and cursing both her and himself in a low voice, or he would clamber into a hayloft, into a barn, and, obstinately shutting his eyes, force himself to fall asleep, though he did not always succeed in achieving that result. Suddenly he would imagine those chaste hands one day twining themselves round his neck, those proud lips responding to his kisses, those intelligent eyes gazing lovingly—yes, lovingly—into his own; his head would go round and he would find an instant of oblivion before his indignation flared up again. As though tempted by the devil, he caught himself thinking all sorts of immodest thoughts. Sometimes, it seemed to him that a change was coming over Anna too, that there was something particular about the expression of her face, that perhaps . . . But at this point he would usually stamp his feet, grind his teeth and shake his clenched fist menacingly under his own nose.

And yet Bazarov was not entirely mistaken. He had excited Anna Sergeyevna's imagination; he had intrigued her, and she devoted much thought to him. In his absence she did not long for him, she did not yearn for him, but his presence always stimulated her; she was glad to be alone with him and glad to converse with him, even when he irritated her or shocked her taste and her refined habits of mind. She behaved as though she wished both to test him and to explore her own depths.

One day, as they were strolling in the garden, he suddenly informed her in a grim voice of his intention to depart in the near future and to visit his father. . . . Anna turned pale as though something had pricked her heart, and pricked it so painfully that she was surprised; she worried for a long time afterwards about the significance of this. Bazarov had told her of his intended departure without any idea of testing her or checking her reaction; he was not in the habit of "fabricating effects." That very morning he had seen his father's steward, Timofeyich, who was by way of being the "uncle" of his childhood. This Timofeyich, an experienced and astute old man, with faded yellow hair, red weather-beaten face and tiny teardrops in his shrunken eyes, had unexpectedly confronted Bazarov, wearing a short coat of greyish-blue cloth, belted with a leather thong, and tarred boots.

"So it's you, old Timofeyich! How goes it?" Bazarov had exclaimed.

"Greetings to you, young master," the old man had begun, smiling joyously, so that his face had suddenly dissolved into wrinkles.

"What have you come for? Were you sent to fetch me or what?"

"If it please your honour, how can that be!" Timofeyich had started to mumble (he remembered his master's strict injunctions when setting off). "I was on the way to town on the master's business when I happened to hear of your honour's being here, so I turned aside from the main road, that is—to have a peep at your honour . . . it wouldn't do to disturb you otherwise."

"Now don't tell fibs," Bazarov interrupted him: "Is this the way to town?" Timofevich looked sheepish and made no reply. "Is my father well?"

"Yes, thank God."

"And my mother?"

"Arina Vlassyevna is very well too, the Lord be thanked."

"No doubt they are expecting me!"

Old Timofeyich hung his small head to one side.

"Ah, your honour, how could they not be expecting you! As God's my witness, my heart's grown sick with watching your parents worry."

"Well, that'll do, that'll do, don't exaggerate. Tell them I'll be coming soon."

"As you will," Timofeyich had replied with a sigh.

As he quitted the house, he had pulled his cap over his eyes with both hands. On getting into the rickety droshky, which had been left standing at the gateway, he had started off at a trot—but not in the direction of the town.

The same evening Anna Sergeyevna was sitting in her study with Bazarov, while Arcady was pacing up and down the music-room, listening to Katya as she played. The princess had retired upstairs; as a rule, she could not bear guests, especially these "new loony ones," as she had dubbed them. In the drawing-room, she merely sulked, but in her own quarters, in the presence of her maid, she sometimes gave vent to such a stream of abuse as made her cap jerk up and down on her head together with her wig. Anna Sergeyevna was well aware of this.

"Why are you thinking of going away?" she began. "What about your promise?"

Bazarov stirred.

"Which promise?"

"You've forgotten then? You were going to give me a few lessons in chemistry."

"What's to be done! My father is expecting me; I can't dawdle here any longer. However, you can read Pelouse and Frémy, *Notions générales de la Chimie*; it's a good book and clearly written. You will find in it everything you need."

"But don't you remember, you tried to persuade me that a book was no substitute for . . . I forget how you put it, but you know what I want to say . . . do you remember?"

"What's to be done!" Bazarov repeated.

"Why must you go?" Anna Sergeyevna asked, lowering her voice.

He glanced at her. She had thrown her head back against the arm-chair and folded her arms, which were bare to the elbow. She looked paler in the light of a solitary lamp, hung over with a gauze-like paper shade. She was swathed in the soft folds of a voluminous white dress; the tips of her feet, which were also crossed, were just visible.

"And why should I stay?" Bazarov replied.

Anna Sergeyevna turned her head slightly.

"What do you mean by that? Aren't you enjoying yourself here? Or do you imagine that no one here will regret your going?"

"Of that I am positive."

Anna Sergeyevna had nothing to say for a moment.

"A pity you think so. However, I don't believe you. You could not have meant it seriously." Bazarov made no move. "Why don't you speak?"

"And what am I to say to you? There's no point in having regrets about people, and even less so about me."

"Why do you say that?"

"I am a serious and uninteresting person. I'm no conversationalist."

"You're angling for a compliment, Eugene Vassilich."

"That is no habit of mine. Don't you know yourself that the refinements of life are beyond my reach—the refinements on which you set so much store?"

Anna Sergeyevna nibbled a corner of her handkerchief.

"You can think what you like, but I shall miss you when you go."

"Arcady is staying behind," Bazarov replied.

Anna Sergeyevna gave a slight shrug of her shoulders.

"I shall miss you," she said.

"Really? In any case you won't miss me for long."

"Why do you assume that?"

"Because you told me yourself that you feel bored only when your routine is upset. You have arranged your life with such blameless rectitude that there could be no place in it for boredom or grief . . . or any disturbing emotions."

"You find that I am blamelessly . . . that is, that I have arranged my life with such rectitude?"

"Exactly so! Now take this, for example: in a few minutes it will strike ten, and I already know in advance that you will send me packing."

"No, I won't. You may stay. Will you open the window? . . . It feels stuffy."

Bazarov got up and pushed at the window. It flew open at once with a rattle. . . . He had not expected it to open so easily; moreover, his hands were shaking. The dark, mild evening peeped into the room with its almost black sky, faintly rustling trees and the fresh fragrance of the pure untrammelled air.

"Draw the blind and sit down," Anna Sergeyevna said. "I'd like to have a talk with you before you depart. Tell me something about yourself; you never talk of yourself."

"I try and chat with you about useful subjects."

"How very modest of you. . . . But I should like to learn something about you, your family, your father, for whom you are forsaking us."

"Why is she talking like this?" Bazarov thought.

"It's not at all interesting," he said aloud, "especially for you; we're obscure sort of folk. . . ."

"And according to you, I am an aristocrat?"

Bazarov raised his eyes and looked at Madame Odintzov.

"Yes," he said with over-emphatic bluntness.

She smiled.

"I can see that you hardly know me, although you assure me that all people are alike and that they are not worth individual study. One day I shall tell you about my life . . . but you must tell me about yours first."

"I hardly know you," Bazarov repeated. "Maybe you

are right; it may be true that every person is an enigma. Now let's take you, for instance: you shun people, you find them a nuisance, and yet here you have invited two students to come and stay with you. Why does a woman of your intelligence and your beauty live in the country?"

"What? How did you put it?" Madame Odintzov cried with animation. "With my . . . beauty?"

Bazarov frowned.

"It doesn't matter," he muttered. "I wished to say that I don't quite understand why you have settled in the country."

"You don't understand. . . . However, you must explain it in some way?"

"Yes. . . . I assume that you remain fixed in one and the same spot because you have been spoilt, you have grown too fond of comfort and all that goes with it, and are quite impervious to anything else."

Madame Odintzov smiled again.

"You are determined to disbelieve in my capacity for enthusiasm?"

Bazarov glanced at her from under his eyebrows.

"Out of curiosity, maybe; not otherwise."

"Indeed? Well, now I understand what brought us together; you are exactly like me."

"Brought us together . . ." Bazarov repeated in a hollow voice.

"Yes! . . . but I forgot that you were intending to go away."

Bazarov rose. The lamp was burning dimly in the middle of the dusky, fragrant and secluded room; the irritating freshness of the nocturnal air came pouring through the blind as it stirred occasionally, and its mysterious whispering seeped through. Anna sat perfectly still, but a secret agitation was gradually invading her. . . . It communicated itself to Bazarov. He suddenly realized that he was alone with a young and beautiful woman. . . .

"Where are you going?" she slowly asked.

Without replying he sank back into his chair.

"So you regard me as a placid, spoilt and self-indulgent creature," she went on in the same tone, without taking her eyes off the window. "But the one thing I know about myself is that I am unhappy."

"Unhappy! Why? You don't mean to say that you attach any importance to slanderous tittle-tattle?"

Madame Odintzov frowned. She felt annoyed at his interpreting her so well.

"These slanders don't even amuse me, and I am too proud to let them upset me. I am unhappy because . . . I have no desire, no longing for life. You look distrustfully at me, you think: there's an 'aristocrat,' covered in lace and seated in a velvet arm-chair. I shall not disguise the fact that I am fond of what you call comfort, but at the same time I have very little desire to live. Interpret this contradiction as you will. However, all this is romanticism in your eyes."

Bazarov shook his head.

"You are in good health, independent, rich. What more do you need? What is it you want?"

"What do I want?" Madame Odintzov repeated, sighing. "I have grown weary and old; I seem to have lived a great age. Yes, I've grown old," she added, gently drawing the ends of her mantilla over her bare arms. Her eyes met Bazarov's, and she flushed slightly. "I have behind me so many memories: my life in Petersburg, prosperity, then poverty, my father's death, my marriage, my trip abroad, it had to be . . . There are plenty of memories, but nothing to remember, and ahead, in front of me, stretches a long, long road, but I have no goal. . . . So I have no desire even to tread the path."

"You are so disillusioned?" Bazarov asked.

"No," Madame Odintzov replied with deliberation. "But I am incomplete. It seems to me that, if I were capable of becoming strongly attached to something . . ."

"You are longing to fall in love," Bazarov interrupted her, "but you are incapable of it: that is your unhappiness."

Madame Odintzov began to inspect the mantilla which covered her arms.

"Am I incapable of love?" she asked.

"Hardly! Only I was wrong to call it unhappiness. The contrary is true, people deserve pity who do fall for that."

"Fall for what?"

"Love."

"And how do you know that?"

"By hearsay," Bazarov retorted angrily.

"You're playing the coquette," he thought to himself. "You are merely bored and want to provoke me out of idleness, but I . . ." And, indeed, his heart was being torn.

"Moreover, you may be too exacting," he said, bending his whole body forward and playing with the fringe of the arm-chair.

"Perhaps. All or nothing is the way I see it. A life for a life. If you take mine, give me yours. And, if you do so, you must have no regrets or afterthoughts. Otherwise I don't want it."

"Indeed?" Bazarov remarked. "There's justice in that, and I am surprised that until now . . . you have not found what you wanted."

"And do you think it's so easy to surrender one's self completely to whatever it might be?"

"Not so easy once you start thinking, biding your time, putting a price on yourself, growing in your own estimation. That is so; but if you stop reflecting, then it's quite easy to surrender."

"But how can one fail to set a value on one's self? If I had no price, who would want my devotion?"

"That's not my affair; it's for the other person to decide on my value. What matters is to be able to surrender yourself."

Anna detached herself from the back of the arm-chair.

"You are talking as if you had experienced it all."

"It arose out of the conversation, Anna Sergeyevna. As you know, all this is not in my line."

"But would you be capable of surrendering yourself?"

"I don't know. I don't wish to boast."

Madame Odintzov did not say anything, and Bazarov fell silent. From the drawing-room came the sound of a piano being played.

"Katya is playing very late to-night," Madame Odintzov remarked.

Bazarov got up.

"Yes, it is quite late," he said. "It's time you were in bed."

"Wait. Why are you in such a hurry? . . . I want to say a word to you."

"What is it?"

"Wait," Madame Odintzov whispered. Her eyes rested on Bazarov; she seemed to be scrutinizing him with great attention.

He took a turn about the room and then, suddenly approaching her, bade her a hurried "Good night." He squeezed her hand so hard that she almost cried out and left the room. She raised her numbed fingers to her lips, blew on them and, rising brusquely and impetuously from her arm-chair, strode rapidly towards the door as though intending to call Bazarov back. . . . A maid entered with a decanter on a silver tray. Madame Odintzov stopped short, ordered her to go away and sat down again, immersed in thought. Uncoiling itself like some dark snake, her hair spread over her shoulders. For a long while yet the lamp burnt on in Anna Sergeyevna's room, and for a long while she remained sitting motionless, only occasionally with her fingers stroking her hands which were now beginning to feel the chill of the nocturnal air.

As for Bazarov, he returned some two hours later to his bedroom, his boots all wet with dew, his hair dishevelled and his expression grim. He found Arcady sitting at the writing-desk, a book in his hands and his jacket all buttoned up.

"You're not in bed yet?" Bazarov asked in a tone almost of regret.

"You were a long time with Anna Sergeyevna to-night," Arcady retorted, without replying to the question.

"Yes, I was with her all the time you and Katya were playing the piano."

"I was not playing . . ." Arcady started to say and then stopped. He felt the tears welling to his eyes, but he did not want to weep in front of his scoffing friend.

XVIII

WHEN Madame Odintzov appeared at tea next day, Bazarov sat for a while hunched over his cup of tea and then suddenly glanced up at her. . . . She turned to face him as if he had given him a jolt, and it struck him that her face had gone slightly pale overnight. She soon retired to her room and did not re-emerge until lunch-time. It had drizzled from early morning and to go walking was out of the question. The whole of the company had gathered in the drawing-room. Arcady had got hold of the *Gazette* and had begun to read aloud from it. The princess, as usual, had reacted by looking amazed at first, as though Arcady were guilty of some indecency, and then she had fixed him with a baleful stare; but he paid no attention to her.

"Eugene Vassilich," Anna Sergeyevna said at last, "come along to my room. . . . I should like to ask you . . . You mentioned a manual yesterday."

She stood up and made for the door. The princess glanced round her with an expression that seemed to say, "Well, well, just look at that!" and then she had glared at Arcady again, but he merely raised his voice and, after exchanging a few glances with Katya, who was sitting beside him, continued to read aloud to her.

With quick steps Madame Odintzov reached her study. Bazarov had followed her promptly without raising his eyes and, as she glided ahead of him, he only caught the gentle swish and rustle of her silk dress. Madame Odintzov sank down into the same arm-chair as she had occupied the previous evening, and Bazarov also sat down on his former chair.

"What was the name of that book?" she began after a short pause.

"Pelouse and Frémy, *Notions générales* . . ." Bazarov replied. "However, I can also recommend Ganot, *Traité élémentaire de la physique experimentale*. The illustrations to that treatise are much clearer and, on the whole, that manual is . . ."

Madame Odintzov held out her hand.

"Eugene Vassilich," she said, "you must pardon me, but I did not ask you to come here to discuss manuals. I wanted to pursue our conversation of yesterday. You left so abruptly. . . . You won't find this boring?"

"I am at your service, Anna Sergeyevna. But, may I ask, what was it we were discussing last night?"

Madame Odintzov glanced at Bazarov out of the corner of her eyes.

"I believe we were discussing happiness. I was telling you something about myself. Incidentally, I have just mentioned the word 'happiness.' Now will you tell me why, even when we are enjoying music, for instance, or a pleasant evening party, or a conversation in agreeable company —why it all seems no more than just a hint of some boundless happiness existing elsewhere rather than actual happiness, or any such happiness as may really be granted to us? Why is it so? Or, maybe, you never feel like that?"

"You know the proverb, 'Happiness is somewhere else,'" Bazarov retorted. "Besides, you yourself told me yesterday that you felt incomplete. As for myself, you are quite right, such thoughts never occur to me."

"Perhaps you think them ridiculous?"

"I don't, but they simply never enter my head."

"You don't mean that? Do you know, I am very anxious to learn what you *do* think about."

"How so? I don't quite understand you."

"Now just listen to me. For a long time I've been wishing to clear up a few matters with you. There is no point in telling you—you know it yourself—that you are not just an average person. You are still young—you have a whole life in front of you. For what are you preparing yourself? What is your future going to be? I mean to say, what goal have you set yourself? Where are you going? What is the purpose animating you? In short, who are you? What are you?"

"You amaze me, Anna Sergeyevna. As you know very well, I am merely a student of the natural sciences, and as for what I am . . ."

"Yes, what are you?"

"I have already told you—a country doctor in the making."

Anna Sergeyevna made an impatient gesture.

"Why tell me that? You don't believe it yourself. Arcady might answer me so, but not you."

"And in what way is Arcady . . ."

"Do stop it! Can you possibly be satisfied with such a modest life? And haven't you always maintained that there is no such thing as medicine? You—with your pride—a country doctor! You are merely trying to put me off with such answers because you have no confidence in me. But do you know, Eugene, I could understand you; once I was poor and full of pride myself; I may have been through quite as many trials as you."

"All that is very well, Anna Sergeyevna, but you must excuse me . . . I'm not accustomed as a rule to talking about myself; and between you and me there is such a gulf. . . ."

"What gulf? Are you going to tell me again that I am an aristocrat? That's beside the point, Eugene Vassilich; I think I have proved to you . . ."

"And besides," Bazarov interrupted her, "why all this eagerness to talk and think about the future, which for the most part does not depend on us? If one gets an opportunity of doing something positive, that's excellent—but if one doesn't, one should at least be content with not chattering about it in advance."

"You call our friendly talk 'chatter.' . . . Or perhaps you don't regard me as a woman worthy of your trust? You must really despise the lot of us."

"I don't despise you, Anna Sergeyevna, you should know that."

"No, I don't know anything . . . but let us suppose that I do understand your reluctance to talk about your future plans; quite apart from that, we could discuss what is happening to you now. . . ."

"Happening!" Bazarov repeated. "As though I were some sort of state or society! In any case, it is all quite uninteresting and, besides, is a man always capable of describing aloud everything that is 'happening' to him?"

"But I don't see why it should be impossible to express everything one has on one's mind."

"Can you do it?" Bazarov inquired.

"I can," Anna Sergeyevna replied after a moment of hesitation.

Bazarov inclined his head.

"You are more fortunate than I," he said.

Anna Sergeyevna looked at him questioningly.

"As you like," she went on. "But something tells me, nevertheless, that we did not meet for nothing and that we shall become the best of friends. I am convinced that this —how shall I call it?—this tension of yours, this reserve, will disappear one day."

"So you have noticed in me this reserve . . . as you put it . . . this tension?"

"Yes."

Bazarov stood up and went over to the window.

"And you would like to learn the cause of this reserve? You would like to learn what is 'happening' inside me?"

"Yes," Madame Odintzov repeated with a sort of as yet unexplained fear.

"And you will not be angry?"

"No."

"No?" Bazarov was standing with his back to her. "Then

I must tell you that I love you stupidly, madly. . . . You have forced me. Now you know."

Madame Odintzov held out both her hands to him, while Bazarov remained standing with his forehead pressed against the window-pane. He was gasping: his whole body was visibly quivering. But it was no quiver of youthful timidity, nor yet the sweet terror of a first avowal that had got possession of him: it was a wave of passion surging through him, a violent and urgent passion, not unlike the symptoms of rage and, perhaps, not unrelated to it. . . . Madame Odintzov was filled with fear as well as a feeling of compassion for him.

"Eugene Vassilich," she murmured at last, and there was a note of involuntary tenderness in her voice.

He spun round, threw a devouring glance at her, and, seizing hold of both her hands, suddenly drew her to his breast.

But she at once disengaged herself from his embrace; an instant later she was already standing distantly in a corner and gazing at him. He rushed towards her. . . .

"You misunderstood me," she whispered hastily in alarm. She looked as though she might scream if he took another step. . . . Bazarov bit his lips and strode out of the room.

Half an hour later, the maid brought Anna Sergeyevna a note from Bazarov; it consisted of a single line: "Must I leave this evening or may I stay until to-morrow?" "Why leave? I did not understand you—you misunderstood me," was Anna Sergeyevna's reply. To herself she thought, "Nor do I understand myself."

She did not show herself till dinner-time. In the meantime she paced up and down her room, with hands clasped behind her back, stopping every now and then either in front of the window or in front of the mirror, slowly mopping her neck with a handkerchief on the spot where she fancied her skin to be burning. She kept asking herself what had impelled her to "force him," as Bazarov had put it, into being frank with her. Had she not really had an inkling of something? . . . "I am to blame," she said aloud, "but I could not foresee it." She kept thinking about it, and blushed each time she remembered Bazarov's almost bestial expression as he had rushed towards her. . . .

"Or . . . ?" she exclaimed suddenly and stopped, giving her curls a shake. . . . She had caught a glimpse of herself in the mirror; the image of her head, as it was flung back, and of the mysterious smile playing on her half-closed, half-opened eyes and lips seemed instantly to tell her something which immediately threw her into confusion. . . .

"No," she resolved at last. "God knows where that might have led, it's no joking matter. A quiet life is better than anything else in the world."

Her inward calm was not shattered; but she felt sad, and once she even burst into tears—she did not know why, but the insult she had suffered was certainly not the cause. She did not feel insulted: on the contrary, she had a feeling of guilt. The pressure of various conflicting emotions—an awareness that her life was on the decline, a longing for novelty—had brought her to the brink of an abyss; and as she peered over it, she saw no abyss but only a void . . . a shapeless chaos.

XIX

FOR all her self-possession and freedom from prejudice, Madame Odintzov felt distinctly ill at ease when she entered the dining-room. However, the dinner passed off fairly happily. Porfiry Platonich arrived and recounted various anecdotes; he had just got back from town. Among other things, he related that the Governor, "Bourdaloue," had issued instructions that officials engaged on special missions should wear spurs in case they might have to be dispatched on urgent business on horseback. Arcady was chatting with Katya in a low voice and, at the same time, he was being diplomatically attentive to the princess. Bazarov preserved an obstinate and gloomy silence. Twice Madame Odintzov glanced at him—straight in the face rather than out of the corner of her eyes, but at the sight of his rigid and glowering features, his lowered eyes, and the imprint of a contemptuous resolve on each line of his face, she thought to herself, "No . . . no . . . no. . . ." After dinner she strolled out with the whole company into the garden where, noticing that Bazarov wished to speak to her, she took a few steps to one side and stopped. Without raising his eyes, he went up to her and said in a hollow voice:

"I must apologize to you, Anna Sergeyevna. You must be angry with me."

"No, I'm not angry with you, Eugene Vassilich," Madame Odintzov replied. "But I am disappointed."

"So much the worse. In any case, I am sufficiently punished. As you will probably agree, I'm in an extremely silly position. You wrote asking me why I must leave. But I cannot stay, nor do I wish to. By to-morrow I shall be gone."

"But Eugene Vassilich, why are you . . ."

"Why am I going away?"

"No, that was not what I wished to say."

"The past cannot be resurrected, Anna Sergeyevna . . . and sooner or later this was bound to happen. Therefore I must go away. As I see it, there's only one condition on which I might have remained; but that can never be fulfilled. If you will pardon my presumption, am I not correct in saying that you do not love me and never will?"

For an instant Bazarov's eyes gleamed from under his dark eyebrows.

Anna Sergeyevna made no reply. "I'm afraid of this man," was the thought that flashed through her mind.

"Farewell then," Bazarov said, as though divining her thought, and he turned back towards the house.

Anna Sergeyevna followed him slowly and, calling Katya, took her by the arm. She remained inseparable from her until evening. She kept away from the card-table and frequently laughed to herself, which contrasted strangely with her pallor and the distraught look on her face. Arcady was puzzled and kept an eye on her, as young men will do, constantly asking himself what it all meant. Bazarov had locked himself in his room; but he put in an appearance for tea. Anna Sergeyevna was longing to say a kind word to him, but was at a loss how to approach him. . . .

An unexpected incident resolved her embarrassment: the butler announced Sitnikov's arrival.

Words fail to describe the fluttering quail-like figure cut by this young "Progressive" as he flew into the room. Having decided with an importunity so characteristic of him to drive into the country to pay a visit to a lady whom he barely knew and who had never invited him, but at whose house, as he had been informed, some intelligent and close friends of his were staying, he was nevertheless stricken to the marrow of his bones with embarrassment on setting foot in the house. Instead of repeating the excuses and greetings he had learnt by heart, he merely stammered some nonsense to the effect that Eudoxia Kukshin had sent him to inquire after Madame Odintzov's health and that Arcady had always spoken of him in terms of highest praise. . . . At this point, he got stuck, and was so flustered that he sat down on his own hat. As no one ventured to show him the door, however, and as Anna Sergeyevna even went so far as to introduce him to her aunt and sister, he soon recovered his equanimity and warbled away in all his glory. The spectacle of paltriness can often prove a useful lesson in life: it may loosen strings that have been pitched too high and sober both self-assured and disinterested feelings by serving to remind one of a possible affinity between them. Sitnikov's arrival had the effect of making everything seem cruder and simpler; the company even supped more solidly and dispersed to their bedrooms half an hour earlier than usual.

"I can now repeat to you," Bazarov said, as he lay in bed, to Arcady, who had also undressed, "what you once said to me: 'Why do you look so sad? Have you just fulfilled a sacred duty?' " Of late a sort of pseudo-easy banter —the sign invariably of secret discontent or suppressed suspicions—had become a habit between our young friends.

"I'm off home to-morrow, to my father's," Bazarov went on to inform him.

Arcady sat up, leaning on his elbow. He felt both surprised and, for some reason, pleased. "Ah," he exclaimed, "doesn't it depress you?"

Bazarov yawned. "Too much knowledge makes one's hair go grey," he exclaimed.

"And what about Anna Sergeyevna?" Arcady pursued.

"What about Anna Sergeyevna?"

"What I mean is: will she let you go?"

"She is not my employer."

While Arcady ruminated, Bazarov stretched himself out, and then turned his face to the wall. For several minutes there was silence.

"Eugene!" Arcady suddenly exclaimed.

"Well?"

"I'm also coming with you."

Bazarov made no reply.

"But I mean to drive on home," Arcady continued. "We'll go together as far as the Khokhlovsky settlement, you'll be able to get a relay of horses at Fedot's. It would give me very great pleasure to make the acquaintance of your people, but I'm afraid to inconvenience them as well as yourself. But you'll visit us again, won't you?"

"I have left my apparatus at your house," Bazarov replied, without turning round.

"Why doesn't he ask me why I'm going away? And quite as unexpectedly as himself," Arcady thought. "Why indeed am I going and why is he?" he pursued his reflections. He could find no satisfactory answer to this question and a feeling of bitterness filled his heart. He found it difficult to break with this life at Nicolskoye, to which he had grown so accustomed; but to have stayed on there alone, would have created a strange impression. "What has happened between them?" he asked himself. "What excuse could I offer for sticking round here in her company after his departure? And anyhow it would only end in my boring her and thus losing my last chance." He began mentally to picture Anna Sergeyevna; then gradually other traits began to emerge in the background of the young widow's lovely features.

"I shall regret leaving Katya too!" Arcady whispered into his pillow, on which he let drop a tear. . . . Then suddenly tossing back his hair, he exclaimed aloud: "Why the devil did that idiot Sitnikov barge in?"

Bazarov stirred in his bed, and gave vent to the following:

"I can see, brother, that you are still stupid. Sitnikov is essential to us. I would have you understand that I need such louts. It is not for the gods to glaze pottery! . . ."

"Oho! . . ." Arcady thought. Only now, at this very instant, was the whole bottomless pit of Bazarov's arrogance and pride revealed to him. "So you and I are gods? Or rather, you are a god and I'm a mere lout, isn't that so?"

"Yes," Bazarov repeated firmly. "You're still stupid."

Next day, when Arcady informed her that he was leaving with Bazarov, Madame Odintzov expressed no particular surprise; she looked distraught and fatigued. Katya gazed at him gravely and silently, and he could not help noticing that the princess went so far as to make a sign of the cross under her shawl, but Sitnikov, on the other hand, was quite taken aback. He had just come down for breakfast, wearing for the occasion a modish costume instead of a Slavophil one; the previous night he had astounded the valet placed at his disposal by the quantity of linen he had brought with him, and now his friends were leaving him in the lurch! He took a few mincing steps, scurried about like a hare driven to the edge of a wood—and suddenly, almost in terror, almost with a shrill cry, declared that he also intended to depart. Madame Odintzov made no attempt to detain him.

"I have a very smooth-running barouche," the unfortunate young man added, turning to Arcady. "I can take you in it, while Bazarov can use your tarantass. That would be even better."

"But I'm going out of your way. It's quite a distance to my place."

"That doesn't matter at all; I have plenty of time and, besides, I have some business to transact in that region."

"Liquor deals?" Arcady inquired a little too contemptuously.

But Sitnikov was in such a state of despair that, contrary to his habit, he did not even simper.

"I can assure you," he muttered, "that my barouche runs very smoothly and there's plenty of room for everyone."

"You must not disappoint Monsieur Sitnikov," Anna Sergeyevna interjected. . . .

Arcady glanced at her and bowed significantly.

The guests took their leave after breakfast. When saying farewell, Madame Odintzov held out her hand to Bazarov and said: "We shall see each other again, shan't we?"

"At your orders," Bazarov replied.

"In that case, we shall see each other."

Arcady was the first to go down the steps and to clamber into Sitnikov's barouche. While a servant was respectfully helping him to get in, Arcady could have thrashed him with the greatest of pleasure or have burst out crying. Then Bazarov took his seat in the tarantass. On reaching the Khokhlovsky settlement, Arcady waited while Fedot, the keeper of the posting-station, harnessed a fresh team of horses; walking up to the tarantass, he smiled as of old and said to Bazarov, "Eugene, do take me with you; I should like to visit your home."

"Get in," Bazarov growled through his teeth.

Sitnikov, who was pacing up and down and whistling cheerfully in the vicinity of the wheels of his barouche, could only gape when he heard these words and saw Arcady coolly retrieve his belongings, get in beside Bazarov and, with a polite bow to his former travelling-companion, shout, "Drive on!" The tarantass rolled away and soon vanished from sight. . . . Sitnikov stared hopelessly at his coachman, but the latter merely flicked his whip over the tail of the off-side horse. Then jumping into his barouche and shouting at a couple of peasants who happened to be passing by, "On with your caps, you idiots!" Sitnikov dragged himself off to town, where he arrived very late that night. The following day, at Madame Kukshin's house, he severely took to task a couple of "nasty and oafish pups."

On joining Bazarov in the tarantass, Arcady pressed his hand warmly and then a long silence ensued. Bazarov seemed to understand and value both the handshake and the silence. He had not slept a wink the whole of the previous night, and for some days past he had neither smoked nor eaten much.

His gaunt profile was sharply and grimly outlined beneath his cap, which was pressed well down over his forehead.

"Well, brother," he said at last, "give me a cigar. And by the way, is my tongue all coated?"

"Quite thickly," Arcady replied.

"I thought so . . . this cigar hasn't any taste. My mechanism has gone to pieces."

"You certainly have altered of late," Arcady remarked.

"Never mind! We'll get over it. I have only one thing on my mind—my mother is so fond of me that she worries to death if I don't grow a pot-belly and eat a dozen times a day. As for my father, he's got his feet on the ground, he's knocked about the world, through thick and thin. No," he added, throwing his cigar into the dusty road, "I must stop smoking."

"It's about sixteen miles to your estate, isn't it?" Arcady inquired.

"Yes, sixteen. But you'd better ask that sage," he said, pointing to the peasant in the driver's seat, one of Fedot's employees.

But the sage in question replied in this wise: "And who would be after knowing it?—the miles hereabouts are not measured." And having said that, he went on swearing in an undertone at the shaft horse for "kicking out with its headpiece"—in other words, for jerking its neck.

"Yes, yes," Bazarov began, "let this be a lesson to you,

my young friend, an instructive example of sorts. The devil take it, how absolutely absurd everything is! The life of each of us hangs by a thread, an abyss may gape beneath us any minute, and yet we go out of our way to cook up all sorts of trouble for ourselves and to mess up our lives."

"What are you driving at?" Arcady inquired.

"I'm not driving at anything, but let me tell you straight from the shoulder that we have been acting very stupidly. What's the point of talking about it! But my clinical observations have already led me to conclude that resistance is the only way of conquering pain."

"I don't quite get you," Arcady said. "It seems to me that you have nothing to complain about."

"If you don't quite get me, then let me tell you this: in my opinion, it's better to break paving-stones than to allow any woman to dominate as much as the tip of your little finger. That's all . . ." Bazarov was on the point of uttering his favourite word—"Romanticism," but he refrained and said instead: "Rubbish. You may not believe me, but it's quite clear that we were drawn into feminine society and found it agreeable; but to give up that society is as refreshing as a cold shower on a hot day. A man should have no time for such trifling: as the Spanish proverb says, 'A man must be ferocious.' Now what about you?" he added, turning to the peasant on the box. "You're a smart fellow; tell me, have you a wife?"

The peasant turned his flat and bleary-eyed face towards the friends.

"A wife, you say? I have one. How could it be otherwise?"

"Do you beat her?"

"The wife, you say? Anything can happen. But we don't beat her without cause."

"That's fine. We . . . and does she beat you?"

The peasant tugged at the reins. "Them's your words, master. You like your joke. . . ." He was evidently quite offended.

"You heard that, Arcady! But you and I have received a thrashing. . . . That's what comes of being so cultured."

Arcady uttered a forced laugh; Bazarov turned away and kept his mouth shut for the rest of the journey.

To Arcady the sixteen miles were more like thirty. But at last, at the foot of a slope, a small village came into view.

It was there that Bazarov's parents lived. Nearby, in the middle of a young birch-tree copse, a gentleman's small house could be perceived under a thatched roof. As they drove past the first of the cottages, they saw a couple of peasants with caps on standing outside and swearing at each other. "For an out-size swine," one of them said, "you're worse than any sucking-pig." "And your wife's a witch," retorted the other.

"By their free and easy ways," Bazarov remarked, "and by their playful turns of speech, you can guess that my father's peasants are not too ground down. And there he is himself coming out on the steps of the house. He must have heard the bells tinkling. It's he, it's he—I can tell him by his shape. Ay, ay! And yet how grey he's grown, poor old chap!"

XX

BAZAROV stuck his head out of the tarantass while Arcady, peering over his friend's head, caught sight of a tall, gaunt-looking individual with tousled hair and sharp aquiline nose standing on the steps of a small house, attired in an old unbuttoned military jacket. He stood there with legs wide apart, smoking a long pipe and squinting at the sun.

The horses came to a stop.

"Here you are at last," Bazarov's father exclaimed, still continuing to puff at his pipe although his trembling fingers could hardly hold the stem. "Now, out you get, out you get, let me embrace you."

He hugged his son again and again. . . .

"Enyusha, Enyusha," a woman's quavering voice rang out. The front door opened and a shortish, stoutish old lady came running down the steps, in a white cap and a brightly coloured blouse. She gave a cry, staggered, and would have fallen if Bazarov had not steadied her. Her plump little hands immediately clasped him round his neck, her head sank against his chest, and the ensuing silence was interrupted only by convulsive sobs.

Old Bazarov breathed heavily and squinted more than ever at the sun.

"Well, that's enough, that's enough, Arina! Stop it now," he exclaimed after exchanging glances with Arcady, who had remained standing motionless near the tarantass; even the peasant driver on his box-seat had turned away his head. "It's quite unnecessary! Do stop it, please!"

"Ah! Vassily Ivanich," the old woman quavered, "it's ages and ages since I've seen my little lord, my darling, my Enyushenka. . . ." And without unclasping her hands she drew away her face, which was all tear-stained, crumpled and melting with emotion; gazing at him again with eyes at once blissful and comic, she clasped her arms once more round his neck.

"Well, yes, of course, it's all very natural," said Vassily Ivanich, "but it would be better if we went in. Eugene has brought a guest. Excuse me," he added, turning to Arcady with a slight scrape of his foot, "but I'm sure you understand, a woman's frailty; yes, and a mother's heart too. . . ."

But his own lips and eyebrows were also twitching, and his chin trembled . . . he was evidently trying to master his emotions and to appear indifferent. Arcady bowed.

"Let's go in, mother, indeed let us," Bazarov said, conducting the old lady, who was overcome by the scene, into the house. Making her sit down in a comfortable arm-chair, he hastily embraced his father once more and then introduced Arcady to him.

"Heartily glad to make your acquaintance," Vassily Ivanich said, "but you mustn't expect too much: we lead a simple, soldierly life here. My dear Arina, do calm yourself, oblige me please: why show yourself so faint-hearted? Our gentleman visitor will form a poor opinion of you."

"My good sir," the old lady managed to stutter through her tears, "I have not the honour of knowing your name . . ."

"Arcady Nicolaievich," her husband prompted in a low but solemn voice.

"You must excuse me, I am a stupid old thing." The old lady blew her nose and bending her head now to the right, now to the left, wiped each eye thoroughly in turn. "You must excuse me. Why, I thought I'd die and never see my da . . . dar . . . ling again."

"Well, your patience has been rewarded, my dear lady,"

Vassily Ivanich took her up. "Tanyushka," he cried, turning to a barefooted girl of about thirteen in a bright red cotton dress, who was peeping from behind the door, "bring a glass of water for the lady—on a tray, do you hear? As for you, gentlemen," he added with a sort of old-fashioned play of civility, "allow me to invite you to pass into the study of a retired veteran."

"Let me embrace you just once more, Enyushenka," Arina Vlassyevna moaned. Bazarov stooped down. "What a handsome lad you've grown!"

"Handsome or not," Vassily Ivanich remarked, "but he looks a man all right—'om fay, as they say. And now, Arina Vlassyevna, I hope that, having satiated your maternal heart, you will take the trouble to satisfy our dear guests, because, as you must know very well, a nightingale cannot live only on fables."

The old lady got up from her arm-chair.

"The table will be laid in a minute, Vassily Ivanich. I shall run along to the kitchen myself and order the samovar to be got ready. We shall have everything, everything. Why, it's three years since I have seen him, since I have given him to eat and drink. It's not easy, is it?"

"Well, attend to it, my little housewife, get it all ready, and don't disgrace us; and as for you, gentlemen, I beg you to follow me. Ah, Eugene, here's Timofeyich coming to greet you. He's delighted too, I expect, the old poodle. What? You're glad, aren't you, you old poodle. Now, pray, follow me."

And Vassily Ivanich fussily led the way, shuffling and flapping along in his well-worn slippers.

His whole house consisted of six minute rooms. One of them—the room into which he conducted our friends—was called the study. The space between the two windows was entirely filled by a table on sturdy legs, heaped with papers that had turned black with ancient dust and looked as if they had been smoked. The walls were hung with Turkish flint-locks, whips, sabres, a couple of maps, a series of anatomical drawings, a portrait of Hufeland, a monogram woven from hair set in a black frame and a diploma under glass. A leather sofa, holed and torn in places, stood between two enormous cupboards of Karelian birch; the shelves were packed with a welter of books, little boxes, stuffed birds, jars, phials; a broken electric battery lay in one of the corners.

"I warned you, my dear guest," the father began, "we are living here, as it were, in a camp. . . ."

"Do stop apologizing all the time," Bazarov interrupted him. "Kirsanov knows very well that we are no Crœsuses and that you don't own a palace. Where shall we lodge him, that's the question?"

"That's no problem, Eugene; we have an excellent room in the wing: our guest will find it quite comfortable."

"So you've had a new wing put in?"

"Indeed we have—on the site of the bath-house," Timofeyich intervened.

"That's to say, next door to the bath-house," the father hastened to interject. "It's summer now. . . . I shall run along and see that everything is put in order; and you, Timofeyich, had better take charge of their baggage. As for you, Eugene, I shall of course let you have my study. *Suum cuique.*"

"Well, that's that! An amusing old man, a heart of gold," Bazarov said as soon as his father had gone out. "He is as eccentric as your father, but in a different way. He's a chatterbox."

"Your mother seems a wonderful woman," Arcady remarked.

"Yes, she has no wiles. Just wait and see what a spread she will give us."

"We were not expecting you to-day, master. We didn't get any beef," said Timofeyich, who had just brought in Bazarov's trunk.

"We can do without beef; 'one can't blame the innocent.' They say poverty is no crime."

"How many serfs does your father own?" Arcady suddenly inquired.

"The property is not his, but my mother's; as far as I remember, there are fifteen."

"Twenty-two in all," Timofeyich remarked with evident displeasure.

There was a sound of shuffling slippers and Vassily Ivanich reappeared on the scene.

"Your room will be ready to receive you in a few minutes," he exclaimed triumphantly. "Arcady . . . Nicolaievich, isn't that how you're pleased to be called? And here is your valet," he added, pointing to a lad who had just entered, dressed in a blue kaftan with ragged elbows and wearing someone else's boots.

"His name is Fedka. Although my son forbids it, I must ask you again not to expect too much. However, the lad can fill a pipe. You smoke, don't you?"

"I usually prefer cigars," Arcady replied.

"How very sensible of you. My preference also goes to cigars, but it's extremely difficult to procure them in these remote parts."

"Stop playing Lazarus," Bazarov again interrupted him. "You'd better sit down here on the sofa and let me have a look at you."

Vassily Ivanich laughed and sat down. His face closely resembled his son's, only the forehead was lower and narrower, the mouth a trifle broader, and he seemed always in motion, perpetually shrugging his shoulders as though his suit were too tight for him under the armpits, blinking his eyes, coughing and twitching his fingers, whereas a certain air of detached immobility was his son's distinguishing trait.

"Play Lazarus!" Vassily Ivanich repeated. "Don't imagine, Eugene, that I wish, as it were, to excite our guest's compassion by complaining of our life here in the wilds. On the contrary, I am of the opinion that no wilds can exist for any thinking person. At least, I do my best, as far as I can, not to grow stale, as they say, and to keep up with the times."

From his pocket Vassily Ivanich pulled out a new yellow silk handkerchief, which he had managed to pick up while running to attend to Arcady's room. Fanning himself with it, he went on: "I am not referring now to the fact that, at some sacrifice to myself, I have established my peasants on a rent-paying system and have transferred my land to them on a profit-sharing basis. I consider that I have done no more than my duty as dictated by common sense, although plenty of other landowners don't even dream of attempting it. But I am speaking now of the sciences, of education."

"Yes, I notice you have a copy of the *Friend of Health* for 1855," Bazarov remarked.

"An old comrade of mine sends them to me for old times' sake," Vassily Ivanich hastily replied. "But to give you an example, we are not without some knowledge of phrenology," he added, speaking more for the benefit of Arcady and pointing to a small plaster head divided up into squares, which was standing on the top of the cupboard. "Even Shönlein has not remained unknown to us—and Rademacher."

"Is Rademacher still regarded as an authority in this province?" Bazarov asked.

Vassily Ivanich coughed. "In the provinces . . . Of course, you know better, gentlemen; how is one to keep up with you? You are here to succeed us. In my day some *humoralist* like Hoffman, some Brown with his *vitalism*—they all seemed quite ridiculous, and yet they too had made a lot of noise in their time. Now someone has taken Rademacher's place in your estimation, and you worship him, but in twenty years' time he will very likely also be a laughing-stock."

"Let me tell you by way of consolation," Bazarov retorted, "that we now laugh at medicine as a whole, and worship no one."

"How can that be? But you intend to become a doctor, don't you?"

"I do, but there is no contradiction involved."

With his middle finger Vassily Ivanich poked about in his pipe, which still contained a little hot ash. "Well, that may be, that may be—I will not dispute it. For who am I? A retired army doctor, *voyla-too,* now turned agronomist. Yes, I served in your father's brigade," he added, turning again to Arcady. "Yes, yes—I have seen many sights in my day. And what circles have I not moved in! What people have I not met! I—the person you are pleased to see before you—I felt Prince Wittgenstein's pulse and Zhukovsky's too! All those people who were with the southern army in the 1814, you know" (hereupon the old doctor pursed his lips significantly), "I knew them all without exception. Yes, but my job was very lop-sided: to be proficient with the lancet, that's all there was to it! Now your grandfather was a very honourable man, a real soldier."

"Come, come, confess he was a first-class blockhead," Bazarov said lazily.

"Ah, Eugene, how can you say such things! Do be considerate. . . . Of course, General Kirsanov was not one of . . ."

"Well, drop him then," Bazarov interrupted him. "As I was driving here, I was very pleased to see your birch-plantation. It has sprouted beautifully."

Vassily Ivanich grew animated. "You must see the garden now! I planted each tree myself. We have fruit-trees, raspberry canes and all sorts of medicinal herbs. However clever you young gentlemen may think your-selves, old Paracelsus put his finger on the truth: *in herbis, verbis et lapidibus*. . . . As you know, I gave up my practice, but a couple of times a week I am obliged to revert to my old pastime. Folk will come for consultation—I can't drive them away. Sometimes a poor man will ask for help. There are no other doctors in the locality. One of our neighbours —just imagine it—a retired major, goes about healing too. I made some inquiries about him: had he studied medicine? They told me, 'No, he hasn't studied, but he does it for the sake of philanthropy.' . . . Ha, ha, ha—for the sake of philanthropy! Ah? Now what do you think of that? Ha, ha, ha!"

"Fedka, fill my pipe for me!" Bazarov said sternly.

"We have another doctor here who once came to visit a patient," Vassily Ivanich went on in a sort of despairing way, "and the patient was already *ad patres*; the servant would not let the doctor in since there was no longer any need for him. The doctor did not expect this and, in his confusion, inquired: 'Tell me, did your master hiccup before he died?' 'Yes, he did.' 'And did he hiccup a lot?' 'Quite a lot.' 'Well, that's fine!' he exclaimed and went off. Ha, ha, ha!"

The old man was alone to laugh; Arcady just managed a smile. Bazarov only puffed at his pipe. The conversation continued in this wise for about an hour; Arcady had time to pay a visit to his room, which turned out to be the ante-room of the bath-house, but it was very cosy and clean. At last Tanyusha came in to announce that the dinner was served.

Vassily Ivanich was the first to get up. "Come along, gentlemen! You must be indulgent to me if I have bored you. Perhaps my good wife will give you better satis-faction."

The dinner, though hastily prepared, turned out to be

excellent and even abundant; only the wine was a trifle dubious, as they say: the almost black sherry, which Timofeyich had bought in town from a merchant of his acquaintance, tasted slightly of copper or resin; and the flies also were a pest. Usually the servant boy chased them away with a leafy branch; but on this occasion the host had sent him away for fear of being misjudged by the younger generation. The mistress of the house had had time to change; she had donned a high cap ornamented with silk ribbons and a pale-blue flowered shawl. On catching sight of her Enyusha, she burst into tears again; but there was no need for her husband to chide her, for she wiped away her tears promptly to avoid staining her shawl. The young men were alone to eat, for the old folk had already dined. Fedka waited at table, obviously encumbered by his unfamiliar boots, and was assisted by a woman of masculine looks, who went by the name of Anfisushka and fulfilled the duties of housekeeper, pantry-maid and washerwoman. Throughout the dinner Vassily Ivanich marched up and down the room and, with a happy and even blissful expression on his face, talked about the grave anxieties roused in him by Napoleon III's policy and the complications of the Italian question. Bazarov's mother paid no attention to Arcady and did not even press him to eat more; with her tiny fist propping her rounded face, to which her puffy little cherry-tinted lips and the moles on her cheeks imparted a very benign expression, she glued her eyes on her son and sighed continuously; she was desperately anxious to learn how long he intended to stay, but was afraid to ask him. "And what if he should say, 'I've come for two days only,'" she thought to herself, and her heart would stop beating. After the roast Vassily Ivanich disappeared for an instant and then returned with an uncorked bottle of champagne.

"Here!" he exclaimed, "even though we do live in the wilds, yet we always have something special in reserve for festive occasions!" He filled three large glasses and a smaller one, proposed a toast to "our invaluable guests," and emptied his glass at one draught in the military fashion. He forced his wife to drink her little glass to the very last drop. When the turn of the jam came, Arcady, who as a rule could not bear anything sweet, nevertheless deemed it his duty to taste four different kinds of freshly made jam. He did this also because Bazarov had bluntly refused to try them and had at once lit a cigar. Then the tea was brought, with cream, butter and cracknels: afterwards the old man led them out into the garden so that they might admire the beauty of the evening. As they passed a certain bench, he whispered to Arcady: "On this spot I love to philosophize, gazing at the sunset: it becomes a recluse. And over there I have planted several trees so greatly favoured by Horace."

"What are the trees?" inquired Bazarov, who had overheard.

"Why . . . acacias."

Bazarov began to yawn.

"I suppose it is time for the weary travellers to fall into the embraces of Morpheus," Vassily Ivanich remarked.

"You mean it's time for us to sleep," Bazarov retorted. "A very just remark that. It is time, indeed it is."

Bidding his mother good night, he kissed her on the forehead, while she hugged him and blessed him thrice stealthily behind his back. Vassily Ivanich conducted Arcady to his room and wished him "such sweet repose as I also have enjoyed in the flower of my youth." And, indeed, Arcady slept excellently in his bath-house anteroom: the place smelt of mint, and two crickets behind the stove competed with each other in drowsy chirping. On leaving Arcady, Vassily Ivanich went into the study where, curling himself up on the sofa at his son's feet, he prepared to have a chat with him: but Bazarov sent him away at once, saying that he felt sleepy, though actually he did not fall asleep until the early morning. With eyes wide open he glared banefully into the gloom; childhood memories had no hold over him and, besides, he had not yet succeeded in shaking off his last bitter impressions. As for his mother, she first of all prayed her fill; afterwards, she spent a long while chatting with Anfisushka who stood in front of her mistress, like a person rooted to the ground, with her one and only eye fixed on her, imparting in a whisper all her impressions and notions regarding the young master. The old mother's head was spinning with joy, wine and cigar smoke; her husband made an attempt to converse with her, but soon, with a hopeless gesture, gave it up as a bad job.

Arina Vlassyevna was a genuine Russian gentlewoman of the old school; she might have lived some two centuries back, in the old days of Muscovy. Very devout and impressionable, she believed in all sorts of omens, fortune-telling, charms and dreams; she believed in the visions of mad prophets, in spirits, in wood-sprites, in the evil eye, in spells, in folk remedies, on "Thursday salt," and in the imminent end of the world; she believed that, if the candles failed to go out at vespers on Easter Sunday, a good crop of buckwheat would result, and that mushrooms stopped growing when seen by the human eye; she believed that water was the devil's haunt, and that every Jew had a bloody mark on his breast. She was afraid of mice, adders, frogs, sparrows, leeches, thunder, cold water, draughts, horses, goats, ginger-haired people and black cats, and deemed crickets and dogs unclean creatures; she ate no veal or pigeon, crayfish or cheese, asparagus or Jerusalem artichokes, hare or, finally, water melon, because a sliced water melon reminded her of John the Baptist's head. The mere mention of oysters made her shudder; she loved food but also kept strict fasts; she slept ten hours out of twenty-four—and did not go to bed at all when her husband happened to have a headache. She read no book except *Alexisa, or the Hut in the Forest*; she wrote one, never more than two, letters a year, but she knew all about housekeeping, preserving fruit and jam-making, although she did not touch anything with her own hands and disliked moving about. Arina Bazarov was very kind of heart and, in her own way, not at all stupid. She was convinced that the gentry were there to give orders and the common people to obey them—and so she felt no repugnance at the sight of servility and obsequience; but she was always mild and gentle with those who served her, no beggar was allowed to pass by without receiving alms and, although at times she was inclined to gossip, she never criticized anyone. In her youth she had been very comely, had played the clavichord and prattled a little in French; but in the course of many years of peregrination with her husband, whom she had married against her will, she had grown stout and forgotten both her music and her French. Her son she both loved and feared to an incredible degree; and as for her estate, she let her husband manage it and never interfered with him: she merely moaned and waved her handkerchief, while her brows shot up higher and higher in alarm, whenever the old man broached the subject of the imminent land reforms and his projects. She was very apprehensive, lived in constant expectation of some great misfortune about to befall them, and burst out sobbing whenever she happened to recall any sorrow. . . . In our time, women like her have grown rare. God alone knows whether that is a matter for rejoicing.

XXI

GETTING out of bed, Arcady flung the window wide open, and Vassily Ivanich was the first object to catch his eye. Wearing a dressing-gown of Bokhara silk, fastened round the waist with a handkerchief, the old man was busily digging in the orchard. Perceiving the young guest and leaning on his spade, he exclaimed: "The best of health! Did you have a good night's rest?"

"Indeed, I had," Arcady replied.

"As you can see, here I am like some Cincinnatus, knocking up a bed for the late turnips. Such are the times we live in—and thank God for that!—each one of us has to provide for his nourishment with his own hands; it's no use relying on others—one must labour oneself. It turns out that Jean-Jacques Rousseau was right. Half an hour ago, my dear sir, you would have seen me in quite a different posture. I had a peasant woman here who complained of 'gripes'—that's what they call it, dysentery is the term we would use, and there was I . . . how shall I put it best? . . . there was I pumping opium into her; I also pulled out a tooth for another woman. I offered to give her an anæsthetic . . . but she wouldn't have it. All that I did gratis—*in amature*. However, I am quite used to that; for I am a plebeian, *homo novus*—not out of Debrett, like my dear spouse. . . . Wouldn't you like to join me here, in the shade, and breathe the morning freshness before breakfast?"

Arcady joined him.

"Welcome once more!" Vassily Ivanich exclaimed, raising his hand to his greasy skull-cap in a military salute. "I know you are accustomed to luxury and pleasure, but the great ones of this world would not disdain to spend a short time under a humble roof."

"Good Heavens," Arcady protested. "What sort of a great personage of the world do you take me for? Nor am I accustomed to luxury."

"I beg to differ," Vassily Ivanich retorted with an amiable grimace. "Although I am already filed away in the archives, I have had some experience of the world—I can spot a bird by the way it flies. In my own way, I am also a psychologist and a physiognomist too. If I had not possessed that gift—if so I may call it—I would have been a failure long ago; they would have just trodden on an insignificant man like me. Let me tell you, compliments apart, that I am sincerely glad of the friendship which I have noted between you and my son. I have just seen him; according to his habit, one you very likely know, he was up very early and off into the country. If you don't mind my curiosity, may I ask if you have known my Eugene long?"

"Since the winter."

"I see. May I also inquire . . . but won't you sit down? May I also inquire, as a father, quite frankly, what is your opinion of my Eugene?"

"Your son is one of the most remarkable men I have ever met," Arcady replied with feeling.

Vassily Ivanich's eyes suddenly opened wide and a faint blush spread over his cheeks. The spade dropped out of his hands.

"So, you suppose . . ." he began.

"I am convinced," Arcady took him up, "that a great future awaits your son, that he will make your name famous. I was sure of that as soon as I met him."

"And how . . . how did you meet him?" Vassily Ivanich inquired, hardly able to speak. A smile of delight had parted his lips and stayed there.

"You would like me to tell you how we met?"

"Yes . . . and moreover . . ."

Arcady launched on an account of their meeting and talked of Bazarov with even greater warmth and enthusiasm than on the evening when he had danced a mazurka with Madame Odintzov.

Vassily Ivanich was all ears, he listened, blew his nose, with both hands rolled his handkerchief into a ball, coughed, ruffled his hair—and, finally, unable to restrain himself any longer stooped and kissed Arcady on the shoulder.

"You have made me perfectly happy," he said, smiling all the while. "I must tell you that I . . . I worship my son; as for my old woman, there is no need even to mention it: she is the mother, of course!—but I dare not show my feelings in his presence, because he dislikes it. He is an enemy to all expressions of emotion; many people even criticize him for this firmness of character and interpret it as a sign of arrogance or insensibility; but men like him should not be measured with a common yardstick, should they now? Here is an example: in his place another would have drawn and drawn on his parents; but would you believe it, he never took a penny too much from us from the day he was born, and that's God's truth!"

"He is quite unselfish and honest," Arcady remarked.

"Yes, exactly, unselfish. But I not only worship him, I am also proud of him, and the whole of my vanity comes to this, that in due course I should like to see the following written in his biography: 'The son of an army doctor who, however, was able to understand him early in life and who spared nothing for his education. . . .' " The old man's voice quavered.

Arcady pressed his hand.

"Now what do you think?" Vassily Ivanich asked him after a pause. "It will not be in the field of medicine that he will attain the fame you prophesy for him?"

"Of course not, although his will be one of the great minds in that field."

"What will be his particular field then, Arcady?"

"It is hard to tell yet, but he is bound to be famous."

"Bound to be famous?" the old man repeated, falling into a reverie.

"Arina Vlassyevna sends me to tell you breakfast is served," Anfisushka called out as she passed them, carrying a great big dish of ripe raspberries.

Vassily Ivanich came to life.

"Will there be any cold cream with the raspberries?"

"Yes, plenty of cream."

"Make sure it's put on ice! Don't stand on ceremony, do help yourself to the raspberries. I wonder why Eugene isn't back yet."

"I am here," Bazarov's voice rang out, coming from Arcady's room.

His father spun quickly round.

"Aha! You called on your friend, but you were too late, *amice*. I have already been having a long chat with him. Now we must go in and have breakfast: mother is calling us. Incidentally, I must have a word with you."

"What about?"

"We have a peasant here who suffers from *icterus*. . . ."

"You mean jaundice?"

"Yes, a chronic and very persistent *icterus*. I have prescribed centaury and St. John's wort, I have made him eat carrots and given him soda; but these are merely palliative measures: something more drastic is required. I know you laugh at medicine, but I'm pretty sure you will be able to give me some sound advice. But we must talk of that later. And now let's go in and have tea."

Leaping nimbly from the bench, Vassily Ivanich started to hum an air from *Robert le Diable*:

A law, a law, a law let's make
To live . . . to live for joy and pleasure!

"What remarkable vitality!" Bazarov said to himself, moving away from the window.

Midday came. From behind a diaphanous curtain of spreading whitish clouds, the sun was scorching. Everything was still: only the cocks crowed lustily in the village, exciting a strange sensation of drowsiness and boredom in all who heard them; and somewhere high up above, in the tree-tops, throbbed the querulous and persistent squeaking of a young hawk. Arcady and Bazarov lay stretched out in the shade of a small hayrick; beneath them they had strewn two or three armfuls of grass that was still green and fragrant though it rustled drily.

"That poplar," Bazarov remarked, "reminds me of my childhood; it grows on the edge of a pit, which is all that remains of the brick shed, and at the time I was convinced that both the pit and the poplar had the powers of a talisman; in their vicinity I was never bored. I failed to understand then that I was not bored just because I was a child. Well, now that I'm grown up, the talisman has lost its charm."

"How long were you here in all?" Arcady inquired.

"Two years running. Then we had our fill of travelling. We led a vagabond sort of life; we mostly traipsed from town to town."

"And has this house been long built?"

"Yes, quite a time. My maternal grandfather had it put up."

"And what was your grandfather?"

"The devil only knows. An army major of sorts. He served under Suvorov, and was always telling us how he had crossed the Alps. No doubt he was making it up."

"That explains the portrait of Suvorov in the drawing-room. I like small houses, such as yours—they are old and warm; and they have a peculiar smell of their own."

"Yes, they're saturated with lamp-oil and clover," Bazarov replied with a yawn. "And the quantities of flies these dear little houses breed . . . Ugh!"

"Tell me," Arcady resumed after a short pause, "you were not badly treated as a child, were you?"

"You have seen my parents," Bazarov replied. "They are not very strict."

"Do you love them, Eugene?"

"Yes, I do, Arcady!"

"They love you greatly!"

Bazarov made no rejoinder for a while. "Do you know what I am thinking?" he asked at last, clasping his hands behind his head.

"No, I don't. What is it?"

"I'm thinking of the happy life they lead! At sixty father is always busy. He talks of 'palliative' measures, treats patients, is generous to the peasants—in short, he is making quite a spree of his old age; and mother has a good time too: her days are so crammed with all sorts of little jobs, sighs and groans, that she never has time to stop and think; but as for me . . ."

"As for you?"

"I keep racking my brains: now here I am lying under this hayrick. . . . The confined space I occupy is so minute when compared with the rest of the universe, where I am not and have no business to be; and the fraction of time I shall live is so infinitesimal when contrasted with eternity, in which I have never been and never shall be. . . . And yet here, in this atom of myself, in this mathematical point, blood circulates, the brain is active, aspiring to something too. . . . What a monstrous thing! How absurd it seems!"

"Allow me to point out," Arcady retorted, "that what you say applies generally to all men . . ."

"Quite right," Bazarov interrupted him. "All I wanted to say was that they, my parents, that is, have their minds occupied and do not worry about their own insignificance. It does not stink in their nostrils . . . while I . . . I feel only bored and angry."

"Angry? Why angry?"

"Why? Why need you ask me? Have you forgotten?"

"I remember everything, but, at the same time, I do not admit that you have the right to be angry. You are unhappy, I agree, but . . ."

"Ah! I can see, Arcady, that your idea of love is no different from that of all the other young men of the new generation: 'Cluck, cluck, cluck, my little hen,' you all exclaim, but when the 'little hen' begins to strut towards you, then you all take to your heels! I am not made like that. But enough. It's a shame to chatter about what can't be helped." He turned over on his side. "Aha! There's a lusty fellow of an ant dragging a dying fly. Drag it along, brother, drag it along! Take notice of her resistance, take every advantage of the fact that, as an insect, you have the right to feel no compassion—unlike us, poor self-divided brethren!"

"You can hardly call yourself that, Eugene!" Arcady exclaimed. "When did you become 'divided'?"

Bazarov raised his head.

"That's the one thing I'm really proud of. I am not 'divided' and no female can break me either. Amen! Full stop! I shan't refer to the subject again."

The friends lay for a while in silence.

"Yes," Bazarov began, "man is a strange creature. When you observe in a detached sort of way the remote life these 'old folk' lead here, it could not seem better. It's eat, drink and be sure you do the right thing in the right way. But it's not really like that; one would only get bored if it were. There is also the need we feel for bothering about other people, even if we do no more than swear at them or suffer them to importune us."

"Life should be so arranged that every moment of it can

be packed with significance," Arcady remarked thoughtfully.

"That's all very well! Significance is sweet, even though it may be false; but we can also come to terms with the insignificant. . . . But all this tittle-tattle, all this petty wrangling, that's the trouble."

"All this wrangling would stop if men refused to admit it."

"H'm . . . you have just uttered an *inverted platitude.*"

"What?" Arcady cried out. "What do you mean?"

"Just this: to say, for example that education is useful is a platitude; but to say that education is harmful is an inverted platitude. It sounds more dashing, but in essence it comes to the same thing."

"But where is truth? On which side?"

"Where? Like an echo, I shall answer where?"

"What a despondent mood you're in to-day, Eugene."

"You don't say so? I've been out in the sun too long, and shouldn't have eaten so many raspberries."

"In that case, it wouldn't be a bad idea to have a nap," Arcady remarked.

"Maybe. But don't stare at me, we all look silly when asleep."

"And do you mind what people think of you?"

"I don't quite know what to reply. A real man does not worry about that; for people do not need to have opinions about a real man; he must either be obeyed or hated."

"Very strange! I don't hate anyone," Arcady replied after a moment's reflection.

"And I hate lots of people. You have a tender wishy-washy heart. Hatred is not in your line. . . . You're timid and have no confidence in yourself. . . ."

"And you?" Arcady interrupted him. "Have you confidence in yourself? Have you such a high opinion of yourself?"

Bazarov remained silent.

"When I meet a man who will not wilt before me," he said with measured deliberation, "then my opinion of myself will change. Hatred! Now here is an example: this morning when you passed the house of Philip, the village bailiff, you remarked: 'What a pleasant, neat-looking house.' And you went on to say: 'Russia will reach perfection when every peasant will own a house like that, and each of us must help to that end. . . .' But I've developed a hatred for that 'every peasant,' that Philip or Sidor, for whose sake I must crawl out of my skin and who will not even thank me for it. . . . And why do I need his thanks? Well, just imagine him living in his neat-looking house while I shall be sprouting weeds. What comes after?"

"Don't go on like that, Eugene. . . . To hear you talking to-day leaves me no alternative but to agree with those who reproach us for having no principles."

"You're talking just like your uncle. There are no principles in general—you haven't tumbled to that yet! There are only sensations. Everything depends on them."

"How's that?"

"Just so. Now take me, for example: my negative attitude is the result of my sensations. If I find pleasure in denying, it's because my brain is so constructed—and that is all there is to it! Why do *I* like chemistry? Why do *you* like apples? Precisely because of our particular sensations. There is a connexion between them. And mankind will never succeed in probing deeper than that. It isn't everyone could tell you that, and next time I shan't tell you as much."

"Not tell me? And is honesty a sensation too?"

"Obviously!"

"Eugene!" Arcady exclaimed sorrowfully. . . .

"Well? What is it? Not to your taste, eh?" Bazarov interrupted him. "No, brother! Once you have made up your mind to scythe, why, you must scythe your very feet from under you! . . . However, we have philosophized quite enough. As Pushkin said, 'Nature wafts upon us the silence of sleep.' "

"He never said anything of the sort," Arcady retorted.

"Well, even if he didn't, as a poet he might and should have said it. Incidentally, he must have served in the army."

"Pushkin was never in the army!"

"Really? But on every page he has, 'Into battle, into battle! For the honour of Russia!' "

"That's pure invention on your part! A downright slander!"

"Slander? As if that mattered! What a word you've picked on to frighten me! However much slander you may heap on a person, he really deserves twenty times as much."

"We'd better have a snooze!" Arcady replied sadly.

"With the greatest of pleasure," Bazarov replied. But neither of them felt like sleeping. A feeling of hostility almost seethed in the young men's hearts. Within five minutes they opened their eyes and exchanged silent glances.

"Look!" Arcady suddenly exclaimed. "A withered maple leaf has left its branch and is falling to the ground; its movements resemble those of a butterfly in flight. Isn't it strange? The saddest and deadest of all things is yet so like the gayest and most vital of creatures."

"Oh, my dearest friend Arcady!" Bazarov cried. "One thing I entreat you; don't talk so beautifully."

"I talk as best I can. . . . Why, that's sheer despotism. If a thought occurs to me, why shouldn't I express it?"

"That's so. But why shouldn't I express my thoughts too? In my opinion, it's indecent to talk beautifully."

"What is decent then? To abuse people?"

"Oho! I can see you're determined to follow in your uncle's footsteps. How that idiot would rejoice if he heard you!"

"What did you call Uncle Paul?"

"I called him an idiot, as was fitting."

"But this is becoming unbearable!" Arcady exclaimed.

"Aha! Your family feelings are manifesting themselves," Bazarov remarked calmly. "I have noticed how very firmly they are embedded in people. Man seems ready to reject everything, to give up every prejudice; but he cannot bear to admit, for instance, that a brother of his, who steals other people's handkerchiefs, is a thief. And let's face it, we do find it incredible, don't we, that any brother of mine, that my brother, should turn out to be no genius?"

"I spoke from a sense of justice and out of no family feeling," Arcady protested hotly. "But since you do not understand that feeling, since you lack that *sensation,* you are incapable of judging it."

"In other words, Arcady Kirsanov is too elevated for my understanding: I am to bow to him and keep mum."

"Shut up, Eugene, please; or we shall end by quarrelling."

"Ah, Arcady! Do me a favour, let's quarrel thoroughly —go the full hog, to the point of annihilation. . . ."

"If we go on like this, we may end up by . . ."

"By fighting?" Bazarov interjected. "What of it? Here, in the hay, in these idyllic surroundings, far from the world and the ken of people—it wouldn't be too bad. But you wouldn't be able to stand up to me. . . . Just wait till I get a grip on your throat. . . ."

Bazarov stretched out his long, tough fingers. . . . Arcady turned round and got ready, as though in fun, to defend himself. . . . But in his friend's face he surprised such a malevolent expression, in his crookedly smiling lips and glinting eyes such a serious threat, that he instinctively felt uneasy. . . .

"Ah, that's where you've got to!" Vassily Ivanich's voice rang out at that instant, and the old army doctor presented himself before the young men, in a homespun linen jacket and a straw hat, also of home-make. "I've been looking for you everywhere, everywhere. . . . But you have picked on an excellent spot and are engaged in a fine occupation. 'Lying on the ground, gazing at the sky. . . .' Do you know —there is something particularly significant in that!"

"I only look at the sky when I feel like sneezing," Bazarov growled and, turning to Arcady, he added in a low voice: "A pity he interfered."

"Shut up," Arcady whispered back, pressing his friend's hand stealthily. "No friendship could bear such strain for long."

"When I look at you, my young friends," Vassily Ivanich said, shaking his head and leaning forward with hands clasped on a cunningly wrought stick of his own handiwork, with the figure of a Turk carved on it by way of a knob, "when I look at you, I can't help admiring you. What strength and flowering youth! How many abilities and talents! Why, the two of you might be . . . Castor and Pollux!"

"There you go—plunging into mythology again!" his son exclaimed. "One can tell at once that you were a Latin scholar in your day! Why, if I remember rightly, you were awarded a silver medal for a Latin composition, weren't you?"

"The *Dioscuri*, the *Dioscuri*!" Vassily Ivanich repeated.

"Enough, father. Don't be sentimental."

"I can allow myself this every once in a while," the old man muttered. "However, gentlemen, I did not seek you out in order to pay you compliments, but, firstly, to announce to you that dinner will soon be ready, and secondly, to warn you, Eugene. . . . You are a man of the world and a judge of people, and you know women too . . . so you must be charitable. . . . Your mother wishes to have a thanksgiving mass celebrated on the occasion of your arrival. Don't imagine that I'm asking you to assist at the mass—it's already over; but Father Alexei . . ."

"Oh, the ecclesiastic?"

"Well, yes, the priest; he is going to be . . . at dinner. . . . I did not expect it and even advised against it . . . but somehow or other that's the way it's happened . . . he would not take the hint. . . . Well, and there was your mother too. . . . And besides, he is a very good and reasonable man."

"I presume he won't eat my portion of the dinner, will he?" Bazarov asked.

"Heavens, what a thing to say!" Vassily Ivanich laughed.

"That's all I ask. I am quite prepared to sit at table with any man."

Vassily Ivanich set his hat straight.

"I was sure in advance," he said, "that you were above prejudice. And here am I—an old man, still alive in my sixty-second year, and I haven't any prejudices either" (Bazarov's father did not dare to admit that he also had wished to have the mass celebrated. . . . He was not a whit less devout than his wife). "And Father Alexei very much wants to make your acquaintance. You will like him, you'll see. He is not against playing a game of cards either, and he is even . . . but let this go no further . . . he is even not averse from smoking a pipe."

"Well, in that case, we'll settle down to a game of whist after dinner, and I'll trounce him."

"Ha, ha, ha! We shall see! Two can play at that game!"

"You don't mean you're going to have a fling as you were in the habit of doing once?"

A blush of confusion spread over Vassily Ivanich's bronzed cheeks.

"Shame on you, Eugene. . . . Let sleeping dogs lie. Well, I am quite ready to confess in front of your friend that I was addicted to that passion in my youth—indeed, I was; and didn't I have to pay for it! However, how hot it is. May I sit down beside you? I'm not in the way, am I?"

"Of course not," Arcady replied.

With creaking limbs, Vassily Ivanich sank down into the hay.

"Your present billet, my dear sirs," he began, "reminds me of my camping days in the army; the field hospitals were also pitched near some hayrick, and that was something to thank God for." He sighed. "I have had a great deal of experience, a very great deal of it in my time. Thus, for instance, let me tell you, if you will allow, a very curious episode during the plague in Bessarabia."

"For which you were awarded the order of St. Vladimir?" Bazarov interposed. "We know, we know. . . . Incidentally, why do you never wear it?"

"But I told you that I have no prejudices," Vassily Ivanich muttered (only the day before he had given orders for the red ribbon to be removed from his jacket). Then he began to describe the episode of the plague. "Why, he's fallen asleep," he suddenly whispered, with a kindly wink, pointing to his son.

"Eugene! Get up," he added loudly. "It's time for dinner. . . ."

Father Alexei, a stout and imposing personage with thick, carefully brushed hair and an embroidered sash girding his mauve silk cassock, turned out to be a very adroit and resourceful man. He took the initiative in hastening to shake hands with both Arcady and Bazarov, comprehending in advance that they had no need of his blessing, and in general he conducted himself without any reserve. Never betraying himself, he managed also to avoid treading on other people's toes; at the right moment he made a joke about Latin as taught in the seminaries and said a word in favour of his bishop; he drank two glasses of wine, but declined a third; he accepted a cigar from Arcady, but abstained from smoking it, saying that he would take it home with him. His only none-too-pleasant feature was the slow and careful gesture he made with his hand when he tried to catch the flies that settled on his face, in the process sometimes crushing them. He took his seat at the green baize table with a moderate show of pleasure, but ended by winning two roubles and fifty kopecks in currency notes from Bazarov: in Arina Vlassyevna's house they had not yet learnt how to reckon in silver. . . .

As usual, she sat near Bazarov (she did not play cards herself), with her fist as ever propping her cheek; she got up only when it was necessary to give an order for some fresh delicacy to be served. She was afraid of showing her fondness for Bazarov, and he did not encourage her to do so; he did not seek endearments from her, and as a result the father had advised her not to "disturb" their son too much. "Young men are not very keen on that sort of thing," he kept repeating to her. There is no need to enlarge on the sort of dinner that was served that day: Timofeyich had employed himself personally at daybreak to drive off in search of some extra special Circassian beef; the steward had driven off elsewhere for turbot, perch and crayfish; for the mushrooms alone the peasant women raked in forty-two kopecks in copper. But Arina Vlassyevna's eyes, which she could not tear away from her son, wore an expression not only of tenderness and devotion; one could also spy in them a shade of sorrow mingled with curiosity and fear; and there lurked, too, a look of resigned reproach.

However, Bazarov was in no mood to probe the significance of his mother's expression; he addressed her but rarely, and then only to ask some brief question. Once he asked her to give him her hand "for luck"; quietly she slipped her soft little hand into his rough and broad palm.

"Well," she inquired after a while, "did it not help?"

"I had worse luck than ever," he replied with a careless smile.

Meanwhile the game of whist was in progress.

"What big risks they do take!" Father Alexei exclaimed in a tone of feigned regret, stroking his handsome beard.

"It's the Napoleonic rule, Father, the Napoleonic rule," Vassily Ivanich interjected, slamming down an ace.

"It brought him to St. Helena," Father Alexei retorted, playing a trump.

"Would you like a little black-currant juice, Enyushicka?" Arina Vlassyevna asked her son.

But he merely shrugged his shoulders.

"No!" he said to Arcady next day. "To-morrow I shall leave this place. I'm bored. I feel like work but I can't work here. I shall go to your part of the country again; I left all my equipment there. In your house I can at least lock myself in. But here, although my father keeps assuring me, 'My study is at your disposal—no one will interrupt you,' he will dog my steps. And I get an uneasy conscience when I lock myself in from him. And mother too. I can hear her sighing next door, and whenever I go out to her, I find I have nothing to say."

"She will be very upset," Arcady replied, "and he too."

"But I shall come back to them."

"When?"

"Oh, on my way to Petersburg."

"I am particularly sorry for your mother."

"Why? Has she won you over with her raspberries and black-currants?"

Arcady looked down at his feet.

"You don't know your mother, Eugene. She's not only a fine character, but also really intelligent. This morning she talked to me for half an hour, and all she said was both interesting and to the point."

"No doubt she was enlarging about me all the time?"

"You were not the only subject of conversation."

"Maybe. As a detached observer you can see more clearly. It's a good sign when a woman can keep up a conversation for half an hour. But I shall depart all the same."

"It won't be so easy for you to break the news to them. They are still discussing plans for us a fortnight ahead."

"I know it won't be easy. Some devil prompted me to tease my father this morning: he gave orders a few days ago to have one of his rent-bound peasants flogged—and an excellent thing too. Yes, yes, don't look at me with such horror—an excellent thing too, because the peasant in question is a most frightful thief and drunkard; but father did not expect that I, as they say, should become acquainted with the facts. It threw him into great confusion, and now I must give him another shock. . . . It can't be helped! Anyway, the wound will heal in time!"

Although Bazarov had said, "It can't be helped!" a whole day passed before he made up his mind to inform his father of his intention. Finally, as he was bidding him good night in his study, he said with a drawn-out yawn:

"Yes . . . I almost forgot to tell you. . . . Will you order our horses to be sent to Fedot's as relays?"

Vassily Ivanich was astounded.

"Is Mr. Kirsanov leaving us then?"

"Yes, and I am going with him."

The old man was completely nonplussed.

"You are going away?" he stuttered.

"Yes. . . . I must go. Will you please see to the horses?"

"Very well. . . ." The old man quavered. "For the relay . . . very well . . . only . . . only . . . Why must you?"

"I must visit the Kirsanovs for a short while. And then I shall come back again."

"Yes! For a short while. . . . Very well." Vassily Ivanich

pulled out his handkerchief and, after blowing his nose, bowed down almost to the ground. "Well? That . . . all that will come to pass. I thought you would stay with us . . . a little longer. Three days. . . . After three years that's . . . that's very little, very little, Eugene!"

"But I assure you that I shall be back very soon. It's essential for me to go."

"Essential. . . . Well? One must do one's duty, first of all. . . . So, we'll have to send the horses? Very well. Your mother and I, of course, did not expect this. She has just procured some fresh flowers, to make your room brighter." (His father did not mention that, as soon as it was light, he had got up barefoot in his slippers, to take counsel with Timofeyich and, pulling out with shaking hands one ragged banknote after another, had instructed him what purchases to make, laying stress particularly on the food and red wines which, as far as he could observe, were most appreciated by the young men.)

"Freedom's the important thing," he went on. "That has always been my rule . . . one must never be an obstacle . . . one must never . . ."

Suddenly, he stopped talking and made for the door.

"We'll see each other very soon, father, I assure you."

But without turning round, Vassily Ivanich merely made a gesture with his hand and went out. Back in the bedroom, he found his wife already in bed, and he began to say his prayers in a whisper so as not to wake her. However, she did wake.

"Is that you, Vassily Ivanich?" she asked.

"It's me, my soul!"

"Have you just come from Yenusha? Do you know, I'm worried if he can sleep comfortably on the sofa. I told Anfisushka to lay your camp mattress on it and the new pillows; I'd gladly give him our feather mattress, but I seem to remember that he does not like too soft a bed."

"Never mind, my dear, don't worry now," her husband replied. "He's comfortable enough. The Lord have mercy on us, poor sinners," he went on saying his prayers in a low voice. He had pity on his old wife; he did not wish to tell her overnight of the sorrow that was in store for her.

Bazarov and Arcady drove off the next day. From early morning an atmosphere of dejection had reigned in the house; the plates dropped out of Anfisushka's hands; even

Fedka was in a state of perplexity, and ended by taking off his boots. Vassily Ivanich fussed about more than ever; he was obviously trying to put a good face on things, talked loudly and stamped his feet, but his face looked drawn and he consistently avoided looking at his son. Arina Vlassyevna sobbed quietly; she would have broken down altogether and lost control of herself had not her husband spent a whole two hours in the morning consoling her. When Bazarov, after repeated promises to return not later than in a month's time, at last tore himself away from their clinging embraces, and took his seat in the tarantass; when the horses moved off, the bells tinkled, and the wheels spun round—when nothing more was left to gaze at, the dust had settled, and Timofeyich, all bent and tottering, had made his way back to his tiny room; when the old folk were alone in the house, which now looked suddenly shrunken and decrepit; the Vassily Ivanich who, only a few instants before, had bravely waved his handkerchief as he stood on the porch, slumped into a chair and let drop his head on his chest.

"He has abandoned us, abandoned us," he quavered. "He has left us; he found us boring. He's all alone now, alone like this finger!" he repeated several times, and each time he thrust out his hand with the forefinger pointing away from the rest.

Then Arina Vlassyevna came to his side and, pressing her grey head to his, said: "It can't be helped, Vasya. A son is like a lopped-off branch. As a falcon he comes when he wills and goes where he lists; but you and I are like mushrooms growing in a hollow tree. Here we sit side by side without budging. But I shall stay with you for ever and unalterably, just as you will stay with me."

Vassily Ivanich removed his hands from his face and embraced his wife, his constant companion, with a warmth greater than he had ever shown her in his youth; she had consoled him in his grief.

XXII

In silence, exchanging only a few trivial remarks now and then, our friends finally drove up to Fedot's. Bazarov was not quite satisfied with himself. Arcady was disappointed in him. Moreover, his heart was full of that inexplicable nostalgia which is familiar only to the very young. The coachman harnessed a fresh relay of horses and, clambering up on his seat, asked them: "Am I to turn right or left?"

Arcady gave a start. The road to the right led to town and then homewards: the road to the left led to Anna Odintzov's.

He glanced at Bazarov.

"Eugene," he asked, "shall we turn left?"

Bazarov looked away.

"What foolishness is this?" he muttered.

"I know it's foolish," Arcady pursued. . . ."But what of it? It's not the first time."

Bazarov pulled his cap over his forehead.

"As you like," he said at last.

"Turn left," Arcady shouted.

The tarantass rolled off in the direction of Nicolskoye. But having resolved to be *foolish,* the friends relapsed into still more obdurate silence, and they even looked sulky.

Judging by the way the butler received them in the porch of the Odintzov house, the friends got an inkling that they had acted unwisely in thus giving way to a sudden impulse. They were obviously not expected. Looking sheepish, they waited for a long time in the drawing-room. Finally, Madame Odintzov came out to see them. She greeted them with her usual courtesy, but expressed surprise at their rapid return and, to judge by her hesitant gestures and speech, she did not seem too pleased. They hastened to declare that they had only dropped in on the way and would set out again in about four hours in the direction of the town. She confined herself to a faint exclamation, asked Arcady to pay her respects to his father, and then sent for her aunt. The princess came in, sleepy-eyed, and this made her wrinkled old face look even more spiteful. Katya, who was feeling unwell, stayed in her room. Arcady suddenly felt that he wanted to see Katya at least as much as Anna Sergeyevna. The four hours were spent in small talk; Anna Sergeyevna listened and chatted without smiling at all. Only when they came to take leave, did she look as if her former friendliness had warmed her heart again.

"I'm suffering from an attack of spleen just now," she confessed. "So don't pay any attention to me and do come back again—I mean this for both of you—in a little while."

Arcady and Bazarov replied with silent bows. Taking their places in the tarantass and without halting on the way, they set off home to Maryino, where they arrived safely on the evening of the following day. During the whole of the journey neither of them so much as mentioned Madame Odintzov's name; Bazarov, in particular, hardly opened his mouth and persisted in keeping his eyes off the roadway, an expression of sour concentration on his face.

At Maryino everyone was extremely glad to see them. The continued absence of his son had begun to disquiet Nicholas Petrovich; throwing up his legs in the air and bouncing up and down on the sofa, he let out a shout when Fenichka ran in and with radiant eyes informed him of the "young gentlemen's" arrival. As to Paul Petrovich, he experienced a certain pleasurable excitement and smiled condescendingly as he shook hands with the returning wanderers. They began to talk and ask questions; Arcady chattered most of all, especially at supper, which was prolonged till well past midnight. Nicholas Petrovich ordered several bottles of port, just fresh from Moscow, to be brought out, and set the pace so fast that his cheeks flushed a raspberry colour, and he laughed in a way that was either childish or nervous. The general gaiety spread to the servants' quarters too. Dunyasha ran to and fro like one possessed, and kept banging the doors; as to Peter, he was still trying to strum a Cossack waltz on a guitar at three o'clock in the morning. The night air resounded with the strumming of plaintive and pleasurable notes; but with the exception of a few short preliminary flourishes, the cultured butler failed to obtain any other effects: nature had denied him an aptitude for music as it had for everything else.

In the meantime, life at Maryino had not been following a smooth pattern, and poor Nicholas Petrovich was having a bad time. Each day the "farm" brought increasing worries—and they were cheerless, stupid worries. The complications with the hired labourers were becoming unbearable. Some of them had insisted on being paid off or on having their wages increased, others had pocketed their advance and decamped. The horses fell sick; the harness simply wore away; the work in the fields had been badly done; the threshing machine ordered specially from Moscow proved too heavy and unusable; another such machine broke down as soon as it was tried; half the cowsheds were burnt out because a short-sighted old woman had gone out on a windy day to fumigate her cow with a burning brand. . . . This old woman later insisted that the disaster had been caused by her master's taking it into his head to start manufacturing "foreign" cheeses and dairy products. The steward grew lazy and began to get stout, as every Russian will when he has his "bread buttered." Whenever he caught sight of Nicholas Kirsanov in the distance, he gave evidence of his energy by throwing a stick at some trotting porkling within reach or by waving his fist threateningly at some half-naked urchin, but for the most part he slumbered. The peasants, who were now supposed to pay rent, were never prompt to meet their obligations and filched their landlord's timber; almost every night the watchman would catch or be obliged to confiscate by force the peasant nags that he found grazing on the meadows of the "farm." Nicholas Kirsanov attempted to institute a system of fines for such encroachments, but the matter usually ended by the master feeding the horses at his own expense before returning them to their owners a day later.

The climax came when the peasants started to squabble among themselves: brothers demanded that the holdings should be split up among them individually and their wives refused to live together under the same roof. Fights boiled up of a sudden and, as though at a word of command, a whole crowd of them would be up on their feet, swarming round the entrance to the office, importuning their master, their faces quite often bruised and bloody and they themselves in a state of inebriation, clamouring for justice and retribution; in an uproar of howling voices, the women's shrill whining would mingle with the men's raucous swearing. Kirsanov did his best to separate the adversaries, shouting till he was hoarse but knowing in advance that it was impossible, in any case, to arrive at any reasonable solution. There was a shortage of hands for harvesting: a neighbouring freeholder, who looked a decent enough fellow, had undertaken to provide reapers at a commission of two roubles per acre and had then cheated Kirsanov in the most shameless fashion. The peasant women on his own estate began to demand extortionate wages and, in the meantime, the corn was going to seed. To make matters worse, while they were still behindhand with the reaping, the local council started to issue threats and to demand full payment of the interest due. . . .

"I simply can't go on like this!" Nicholas Petrovich had exclaimed despairingly more than once. "It's impossible for me to fight them on my own and my principles forbid me to send for the police; yet nothing can be done without the threat of penalties!"

"Du calme, du calme," his brother Paul counselled, purring, frowning and tugging at his moustaches.

Bazarov held himself aloof from these domestic "wrangles"; nor was it his business as a guest to interfere in matters which did not concern him. The day following his arrival at Maryino he became engrossed in his frogs, his infusoria, and his chemical compounds, and spent all his time over them. Arcady, on the other hand, considered it his duty, if not to assist his father, at least to appear ready to help him. He listened to him patiently and, on one occasion, even ventured to give him some advice, not so much in the hope of its being taken to heart as in order to demonstrate his interest. He felt no repugnance for farming: he even found pleasure in thinking of agriculture as a possible occupation for himself, but at this time his head was still full of other projects. To his own amazement, Arcady found himself constantly thinking of Nicolskoye. Formerly he would merely have shrugged his shoulders if anyone had suggested that he would feel at a loose end under the same roof as Bazarov, and what a roof too!—that of his own parents; but he now felt bored and attracted elsewhere. He decided that he must try and work off his tedium by indulging in long and exhausting walks, but that did not help either.

One day, while talking to his father, he found out that Nicholas Petrovich had in his possession a few letters of

some interest, written once upon a time to his late wife by
Anna, Madame Odintzov's mother. Arcady did not leave
his father in peace until he was shown these letters, for
which Nicholas Petrovich was obliged to rummage in twenty different boxes and trunks. On getting possession of
these partly mouldering sheets of paper, Arcady seemed
to calm down, as though he had set himself some definite
goal. "I mean this for both of you," he whispered often to
himself, recalling Anna Sergeyevna's phrase. "She added
that herself. I'll go, I will, and the devil take the consequences!" But then, remembering their last visit, the cool
reception and the ensuing embarrassment, he was overcome with hesitation. The "dare and venture" of youth, the
secret desire to try his luck, to measure his strength all by
himself, without any patronage, finally prevailed.

Ten days had not passed since his arrival in Maryino,
when, on the pretext of studying the Sunday-schools, he
was off at a gallop again to town and, from there, to Nicolskoye. Ceaselessly urging on his driver, he rushed to his
destination, like a young subaltern into battle: he felt at
once terrified and gay, and was devoured with impatience.
"But above all—I must not worry about it!" he kept repeating. His driver turned out to be a dashing fellow; pulling
up at a roadside inn, he would say: "One for the road?" or
"Shall we have one?" But once *having had one,* he did not
spare the horses. Then, at last, the high roof of the familiar
house came into view. . . . "What am I doing?" flashed of
a sudden through Arcady's head. "Hadn't I better turn
back?" But the troika sped smoothly on; the driver was
encouraging the horses and whistling at them. Already the
bridge was thundering under the hooves and the wheels,
already the alley of trimmed fir trees was running forward
to meet him. . . . A lady's rose-coloured dress gleamed
among the dark foliage, and a young face peeped from
under the light fringe of a parasol. . . . He recognized Katya,
and she recognized him. Arcady ordered the driver to halt
the galloping horses and, jumping out of the carriage, went
to meet her.

"It's you!" she exclaimed, a blush gradually suffusing her
face. "Let's go and find my sister, she's here in the garden;
she will be very pleased to see you."

Katya conducted Arcady through the garden. Their meeting struck him as a particularly happy omen; so delighted

was he to see her that she might have been a close relative. Everything had turned out so well: there had been no formalities, no butler to announce him. At the turning of the path, he caught sight of Anna Sergeyevna. She was standing with her back to him. On hearing their steps, she slowly turned her head.

Arcady was on the point of feeling embarrassed again, but her very first words immediately reassured him.

"Good day to you, fugitive!" she said in her calm, affectionate voice, coming forward to meet him, smiling and screwing up her eyes from the sun and wind. "Where did you unearth him, Katya?"

"I have brought you something, Anna Sergeyevna," he began, "something you were far from expecting . . ."

"You have brought yourself—and that is the best you could do."

XXIII

AFTER seeing Arcady off with mocking solicitude, letting him understand that he was not in the least deceived as to the real purpose of his journey, Bazarov isolated himself completely and feverishly fell to work. He avoided arguments with Paul Petrovich, particularly as the latter now assumed an excessively aristocratic air in his presence and gave vent to his opinions in grunts rather than words. On one occasion, however, Paul Petrovich did venture to engage in controversy with the Nihilist on the then fashionable topic of the rights of the Baltic Barons, but he soon thought better of it and, pausing suddenly in the middle of his discourse, remarked with frigid politeness: "But what's the use? We fail to understand each other; or, at least, I have not the honour to understand you."

"No wonder!" Bazarov exclaimed. "Man is capable of understanding everything—the vibration of ether and the radiation of the sun; but he can never comprehend why another person should blow his nose in a manner different from his own."

"What? Are you trying to be witty?" Paul Petrovich remarked questioningly and walked away.

However, he did sometimes ask Bazarov's permission to watch his experiments, and once he even moved his generously scented face, washed with the finest of soaps, close to the microscope to observe a transparent protozoon swallow a green speck of dust and fussily masticate it with the help of some very dexterous, fist-like organs attached to its throat. Nicholas Petrovich dropped in to see Bazarov more frequently than his brother; he would have come every day "to school himself," as he put it, if the management of his estate had not made such great demands on his time. He did not disturb the young naturalist: he would sit down somewhere in a corner and watch him attentively, asking a cautious question now and then. At table, he did his best to turn the conversation to physics, geology or chemistry, for every other topic, even farming, to say nothing of politics, might have led to a clash if not to mutual recrimination. Nicholas Petrovich divined that his brother's hatred of Bazarov had in no way diminished. A trifling incident, one of many, confirmed this hypothesis. Here and there in the neighbourhood, cholera had broken out, and had even "weeded out" a couple of inhabitants from Maryino. One night Paul Petrovich felt violently indisposed. But he bore his pains until the morning without resorting to Bazarov's medical skill—and, when he saw him on the following day, pale as he still was, but with his hair carefully groomed and his cheeks clean-shaven, he retorted to Bazarov's question, "Why didn't you send for me?" by saying, "But I seem to recall your saying that you have no faith in medicine." So the days passed. Bazarov applied himself to his work steadily and grimly . . . and yet there was a person in Nicholas Petrovich's household with whom, though he did not open his heart fully, he at least enjoyed chatting. . . . That person was Fenichka.

He usually met her early in the morning, in the garden or the courtyard: he never ventured to visit her room, and, for her part, she only once went as far as his door, to inquire if she should bathe Mitya or not. Not only was she not afraid of him and had every confidence in him, but she also felt less constrained and more able to talk in his presence than in that of Nicholas Petrovich. It is hard to explain why this was so; perhaps because she sensed unconsciously that Bazarov was quite free from aristocratic prejudice, from that consciousness of superiority which is both alluring and intimidating. In her eyes he was an excellent doctor and a forthright man. She felt no shame at nursing her baby in his presence, and on one occasion, when she suddenly felt faint and developed a splitting headache, she accepted a spoonful of medicine from his hands. When Nicholas Petrovich was about, she seemed to avoid Bazarov —out of no duplicity but simply from a sense of decency. More than ever she was apprehensive of Paul Petrovich: of late he had begun to keep an eye on her; and he would suddenly confront her, as though he had sprung out of the ground behind her back, in an English-cut suit, his face set and suspicious, and his hands in his pockets.

"It's like having a cold shower," Fenichka complained to Dunyasha, while the latter only sighed and let her mind stray to another "heartless man." Without suspecting it, Bazarov had become the "ruthless tyrant" of Dunyasha's soul.

Fenichka liked Bazarov, and he liked her. Even the expression of his face seemed to change when he talked to her: it grew brighter, almost assuming a look of good-nature, and his manner, ordinarily so casual, became playful and considerate. Fenichka looked prettier every day. There comes a period in the life of young women when, of a sudden, they begin to flower and blossom like summer roses; such a time had come for Fenichka. Everything contributed to this, even the sultry heat of July, which was then raging. Wearing a flimsy white dress, she looked whiter and more diaphanous than ever: the sun had not tanned her, but the heat, from which she could not shield herself, had made her cheeks and ears go a faint pink and, infusing her whole body with gentle languor, was reflected in the dreamy torpor of her bewitching eyes. She could barely get on with her work; her hands kept slipping to her knees. She could hardly take a step, and kept moaning and complaining with an amusing show of helplessness.

"You should bathe more often," Nicholas Petrovich would say to her. He had rigged up a large bathing-tent over one of the ponds which had not yet dried up.

"Oh, Nicholas Petrovich! But I'd die before I ever got there, and I'd die again on the way back. There is no shade at all in the garden."

"You are quite right, there is no shade," Nicholas Petrovich would reply, mopping his forehead.

One day, as Bazarov was returning from a stroll at about seven in the morning, he came across Fenichka in the lilac arbour, which had stopped flowering long ago but was still thickly covered with green leaves. She was sitting on a bench and, as usual, wore a white kerchief on her head; beside her lay a large bunch of red and white roses still sprinkled with dew. He bid her good morning.

"Ah, Mr. Bazarov!" she exclaimed and, in order to see him, raised the edge of her kerchief a trifle, baring her arm to the elbow as she did so.

"What are you doing here?" Bazarov inquired, sitting down beside her. "Are you making a bouquet?"

"Yes, for the lunch table. Nicholas Petrovich is fond of flowers."

"We have plenty of time before breakfast. What a lot of flowers!"

"I have just picked them, before it was too hot for walking. Now is the only time I can breathe. This heat makes me sick. I'm afraid of falling ill."

"That's sheer fantasy! Let me feel your pulse." Bazarov took her hand, felt her evenly throbbing pulse and did not even bother to count the beats. "You'll live to be a hundred," he said, letting drop her hand.

"Ah, God forbid!" she exclaimed.

"Why not? Don't you want to live a long life?"

"Yes, but not a hundred years! We had a granny of eighty-five—and what a martyr she was! Black as soot, deaf, hunchbacked, coughing all the time; she was only a burden to herself. What sort of a life is that!"

"So it's better to be young?"

"But of course."

"Why should it be better? Tell me!"

"Why? Oh, because being young, I can do anything—I can come and go, and carry things, and I don't have to rely on anyone. . . . What could be better?"

"But I don't mind whether I am young or old."

"How can you say that—'I don't mind?' I simply don't believe you."

"But judge for yourself. What need have I of youth? I live all alone, have no ties. . . ."

"It all depends on yourself."

"That's just the point—it doesn't! If only I could find someone to take pity on me."

Fenichka looked sideways at Bazarov, but made no rejoinder. "What is the book?" she inquired after a short pause.

"This? It's about science, a very learned book."

"And you study all the time? Don't you get tired of it? I expect you must know everything by now."

"Evidently not. Just try and read a few pages of this."

"Why, I shouldn't understand anything. Is it in Russian?" Fenichka asked, picking up the heavily bound volume in both hands. "What an enormous book!"

"It's in Russian."

"All the same, I shan't understand anything."

"I didn't give it to you that you might understand it. I only want to watch you as you read. When you read, the tip of your nose twitches most endearingly."

Fenichka, who was about to construe in a low voice an article "On Creosote," which she happened to turn up, burst out laughing and threw the book down . . . it slipped from the bench and fell to the ground.

"I like you also when you laugh," Bazarov pursued.

"Don't say things like that."

"I like you when you talk. It reminds me of a babbling brook."

Fenichka turned away her head.

"What a man you are!" she exclaimed, fingering the flowers. "Why do you bother to listen to me? You are accustomed to very bright ladies."

"Ah, Fenichka, do believe me: all the brightest ladies in the world are not worth your little elbow."

"What a fancy you have!" Fenichka whispered, clasping her hands.

Bazarov picked the book up from the ground.

"This is a medical book. Why do you throw it about?"

"A medical book?" Fenichka repeated, turning to face him. "Do you know? Why, ever since you gave me those drops for Mitya, do you remember, he's been sleeping ever so soundly! I don't know how to thank you; you are so very kind, really you are."

"Doctors usually charge a fee, you know," Bazarov remarked with a smile. "As you are aware, doctors are quite a greedy crowd."

Fenichka raised her eyes: they looked even darker in the dazzling light which was reflected on the upper part of her face. She was not quite sure if he were joking or not.

"If you like, we will gladly . . . I shall have to ask Nicholas. . . ."

"So you think I want money?" Bazarov interrupted her. "No, it's not money I want from you."

"What then?" Fenichka asked.

"What?" Bazarov repeated. "Try and guess."

"I'm not much good at guessing!"

"Well, let me tell you then; I want . . . one of those roses."

Fenichka laughed again and threw up her hands, so amused she was at Bazarov's wish. But though she was laughing, she also felt flattered. Bazarov stared closely at her.

"By all means, by all means," she brought out at last and, stooping over the bench, began to sift the roses. "Which do you prefer? Red or white?"

"A red one, and not too large."

"Here, take this," she said, sitting up. Then jerking back her outstretched hand and biting her lips, she peered at the entrance of the arbour, straining her ears.

"What's the matter?" Bazarov inquired. "Is it Nicholas Petrovich? . . ."

"No. . . . He's out on the farm . . . and anyhow I'm not afraid of him . . . but there's Paul Petrovich. . . . It seemed to me . . ."

"What?"

"He seems to be prowling about. No. . . . There's no one there. Now, please take it," Fenichka said, giving Bazarov a rose.

"And why should you be afraid of Paul?"

"He frightens me. It's not that he says anything—he doesn't, but he keeps staring at me in such a knowing way. You don't like him either. Do you remember how you always used to argue with him? I had no idea what it was about, but I could see that you were twisting him round your little finger. . . ."

Fenichka illustrated with her hands how she thought Bazarov dealt with Paul Petrovich.

Bazarov smiled.

"And what would you have done if he had begun to get

the better of me?" he asked. "Would you have taken my side?"

"Who am I to meddle? No. No one could get the better of you."

"You think so? But I know a little finger that could topple me over like a feather if it wanted."

"Whose finger?"

"You pretend not to know? What a wonderful scent this rose has. Just smell it."

Fenichka stretched her slender neck forward and put her face close to the flower. . . . The kerchief fell from her head upon her shoulders, disclosing a wavy mass of black, glossy and slightly rumpled hair.

"Just a minute. I want to smell it too," Bazarov exclaimed, and, stooping forward, kissed her warmly on her parted lips.

She quivered, pressing both her hands against his chest, but her pressure was feeble, and he was able to renew and prolong the kiss.

There was a sound of a dry cough behind the lilac shrubs. Fenichka instantly edged away to the other end of the bench. Paul Petrovich showed himself, made a slight bow, and, exclaiming in a sort of jaundiced and dejected tone, "So that's where you are!" walked away. Fenichka at once gathered up all the roses and fled from the arbour.

"How could you!" she whispered as she departed. Her whisper conveyed a note of sincere reproach.

Bazarov recalled another recent scene: his conscience pricked him and he experienced a feeling of contempt mingled with regret. But he immediately shook his head, congratulated himself sardonically on his "own formal entry into the ranks of the gay Lotharios," and marched off to his room.

In the meantime, Paul Petrovich had left the garden and walked as far as the copse. He remained there for quite a while. When he came back for breakfast, his face looked so clouded that Nicholas Petrovich inquired with solicitude if he was feeling quite well.

"As you know, I am sometimes subject to bilious attacks," was Paul Petrovich's calm reply.

XXIV

Two hours later he knocked at Bazarov's door.

"Pardon me for interrupting your scientific researches," he began, sitting down on a chair by the window and leaning with both hands on a handsome cane with an ivory knob (he usually did not carry a cane), "but I have to ask you to spare me five minutes of your time . . . no more."

"My time is at your disposal," replied Bazarov, whose face had twitched as soon as Paul Petrovich crossed the threshold.

"Five minutes will be ample. I have come to put a question to you."

"A question? What is it?"

"I shall explain if you will be good enough to listen. In the early days of your stay in my brother's house, before I denied myself the pleasure of talking with you, I had occasion to hear you express opinions on many subjects; but, as far as I can remember, you have never made any reference to single combats or duelling in general, either in conversation with me or in my presence. May I inquire what your views are on this subject?"

Bazarov, who had risen to receive Paul Petrovich, sat down on the edge of a table and crossed his arms.

"This is what I think," he replied. "From the theoretical point of view duelling is stupid; but from the practical point of view—well, that's another question."

"That is to say, you mean, if I understand you correctly, that in practice, whatever your theoretical view of duelling may be, you would not suffer yourself to be insulted without demanding satisfaction!"

"You have fully grasped my meaning."

"Very well. I am pleased to hear you say so. Your words have rescued me from a dilemma."

"From indecision, you mean."

"As you like. I am trying to express myself in a way you will understand; I . . . I am no seminary rat. What you say will spare me from resorting to a certain unfortunate necessity. I have decided to fight you."

Bazarov stared at him round-eyed.

"To fight me?"

"Precisely."

"And for what reason, may I inquire?"

"I could explain," Paul Petrovich began. "But I would prefer not. I think you are in the way here. I cannot stand you, I despise you, and if that is not enough for you . . ."

Paul Petrovich's eyes flashed. . . . Bazarov's glinted too.

"Very well then," he articulated slowly. "Further explanations are superfluous. You have succumbed to the fantasy of testing your chivalrous spirit on me. I could have denied you that pleasure, but I shall let you have your way!"

"I am most grateful to you," Paul Petrovich replied. "I hope that you will now accept my challenge without forcing me to resort to compulsory measures."

"That is to say, if we dispense with allegory, you would resort to that cane?" Bazarov coolly remarked. "You are quite right. There is no need for you to affront me. Nor would that have been without some peril to you. You may remain a gentleman. . . . I also accept your challenge like a gentleman."

"That's fine," Paul Petrovich exclaimed, putting his cane into a corner. "It now remains for us to discuss the conditions of the duel; but, first of all, I should like to know whether you consider it necessary for us to have recourse to the formality of a slight dispute which might serve as an excuse for my challenge?"

"No, we had better dispense with the formalities."

"I am of that opinion myself. I also assume that it would be out of place to probe into the real reasons for our encounter. We just can't bear each other. Isn't that enough?"

"Isn't that enough?" Bazarov echoed him ironically.

"As to the conditions of the duel, we shall be without seconds . . . for where can we procure them?"

"Exactly. Where can we procure them?"

"I have the honour to suggest the following: let us fight early to-morrow morning, at six o'clock, behind the copse, with pistols, at ten paces on each side of the barrier. . . ."

"At ten paces? All right. Let that be the distance over which we shall hate each other."

"We can make it eight," Paul Petrovich remarked.

"We can. Why not?"

"We shall fire two shots and, as a precaution, each of us

must put a letter in his pocket, holding himself responsible for his own demise."

"I don't altogether agree with that," Bazarov replied. "It's beginning to smell rather like a French romance, a bit improbable."

"Perhaps. However, you will agree that it would be unpleasant to be suspected of murder?"

"I agree. But there is a way of avoiding that depressing approach. We have no seconds, but we have a witness."

"May I inquire who it will be?"

"Why, Peter."

"Which Peter?"

"Your brother's valet. He is quite up to the standards of contemporary culture, and would play his part, and all it entailed in these circumstances, quite *comme il faut.*"

"I have the impression that you are joking, my dear sir."

"Not at all. If you will ponder on my suggestion, you will conclude that it is full of common sense and simplicity. Murder will out, but I shall take it on myself to coach Peter in a befitting manner and to deliver him on to the battlefield."

"You like joking," Paul Petrovich said, rising from his chair. "But after the amiable readiness you have displayed, I have no right to insist further. . . . So everything is in order. . . . By the way, have you any pistols?"

"How should I have pistols? I am no warrior."

"In that case I shall have to offer you a set of mine. You may rest assured that I have not used them these five years."

"That is very comforting news."

Paul Petrovich picked up his cane. . . .

"To conclude, my dear sir, it only remains for me to thank you and to allow you to resume your studies. I have the honour to take leave of you."

"Until I have the pleasure of meeting you again, my dear sir," Bazarov said as he conducted his visitor to the door.

Paul Petrovich went out, leaving Bazarov standing at the door. The latter suddenly exclaimed: "The devil take it! How beautiful and how stupid! What a farce we have thumped through! Circus dogs could not have done their turn any better. And there was no getting out of it; he would have hit me at the slightest provocation, and then . . ." (At the very thought Bazarov turned pale; all his pride reared up within him.) "Then I should have had to strangle him as I might a kitten." He went back to his microscope, but his heart had been stirred, and he now lacked the composure essential for precise observation. "He must have seen me with Fenichka this morning," he thought. "But is it for his brother's sake that he intervened in this fashion? And is a kiss so very important? There must be something else behind it. Bah! Perhaps he is in love with her himself? Of course, he is in love; it's as clear as daylight. What a complication, just imagine! . . . What a mess!" he decided at last. "It's a mess from whichever angle one may look at it. In the first place, I shall have to risk my own head, and then I shall have to go away anyhow; and there is also Arcady . . . and that angelic Nicholas Petrovich. It's a mess, a holy mess."

The rest of the day passed somehow, uneventfully and limply. Fenichka might never have existed; she kept to her room like a mouse to its hole. Nicholas Petrovich looked worried. He had received a report that a blight had set in among the wheat crop on which he had set so much store. Paul Petrovich's icy politeness had a crushing effect on everyone, including even Prokofyich. Bazarov began to write a letter to his father, but tore it up and threw it under the table. "If I die," he thought, "they will hear of it; but I shall not die. No, I shall be about for a long time yet." He ordered Peter to present himself next morning as soon as it was light on a matter of some urgency. For some reason, Peter had got it into his head that Bazarov wished to take him to Petersburg. Bazarov went to bed late, and throughout the night was a prey to confused dreams. . . . Madame Odintzov kept looming before him: she assumed the likeness of his mother and was followed by a kitten with black whiskers; the kitten turned out to be Fenichka; and Paul Petrovich merged into a dense forest, which he nevertheless had to fight. At four o'clock Peter woke him; he dressed at once and went out with him.

It was a glorious, fresh morning; tiny mottled clouds stood out, like fleecy lambs, in the transparent azure of the sky; fine beads of dew lay sprinkled over the leaves and grasses, glittering like silver among the cobwebs; the rosy tints of dawn still seemed to cling to the moist dark earth; from the depths of the sky larks showered their songs. Bazarov reached the copse, sat down on the edge of it in the shade, and only then divulged to Peter what service he expected of him. The cultured valet was scared to death; but Bazarov calmed his fears by assuring him that he would have nothing to do except stand at a distance and look on, and that he would incur no responsibility. "And yet," he added, "just think of the important part you will have to play!" Peter threw up his hands, stared at his feet and, all green with fright, leaned back for support against a birch tree.

The road from Maryino skirted the copse; a light dust lay on it, undisturbed by wheel or foot since the previous day. Bazarov could not help glancing down the road, plucking as he did so tufts of grass, and chewing them, repeating to himself, "This is sheer idiocy!" The early morning chill made him shudder a couple of times. . . . Peter glanced at him dismally, but Bazarov only grinned back at him; he was showing himself no coward.

A thud of hooves could be heard in the wood. From behind the trees a peasant emerged. In front of him he was driving a couple of horses hobbled together and, as he went past Bazarov, he stared at him in a strange sort of way without doffing his cap—a circumstance which Peter evidently interpreted as a bad omen. "That fellow is up early too," Bazarov thought, "but at least he is up on business, while we . . . ?"

"They seem to be coming," Peter whispered of a sudden.

Bazarov raised his head and caught sight of Paul Petrovich. Wearing a light check jacket and snow-white trousers, he strode rapidly down the road; under his arm he carried a box wrapped in green cloth.

"I'm so sorry. I believe I have kept you waiting," he said, bowing first to Bazarov and then to Peter, in whose person he for an instant respected something in the nature of a second. "I did not want to wake my valet."

"It doesn't matter," Bazarov replied. "We have just arrived ourselves."

"Ah! so much the better!" Paul Petrovich looked round him. "There is no one about, no one to disturb us. . . . Shall we proceed?"

"By all means."

"I assume that you require no further explanations?"

"I don't."

"Would you like to load the pistols?" Paul Petrovich inquired, taking them out of the box.

"No! You had better do that. I shall measure out the paces. I have longer legs," Bazarov added with a smile. "One, two, three . . ."

"Mr. Bazarov, sir," Peter stammered with difficulty (he was shaking as in a fever), "by your will, I shall now stand aside."

"Four . . . five . . . Yes, stand aside, my good man, stand aside, you may even stand behind a tree and stop your ears; only don't shut your eyes; and if anyone falls, run forward and help them up. Six . . . seven . . . eight . . ." Bazarov came to a halt. "Is that enough?" he asked, turning to Paul Petrovich, "or shall I throw in a couple more paces?"

"As you like," the other replied, stuffing in the second bullet.

"All right, we'll make it two more." Bazarov drew a line on the ground with the toe of his boot. "There's the barrier. By the way, how many paces shall we stand away from it? That's important. We did not discuss it yesterday."

"Ten I should think," Paul Petrovich replied, handing both pistols to Bazarov. "Will you deign to make your choice?"

"I will deign. But you must agree, Paul Petrovich, that our single combat is extraordinary to the point of being comic. Just have a look at our second's physiognomy."

"You are still bent on joking," Paul Petrovich replied. "I do not deny the strange circumstances of our duel, but I consider it my duty to warn you that I intend to fight seriously. *A bon entendeur, salut!*"

"Oh, I don't doubt for a moment that we are both resolved to annihilate each other; but why shouldn't we laugh, too, and combine *utile dulci*? Let's do it: you will address me in French, and I shall reply in Latin."

"I mean to fight quite seriously," Paul Petrovich repeated, taking up his position. Bazarov, for his part, counted off ten paces from the barrier and then came to a stop.

"Are you ready?" Paul Petrovich asked.

"Yes, I am."

"Let us begin."

Bazarov moved forward slowly while Paul Petrovich advanced towards him, his left hand in his pocket and his right gradually raising the pistol. . . . "He is aiming straight at my nose," Bazarov thought to himself, "and how carefully he's aiming too, the bandit! What a horrible sensation. I shall fix my eyes on his watch chain. . . ." Something hissed close to Bazarov's ear, and at that very moment a shot rang out. "I heard it, so I must be all right then." The thought had just time to flash through his head. He took another step and, without aiming, pressed the trigger.

Paul Petrovich gave a slight start and his hand went to his thigh. A trickle of blood flowed down his white trousers.

Bazarov threw away his pistol and approached his adversary. "Are you wounded?" he inquired.

"You had the right to summon me to the barrier," Paul Petrovich said. "This is only a scratch. According to the conditions, each of us has another shot."

"You must excuse me, but that will have to wait till next time," Bazarov replied, putting his arm round Paul Petrovich who was beginning to grow pale. "Now I am no duellist but a doctor, and I must begin by inspecting your wound. Peter! Come here, Peter! Where have you got to?"

"That's sheer nonsense. . . . I don't need any help," Paul Petrovich said, spacing out his words, "and . . . we must . . . again . . ." He was about to tug at his moustache, but his arm sagged, his eyes rolled back, and he lost consciousness.

"Here's a novelty! A swoon! As though there were cause!" Bazarov involuntarily exclaimed, letting Paul Petrovich sink to the ground. "Let's see the damage." He pulled out his handkerchief, wiped the blood, and probed all round the wound. . . . "The bone's intact," he muttered through his teeth. "The bullet has gone through but quite near the surface; one of the muscles, the *vastus externus,* must have been grazed. You will be dancing within three weeks if you feel like it! . . . Ah, a swoon! Ugh, what weak nerves these people have! Just look, how thin-skinned he is!"

"Is he killed?" Peter's quavering voice came fluttering behind his back.

Bazarov looked round.

"Go along quickly and fetch some water, my man. As for him, he'll survive both of us."

But the highly cultured servant did not seem to grasp

his words and remained rooted to the spot. Paul Petrovich slowly opened his eyes.

"It's the end of him!" Peter whispered, making the sign of the cross.

"You're quite right. . . . What an idiotic face!" the wounded gentleman exclaimed, forcing a smile.

"Go and fetch some water, you devil!" Bazarov yelled.

"There's no need. . . . It was only a momentary vertigo. . . . Will you help me to sit up? . . . like that. . . . This scratch only needs a bandage. I can walk home, or the droshky can be fetched. If you are agreeable, we will not renew the duel. You have conducted yourself very nobly . . . to-day, you must note."

"There's no need to dwell on the past," Bazarov replied. "As to the future, it's not worth while racking your brains over it, for it is my intention to depart at once. Now you must allow me to bandage your leg; your wound is not dangerous, but it would be advisable to stop the bleeding. But first of all we must revive this poor mortal."

Bazarov shook Peter by his collar and sent him off to fetch the droshky.

"Take care and don't alarm my brother," Paul Petrovich instructed him. "Don't you dare to say a word to him about this."

Peter rushed off. While he was seeking the droshky, the adversaries sat on the ground without exchanging a word. Paul Petrovich tried to avoid looking at Bazarov; he was reluctant to make peace with him; he was ashamed of his own arrogance, of his failure; he was ashamed of what he had done, although he felt that the incident could not have ended more propitiously. "At least he will not stick round here any longer," he consoled himself, "and that is something to be grateful for." The heavy, awkward silence persisted. They both felt embarrassed. Each of them realized that the other read his thoughts. Such awareness is agreeable between friends, but most disagreeable between enemies, especially when it is impossible for them to thrash it out or to part.

"Have I bandaged your leg too tightly?" Bazarov inquired at last.

"No, it's all right, perfect," Paul Petrovich replied, adding after a while: "We shan't be able to hide this from my brother. We shall have to tell him that we fell out over politics."

"Very well," Bazarov agreed. "You can tell him that I was abusing all Anglomaniacs."

"Excellent. Now what do you suppose that fellow is thinking about us?" Paul Petrovich went on, pointing to the peasant who had driven his hobbled horses past Bazarov a few minutes before the duel and who, as he was now trudging back along the road, played up at the sight of the gentry and doffed his cap.

"Who can tell!" Bazarov replied. "Very likely he is not thinking at all. The Russian peasant is in truth that mysterious Unknown, about whom Mrs. Radcliffe talked so much once upon a time. Who can understand him? He does not understand himself."

"Ah, so that's what you think!" Paul Petrovich began, but suddenly exclaimed: "Look what that idiot, Peter, has done! There's my brother coming at full speed!"

Bazarov turned round and perceived Nicholas Petrovich sitting pale-faced in the droshky. Before it had time to pull up, he leapt out and rushed towards his brother.

"What's the meaning of this?" he cried in an agitated voice. "Eugene Vassilich, I ask you, what does it mean?"

"It's nothing," Paul Petrovich replied. "A pity you were disturbed. Mr. Bazarov and I had a slight altercation, and I have paid slightly for it."

"For heaven's sake! What was it all about?"

"How am I to explain? Mr. Bazarov referred disrespectfully to Sir Robert Peel. I hasten to add I alone am to blame for all that has happened, and Mr. Bazarov has conducted himself perfectly. It was I who challenged him."

"But you are bleeding, my dear!"

"And did you suppose that I had water in my veins? This blood-letting might even do me some good. Isn't that so, doctor? Now help me to get into this droshky and don't look so gloomy. I shall be quite recovered by to-morrow. Fine! Off we go, coachman!"

Nicholas Petrovich followed the droshky on foot; Bazarov was on the point of staying behind. . . .

"I must ask you to attend to my brother," Nicholas Petrovich said to him, "until we fetch another doctor from town."

Bazarov silently nodded.

An hour later Paul Petrovich lay stretched out in bed

with a skilfully bandaged leg. The whole household was in a state of panic. Fenichka had fainted. Nicholas Petrovich wrung his hands in silence while Paul Petrovich continued to laugh and joke, especially with Bazarov; he had donned a fine cambric shirt, a fashionable morning jacket and a smoking-cap, and, forbidding the blinds to be pulled down, jokingly complained of having to abstain from food.

By night-time he had developed a temperature and his head ached. Then the town doctor arrived. Nicholas Petrovich had paid no heed to his brother, nor had Bazarov wished him to do so; the latter sat about in his room all day, looking bilious and angry, and only went in to see the invalid for a moment every now and then. He happened to run into Fenichka a couple of times, but she jumped out of his way in horror. The new doctor recommended cooling drinks and, incidentally, confirmed Bazarov's diagnosis that there was no danger of complications. Nicholas Petrovich told him that his brother had been careless and had wounded himself. To this the doctor had replied, "H'm!" but on receiving there and then twenty-five roubles in silver exclaimed: "You don't say so! That happens often enough. Exactly so!"

No one in the house undressed or went to bed. Nicholas Petrovich kept tiptoeing into his brother's room and tiptoeing out again; Paul Petrovich would doze off, groan gently, or say to him in French, *"Couchez-vous,"* and then ask for a drink. Once Nicholas Petrovich made Fenichka take him a glass of lemonade; Paul Petrovich stared at her fixedly as he emptied the glass. By morning the fever had become a little more pronounced and a slight delirium had set in. At first Paul Petrovich talked wildly; then he suddenly opened his eyes and, seeing his brother standing by the bed and stooping anxiously over him, said, "Isn't it true, Nicholas, that Fenichka has something in common with Nelly?"

"Which Nelly, Paul?"

"Why do you ask? With Princess R. of course. The top part of her face especially. *C'est de la même famille.*"

Nicholas Petrovich made no reply, but inwardly he wondered at the persistent vitality of his elderly brother's sentiments. "So this is how it has all come back," he thought to himself.

"Ah, how I love that worthless creature!" Paul Petrovich

moaned, dejectedly clasping his hands behind his head. "I will suffer no upstart to touch . . ." he muttered a few moments later.

Nicholas Petrovich only sighed; he had no suspicion to whom these words might refer.

Next morning, at about eight o'clock, Bazarov came to see him. He had already had time to pack his belongings and to set at liberty all his frogs, insects and birds.

"You have come to take leave of me?" Nicholas Petrovich asked, rising up to meet him.

"That is so."

"I understand you and fully approve what you are doing. My poor brother is, of course, to blame; he has been punished for it. He told me himself that he had made it impossible for you to act otherwise. I am ready to believe that you could not avoid this duel, which . . . which to a certain extent was undoubtedly due to the persistent antagonism between our mutual outlooks." (Nicholas Petrovich was getting entangled in his words.) "My brother is a man of the old school, hot-tempered and heady. . . . Thank God, the matter ended no worse. I have taken all the necessary steps to avoid publicity. . . ."

"I shall leave my address with you in case of any unpleasant developments," Bazarov remarked casually.

"I hope there will be none. . . . I very much regret that your stay in my house has ended . . . in this fashion. I feel all the more aggrieved, since Arcady . . ."

"No doubt I shall be seeing him," said Bazarov, whom every sort of "explanation" and "protestation" never failed to irritate. "If I don't, I beg you to give him my greetings and to ask him to accept my regrets."

"And I beg . . ." Nicholas Petrovich replied with a bow. But Bazarov had gone out without waiting for him to finish his sentence.

On learning that Bazarov was about to depart, Paul Petrovich expressed the wish to see him and shook hands with him. But even on this occasion Bazarov remained as cold as ice; he realized that Paul Petrovich wished to appear magnanimous. He did not succeed in bidding farewell to Fenichka: he was only able to exchange a few glances with her through a window. Her face looked very sad to him. "A lost soul most likely," he said to himself. . . . "Yet she may scramble out of it somehow!" Peter, on the other hand, was so moved that he wept on his shoulder until Bazarov cooled his ardour by asking him whether "his eyes were not in a damp spot." Dunyasha was obliged to take refuge in the copse in order to conceal her feelings. The man responsible for all this grief clambered into a cart, lit a cigar, and when, as the road branched off after the fourth mile, he saw for the last time the Kirsanovs' domain and the new manor house spread out in a straight line, he spat and muttered to himself, as he wrapped his overcoat more closely round him,

"These damned gentry!"

Very soon Paul Petrovich's condition had improved for the better; but he was obliged to keep to his bed for another week. He bore his "imprisonment," as he called it, philosophically, but he fussed about his toilet overmuch and had all his articles of apparel sprinkled with eau-de-Cologne. Nicholas Petrovich read the papers to him; Fenichka attended to him as before, bringing him chicken broth, lemonade, soft-boiled eggs and tea; but a secret terror gripped her each time she entered his room. Paul Petrovich's unexpected action had frightened all the folk in the house and her above all; only Prokofyich did not lose his presence of mind and argued that, in his day, the gentry used to duel—"the gentry only amongst themselves, while they had the like of them outsiders thrashed in the stables for their insolence."

Fenichka felt almost no twinges of conscience; but she was tortured at times when she pondered on the real cause of the dispute; and Paul Petrovich, too, was in the habit of staring at her so strangely . . . that, even when her back was turned, she could feel his eyes upon her. Her state of continuous inward alarm had made her grow thinner, though, as is often the case, she looked even prettier.

One day—it was morning—Paul Petrovich felt much better and moved from his bed to the sofa. After inquiring about his health, Nicholas had gone off to the threshing-floor. Then Fenichka came in with a cup of tea and, setting it down on the table, was about to leave the room. Paul Petrovich detained her.

"Why are you in such a hurry, Fenichka?" he began. "Have you things to do?"

"No. . . . I must pour out the tea."

"Dunyasha can do that without you; come and sit for

a while with an invalid. By the way, I should like to have a chat with you."

Fenichka sat down without a word on the edge of an arm-chair.

"Listen," Paul Petrovich said, tugging at his moustaches. "I have long wanted to ask you a question. Are you frightened of me?"

"I? . . ."

"Yes, you. You never look me straight in the face. It's as though you were not clear of conscience."

Fenichka blushed, but glanced at Paul Petrovich. He seemed very strange to her, and her heart quivered gently.

"But your conscience is clear?" he asked her.

"Why shouldn't it be?" she whispered.

"Who knows? However, who is there you could have offended? Me? That is improbable. Other people in the house? That's also unlikely. My brother, perhaps? But you love him, don't you?"

"Yes, I do."

"With all your soul? With all your heart?"

"I love Nicholas Petrovich with all my heart."

"You really mean it? Look at me, Fenichka" (it was the first time he called her by that name). "You know, lying is a major sin!"

"I am not lying. If I did not love Nicholas, I would have nothing to live for."

"And you would not exchange him for anybody?"

"For whom could I exchange him?"

"One never knows! For the gentleman who has just left, for example?"

Fenichka got up.

"Great Heavens, why do you torment me? What have I done to you? How can you say such things? . . ."

"Fenichka," Paul Petrovich said in a lugubrious voice, "I saw everything. . . ."

"What did you see?"

"Why, over there . . . in the summer-house."

Fenichka blushed crimson to the roots of her hair and the tips of her ears.

"But how was I to blame?" she asked with difficulty.

Paul Petrovitch sat up.

"You are not to blame? No? Not at all?"

"Nicholas Petrovich is the only person I love in the

whole wide world, and I shall love him for ever!" she
burst out with unexpected force, while sobs rose to her
throat. "And as to what you saw, on the Day of Judgment
I shall myself be able to say that I did no wrong; and I
would rather die at once rather than be suspected of such a
thing, of such behaviour behind my benefactor's back, your
brother's back. . . ."

But at this point her voice failed her, and she felt Paul's
hand gripping and pressing hers. . . . She looked at him
and turned to stone. He had grown paler than ever; his
eyes glittered, and what was even more astonishing, a
lonely, heavy tear rolled down his cheek.

"Fenichka!" he gasped in a sort of wondering whisper.
"Love him, do love my brother! He is so very kind and
good! Don't betray him for anyone in the world. Don't
heed anyone else! Just think! What could be more terrible than love unrequited! Never forsake my poor dear
Nicholas!"

Fenichka's eyes had dried and her fear had passed—so
great was her amazement. But imagine her feelings when
Paul Petrovich himself pressed her hand to his lips, and
kept it there, without kissing it but only sighing feverishly. . . .

"Oh, Lord," she thought, "has he had a fit?"

At that instant the whole of his wasted life quivered inside him.

The stairs creaked beneath rapid footsteps. . . . He
pushed her aside, and fell back on the pillow. The door
opened, and Nicholas, cheerful, fresh and rosy-cheeked,
appeared. Mitya, fresh and rosy-cheeked as his father, was
jumping up and down in his arms in only a shirt, while his
bare feet clutched at the large buttons of his father's country
overcoat.

Fenichka threw herself at Nicholas Petrovich and, clasping her arms round him and their son, let her head drop on
his shoulder. Nicholas Petrovich was surprised: the shy
and modest Fenichka normally never showed her affection
in the presence of a third person.

"Is anything the matter?" he asked and, glancing at his
brother, handed Mitya over to her. "You're not feeling
worse, are you?" he inquired, going up to Paul Petrovich.

The latter hid his face in a cambric handkerchief.

"No . . . it's all right . . . it's nothing. . . . On the contrary, I feel much better."

"A pity you were in such a hurry to change over to the sofa. Where are you going now?" Nicholas Petrovich added, turning to Fenichka; but she had already banged the door behind her. "I was going to show you my little champion; he wanted to see his uncle. Why did she take him away? But tell me, what's the matter? Did anything happen between you, tell me?"

"Brother!" Paul Petrovich said solemnly.

Nicholas Petrovich started. He felt pained, he knew not why.

"Brother," Paul Petrovich repeated, "give me your word that you will fulfil a certain request of mine."

"What request? Tell me."

"A most important one. As I see it, your whole happiness depends upon it. I have pondered a great deal on what I am now going to say to you. . . . Brother, you must do your duty, that of an honest and noble man; you must put an end to the temptation and bad example you are setting —you, the best of men!"

"What are you driving at, Paul?"

"Marry Fenichka . . . she loves you; she is—the mother of your son."

Nicholas Petrovich stepped back and threw up his hands.

"Is it you, Paul, I hear saying this? You, whom I always regarded as a resolute opponent of such marriages! And now you recommend it! But don't you realize, it was only out of respect for you that I have not long ago fulfilled what you have now very justly described as my duty?"

"A pity you respected my judgment in this case," Paul Petrovich answered with a wan smile. "I'm beginning to think that Bazarov was right after all in reproaching me for my aristocratic outlook. No, my dear brother, enough of cutting capers and thinking of etiquette: we are already elderly, peaceful folk; it's high time we put aside all pretensions. So be it, as you say, let us fulfil our duty; I am sure we shall also find happiness."

Nicholas Petrovich rushed to embrace his brother.

"At last you have opened my eyes!" he exclaimed. "I wasn't wrong to maintain that you were the kindest and wisest of men; but now I realize that you are as reasonable as you are generous."

"Calm yourself, calm yourself," Paul Petrovich interrupted him. "Be careful now and don't press on my leg—the leg of your reasonable brother, who fought a duel, like any lieutenant, when on the verge of fifty. And so, we have settled the matter; Fenichka will be my . . . *belle sœur.*"

"My dear Paul! But what will Arcady say?"

"Arcady? Why, he'll be simply delighted! Marriage is not a principle he upholds, but his feeling of equality will be flattered. Yes, indeed, why have we still got all these castes *au dix-neuvième siècle?*"

"Ah, Paul, Paul! Let me kiss you again. Don't be alarmed about your leg, I shall be very careful."

The brothers embraced.

"Now what do you think? Should we not inform her at once of your intention?" Paul Petrovich asked.

"Why hurry?" Nicholas Petrovich retorted. "Why? Have you already discussed it?"

"Discussed it? *Quelle idée!*"

"Well, everything is in order then. First you must get better; we shall not overlook this, we must think it over, consider it. . . ."

"But you have already decided?"

"Of course I have, and I thank you from the bottom of my heart. But now I must leave you; you must rest; all this excitement is bad for you. . . . We shall talk it over very soon. Now go to sleep, my dear, and may God grant you health!"

"Why does he thank me?" Paul Petrovich thought when left alone. "Doesn't it depend entirely on him? As for myself, I shall go off somewhere as soon as he gets married, as far as possible, to Dresden or Florence, and there I shall stay till I fade away."

Paul Petrovich moistened his forehead with eau-de-Cologne and closed his eyes. In the radiant light of day, his handsome, wasted head reclined on the white pillow like the head of a corpse. . . . Indeed, he was a corpse.

XXV

IN the shade of a lofty ash tree, Katya and Arcady were sitting on a turf bench in the garden at Nicolskoye; allowing her elongated body to assume an elegant posture known to sportsmen as the "Hare's stance," Fifi had chosen a spot for herself on the ground nearby. Arcady and Katya were both silent; in his hands he held a half-open book, and she was engaged in picking crumbs from the bottom of her basket and throwing them to a small family of sparrows which, with the cowardly persistence characteristic of them, hopped about and chirped right under her feet. A faint rustling breeze among the foliage of the ash tree was shifting pale-gold patches of sunlight back and forth over the shadowy path and over Fifi's tawny back; Arcady and Katya were both immersed in unrelieved shadow: only now and then did a bright gleam of sunshine illumine her hair. They were both silent; but their very silence and the way they sat together spoke eloquently of their confiding intimacy; each looked unmindful of the other and yet full of an inward joy at being so close together. The expressions on their faces had altered, too, since we had last seen them; Arcady appeared more collected, Katya more lively and enterprising.

"Don't you think," Arcady began, "the Russians have been right to name the ash tree *yasen, yasen*—lucent? No tree is as lucent when the sun shines."

Katya looked up and said, "Yes," and Arcady thought, "She at least does not reproach me for using beautiful language."

"I don't like Heine," Katya said, with her eyes indicating the book in Arcady's hands, "when he is either sarcastic or plaintive. I prefer his pensive and nostalgic moods."

"And I prefer his gibing tone," Arcady remarked.

"That's the residue of your sardonic turn of mind."

("Residue!" Arcady thought. "If only Bazarov could hear that!")

"You just wait," Katya went on, "we shall transform you."

"Who will transform me? You?"

"Who? Why, my sister, and Porfiry Platonich, with whom you have now stopped quarrelling, and auntie, whom you accompanied to church the day before yesterday."

"I couldn't very well refuse! And as for Anna Sergeyevna, you must remember that she agrees with Eugene on many points."

"My sister was under his influence then, just as you were."

"As I *was*! Why? Have you noticed any signs of my breaking away from that influence?"

Katya made no reply.

"I know," Arcady went on, "you never took to him."

"I am not in a position to judge him."

"Do you know what, Catherine Sergeyevna? Every time I hear you say that, I disbelieve you. . . . There is no man living who is not capable of being judged by any of us! You are merely quibbling."

"Very well, then let me tell you that he . . . it's not that I don't like him, but I have no contact with him. It's as though I had nothing in common with him . . . just as you haven't either."

"Why do you think that?"

"How am I to explain? . . . He's like a wild beast, we're just domestic animals."

"Am I a domestic animal too?"

Katya nodded her head. Arcady scratched behind his ear.

"Now listen, Catherine Sergeyevna. You are really being very offensive."

"Why? Would you prefer to be a wild beast?"

"Not wild, but strong and energetic."

"You can't just wish that. . . . Your friend does not *wish* it, he *is* like that."

"H'm! So you assume that he has exercised a great influence on Anna Sergeyevna?"

"Yes. But no one can dominate her for long," Katya added softly.

"Why do you think so?"

"She is very proud. . . . I didn't mean that. . . . I meant that she sets great store by her independence."

"Who doesn't?" Arcady asked, while the thought flashed through his mind, "What's he got to do with it?" "What's she got to do with it?" was the thought that also occurred to Katya. The same ideas tend to occur simultaneously to young people who are in the habit of seeing each other often and of being on terms of intimacy.

Arcady smiled, and coming a little closer to Katya whispered to her:

"Now confess, you are a bit frightened of *her*."

"Of whom?"

"*Her*," Arcady repeated significantly.

"And you?" Katya asked him in her turn.

"I also. You will note I said 'I also.' "

Katya wagged a finger at him.

"I'm surprised at you," she began. "My sister has never been so well disposed to you as just now; a great deal more so than when you first arrived."

"You don't mean it!"

"And you haven't noticed it? Aren't you pleased?"

Arcady reflected for a moment.

"What have I done to win Anna Sergeyevna's favour? Perhaps it's because I brought her your mother's letters?"

"That may be one reason; but there are others which I shan't tell you."

"Why won't you?"

"I won't."

"Oh, I know how stubborn you are."

"I am stubborn."

"And observant."

Katya glanced sideways at Arcady.

"Perhaps you find that irritating? What are you thinking about now?"

"I was wondering how you had acquired that acute sense of observation which is so much a part of you. You are so shy and distrustful; you keep everyone at bay. . . ."

"I have lived so much alone, and willy-nilly that stimulates the imagination. But do I keep everyone at bay?"

Arcady cast a grateful glance at Katya.

"That is all very fine," he continued, "but people in your position, I mean persons of your means, have this gift but rarely; it's as hard for them to see the truth as for a Tsar."

"But I'm not rich."

Arcady was astonished and failed to grasp at once what Katya had said.

Then it dawned on him. "The property is really her sister's," he thought, and the idea did not displease him.

"How well you put it!" he exclaimed.

"What do you mean?"

"You put it so well—quite simply, without any embarrassment or undue emphasis. Incidentally, I imagine that there must be something distinctive, a sort of feeling of pride in a person who realizes and acknowledges his poverty."

"Thanks to my sister, I have been spared the experience of poverty; I referred to my situation only because it cropped up in the conversation."

"So be it! But you must admit that you have just a particle of the pride I referred to a moment ago."

"For instance?"

"For instance—excuse me for asking the question—but you would not consent to marry a rich man, would you?"

"If I loved him very much. . . . No, maybe, even then I wouldn't accept him."

"Ah, you see!" Arcady exclaimed, adding after a while: "And why wouldn't you accept him?"

"Because even folk-songs tell one that such a marriage does not make a happy pair."

"Perhaps it's your ambition to dominate or . . ."

"Oh, no! Why do you say that? On the contrary, I am ready to yield, I can understand that; that is happiness, but a life of utter submission. . . . No, I've had my fill of it, as it is."

"Your fill of it, as it is," Arcady repeated. "Yes, yes," he went on, "I can see you're of the same stock as Anna Sergeyevna; you are quite as independent as she is, but more secretive. . . . I am positive that you would never be the first to declare your feelings, however overpowering and holy they may be. . . ."

"How could it be otherwise?" Katya inquired.

"You are quite as intelligent; you have as much character, if not more than she. . . ."

"Please don't draw comparisons between me and my sister," Katya hurriedly interrupted him, "I stand to lose. You have evidently forgotten that my sister is beautiful as well as intelligent, and . . . you especially, Arcady, should not say such things, with such an assumed air of seriousness into the bargain."

"What do you mean by 'you especially'? And why do you suppose that I am not serious?"

"Of course you are not serious."

"You think so? And what if I do believe in what I am saying? If I feel that I have not even expressed myself forcibly enough?"

"I don't quite understand you."

"Really? Well, it's as clear as daylight now: to be precise, I find that I praised your sense of observation too highly."

"What do you mean?"

Arcady turned away without replying, while Katya found a few more crumbs in the basket and began to throw them to the sparrows; but she jerked her arm too violently, and the sparrows flew off in alarm before they had time to peck at the crumbs.

"Catherine Sergeyevna!" Arcady exclaimed of a sudden. "It may be all the same to you, but I should like to state that, far from having any preference for your sister, I wouldn't exchange you for anyone else in the world."

As though frightened of the words that had just burst from his lips, he got up and quickly walked away. Katya let drop both her hands and the basket into her lap, and for a while sat with drooping head, gazing after Arcady. Gradually her cheeks were suffused with scarlet; but her lips remained unsmiling, and her dark eyes shone with perplexity and another as yet nameless feeling.

"Are you alone?" Anna Sergeyevna's voice rang out close by. "I thought you went into the garden with Arcady."

Katya showed no haste as she looked round at her sister (dressed elegantly and with careful taste, Anna stood on the path, tickling Fifi's ears with the point of her open parasol), and with deliberation said: "I am alone."

"I can see that," the other replied, laughing. "Then he must have gone in."

"Yes."

"Were you reading together?"

"Yes."

Anna Sergeyevna took Katya under the chin and raised her face.

"You did not quarrel, I hope?"

"No," Katya replied, gently disengaging herself from her sister's hand.

"What a solemn answer! I expected to find him here and was going to ask him to take a stroll with me. He has begged me so often to go for a walk with him. By the way, your new boots have just arrived from town, go and try them on: I noticed yesterday that your old pair were quite worn out. In general, you don't pay enough attention to your footwear and you have such pretty little feet! And you have such lovely hands too—only they are a trifle too large; so you must make the most of your feet. But you are no coquette."

Anna Sergeyevna went down the path, her attractive dress making a slight rustling sound; Katya rose from the bench and, picking up the volume of Heine, went her way too—but not to try on her boots.

"Pretty little feet," she thought to herself as she slowly and lightly mounted the stone steps of the terrace, which was scorching in the sun. "Pretty little feet, you say. . . . Well, he will find himself kneeling at those very feet."

But at once she felt ashamed of herself, and nimbly ran upstairs.

As Arcady was walking down the corridor towards his room, the butler caught up with him and announced that Mr. Bazarov was waiting for him.

"Eugene!" Arcady muttered almost apprehensively. "How long has he been here?"

"He has just arrived. He ordered me not to announce him to madame, but to take him straight to your room."

"Can anything have happened at home?" was Arcady's first thought as he ran hurriedly upstairs and flung open the door of his room. On seeing Bazarov, he was reassured, although a more experienced eye would probably have discerned many signs of an inward perturbation in the unexpected visitor's normally energetic but somewhat sunken face. He was sitting on the window-sill, a dusty overcoat slung over his shoulders and a cap pulled over his eyes; he did not get up even when Arcady, with noisy exclamations, flung his arms round his neck.

"How unexpected! What fates bring you here?" he kept repeating as he fussed about the room, like a person who imagines that he is delighted and wishes to demonstrate the fact. "There's nothing wrong at home, is there? Everyone's well, I suppose?"

"Everything is all right at home, but not everyone is well," Bazarov replied. "Now don't be such a chatterbox, but tell them to bring me a drink of *kvas*. Sit down and listen to what I have to tell you very briefly but, I hope, forcibly."

Arcady calmed down and heard Bazarov describe his duel with Paul Petrovich. Arcady was greatly astonished and even depressed; but he did not think it necessary to disclose this; he contented himself with inquiring whether his uncle's wound was really a slight one. On being assured that the wound was extremely interesting in every respect except the medical one, he forced a smile in spite of a feeling of anguish and shame. Bazarov seemed to have an inkling of this.

"Yes, brother," he said, "that's what comes of living among these feudal barons. You are liable to become like them and to join in their knightly tourneys. Well, I'm off to visit my pater," Bazarov concluded, "and I just dropped in to see you on the way . . . 'in order to inform you of all this' I might have said, if I did not think it stupid to tell useless lies. No, I dropped in here—the devil alone knows why! You see, sometimes it pays a man to grab himself by a tuft of hair and jerk himself out as one might pull a radish from its bed. A few days ago I succeeded in doing this. But I was overcome with a desire to have one more peep at what I was leaving behind—at the bed in which I was rooted."

"I hope these words don't apply to me," Arcady protested with emotion. "I hope you do not intend to cut yourself off *from me.*"

Bazarov stared at him fixedly, almost piercingly.

"And would that upset you very much? My impression is that *you* have already cut yourself off from me. How fresh and spruce you look. . . . Your affairs with Anna Sergeyevna must be making excellent progress."

"What affairs of mine with Anna Sergeyevna?"

"Wasn't it for her sake that you left town and·came here, my little warbler? Incidentally, how are those Sunday-schools getting on? Aren't you in love with her? Or do you want to appear modest now?"

"Eugene, you know I have always been frank with you; I assure you, I swear you are mistaken."

"H'm! That's a new one," Bazarov exclaimed under his breath. "But you mustn't excite yourself, I don't care a jot. A romantic might say, 'I feel our ways are beginning to diverge,' but I tell you quite plainly that we have palled on each other."

"Eugene . . ."

"My dear, that's no misfortune; the world is full of things that pall on one. And now I wonder whether it isn't time for us to say farewell. Ever since I've been here, I have felt sick, as though surfeited by too much reading of Gogol's letters to the wife of the Governor of Kaluga. Incidentally, I gave orders for the horses not to be unharnessed."

"But look here, this is impossible!"

"Why?"

"Quite apart from me, it would show a great lack of respect for Anna Sergeyevna, who would certainly wish to see you."

"Well, you're mistaken there."

"On the contrary, I am convinced that I am right," Arcady protested.

"Why pretend? And since we have come to that point, didn't you call in here for her sake?"

"The observation may be just, but you are nevertheless mistaken."

But Arcady was right. Anna Sergeyevna did want to see Bazarov, and she sent the butler to ask him to call on her. Bazarov changed his clothes before seeing her: as it turned out, he had packed his new suit in such a way as to have it handy.

Anna Sergeyevna received him in the drawing-room and not in the study where he had so unexpectedly confessed his love for her. She graciously extended the tips of her fingers to him, but her face showed signs of uncontrollable tension.

"Anna Sergeyevna," Bazarov hastened to say, "I must begin by reassuring you. You see before you a simple mortal, who has already recovered his senses and who hopes that others, too, have forgotten his foolishness. I am now going away for a considerable period and, as you will agree, though I am no tenderfoot, the idea that you may still remember me with disgust would be an unhappy one for me to carry away."

Anna Sergeyevna gave a deep sigh, such as a climber might utter on reaching at last a high mountain peak, and then a smile lit up her face. For a second time she extended her hand to Bazarov and returned the pressure of his own.

"Let sleeping dogs lie," she replied, "especially as, to be quite frank, I was also to blame, if not by being coquettish, then in some other fashion. In short, let us be friends as before. The past was a dream, wasn't it? And who ever remembers dreams?"

"Who indeed? And, besides, love . . . Why, it's merely an imaginary feeling."

"You don't say so? I'm very glad to hear it."

So spoke Anna Sergeyevna, and so spoke Bazarov. They both believed that they spoke the truth. But did their words really contain truth, complete truth? They could not be sure of that, nor could the author. But their conversation sounded as if they understood each other perfectly.

In the course of it, Anna Sergeyevna inquired what Bazarov had been doing at the Kirsanovs'. He was on the point of telling her about his duel with Paul Petrovich, but restrained himself at the thought that she might think he was trying to show off, and told her instead that he had been working all the time.

"And I had a fit of depression, Heaven knows why," Anna Sergeyevna said. "Then I recovered; your friend Arcady arrived, and I fell into my groove again, the part that suits me."

"And what is that part, may I ask?"

"That of an aunt, governess, mother, call it what you like. By the way, you know, I had never previously fathomed your close friendship with Arcady; I used to attach very little significance to him. But now I know him better and am convinced of his intelligence. . . . But, above all, he is young, young . . . not like you and me, Eugene Vassilich."

"Is he as shy as ever in your company?" Bazarov inquired.

"Why? Was he . . ." Anna Sergeyevna started to say but, after a moment of reflection, added: "He is more confiding now, he talks to me. Formerly he used to avoid me. However, I did not seek his company either. He's more friendly with Katya." A feeling of gloom came over Bazarov. "Women can't help lying!" he thought to himself. "You were saying that he avoided you," he exclaimed with a chilly smile, "but it was probably no secret from you that he was in love with you?"

"What? He too?" burst from Anna Sergeyevna's lips.

"He too," Bazarov repeated with a meek bow. "You don't mean to say that you hadn't realized it, that I am telling you something new?"

Anna Sergeyevna lowered her eyes.

"You are mistaken, Eugene Vassilich."

"I don't think so. But perhaps I should not have broached the subject." "Now don't lie in the future," he added to himself.

"Why should you not have broached it? But I think that even here you attach too much significance to a momentary impression. I am beginning to suspect that you are inclined to exaggerate."

"Let's drop the subject, Anna Sergeyevna."

"Why should we?" she retorted, while at the same time changing the topic. She still felt ill at ease with Bazarov, although she had told him, and had assured herself, that the past had been forgotten. She experienced a slight pressure of fear when engaged in the simplest conversation with him or even when joking with him. Such is often the case with people who are travelling in a ship at sea: they talk and laugh heedlessly just as they would on solid ground; but at the slightest stoppage, the least sign of anything out of order, their faces will at once reflect a feeling of extraordinary alarm, thus showing their persistent awareness of a persistent danger.

Anna Sergeyevna's talk with Bazarov did not last very long. She grew thoughtful, made vague replies, and at last suggested that they should pass into the drawing-room where they found the princess and Katya. "And where is Arcady Nicolaievich?" the lady of the house inquired. On learning that he had not been seen for over an hour, she sent a servant to look for him. He was not easily to be found: he had penetrated into the very depths of the garden and, with his head propped on his folded hands, sat there plunged in thought. His reflections were profound and grave, but not despondent. He knew that Anna Sergeyevna was closeted alone with Bazarov, but he felt less jealous than before; on the contrary, his face looked calm and radiant; his features betrayed amazement and joy, as though he had come to some decision.

XXVI

THE late Mr. Odintzov had disapproved of innovations, but had tolerated a "certain display of noble taste"; as a consequence he had built something in the nature of a Greek portico, constructed of Russian brick, on a spot in his garden between the hothouse and the pond. On the blind, back wall of this portico six niches had been prepared for the statues which Odintzov had intended to order from abroad. These statues were intended to represent Solitude, Silence, Meditation, Melancholy, Modesty and Sensibility. One of these statues, that of the goddess of Silence with a finger held to her mouth, was actually delivered and set up. But the very same day her nose was chipped off by some of the farm lads and, although the local plasterer had offered to take it upon himself to patch up a nose "twice as good as her old one," Odintzov had had her stored away, and the goddess found herself relegated to a corner of the threshing-barn, where she remained standing for many years, exciting the superstitious awe of the peasant women. The façade of the portico had long overgrown with thick shrubbery: only the capitals of the columns could be perceived jutting out above the tangle of foliage. Inside the portico itself it was cool even in the midday heat. Anna Sergeyevna had avoided the spot ever since she had come across a hedgehog there, but Katya made frequent use of it and often sat on the roomy stone bench under one of the niches. Here, in the cool shade, she read and worked, or surrendered herself to that sensation of perfect peace with which we are all presumably familiar and whose charm lies in a barely conscious and silent observation of the sweeping wave of life that for ever rolls all round us as well as within us.

On the day following Bazarov's arrival, Katya was seated on her favourite bench while Arcady sat beside her. He had persuaded her to accompany him to the portico.

There was still an hour to go before breakfast; the dewy morning had already surrendered to the heat of day. Arcady's face wore the same expression as on the previous day, but Katya's showed signs of worry. Immediately after morning tea, her sister had called her into the study and, following that preliminary display of affection which invariably alarmed Katya a little, had counselled her to be more guarded in her manner towards Arcady and, in particular, to avoid those solitary talks with him which, according to her, had already been remarked on by her aunt and the whole of the household. Moreover, Anna Sergeyevna had already felt out of sorts the previous evening; and Katya herself felt ill at ease, as though conscious of her own guilt. Thus, when she had acceded to Arcady's fresh request, she promised to herself that this would be the last time.

"Catherine Sergeyevna," he began with a certain bashful fluency, "ever since I have had the good fortune to stay in the same house as yourself, I have had occasion to discuss many topics with you, and yet there is an important . . . question I have not yet broached. Yesterday, you remarked that I had altered since my stay here," he added, catching but at the same time avoiding the questioning look that Katya had fixed upon him. "I have indeed altered in a great many respects, and you yourself know that better than anyone else—you know it, for it is really to you I owe this transformation."

"I? . . . To me?" Katya stammered.

"I am no longer the cocksure youth I was when I first arrived here," Arcady went on. "It's not for nothing I have just turned twenty-three. As before, I have every wish to lead a useful life, and I still want to devote all my energies to the pursuit of truth; but I can no longer seek my ideal where I did before; I can perceive it now . . . much closer to hand. Until recently I failed to understand myself, I set myself tasks above my capacity. But quite recently my eyes were opened, thanks to a certain emotion. . . . I know I am not expressing myself very clearly, but I hope you will understand me. . . ."

Katya made no reply, but she stopped looking at Arcady.

"I assume," he continued with greater emotion, while a chaffinch, perched in the foliage above his head, poured out its enraptured song, "I assume it is the duty of every honest man to be quite frank with those . . . with those who . . . in a word, with those whom he holds dear, and so I . . . I intend . . ."

But at this point Arcady's eloquence betrayed him; he stammered, grew confused, and was obliged to stop for a while; Katya still kept her eyes lowered. She looked as if she failed to understand where all this was leading and waited to be enlightened.

"I can see that I am going to surprise you," Arcady resumed, gathering strength, "all the more so, since this emotion of mine has some bearing . . . some bearing, you will note, on you. I seem to remember your reproaching me yesterday with a lack of seriousness," Arcady pursued, looking like a man who had just plunged into a bog and feels himself sinking deeper and deeper with each step he takes, but who nevertheless presses on in the hope of getting across more quickly. "That reproach is often levelled . . . is often applied to young people even when they no longer merit it; and if I had more confidence . . ." ("Help me now, why don't you help me!" Arcady inwardly exclaimed in desperation, but Katya sat on as before without even turning her head.) "If I might hope . . ."

"If I were only convinced of the truth of what you say," Anna Sergeyevna's clear voice rang out at that moment.

Arcady at once stopped talking, and Katya grew pale. A path ran past the shrubbery which concealed the portico. Along it Anna Sergeyevna was strolling with Bazarov. Katya and Arcady could not see them, but they could hear each word they uttered, the rustling of their dress and the sound of their breathing. They advanced a few steps and then, as though deliberately, came to a halt right in front of the portico.

"Now you see," Anna Sergeyevna went on, "we both made a mistake; we are no longer young, either of us, and I in particular; we have experienced much and are tired; we are, both of us—why be modest?—intelligent: we became interested in each other, our curiosity was roused . . . and then . . ."

"And I went stale," Bazarov interjected.

"You know very well that was not the reason why we parted. But whatever it might have been, we felt no absolute need of each other, and that was the main reason. . . . We were . . . how shall I put it? . . . too alike. We failed to recognize that at once. On the other hand, Arcady . . ."

"You feel the need of him?" Bazarov asked.

"Don't talk like that, Eugene Vassilich. You told me

yourself that he was not indifferent to me, and I myself have always had the impression. I realize that I am old enough to be his aunt, but I have no wish to conceal from you that he has been in my thoughts more often. I find his fresh and youthful sentiments quite delightful. . . ."

" 'Enchanting' is the word more commonly used in such contexts," Bazarov interrupted her; a trace of anger could be detected in his calm but hollow voice. "Yesterday Arcady was secretive with me; he did not mention either you or your sister. . . . A revealing symptom that."

"He treats Katya like a brother," Anna Sergeyevna said. "And that is what I like about him, though perhaps I shouldn't allow them to be so intimate."

"Are you speaking as . . . a sister?" Bazarov drawled.

"Of course . . . but why are we standing here? Let's walk on. What a strange conversation we're having, don't you think? Could I ever have expected to speak to you in this way? You, I am afraid of you . . . and yet at the same time, I trust you, because fundamentally you are very kind."

"In the first place, I am not at all kind; and in the second, I don't mean anything to you now, and that's why you think me kind. . . . It's like placing a wreath at a corpse's head."

"Eugene Vassilich, it isn't in our power . . ." Anna Sergeyevna began to say; but a breeze rustled among the foliage and wafted her words away.

"Of course, you are free," Bazarov was heard to say after a while. But the rest was lost, the steps faded away . . . and silence supervened.

Arcady turned to face Katya. She was sitting in the same position as before, only her head had sunk even lower.

"Catherine Sergeyevna," he said in a trembling voice, clenching his fists, "I love you for ever, irrevocably, and I love only you. I wish to tell you this, to learn what you think, and to ask your hand; I am not rich, but I am prepared to make every sacrifice. . . . Why don't you reply? Do you believe me? Do you think I am speaking lightly? But just remember these last few days! Aren't you convinced that everything else—yes, everything else, has long ago melted into thin air? Look at me now, just say one word . . . I love . . . I love you . . . you must believe me!"

Katya's eyes looked grave and radiant as she glanced up at Arcady and, after reflecting for an instant, she replied with barely a smile, "Yes."

Arcady leapt from the bench.

"Yes! You said 'yes,' Catherine Sergeyevna! But what do you mean? That I love you? That you believe me? . . . Or . . . or . . . I dare not say it. . . ."

"Yes," Katya repeated, and this time he understood her. He grasped her long, lovely hands and, breathless with joy, pressed them to his heart. He could hardly stand on his feet and kept repeating, "Katya, Katya . . . ," while she, in her perfect innocence burst out crying, laughing the while at her own tears. Who has not seen such tears in the eyes of his beloved has never experienced the degree of terrestrial happiness of which man is capable when stunned with gratitude and overcome with shyness.

Early next morning Anna Sergeyevna gave orders for Bazarov to be summoned to her study and, with a forced laugh, handed him a folded letter. It was from Arcady: in it he asked for her sister's hand.

Bazarov quickly scanned the letter and made an effort to hide the feeling of spiteful pleasure which momentarily flared up in his breast.

"So that's it," he exclaimed. "And as recently as yesterday you assumed that he had only a brotherly regard for Catherine Sergeyevna. What will you do now?"

"What do *you* advise me to do?" Anna Sergeyevna asked him, continuing to laugh.

"I assume," Bazarov replied, also with a laugh, although, like Anna, he felt anything but gay and far from amused. "I assume that we must give the young couple our blessing. It's a good match in every way; Kirsanov is quite well off, an only son, and his father is decent enough—he's not likely to offer any objections."

Anna Sergeyevna paced up and down the room, her face alternately going white and red.

"You think so?" she said. "Well, I see no obstacles. . . . I'm glad for Katya's sake . . . and Arcady Nicolaievich's. Naturally, I shall wait for the father's reply. I shall send Arcady in person to parley with him. As it happens, I was right yesterday when I told you that we were growing old, both of us. . . . How was it I noticed nothing? I'm surprised at myself!"

Anna Sergeyevna laughed again, and then at once turned away.

"Young folk are very wily these days," Bazarov remarked, laughing also. "Well, good-bye," he started to say after a pause. "I hope you will bring this affair to a very happy conclusion. I shall show my joy from afar."

Madame Odintzov turned quickly to face him.

"Are you going away? Why not stay *now*? Do stay . . . you are such an amusing conversationalist. . . . Talking to you is like walking on the edge of a precipice. At first one is frightened, then one picks up courage. Do stay."

"Thank you for suggesting it, Anna Sergeyevna, and also for your flattering opinion of my conversational talent. But I find that I have been mixing too long already in company alien to me. Flying-fish can stay in the air for a while, but very soon they must dive back into the water; with your permission I must also plunge back into my real element."

Madame Odintzov stared at Bazarov. A bitter smile twisted her pale face. "This man loved me once," she thought—and a feeling of compassion for him swept over her as, with every token of sympathy, she offered him her hand.

But he saw through it. "No!" he exclaimed, stepping back. "I may be poor, but till now I have never accepted charity. Good-bye, and look after yourself."

"I am positive this is not our last meeting," Anna Sergeyevna replied as he bowed and left the room.

"So you have taken it into your head to make yourself a nest," he said that day to Arcady, squatting on the floor and packing his valise. "Well? It's a good thing. Only you shouldn't have been so crafty. I expected you to pursue a different line. Or, maybe, you were yourself staggered by it all."

"I was not exactly expecting this outcome when I took leave of you," Arcady replied. "But why are you being so crafty yourself and saying, 'It's a good thing,' when I know perfectly well your opinion of the engagement?"

"Ah, dear friend, how you do express yourself!" Bazarov exclaimed. "Just look at what I am doing: just because there's room in the valise here am I stuffing it with hay: it's the same with our life's valise: we pack it full of anything that comes to hand, just to avoid leaving an empty space. Don't be offended, please: you will probably remember the opinion I have always entertained of Catherine Sergeyevna. Some young ladies have the reputation of being clever because they sigh cleverly: but your young lady can look after herself, and do it so well that she will look after you too—well, that's how it should be." He banged down the lid of the valise and rose from the floor. "And now, in parting, let me tell you again—there is no point in deceiving ourselves—that we are parting for good, and you know that yourself . . . you have acted wisely; you were not made for our bitter, harsh and unsettled life. You have only youth, ardour and passion, but no arrogance or vehemence; and for the ends we pursue, that is quite useless. Your fellow noblemen cannot get much further than well-bred resignation or well-bred indignation, and that's just trivial. For instance, the likes of you won't stand up and fight—and yet you imagine you're heroes—but we insist on fighting. Yes, that's the trouble! The dust of us would bite your eyes out, the dirt of us would soil you, and anyhow you haven't reached our stature yet; unconsciously you admire yourselves, you find pleasure in railing against yourselves; but we find all that boring—give us fresh victims! We are made to break other men! You may be a good lad; but you're too soft, a liberal gentleman—*ay volla too,* as my father would say."

"Is this our final farewell, Eugene?" Arcady mournfully asked. "And have you nothing more to say to me?"

Bazarov scratched the back of his head.

"Yes, I have," he exclaimed. "I have other things to say to you, but I shan't say them now because that would be sheer romanticism: it would be too sugary. Get married as quickly as you can; start a nest of your own, and beget plenty of children. They are bound to have brains, if only because they will be born in the right age—not as we were. Ah! The horses are ready, I see, time to be off! I have said good-bye to everyone. Well? Shall we embrace?"

Arcady threw his arms round the neck of his former mentor and friend, and the tears flooded to his eyes.

"What it is to be young!" Bazarov said calmly. "I have every confidence in Catherine Sergeyevna. Just you wait, she will console you soon enough."

"Farewell, brother!" he said to Arcady after climbing into the cart and, pointing to a pair of jackdaws sitting side by side on the stable roof, added: "There's a fine example for you! Take it to heart!"

"What do you mean?" Arcady asked.

"What? Are you so weak in natural history? Or have you forgotten that the jackdaw is the most respectable of family birds? Let him be your model! . . . Farewell, *signor.*"

With a rattle the cart rolled away.

Bazarov had spoken the truth. While conversing with Katya that evening, Arcady became completely oblivious of his former mentor. He was already beginning to submit to her, and Katya sensed this without being surprised. Next day he had to drive to Maryino to see his father. Anna showed no desire to disturb the young people, and it was only for the sake of decorum that she did not leave them alone for too long. The news of the impending wedding had plunged the princess into a state of terrible rage, and very considerately Anna Sergeyevna kept her out of the way. At first, she was afraid lest the spectacle of their happiness might not prove a trifle painful; but, as it turned out, the opposite was true: far from paining her, their happiness engrossed and finally won her over completely. This made Anna Sergeyevna rejoice in spite of her depression. "Bazarov was evidently right," she thought, "it was curiosity, mere curiosity, a partiality for a quiet life, and egoism . . ."

"Children!" she exclaimed aloud. "Tell me, is love an imaginary feeling?"

But neither Katya nor Arcady grasped what she meant. They fought shy of her; they could not forget the conversation which they had inadvertently overheard. However, very soon Anna Sergeyevna was destined to reassure them; nor did it prove difficult for her, for she had recovered her peace of mind.

XXVII

BAZAROV's old parents were all the more overjoyed at their son's arrival as they had hardly expected him. Arina Vlassyevna was so excited and fussed so much about the house that Vassily Ivanovich promptly likened her to a partridge: the tuft of her short blouse really did give her a bird-like air. He contented himself with a few vague grunts and with chewing the amber mouthpiece of his pipe; gripping the back of his neck, he swivelled his head round as though trying to verify that it was well screwed on, opened his mouth wide and guffawed noiselessly.

"I have come to stay for a whole six weeks, old chap," Bazarov informed him. "I want to work, so please don't be in my way."

"You'll forget the look of my face, that's how I shall be in your way!" Vassily Ivanovich retorted.

He fulfilled his promise. After lodging his son in the study as before, he not only kept out of the way but also restrained his wife from any superfluous displays of tender emotion. "Last time, we got a little on Yeniushka's nerves, my dear," he said to her. "We must be more prudent now." The old lady agreed with her husband, but derived very little benefit from it, for now she saw her son only at table and was much too intimidated to talk to him. "Yeniushinka!" she would call out every now and then—but before he had time to look round, she would pick at the tassels of her handbag and murmur: "Oh, it's nothing, nothing at all, just an exclamation!" And then she would go to her husband and, putting her hand under her chin, say: "My dear, how can I find out what Yeniushka would like for dinner? Cabbage or beetroot soup?" "Why didn't you ask him yourself?" "Oh, I'd only annoy him!" However, very soon Bazarov stopped locking himself in: the fever of work dropped away from him, and gave way to gloomy nostalgia and aching restlessness. A strange fatigue was apparent in all he did; even his normally firm and impetuously resolute stride had altered. He stopped taking long walks and began to look round for distraction; he now took his tea in the drawing-room, sauntered about the orchard with his father and had "silent smokes" with him; once he even asked after Father Alexei. At first, his father was delighted at this change, but his joy was short-lived.

"Yeniushka is breaking my heart," he confided dolefully to his wife. "It's not that he is dissatisfied or angry, that wouldn't matter so much, but he seems upset and sad—that is what's so dreadful. He keeps mum all the time; I'd rather he lost his temper with us. He's losing weight, and the colour of his face is none too healthy."

"Oh Lord, Oh Lord!" the old woman whispered. "I'd

hang a holy charm round his neck, but he wouldn't let me."

With great discretion, Vassily Ivanovich tried several times to question Bazarov about his work, his health, and about Arcady. . . . But Bazarov's replies were reluctant and casual and, once, observing that his father was gradually trying to worm something out of him in conversation, he said with chagrin: "Why do you always tiptoe after me? It's worse than ever."

"Never mind, I didn't mean it!" the wretched father hastily replied. So his politic approach bore no fruit.

One day, in the hope of stirring his son's sympathy, he broached the subject of the imminent emancipation of the serfs and of progress; but the latter only answered indifferently: "As I was walking yesterday by the side of a fence, I heard some local lads bawling, instead of some old song, this new refrain:

> The appointed hour is drawing nigh,
> And love comes welling to the heart. . . .

That's progress for you."

Occasionally, Bazarov went for a stroll to the village and, in his usual bantering tone, engaged some peasant in conversation.

"Well, old man," he would say to him, "tell me about your notions of life. They say that the whole power and future of Russia depends on you folk, and that you will open a new period of history—you will give us a real language and laws." Thus addressed, the peasant would either make no reply at all, or would answer somewhat in this strain: "That we might . . . also, it depends . . . more or less on the limitations imposed on us."

"Now you must explain to me the foundations of your world," Bazarov would interrupt him. "Is your world the same as rests on three fishes?"

"It's the earth, master, that is stood on three fishes," the peasant would explain reassuringly, in a good-natured patriarchal, sing-song voice. "But as against our, so to say, world there is set up, as we well know, the will of the gentry; that is why you are our fathers. And the more exacting the master, the better is the peasant pleased."

After hearing a peasant deliver himself thus, Bazarov on one occasion shrugged his shoulders contemptuously and turned his back on him, and the peasant went on his way.

"What were you palavering about?" another peasant asked him, a middle-aged man of sulky mien, who, as he stood on the porch of his cottage, had followed from a distance his encounter with Bazarov. "Was it about the arrears you were talking?"

"It wasn't about the arrears, mate!" the first peasant replied in a voice which had already shed all trace of patriarchal sing-song, and had, on the contrary, assumed a note of harsh independence.

"I was just having a few words with him; my tongue needed loosening a bit. A master's always a master, we know that; they ain't got much understanding."

"How could they!" the other peasant replied and, tilting back their caps and loosening their belts, they began to discuss their own affairs and needs. Alas! This self-assured Bazarov, who had shrugged his shoulders so contemptuously, this Bazarov who prided himself on being able to talk to peasants (as he had boasted when arguing with Paul Petrovich), had no suspicion that in their eyes he was something in the nature of a mere jack-pudding.

However, at last he did find something to preoccupy him. One day, in his presence, his father was bandaging a peasant's injured leg, but the old man's hands shook so much that he had some difficulty in applying the bandages; his son came to his assistance, and from that day on helped him regularly with his patients, but he never ceased to mock at the remedies he suggested or at his father's eagerness to apply them. But Bazarov's mockery did not upset his father in the least; they even brought him some comfort. With two fingers gripping his soiled dressing-gown in the region of his belly, and puffing away at his pipe, he listened to Bazarov with evident enjoyment; the greater the venom of his son's quips, the more humour there was in the happy father's laughter, as he showed every one of his blackened teeth. Occasionally, he even began to repeat some of these obtuse and pointless sallies, like the one, for instance, which without rhyme or reason he repeated for several days on end: "Well, that's only the ninth degree!" He did so because his son had used the expression when he heard that he was in the habit of going to early mass.

"Thank God! He's shaken off his dejection!" he whispered to his wife. "The way he told me off to-day was a marvel!"

The idea of having his son as an assistant filled him with enthusiasm and brimmed him with pride. "Yes, yes," he would say to some peasant woman, in a long, loose-fitting peasant coat and horned head-dress, thrusting a bottle of Goulard water or a pot of madwort ointment into her hands, "you should praise the Lord every minute of the day, because my son is staying with me; do you realize that you are being treated according to the very latest scientific and modern methods? The Emperor of the French, Napoleon III himself, has no better doctor." The peasant woman who had come to complain of being "hoisted in the gripes" (she was unable, however, to explain the significance of these words), kept bowing low and fumbling in her bosom for the doctor's fee—the four eggs that lay there wrapped in an odd bit of linen.

One day Bazarov even extracted a tooth from an itinerant pedlar of gaudy fabrics, and, although this tooth was normal, the father preserved it as a rare specimen and, when showing it to Father Alexei, kept repeating over and over again:

"Just look at those roots! How strong Eugene must be! He jerked the pedlar right up into the air. . . . I believe he could pull up an oak tree! . . ."

"Excellent!" Father Alexei responded at last, at a loss what to reply or how to cope with the old man's ecstasy.

One day a peasant from a neighbouring village drove up, bringing a brother of his, who had contracted typhus. Lying on a heap of straw, the unfortunate man was on the point of death, his body was covered with purple patches, and he had long ago lost consciousness. Vassily Ivanich expressed regret that it had occurred to no one to seek medical advice sooner, and pronounced against any hope of recovery. As a matter of fact, the peasant failed to get his brother home— he died in the cart on the return journey.

Three days later, Bazarov walked into his father's room and asked him if he had any silver nitrate.

"I have some. What is it for?"

"I need it . . . to sterilize a cut."

"For whom?"

"For myself."

"What? For yourself! What's happened? What sort of a cut is it? Show me it."

"Here it is, on my finger. This morning I drove out to the village—you know the one from which the typhus patient was brought. For some reason, they were getting ready to perform an autopsy, and I thought I'd get some practice."

"Well?"

"So I got permission from the district doctor to do it, and then I cut myself."

Vassily Ivanich suddenly turned quite pale and, without a word, hurried into his study, returning immediately with a little silver nitrate. Bazarov was about to take it and go off.

"For God's sake!" Vassily Ivanich exclaimed. "Let me do it myself."

"You're a great one for practice," Bazarov replied with a smile.

"It's no joking matter, please. Show me your finger. It's not a big cut. Is it painful?"

"Press harder; don't be afraid."

Vassily Ivanich paused.

"What do you think, Eugene? Wouldn't it be better to sear it with a hot iron?"

"That should have been done before. Actually, even silver nitrate is useless now. If I'm infected, then it's already too late."

"What do you mean . . . too late?" The old man was barely able to utter these words.

"What do you expect! It's over four hours since it happened."

Vassily Ivanich burned the cut a little more.

"But hadn't the district doctor any caustic?"

"No, he hadn't."

"My God, how's that? A doctor—and yet without such an essential thing!"

"You should have seen his lancets," Bazarov said, and then went out.

Till late that evening, and all through the following day, Vassily Ivanich picked on every excuse to penetrate into his son's room and, though he made no reference to the cut and even attempted to chat quite casually with him on various topics, stared so persistently into his eyes and watched him so anxiously that Bazarov finally lost his patience and threatened to depart. Vassily Ivanich thereupon promised not to worry him, particularly as Arina Vlassyevna, from whom he naturally kept everything back, had already begun to ask him why he was sleeping so badly and what had come over him. For two whole days he held himself in check, although his son's appearance, which he kept under stealthy observation, was very far from satisfying him. . . . But on the third day, at dinner, he could contain himself no longer. Bazarov was sitting with eyes lowered and without tasting a single dish.

"Why don't you eat, Eugene?" he asked, assuming a casual expression. "The food seems well cooked."

"I don't feel like it, that's why."

"You have no appetite?" he asked, adding timidly: "And does your head ache?"

"It does. Why shouldn't it?"

Arina Vlassyevna sat up and took notice.

"Please don't be angry, Eugene," Vassily Ivanich went on, "but will you let me feel your pulse?"

Bazarov stood up.

"I can tell you, without your feeling it, that I have a temperature."

"And do you feel feverish too?"

"Yes, I do. I'd better go and lie down; will you send me up some lime tea? I must have caught a chill."

"That's why I heard you coughing last night," his mother said.

"I've got a chill," Bazarov repeated and went off.

While Arina Vlassyevna was preparing the lime tea, the old man strode into the next room and there silently tugged at his hair.

That day Bazarov did not get up again and passed the whole of the night in a state of half-conscious, heavy slumber. On opening his eyes with an effort at about one o'clock in the morning, he perceived his father's pallid face bent over him in the glimmer of the icon-lamp, and bade him go away; the latter complied, but was soon back on tiptoe, and partly concealing himself behind the door of a wardrobe, stood there, unable to tear his eyes away from his son. Arina Vlassyevna also did not go to bed and, opening the study door, would come in to hear "how Enyusha was breathing" and also to have a peep at her husband. She could only catch a glimpse of his hunched, motionless back, but this brought her some relief. Next morning, Bazarov made an attempt to get up, but felt giddy and his nose began to bleed; he went back to bed. Vassily Ivanich silently attended to his wants; Arina Vlassyevna came in now and then to ask how he felt. He would reply "Better," and turn his face to the wall. Vassily Ivanich would wave her away with both arms; biting her lips to hold back her tears, she would leave the room. It was as though sudden darkness had descended on the house; everyone's face looked drawn and everything was strangely still; a raucous cock had been removed from the yard and carried into the village; for a long time the bird remained perplexed at being treated in this fashion. Bazarov continued to lie in bed, his face tucked up to the wall. Vassily Ivanich attempted to ask him questions, but they only exhausted Bazarov, and the old man was reduced to sitting still in an arm-chair, now and then cracking his fingers. Off and on, he would go into the garden for an instant, stand for a while there, like a piece of statuary, stricken with unutterable amazement (this expression did not leave his face for a moment); then he would return to his son's room, avoiding as best he could his wife's anxious questioning on the way. At last, she managed to seize hold of his hand and ask him feverishly, almost menacingly: "What is the matter with him?" He managed to collect himself and to force a smile in reply; but to his horror, instead of a smile, a hollow laugh unexpectedly burst from his lips. Early next morning, he sent for a doctor. In case he might take umbrage, he thought it right to warn his son of this step.

Bazarov suddenly turned on the sofa, stared fixedly and dully at his father, and asked him for a drink of water. As he handed a glass of water to him, his father profited by the opportunity to feel his forehead. It was simply blazing.

"I'm in a bad way, old chap," Bazarov began. "I've caught the infection. In a few days, you will have to bury me."

Vassily Ivanich staggered as though he had been kicked on his legs.

"Eugene!" he whispered. "What do you mean? . . . God forbid! You've got a chill. . . ."

"That'll do," Bazarov interjected in a deliberate voice. "No doctor should talk like that. You know very well all the symptoms of the disease."

"Where are the symptoms . . . of the disease, Eugene? . . . I ask you!"

"And what is this?" Bazarov said, pulling back the sleeve of his shirt and showing his father the ominous red patches which had burst out on his skin.

Vassily Ivanich gave a shudder and froze with fear.

"Assuming," he brought out at last, "assuming . . . that . . . that this is something in the nature . . . of an infection . . ."

"Pyæmia," his son prompted.

"Well, yes . . . something . . . in the nature . . . of an epidemic . . ."

"Of pyæmia," Bazarov repeated sternly and distinctly. "Oh have you forgotten your lecture-notes?"

"All right, all right, as you wish . . . But we shall cure you in any case."

"Stuff and nonsense," Bazarov retorted. "However, that's not the point. I did not expect to have to die so soon; it really is rather an unpleasant accident. Mother and you must now make the best of your strong religious convictions; here is your chance to put them to trial." He took a few more sips of water. "May I ask you to do something for me . . . while I can still think clearly? To-morrow or the day after, my brain, as you know, will hand in its resignation. Even now I'm not quite sure whether I am making myself clear. When I was lying down, I seemed to see a pack of red hounds frisking round me, and you were setting them against me as if I were a woodcock. I feel drunk. Do you understand me clearly?"

"Of course, Eugene. You are talking quite normally."

"So much the better. You told me that you had sent for the doctor. . . . That brings you some comfort. . . . Now comfort me too; send a messenger . . ."

"To Arcady," the old man picked him up.

"Who is Arcady?" Bazarov inquired as though reflecting. . . . "Ah, yes! That fledgling! No, leave him in peace: he's a jackdaw by now. Don't be astonished, this is no delirium. But please send a messenger at once to Madame Odintzov, Anna Sergeyevna, there's a lady landowner of that name. . . . Have you heard of her?" (The old man nodded.) "'Bazarov sends his respects and wishes to inform her that he is dying,' You will do that for me?"

"Of course I will. . . . But how can you die, Eugene?

. . . Judge for yourself! What will justice mean if that happens?"

"I don't know. But do send the messenger."

"This very minute. I'll write her a line myself."

"No, why should you? Tell her simply that I send my respects, that's all that is needed. And now I shall return to my hounds again. How strange! I want to concentrate and think of death, but I can't even do that. I merely see a patch of sorts . . . and that's all."

He turned over again heavily facing the wall. On leaving the study, Vassily Ivanich got as far as his wife's bedroom and collapsed there on his knees in front of the icons.

"Pray, Arina, pray!" he moaned. "Our son is dying."

The doctor, the same district practitioner who could produce no caustic when it was required, came along and, after examining the patient, advised them to adopt a prophylactic treatment, and followed this up with a few words on the possibility of recovery.

"And did you ever happen to observe that anyone in my present condition has ever *failed* to reach the Elysian fields?" Bazarov asked and, suddenly gripping the foot of a heavy table next to the sofa, shook it and made it budge.

"My strength. . . . I still have some strength left, and yet I must die . . ." he said. "An old man, at least, has had time to become disenchanted with life, but I . . . Yes, just try and repudiate death. It repudiates you, and that's all there is to it! Who is that crying there?" he went on after a while. "Mother? Poor soul! For whom will she now make her wonderful broths? You also seem to be snivelling, Vassily Ivanich? Well, if Christianity is no help, at least try and be a philosopher, a stoic, maybe! Didn't you once boast to me that you were a philosopher?"

"A fine philosopher I am!" Vassily Ivanich sobbed as the tears streamed down his cheeks.

With every hour Bazarov grew worse; as normally happens in cases of surgical poisoning, the infection spread rapidly. But he had not yet lost consciousness and could grasp what was being said; he was still putting up a fight. "I refuse to be delirious," he whispered, clenching his fists. "How absurd!" And he would at once add: "Now, what is the balance, if we deduct ten from eight?" His father strode about the room like a madman, suggesting one remedy after another, and repeatedly covering his son's feet. "We must wrap him in cold sheets . . . give him an emetic . . . a mustard-plaster for his stomach . . . a bleeding," he would exclaim with great intensity. The doctor, who had stayed on at his request, agreed to all his suggestions, gave the patient lemonade, and for his own use wheedled now a pipe full of tobacco, now "something strong and warming," in short, a portion of vodka. The mother kept vigil on a low bench near the door and every now and again went off to say her prayers; a few days ago, a small hand-mirror had slipped from her grasp and splintered, and this she had always interpreted as a bad omen; even Anfisushka could find no words to console her. Timofeyich had departed with the message for Madame Odintzov.

Bazarov spent an uncomfortable night. . . . A relentless temperature tormented him. Morning brought some relief. He begged his mother to comb his hair, kissed her hand, and drank two mouthfuls of tea. His father felt slightly cheered.

"Thank God!" he repeated. "The moment of crisis has come . . . the crisis has come."

"Just imagine!" said Bazarov. "What does the word mean? It has just occurred to you: 'crisis' you say, and feel relieved. It's amazing the trust men still put in words. You may dub a man a 'fool' for instance, without laying hands on him, and yet he will feel out of sorts; but if you call him a 'brainy chap' and give him no money—then he will be simply delighted."

This little tirade, reminiscent of Bazarov's previous sallies, greatly moved his father.

"Bravo! Excellently spoken, splendid!" he exclaimed, pretending to clap his hands.

Bazarov smiled wryly.

"What do you think?" he asked. "Is the crisis past or just beginning?"

"You feel better, that's what I think. That's why I'm so glad," Vassily Ivanich replied.

"That's fine; there's no harm in rejoicing. And did you send the message to her, you remember? Did you send it?"

"Of course I did."

The turn for the better did not last long. The disease made headway again. Vassily Ivanich spent all his time at his son's bedside. He looked himself as if he were the victim of extraordinary tortures. Several times he was on the point of saying something—but the words stuck in his throat.

"Eugene!" he gasped at last. "My son, my dear, dear son."

This unexpected form of address affected Bazarov. He turned his head slightly and, apparently trying to throw off the pressure weighing down upon him, called out: "What is it, father?"

"Eugene," Vassily Ivanich continued, sinking on his knees by the bed, although Bazarov had not opened his eyes and could see nothing. "Eugene, you are better now; by God's grace you will recover; but make the most of this moment, give your mother and myself some consolation, do your duty as a Christian! It's terrible for me to have to say this to you; but more dreadful still . . . it will be for eternity, Eugene . . . just think what that means. . . ."

The old man's voice trailed off as a strange expression flitted over his son's face, while he continued to lie there with eyes closed.

"I have no objection if that will help to console you," he replied at last. "But there seems no point in hurrying yet. You said yourself that my condition had improved."

"It has, Eugene, it has: but who knows, it's all in God's power, but if you do your duty . . ."

"No, I prefer to wait," Bazarov interrupted him. "I agree, the crisis has set in. But if we are both mistaken, it won't matter! Extreme unction can be administered even to the unconscious."

"Don't say that, Eugene. . . ."

"I'll wait. But now I want to sleep. Please leave me alone."

And he put his head back in the former position.

Rising from his knees, the old man sat down in the armchair and, holding his chin, began to bite his fingers. . . .

Suddenly his ears caught the rumble of a sprung carriage, a rumble that can be heard very clearly in the fastness of the country. Nearer and nearer the light wheels rolled; very soon the snorting of horses could also be heard. . . . The father jumped up and rushed to the window. A barouche, drawn by four horses, drove into the courtyard of the small house. Without understanding clearly the significance of what was happening, he ran out on to the steps, brimming over with senseless joy. . . . A footman in livery was opening the carriage door; a lady in a black veil and black mantilla stepped down. . . .

"I am Madame Odintzov," she said. "Is Eugene Vassilich still alive? Are you his father? I have brought my doctor with me."

"Benefactress!" Vassily Ivanich exclaimed and, seizing her hands, pressed his lips feverishly to them, while the doctor, whom Anna Odintzov had brought, a squat man in glasses and with a German face, was climbing out of the barouche without any sign of haste.

"He is still alive, my Eugene is alive, and now he will be saved! Wife! Wife! . . . A heavenly angel has . . ."

"Oh Lord, what is it?" the old lady stuttered, running out of the drawing-room. Failing to understand anything, she threw herself at once at Anna Sergeyevna's feet and, like a crazy woman, began to kiss her dress.

"What is this! What are you doing!" Anna Sergeyevna kept exclaiming; but Arina Vlassyevna paid no heed to her, and Vassily Ivanich went on repeating: "Angel! Angel!"

"*Wo ist der Kranke?* And the pashient is where?" the doctor inquired at last not without a touch of indignation.

Vassily Ivanich collected himself.

"Here, here, please follow me, *würdigster Herr Kollege,*" he added, drawing on his memories of the past.

"Eh!" the German said with a sour look.

Vassily Ivanich led him into the study.

"Here is the doctor whom Anna Sergeyevna Odintzov has brought," he said, bending down to his son's ear. "And she is here herself."

Bazarov suddenly opened his eyes.

"What did you say?" he asked.

"I said that Madame Odintzov has arrived and has brought this gentleman—a doctor."

Bazarov looked round.

"So she's here. . . . I want to see her," he said.

"You will see her, Eugene, but, first of all, you must have a word with the doctor. Our own doctor is no longer here, so I must tell him the whole history of your illness, and then we shall consult together."

Bazarov glanced at the German.

"Well, get on with it then, only don't spout Latin. I know quite well the meaning of *jam moritur*."

"Der Herr scheint des Deutschen mächtig zu sein," the new successor of Æsculapius started off, turning to Vassily Ivanich.

"Ich . . . habe . . . No, we had better talk Russian," the old man replied lamely.

"Ah, ah! Zo dat iz how it iz. . . . Pleeze. . . ." And so the consultation began.

Half an hour later, in the company of Vassily Ivanich, Anna Sergeyevna entered the study. Her doctor had already told her in a whisper that there was no hope for the patient's recovery.

Her eyes sought Bazarov . . . and she stopped in the doorway, taken aback by his feverish and, at the same time, deathly pale face, and by the turbid eyes that were now fixed upon her. She was really alarmed, overcome by a chilly and haunting fear: then it instantly occurred to her that she would have behaved very differently if she had really loved Bazarov.

"Thank you," Bazarov pronounced with an effort. "I did not expect it. It is a good deed. We meet again, as you foretold."

"Anna Sergeyevna was so kind . . ." his father began to say.

"Father, leave us," his son interrupted him. "Anna, you don't mind, do you? Now that . . ."

He nodded his head at his powerless, supine body.

Vassily Ivanich went out.

"Well, I must thank you," Bazarov repeated. "It was a royal gesture. They say kings visit the dying."

"Eugene, I hope that . . ."

"Ah, Anna Sergeyevna, let us speak the unvarnished truth. I'm done for. The wheel has run over me. As it turns out, there was no point in worrying about the future. Death is an old jester, but every man sees him in a fresh guise. Up to now, I have felt no fear. . . . Soon I shall lose consciousness, and then the lid will be clamped down!" (He waved his arms feebly.) "Well, what shall I say to you? . . . I was in love with you! That made little sense before, even less now. Love has a body, and my particular body is already disintegrating. It would be better if I told you—what a glorious woman you are! How beautiful you look standing there, so lovely. . . ."

Anna Sergeyevna involuntarily shuddered.

"No, don't be alarmed. . . . Just sit down over there. . . . But don't come near me—the disease is infectious."

Anna Sergeyevna quickly crossed the room and sat down in an arm-chair by the sofa on which Bazarov was lying.

"Great-heart!" he whispered. "Oh, how close you are, how young, and fresh, and pure . . . here in the middle of this sick-ridden room! . . . Well, we must say our farewells now! May you live long, that's the best of all things, and make the most of it while there's time. Take a good look at this ghastly sight, at this still writhing worm, crushed and yet glaring at you. And yet once he also dreamt of all the things he might accomplish, and believed he was immortal. Why should he die? He used to think 'I have a task to perform, I am a giant!' And now this giant's only task is to die a decent death, and that is no one else's business. . . . All the same, I shan't put my tail between my legs now."

Bazarov was silent and began to grope for his glass. Without taking off her gloves and breathing apprehensively Anna handed him a glass of water.

"You will soon forget me," he began again. "A dead man is no companion to the living. My father may tell you what a loss I shall be to Russia. . . . That's bosh, but don't disillusion the old man. A child must find something to console it, you know that. And be kind to my mother. You will not find the like of them in all the whole great world, in daylight even, and with the help of a lamp. . . . Does Russia need me? No, clearly she doesn't. Whom does she need? She might need a cobbler, a tailor too, a butcher . . . he sells meat . . . a butcher . . . wait a moment, I'm becoming involved. . . . I can see a forest here. . . ."

Bazarov put his hand to his forehead.

Anna Sergeyevna bent over him.

"Eugene, I am here."

He at once took her hand and raised himself.

"Farewell!" he exclaimed with unexpected force, and his eyes flashed a last gleam. "Farewell. . . . Listen. . . . I never kissed you then. . . . Ah, breathe on the dying flame, let it go out. . . ."

Anna Sergeyevna pressed her lips to his forehead.

"Enough!" he exclaimed, and sank back on the pillow. "Now ... darkness. ..."

Anna Sergeyevna tiptoed out of the room.

"Well?" The father asked her in a whisper.

"He's fallen asleep," she replied barely audibly.

Bazarov was fated to wake no more. By evening he sank into a state of complete coma, and died on the following day. ... Father Alexei performed the last rites. When extreme unction was being administered and the holy oil touched his breast, one of his eyes opened: and it seemed as though at the sight of the priest in his vestments, the smoking censer, and the candles in front of the icon, something like a shudder of horror was momentarily reflected in his pallid face.

When at last he had sighed his last sigh, and the house became filled with general lamentation, Vassily Ivanich suddenly had a fit of frenzy.

"I said I'd rebel," he shouted hoarsely, his face all burning and distorted, waving his clenched fist in the air as though threatening someone. "I will rebel," he shouted, "I will!" But all in tears, Arina Vlassyevna clasped her arms round his neck, and they both fell prone on the ground. "And so," as Anfisushka related afterwards in the servants' quarters, "they bowed their dear heads, like lambs at noonday."

But the noonday blaze dies away, and is succeeded by the evening and then the night; and returning there, in that peaceful retreat, the tormented and the weary find their sweetest sleep.

XXVIII

SIX months passed. White winter was at its height, with its relentless silence of cloudless frosts, firm crunching snow, rosy hoar-rimed trees, pale emerald skies, curls of smoke above the chimneys, puffs of steam from doors quickly opened and shut again, glowing frost-bitten faces, and the jerky trotting of nags chilled to the marrow of their bones. The January day was already drawing to a close;

more and more firmly the evening chill compressed the congealed air, and the blood-red sunset rapidly dwindled. In the house at Maryino, the lights were being lit. In a black tailed coat and white gloves, Prokofyich was laying the table for seven with unwonted ceremony. A week ago, in a small parish church, two weddings had been celebrated without fuss and almost without witnesses—those of Arcady and Katya, Nicholas Petrovich and Fenichka: and, this day, Nicholas Petrovich was giving a farewell dinner for his brother Paul, who was setting out to Moscow on business. Anna Sergeyevna was already in Moscow: having generously endowed the young couple, she had gone there immediately after the wedding.

Punctually at three o'clock they all gathered round the table. Mitya had his place among them too, and could now boast of a nanny in a showy head-dress. Paul Petrovich was throning it between Katya and Fenichka: the "husbands" had found a nook for themselves beside their wives. Of late a change had come over our old friends; they appeared to have grown more handsome and mature. Paul alone looked leaner and this, incidentally, gave an air of great elegance, of the "grand seigneur," to his expressive features. . . . Fenichka too had altered. Wearing a refreshing silk dress, a wide velvet bandeau round her hair, a gold chain on her neck, she sat still and respectful, full of solicitude towards herself, towards everyone round her, and kept smiling as though she wished to say: "Pardon me, it's not my fault." But she was not the only person to smile—they all smiled, and they all looked apologetic; they felt a little awkward, a trifle sad, but at bottom very happy. They attended to each other's wants with an air of amusing consideration as though they had conspired to act in some good-natured comedy. Of them all, Katya was most at ease: she glanced about her with a trusting air, and it was noticeable that Nicholas Petrovich had already become devotedly attached to her. Towards the end of the meal he rose and, raising his wine-glass, turned to Paul Petrovich.

"You are forsaking us . . . forsaking us, dear brother," he began. "Of course, it will not be for long, but still I cannot but express to you what I . . . what we . . . how much I . . . how much we . . . But the trouble is I'm not very good at making speeches! Arcady, you'd better do the rest."

"I can't, daddy; I'm not prepared."

"As if I was prepared! Well, brother, allow me then quite simply to embrace you, to wish you all the best, and do come back to us as soon as you can!"

Paul Petrovich embraced them all, Mitya of course included; moreover, he kissed Fenichka's hand, which she had not yet learnt to hold out properly. Drinking out of the glass that had been refilled with wine, he exclaimed with a deep sigh, "May you all be very happy, dear friends! *Farewell!*" This tail-phrase in English passed unnoticed, but all present showed signs of emotion.

"To Bazarov's memory," whispered Katya into her husband's ear as she clinked glasses with him. By way of a reply Arcady squeezed her hand warmly, but did not venture to propose the toast aloud.

This seems to be the end. But perhaps some of our readers would like to learn what each of the characters we have portrayed is doing now at this very moment. We are ready to oblige.

Recently Anna Sergeyevna married, out of conviction rather than love, a man who promises to be one of Russia's leading figures, a very able lawyer of a vigorous and practical turn of mind, resolute will and remarkable gifts of eloquence—a man still young and generous, but also cold as ice. They live in the greatest harmony and may one day achieve happiness or even love. Princess K died, forgotten by all on her deathbed. The Kirsanovs, father and son, have settled down at Maryino. . . . Their affairs have taken a turn for the better. Arcady has become passionately engrossed in estate-management, and the "farm" is already bringing in a considerable income. Nicholas Petrovich has become an arbitrator on land reforms and is hard at work; he is constantly touring his district; he indulges in long speeches (he is of the school that believes that peasants should receive "instruction," that is to say, that they must be worn down by frequent repetition of one and the same phrase). But to speak the truth, he fails to give complete satisfaction either to the cultured gentry, who now talk flauntingly, now despondently, about 'mancipation (giving the *an* a nasal French twist), or to the uncultured ones, who unceremoniously vituperate against "this 'mancipation." He is too soft for either camp. Katya has given birth to a son, Kolya, while Mitya is already a sturdy scampering boy and prattles away loquaciously. Next to her husband and Mitya, Fenichka adores no one more than her daughter-in-law, and whenever Katya sits down at the piano she is only too delighted to spend the whole day in her company. We must say a word about Peter. He is grown quite starchy with stupidity and self-importance, and drawls out all his o's likes au's: *"Nau* I shall *gau,"* he says. But he has also married and, together with his bride, has appropriated to himself quite a decent dowry. His wife is the daughter of a city market-gardener: she had previously turned down two eligible suitors for no other reason than their lack of a watch; Peter could not only boast of a watch, he even had a pair of patent leather boots.

On the Brühl terrace at Dresden, between two and four o'clock in the afternoon, at the most fashionable hour for promenading, you may come across a gentleman of some fifty years of age, already quite grey and apparently suffering from gout, but still handsome, elegantly dressed, and having that air of distinction which a man can only acquire as a result of long intercourse with the higher ranks of society. Paul Petrovich, the gentleman in question, had left Moscow and gone abroad for the sake of his health, and then stayed on in Dresden, where he frequents chiefly English people and Russian visitors. His manner with the English is simple, almost modest, but not undignified: they find him a bit of a bore, but respect him as *"a perfect gentleman."* He is less inhibited with Russians, unburdens his spleen to them, jests at his own expense and theirs, but he does all this with a certain air of charm, ease and breeding. He is a Slavophil in outlook: as we are well aware, this is considered *très distingué* in higher society. He reads nothing Russian, but keeps on his writing-desk an ashtray in the form of a peasant bast-shoe. Our tourists frequent him a great deal. While "temporarily in the opposition," Matvey Kolyazin paid a magisterial visit to him as he passed through Dresden on his way to the Bohemian watering-places; and the local inhabitants, whom he frequents but little, almost venerate him. No one is more successful than the Herr Baron von Kirsanov in obtaining easily and expeditiously tickets for the court choir, the theatre, and such places. He continues to do good works, within his capacity; he still causes a stir in a small way; it was not in vain that he had been a social lion once upon a time; but life seems to weigh

heavily on him . . . more heavily than he himself will admit.
. . . A mere glimpse of him in the Russian Church confirms
this, as he leans in some corner against the wall, immersed
in thought and remaining motionless for long periods with
tightly drawn lips, before he starts up of a sudden and begins almost imperceptibly to make the sign of the cross. . . .

Madame Kukshin also found herself abroad. She is now
in Heidelberg, a student no longer of the natural sciences
but of architecture, in which, as she declares, she has discovered some new laws. She is as friendly with students as
ever, especially with young Russian physicists and chemists,
who crowd Heidelberg and at first astonish the naïve
German professors by their sober outlook on the world,
only to amaze them subsequently by their complete inactivity and absolute sluggishness. In the company of two or
three such students of chemistry, who cannot distinguish
between hydrogen and nitrogen, though they bubble over
with critical negation and self-importance, and in the company also of the great Elyseyevich, Sitnikov, who is aiming
at greatness, gads about Petersburg and, as he assures us, is
engaged in furthering Bazarov's "cause." Rumour has it
that he recently received a drubbing, but came out of it
quits: in an obscure little article, tucked away in an obscure
little periodical, he hinted that the person who had assaulted
him was a coward. This he calls irony. His father still em-
ploys him on errands, and his wife treats him like a fool . . .
and a *littérateur*.

In one of the far corners of Russia stands a small village
graveyard. Like most of our graveyards it looks dismal:
weeds have long overgrown the ditches round it, the drab
wooden crosses sag and rot beneath their once freshly
painted gables; the tombstones are all askew, as though
someone were pushing them from below; two or three
scanty fir trees barely afford some meagre shade; sheep
wander at will over the graves. . . . But in their midst stands
a grave untouched by any human being, untrampled by any
animal: only the birds at dawn perch and sing on it. An
iron railing fences it in; two fir trees have been planted
there, one at each end; in that grave Eugene Bazarov lies
buried. Often from a nearby village a tottering old couple,
man and wife, make their way here. Supporting each other,
they walk with heavy steps; on reaching the railing, they
fall down upon their knees, and long and bitterly they

weep, and long and yearningly they gaze at the mute tomb-
stone beneath which their son is lying; exchanging a brief
word, they brush the dust from the stone, set a branch of a
fir tree right, and then resume their prayers, unable to tear
themselves away from this spot where they feel themselves
so close to their son and their memories of him. . . . Can
it be that their prayers, their tears, will remain unanswered?
Can it be that love, sacred and devoted love, is not omnip-
otent? Oh, no! However passionate, sinful and rebellious
the heart wrapped away in that grave, the flowers that blossom there peep at us tranquilly with innocent eyes: they
speak to us not only of all-embracing peace, of the vast repose of "indifferent" nature; they tell us also of everlasting
reconciliation and life without end. . . .

SELECTED READING LIST

Other Books by IVAN TURGENEV

The Hunting Sketches, 1852 (Signet
CT135)
Rudin, 1856 Novel
A Nest of Gentlefolk, 1858 Novel
On the Eve, 1860 Novel
First Love, 1860 Novel
Smoke, 1867 Novel
The Torrents of Spring, 1871 Novel
Virgin Soil, 1877 Novel

Selected Biography and Criticism

Freeborn, Richard. *Turgenev: The Novelist's Novelist.* New York and London:
Oxford University Press, 1960.

Gettmann, R. A. *Turgenev in England
and America.* Urbana, Illinois: University of Illinois Press, 1941.

Magarshack, David. *Turgenev: A Life.*
New York: Grove Press; London:
Faber & Faber, Ltd., 1954.

Yarmolinsky, Avrahm. *Turgenev: The
Man, His Art and His Age.* New
York: The Orion Press, Inc., 1959;
London: Andre Deutsch, Ltd., 1960.